DNX
Copyright © 2023 by K. Savage.
All rights reserved. No part of this book may be used or reproduced in any manner whatsoever without written permission except in the case of brief quotations embodied in critical articles or reviews.

This book is a work of fiction. Names, characters, businesses, organizations, places, events and incidents either are the product of the author's imagination or are used fictitiously. Any resemblance to actual persons, living or dead, events, or locales is entirely coincidental.

For information contact:
http://www.starshinecreations.com

Pangea Space Station Map by Lux Vestra Art

ISBN: 979-8-9880516-0-2

First Edition: June 2023

10 9 8 7 6 5 4 3 2

DNX

IN THE DISTANT FUTURE, EVERYTHING IS PLANNED AND PERFECTED BY SCIENCE, DOWN TO YOUR DNA. THE ONLY THING THAT MAKES YOU SPECIAL ARE THE SECRETS YOU KEEP...

BY K. SAVAGE

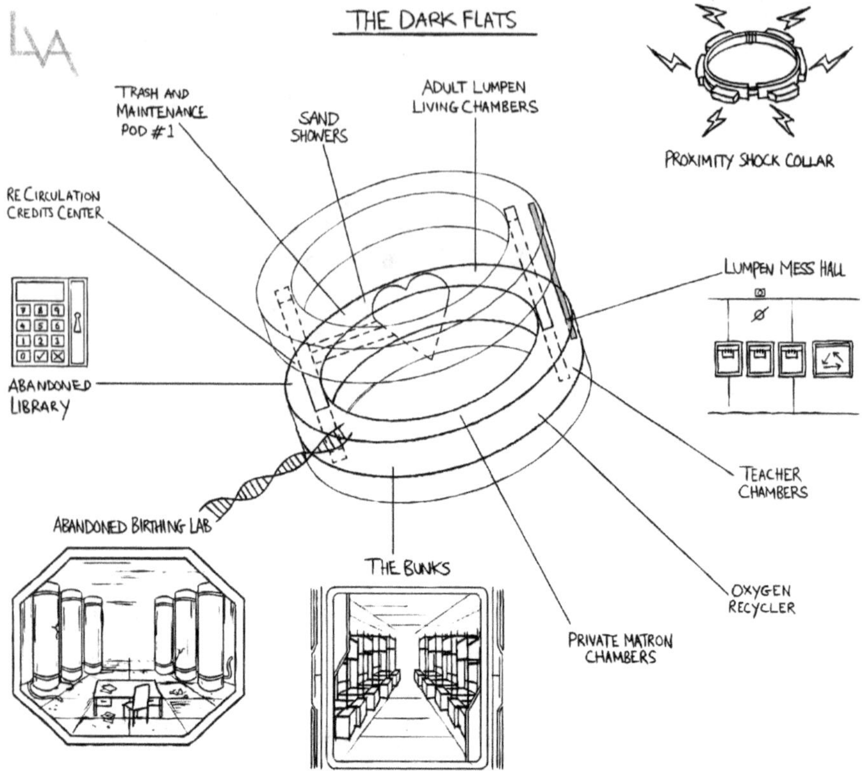

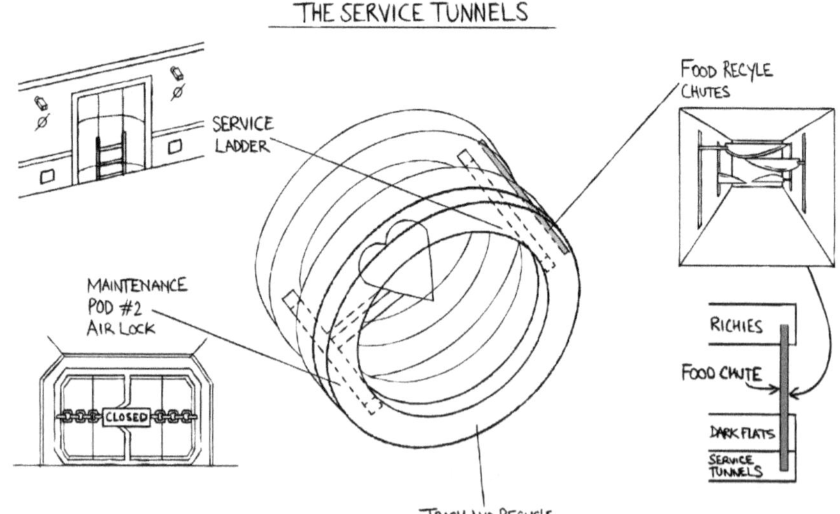

THE DARK FLATS
PROXIMITY SHOCK COLLAR
TRASH AND MAINTENANCE POD #1
SAND SHOWERS
ADULT LUMPEN LIVING CHAMBERS
RE CIRCULATION CREDITS CENTER
LUMPEN MESS HALL
ABANDONED LIBRARY
TEACHER CHAMBERS
OXYGEN RECYCLER
ABANDONED BIRTHING LAB
THE BUNKS
PRIVATE MATRON CHAMBERS
THE SERVICE TUNNELS
FOOD RECYLE CHUTES
SERVICE LADDER
MAINTENANCE POD #2 AIR LOCK
CLOSED
RICHIES
FOOD CHUTE
DARK FLATS
SERVICE TUNNELS
TRASH AND RECYCLE

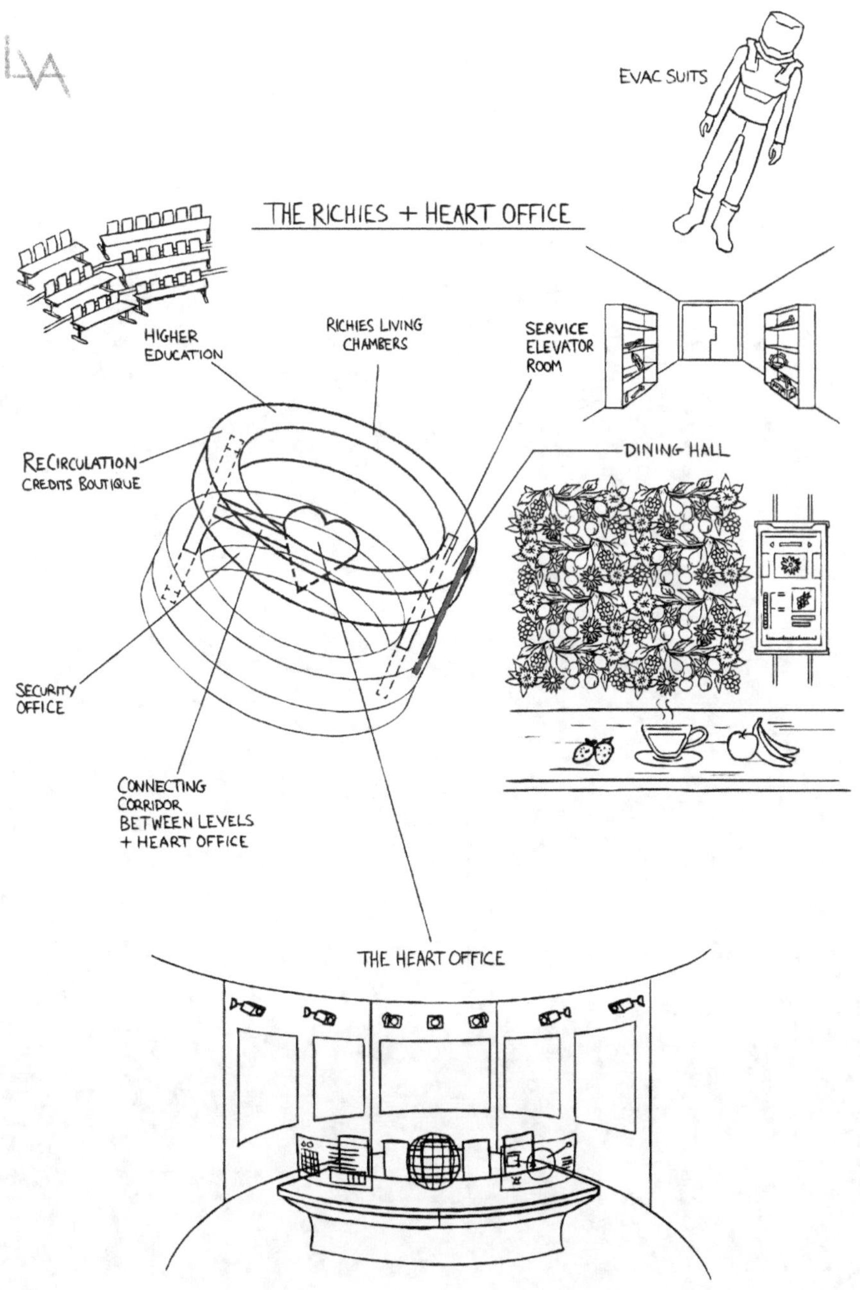
EVAC SUITS
THE RICHIES + HEART OFFICE
HIGHER EDUCATION
RICHIES LIVING CHAMBERS
SERVICE ELEVATOR ROOM
ReCirculation
CREDITS BOUTIQUE
DINING HALL
SECURITY OFFICE
CONNECTING CORRIDOR BETWEEN LEVELS + HEART OFFICE
THE HEART OFFICE

Prologue

Being summoned to the Heart Office in the center of the space station isn't necessarily a good thing. Occasionally, the Council of Elders would broadcast job promotions on the live stream displayed on every screen in Pangea, but those were rare. Most summonses were due to a violation, meaning that punishment was imminent. It was especially true for the Lumpen, the lower class that lived in the Dark Flats. That was one of the first life lessons that Silas Kline had learned.

When Silas was 17, he watched on the screen in the work-study classroom as his friend Dorro was sentenced in the Heart Office. The Elders live streamed Dorro's journey from various angles of the functioning cameras on board. Dorro had committed a crime by eating from another person's ration tray. The rations were left over on Silas' tray. He saw no harm in letting Dorro eat what would otherwise be discarded. It was against the laws of Pangea. Silas remembered when Dorro received the notification, he was summoned to the Heart Office and felt like it was happening again, except to him.

Silas shuddered and swallowed hard as he remembered seeing the terror in Dorro's eyes when the Council had sentenced him to 4 months in Solitary Containment.

It was the isolation that had driven Dorro insane. He hadn't seen another human being for 120 straight days. When he was released from Containment, he looked like he had aged over ten years. He behaved like a different person.

Silas would try to talk to Dorro about his experience, but all Dorro would say was, *"I'd rather die than go back."* Those words echoed loudly in Silas' mind with each step he took toward the Heart Office. The broadcast of Dorro's sentencing had been almost 16 years ago, but the images Silas remembered were vivid and fresh. The guilt was something he had carried with him ever since.

Silas' job as a general education teacher to the Lumpen children came with a few perks, including not having to wear a Proximity Shock Collar. However, his position did not exempt him from being monitored or judged by the Council. He tried to remember if he had done something recently to break any laws. Still, his mind was overwhelmed with memories of the live stream of Dorro's condemnation.

Standing outside the Heart Office, he breathed deeply to calm his racing heart. It didn't work, and he exhaled with a deep sigh. He swiped his right wrist over the door scanner. Processing the Identity Information embedded in the chip under his skin took a moment. When the scanner completed processing, it turned green, and the massive door before him opened with a loud clang. There was a hydraulic hiss before it slid to the side to reveal a circular office with white walls and a transparent ceiling that looked out into space. Silas could see a partial view of the blackened surface of Old Earth and its Moon that Pangea orbited. There was a desk in the middle of the room where the Council sat waiting for him.

"Thank you for joining us today, Mr. Kline." The older woman sitting at the desk directly before him kindly said while remaining seated. Her short white hair slicked back against her head, and her confidence ruled the room.

"Please, call me Silas. Thank you for inviting me. I've never been in the Heart Office before." Silas looked around the room, noticing the several cameras that recorded everything happening in the office. His eyes landed on the multiple screens on the curved walls behind the five Council members. Silas was taken aback when he saw himself on the screens displaying this moment. He blushed with embarrassment when he remembered that this meeting might be live streamed as Dorro's had been. Silas quickly shifted his gaze down to meet the eyes of the woman who welcomed him. He recognized her as Intra, who makes the daily station announcements. While all the Elder members were considered equal, Intra had a more demanding presence on Pangea.

"We have summoned you to discuss a classified assignment for which we need your skill set. It is a top priority and the outcome will benefit everyone who lives on Pangea." Intra said plainly.

"What kind of assignment? My skills?" He questioned the table of Council Members.

"We have seen your work with the children from the Dark Flats. We want to apply your abilities to this special project in addition to your regular duties." Intra told him.

"I'm not sure I understand. What kind of classified assignment would you need a teacher for?" He asked. She paused before responding.

"You must verbally consent to a nondisclosure agreement. You must not repeat anything outside of these walls. If you agree, please say your name, date, and consent for the official records," she stated factually. Silas could not refuse.

"I'm Silas Kline, today is January 16th, 2318, and I consent to the NDA," Silas said reluctantly. He had heard stories from other Lumpen about what happens if you disagreed with the Council, and he didn't want to end up dead.

"Wonderful. Let's proceed." Intra said, using her left hand to gesture above the desk. The screens behind the Council changed from the image of him in the office in to a file containing relevant information and a photo of a teenager.

Intra continued, "This file will be sent to your Onboard Communicator when we conclude here. Your assignment is to conduct a series of specialized tests that our scientists have generated and evaluate the results of this pupil. You will also be teaching the basic curriculum needed to prepare them for the work-study program when they reach the eligible age in two years. We require weekly progress reports based on your evaluations and test responses. Do you have any questions?"

Silas took a moment, looked at the screens, and read what he could, "Age 15 is the minimum age for work-study. The pupil is 13, so who has been their teacher until now?"

"The previous teacher has been promoted to the Aristocrat level, and you will be their replacement," Intra said curtly.

"Will I get promoted when I complete the assignment?" He asked hesitantly. Silas was a little stunned that this meeting even mentioned a promotion. He never thought as a teacher, he would get that opportunity. He had been wondering what would happen when the last of his current class reached 18. There haven't been any new births on board in 5 years. The youngest person in his class was 13 instead of the usual age of 10.

"That's a perfectly acceptable question, although I am surprised you don't have questions regarding the pupil or types of tests." Intra looked at Silas with an unblinking stare to gauge his response.

"I've been administering tests and dealing with children for 18 years, since I was in work-study. I haven't yet seen a test that I can't conduct." Silas said proudly.

"Yes, you are qualified." Intra validated him before she continued, "Due to the importance of this assignment, we are prepared to issue the same compensation that your predecessor received. A promotion to the Aristocrats level, which includes living chambers for one, the privilege of teaching higher education, and a significant bonus upon successful completion."

"If I'm married upon completing this assignment, can I take my spouse?" He asked.

The Council of Elders looked at each other around the desk, gauging his request. Every silent moment ticked by made Silas' stomach knot up with fear. Sweat began to form at his hairline despite being in the chilly office.

"Yes, we will permit a contracted partner to move with you. Please be advised that they will not have a job provided to them as you will. That means that they will have to test into a higher-level opportunity." Intra paused, and a smile began to curl the corners of her mouth. "Of course, all of this depends on the successful assignment."

"Why did you emphasize 'if the assignment is successful' twice? How are we defining success?" He asked.

"Now, those are good questions." Silas detected a condescending tone in Intra's voice. She made another gesture above the desk, and the screens behind her changed to a solar system map. Another member of the Council, a woman with wavy long faded red hair that touched her shoulders, spoke next.

"You must understand," she said from her seat at the end of the desk, "This assignment is a matter of life and death for everyone on board. This pupil is the newest generation of our modified DNX, which our scientists have worked endlessly on this project. The goal is to move the remaining human race to a new planet instead of this space station. We need to conduct tests to see what specific alterations are best. Then we will provide those same upgrades as a booster shot for everyone on board." Her voice was kind and confident as she spoke to Silas, and he felt at ease.

"Thank you for putting it so simply, Codex," Intra said, looking at the woman at the end.

"It sounds like cutting-edge technology, being able to upgrade our DNX so long after completing our gestation in the Birthing Lab. It sounds impossible. What kinds of upgrades are these?"

"That information is irrelevant to your assignment," Intra said sternly.

"Is there anything else I need to know?" He asked timidly.

"The deadline for the weekly reports will be every Saturday before midnight," Codex explained. "You are only permitted to teach the established curriculum and tests we provide you. You must follow the exact instructions as specified. No one else is to know about this assignment, including this pupil. They should believe that they are ordinary so that we can properly evaluate the skills and social responses that occur during and after the testing. Then we will compare those results to your other pupils."

"The control group," Intra added.

"That sounds more like an experiment than an assignment," Silas stated.

"You may call it an assignment or an experiment." Intra began. "Science is part of our everyday life on Pangea. It is unnatural for humans to live in outer space. Every person on board was created in the Birthing Lab using DNX crafted by scientists. The critical fact is that this child can advance the human race exponentially in a fraction of the time."

"We will colonize a new planet to improve everyone's quality of life. Humanity will owe you an outstanding debt for your hard work, and you'll live forever in our history books." Codex added.

Silas took a moment to look at the map displayed on the screens. His youthful self was enticed by the possibilities on other planets and exploring. The thought that he would end up in the books he taught excited him instead of the fear he had felt before the meeting.

"When do I start?" Silas asked with his eyes still on the screens.

"Immediately," Intra said with satisfaction.

Chapter 1
Nitris

Ding, ding, ding.

A computer chime rang across the speakers on board.

"Good morning, residents of Pangea! Today is March 1st, 2320, and the time is 06:00 hours UTC. It is time to start your day. New schedules have been sent to your Onboard Communicator," the geriatric voice of Intra from the Council of Elders announced on the station-wide broadcast.

Alerts filled the Bunks, followed by teenagers groaning in response to their OC notifications.

"I have a special announcement." Intra continued, "With the start of this new month, the Lumpen youths begin their first day of work-study. Be prepared to see them accompanying their adult supervisors as they learn the most important jobs all over Pangea."

The recording of Intra paused. Maybe she was expecting applause, but all I heard were sighs and groans that filled the room.

"Please proceed to get proper nourishment and cleanse within the current hour before beginning the day promptly at 0700 hours. Adults report to your work spaces, and adolescents report to designated classrooms. Your imperative contribution is necessary to ensure the safety of everyone." Intra's announcement ended with the same chime it had started.

That last line of the announcements always made me cringe a little. I didn't see how my contribution would protect anyone. I pulled the thin blanket over my head and closed my eyes. The teenagers began to gather what they needed for the day and exited the Bunks. Some would go towards either the Mess Hall or the Sand Showers. It is one of the few interim hours of the day when we can choose for ourselves what order we want to do things.

"All my older teenagers can proceed with your day as usual. Everyone starting work-study for the first time today, please look at your OC for your updated schedule for this month and let me know if you have any questions." The bright, optimistic voice of Ms. Verban, the tall woman with short curly brown hair who was the matron for all the children in the Dark Flats, announced to us. She always made me feel safe.

I sat up in bed and looked around the Bunks, where all of us unwanted children of Pangea live. It used to be bigger and could fit twice as many children as it contains now. The oldest always have to sleep near the door because they are more useful in an emergency than the younger children. I'm glad to be the youngest because I sleep in the back.

My skull felt like it had been split into two pieces right down the center. I rubbed my forehead, where I had a headache. I had that strange nightmare again. It has been happening more frequently, but it's starting to bring these pains. I don't remember much detail about them. I recognize that I'm standing outside of the abandoned Birthing Lab, trying to look into the dark window. I strain my eyes to focus on the dark. That is when I made eye contact with glowing blue eyes that felt like they were burning into my soul. I felt my whole body shake and rubbed my arms. Everyone else was already starting their day.

"Watch out, Richies. The Lumpen children will finally see your level." Taliah said while she pulled her curly red hair into a bun. She sleeps on the top bunk across the aisle from me.

"Taliah, you know that term is frowned upon." Ms. Verban warned her.

"You are absolutely correct, Ms. Verban." Taliah replied with sarcasm, then announced, "Everyone, if you see a Richie, make sure you don't call them a 'Richie'. You'll hurt their feelings or something." She snorted as she jumped down from her bunk and gathered her clothes to go to the Sand Showers.

"Hey, Ms. Verban, how come this month's schedule seems twice as long as last month's?" Justice asked. She was still looking at the new schedule and scrolling on her OC. Her long wavy blonde hair fell in front of her eyes. With a hair flip, she moved it aside to keep reading her OC. She sleeps under Taliah, and they are best friends.

"That is an accurate observation, Justice." Ms. Verban replied. "Now that everyone here is 15 years old, you're considered of working age. Only the initial rounds of the work-study program will be every day of the week. Thus, allowing an adequate amount of time to learn the various jobs. Then everyone will test for all the jobs they learned at the end of this work-study cycle."

"Better pay attention in work-study, kiddos. You don't want to end up cleaning the suction toilets for the Richies." Cyran teased the others as she walked to meet her girlfriend, Justice. I watched as her long straight black hair bounced with each step down the aisle.

"Don't be an air-suck, Cyran. No one listens to you. Thankfully, we only have to deal with you until you turn 18." Taliah said as she intentionally bumped past Cyran hitting her shoulder.

"*Don't be an air-suck.*" Cyran rolled her brown eyes and said mockingly before she extended her hand to help Justice out of bed.

"I will miss you when you move out of here." Justice pouted as she grabbed Cyran's hand to stand up.

"It's not like I'll be a million miles away." Cyran offered.

"It'll seem like it," Justice replied. "At least until I'm old enough that we can live together. It's always so dark and eerie with the green emergency lights on the floor. I hope our chambers have working lights." Justice said. They kissed before walking down the aisle after Taliah.

The bunk beds didn't have ladders, so we had to hoist ourselves up and down using our assigned trunks. I kept mine flush against the wall and used it to get in and out of bed. The small metal trunk is 30 centimeters by 60 centimeters and contains everything I owned, which isn't much. My bunk mate, Apollox, kept his trunk on the end. Using his trunk to get in and out of my bed felt rude. I tried to find my least holey shirt for class and then work-study afterward. I heard soft steps behind me and turned while I was hunched over, looking in my trunk. I saw Ms. Verban had walked the room length to check and confirm that the Bunks were empty. I had been waiting for the opportunity to talk to her.

"Ms. V?" I asked in a low voice, trying not to startle her.

"Oh! Nitris, I didn't see you there. You frightened me." Ms. Verban said, with a quick inhale as she placed her hand on her chest.

"It's okay. I'm used to not being seen." I said as I hung my head down and looked at the floor.

"Is everything alright? Did you have a question about the new schedule for this month?" Ms. Verban asked as she returned to the moment.

"Why do we have to do work-study every day of the week? We only had classes on the weekdays." I asked in a timid voice. I didn't want to sound disrespectful. Ms. Verban had been kind to me for as long as I could remember. She was the Matron to all of the Lumpen children who were created but never adopted.

"When you move out of The Bunks and have to work your main job, it will be on a rotating schedule." She answered. "Nobody gets weekends off. That is why I'm always here regardless of what day of the week it is. It's part of being an adult."

"How did you know what job you wanted to do?" I asked her.

"I didn't know what job I wanted to do until I was in work-study and saw the variety of necessary tasks. Every job is important and has to be done to ensure the safety of everyone on board." She sounded just like Intra. We all had been trained to say that.

"What must I do to test into a more advanced job instead of the usual Lumpen tasks?" I couldn't look her in the eyes when I asked. Instead, I looked at my OC schedule to see if I had any other questions.

"The better you perform the jobs assigned to you during work-study and excel in the standard tests, you will gain more ReCirculation Credits. You can save up those points and pay for the advanced testing for placement into a higher position." Ms. Verban said.

"Is that what you did to be in charge of The Bunks?" I asked and looked up to meet her comforting green eyes. Her defined cheekbones accentuated her natural beauty, and I knew that would never be the case for me.

"I did many things to be in charge of The Bunks," Ms. Verban began, "I worked a lot of overtime in my work-study. I took as many free job placement tests as possible to make sure I was making the correct choice for my future. Before the lockdown started seven years ago, things were different. We were able to do multiple jobs at the same time. I would teach the infants, through age 9, the basics of reading and math. I also assisted in the adoption of newborns from the Birthing Lab. It was gratifying working with all of the children." She trailed off and looked like she remembered an excellent time long ago.

"What do you do now that there are no younger children and the Birthing Lab has been deactivated?" I asked.

"During the day, while you kids are out of The Bunks, it is my job to assist other workers in the Dark Flats." She said, "Sometimes I help Ms. Cora with the adult PSCs. She is getting slower with age. The PSCs must be attached promptly with precise placement to avoid accidental shocks. Most importantly, I do my rounds in the Dark Flats and ensure you kids stick to your schedule. You should get a move on to the Mess Hall so you won't be late." She patted me on my arm to urge me towards the door. We walked side by side out of The Bunks.

I thought about the rations and how there are days when I don't even know how I get from one place to another. It's like I wake up and I'm in Mess Hall or at my desk in the classroom with no recollection of how I got there.

When I realized that I had been quiet for a while, I tried to reignite the conversation, "If I do my best to keep my head down and not cause any problems, will things get easier when I'm out of The Bunks and working all the time?"

"It is tough to be working all the time and constantly doing something without a break, but you will get through it. Take the next couple of years until you turn 18 to learn as much as you can about how the station operates. The more you know, the more valuable you are, which means the more types of work you can do. You can make an impact just by doing a good and safe job." Ms. Verban said as we continued our walk towards the Mess Hall.

"Do you still have a meditation class? Or does that stop when I turn 18 and move out of The Bunks?" I asked with concern about my favorite time of the day.

"We still have meditation, but we don't call it a

'class' when we are adults. After working 6 hours, we get a half hour for meditation to mentally prepare us for the last 6 hours of our shift and help reduce oxygen and ration use. It is calming to sit in my chambers alone and meditate." She said.

"That sounds nice. I wish I could live alone like you." I told her as we walked passed her old classroom that was now closed.

"It might seem that way after having grown up in The Bunks myself, but sometimes I wish I was married and living with someone special," She said as she looked down the hallway towards Mr. Kline's classroom.

"Like Mr. Kline?" I asked. I had seen the way they look at each other and it felt special.

"Shh, don't tell anyone," she said and blushed, "Lumpen are only allowed to have contractual relationships and reside in the same chambers."

"I can keep a secret," I said. I extended my hand as a fist with my pinky raised. Ms. Verban was the teacher that taught us about a pinky promise, and it is more vital than a regular promise. She knew the hand gesture and locked her pinky finger with mine, and we shook on it.

We walked silently past Mr. Kline's classroom. As we walked by the abandoned Earth Labs, I remembered when Mr. Kline told us they used to work on creating natural resources that used to be found on Earth. Before we got to the Lumpen Mess Hall, I asked Ms. Verban something personal about her life on board.

"Did you ever get to go to the Library and touch a real book made of paper?" I asked the question on my mind, but I was too afraid to ask it in front of my peers.

"I think this is the most we've talked on a personal level since I taught you about a pinky promise when you were 6. Do you remember why I taught it to you?" Ms. Verban changed it up and asked me a question.

"Yes, I remember, but because it was a pinky promise not to say anything. That means that I can't repeat the story without breaking the pinky promise." I replied, remembering the day Ms. Verban held my hand while I cried because I learned I had no more adoption chances. She read me a fairy tale called 'Rapunzel'. It was a secret because fictional writing could no longer be accessed on our OCs due to the lockdown. We were told it was a waste of resources. I looked up around us to see if anything seemed out of place. The Dark Flats were dilapidated, with the lights flickering on and off. Still, I didn't want to risk saying anything if there were functioning cameras around us.

"I'm glad that you remember, and it's a good idea not to say anything that can be incriminating," Ms. Verban said with a laugh. She didn't seem worried if anyone heard the story, but it was something close to my heart, and I wanted to keep our secret.

We walked a few more steps in silence before Ms. Verban said, "To answer your question, yes, I have been in the Library, but I didn't get to touch a paper book. I haven't been there since I was 12 years old. I'd go there with my best friends Dorro and Silas. We would skip the evening Sand Showers, eat our rations fast to get to the Library, and look up videos of performances from all over the world. We must have watched 'The Nutcracker' a million times, not just the same version, but all these different performances from all the different countries. My favorite was watching the 'Dance of the Sugar Plum Fairy'. The guys might deny it today, but I think it was their favorite after the Mouse King." Ms. Verban said. She seemed to be in the memory more than walking the hall with me.

"I don't know what half of those words mean, but it sounds like you had a lot of fun. I didn't think that was possible anymore." I said and shrugged my shoulders.

"It was fun, but that was before the free Library media was moved to rent in the ReCirculation Center in exchange for Credits. It's too expensive to watch all of the classics now." She said with a sad exhale.

"Your friends sound like fun. Where do they work now?" I asked. Trying to imagine Ms. Verban younger than I am now was a challenge.

"Silas is your teacher, and Dorro works in the laundry facility at the end of the Adult Chambers. I will help out there this morning to get more overtime credits since I don't have any younger children to teach," She said with a smile and nudged me with her elbow.

"Silas is Mr. Kline?" I said, shocked.

"Why is that so hard to believe?" She asked and let out a laugh.

"I didn't know he had a first name," I said, embarrassed that I hadn't thought about it before.

"Yes, he does, and so do I." She said as she grabbed my hand, shook it, and continued, "I'm Jexa Verban. Nice to meet you, Nitris."

This brought up more questions that I wanted to ask her.

"Why do you have a last name if you were raised in the Bunks? I thought you had to be adopted to get a last name." I asked, without letting her hand go. It was soft and delicate, like she hadn't been laboring her whole life.

"Last names help establish boundaries and respect," she told me, "All the Gen-Ed and work-study teachers I had growing up were either Mr., Ms./Mrs., or Mx. depending on if they had a spouse or were single. We can also chose to not have a last name and be addressed with the prefix and first name instead. The adults that I grew up with preferred to have the prefix in front of their first name and would choose a last name together if they signed a contractual living agreement."

We had reached the Mess Hall entrance, and I knew I had to go in and eat.

"Thanks for talking with me. Are you coming in?" I asked one last question.

"Not this morning. I'm fasting and saving up my Credits," Ms. Verban answered.

"So you can watch the Fairy Dance again?" I asked with a smile.

"Something like that. Have a good morning Nitris and don't forget that it's the first work-study day. You have many jobs to learn about." She said, then waved goodbye to me as she walked past the Mess Hall towards the adults' living area.

I swiped my wrist at the scanner on the front of the dispenser. The rations oozed out of the tube onto the metal tray I picked up when I entered. The rations were the same plain gray goo I'd had my entire life. At least our water tasted okay. It was made on board and had a dispenser in every room I've seen in the Dark Flats.

I considered what Ms. Verban had said about spouses. I had no delusions of finding "love" on

Pangea, so I thought it best to start with making a friend. I took the tray and scanned the room for an open seat. I would need to find a flatmate in a few years, and my best chance was with someone here. If I was lucky, maybe we could have alternate shifts and not have to interact much.

At one table in the back corner away from the entrance sat a group of 6 teens between 15-17 years old, three girls and three boys. They all sat at the same table, whispering to one another. The three girls looked out into the crowd with their backs against the wall. I made eye contact with the girl in the middle, Taliah.

I could overhear Taliah talking about how she would get out of The Dark Flats and make something for herself by testing the highest in work-study. She gave me an odd look and broke eye contact to look at Justice beside her. They must be talking about me. I gave up for the day and sat at an empty table in the middle of the room to eat my rations.

I was never hungry. I knew I was supposed to eat because the computer told me to, but there were some days that I felt like I could go without any food and be fine. More often than not, I couldn't finish my rations and recycled them into the food chute. I kept my head down and focused on my plate as if I would find the answers to life in the goo if I stared hard enough.

Chapter 2
Mr. Kline

Ding, ding, ding.

The computer chimed with the notification to start class. I looked at the 11 teenagers in my class and noticed an empty chair in the back. I went to my desk and picked up my OC to begin class. When I looked up again, the seat was filled by Nitris.

"I'm going to pretend I didn't see that, Nitris," I warned them sternly.

"I'm sorry, Mr. Kline. Please don't deduct Credits from my participation in today's class." They whimpered with fear in their voice.

"Don't let it happen again. We can't have the top student lose first place because they were a few moments late." I told them.

"That's unfair to the rest of us who arrived on time." Taliah spat the words under her breath just to be cruel.

I didn't feel like dealing with her. I didn't even look up from my OC. I reviewed the updated syllabus that I received that morning.

"According to the new schedule, we are going to be reduced to 1 hour per subject from 07:00 through 12:00," I said, reading off the OC. "This will allow an adequate amount of time to cover General Education. Then, I will prepare everyone for work-study before sending out the station assignments. That means we will have to move faster to cover the same amount of information that we would in our old 2 hour classes. We are starting today with Science." I said, clicked the digital workbook file I made for today, and hit send on my OC.

The classroom lit up with screens coming to life and notifications going off as the students got the digital workbook to follow along with as I brought up my lecture notes. The older children sit on one side of the room and don't have to participate in the lecture because they've heard it before. They only need to complete their workbook to get participation credits. Some fall asleep, but I let them use the time however they want.

"Mr. Kline, this looks more like biology than science," Taliah said while scanning her workbook.

"It is a bit of both. We use science daily to keep us alive on Pangea. Still, we have also altered our biology to adapt to space conditions." I told her and remembered when Intra first told me that same line two years ago.

"Oh! Because scientists developed the DNX that is used to create us!" Taliah concluded faster than the rest of the class. She is always one step ahead during the lectures but sometimes struggles during the tests. That is why she is second in the class ranking.

"Yes, our DNX, but also all the various machines and computer programs constantly running to keep Pangea operational. It fits into why the work-study program is so important. Every person in this room will be doing a job to help maintain and protect everyone's life on Pangea," I said as I brought up the first image on my OC. I sent the picture to the holographic display in the center of the room. "Holo, run program" I ordered, then the holo projected the image from my OC, a DNA double helix rotating.

"Why is that service ladder twisted?" Apollox asked from the back row.

"I like that, 'ladder', I'll use that to describe it. The DNA double helix comprises two strands held together by bases. Think of it like two ladders connected, one going up and one going down. Each step is made up of a base to create a 'rung'. The rungs are the thin, vertical bars that connect each pair of steps. The bases and rungs are the two groups of letters in DNA: adenine (A), cytosine (C), guanine (G), and thymine (T) — in various ways to spell out three-letter 'codons' that specify which amino acid is needed at each position within a protein." I explained the image on the holo.

I looked around the room. Taliah was taking notes on her OC, and Justice looked over her shoulder to see what she had written. Nitris seemed to grasp what I was talking about without taking any notes. I looked at Apollox and saw him struggling to get what we were discussing.

"Where is the X in the ladder?" Apollox raised his hand and asked.

"This is what the old DNA helix looked like before our founding scientists figured out how to adapt our DNA to be more efficient. It was necessary to ensure that the human race will live on," I said. I brought up a second image on the holo and displayed it next to the DNA.

"This is our DNX helix. Apollox, can you see the difference?" I wanted to see if he was able to keep up.

"I think so. There are more rungs on our ladder than there used to be." He said, trying to confirm that he understood.

"You're correct! Who can tell me why there are more rungs now than there used to be?" I asked the class, knowing that Taliah would raise her hand first. I tried to see if I could challenge someone else to answer.

"We have to do more now that we live in space. Supplies like food and water are limited to what we can produce on board," Nitris said without raising their hand.

"Yes, and what other things do we have to worry about because we are limited?" I asked the class, trying to engage them.

"Population control because it affects all of our resources like food, oxygen, and energy," Taliah answered satisfactorily.

"Is that why we are made in the Birthing Lab?" Apollox asked.

"Now you're getting it." I was pleased that he seemed to understand.

"I don't feel like I'm getting it," Justice asked with confusion. "How do more rungs help with our supplies and population?" Math is her strongest subject, but the ladder rungs didn't add up to her.

"The additional rungs are alterations our scientists created," I explained. "They're identified with an X. The X is for spliced modified genes from when Pangea was first assembled from the seven other stations and smaller shuttles. These additional rungs allow us to live with less. We don't eat, drink, or sleep as much as humans did back on Earth in 2020. Using DNX, scientists could create all of us in an incubator with a shorter gestation period than birthing children on Old Earth. We were all created in the same place, and the gestation process only took four months."

"Did they have Birthing Labs on Old Earth?" Apollox asked.

"The Birthing Labs are unique to Pangea," I said. I began to explain everything I knew about how reproduction used to work. "On Old Earth, women gave birth after the gestation period of nine months. Our Scientists knew that strict population control would be essential to humankind's survival in space." I said as I brought up my notes on my OC.

"They were also able to eliminate other biological problems as well," I continued, "Before DNX, women would menstruate every month for about a week. That is when the body replaces the uterus lining to prepare for a baby, in the form of blood. That meant every woman would need additional supplies to control their bleeding. Also, pregnant women would eat twice their normal amount to help feed the child growing inside of them, which would deplete food supplies faster."

"There was blood every month? The child grew *inside* of the woman?" Apollox asked with shock.

"Yes. Can you see how these things would have been an issue on a space station with limited supplies?"

I asked, trying to lead him to the answer.

"Gross!" Apollox said with disgust.

"DNX was modified so that we are all born sterile," I said. Apollox looked confused. He is a bit slower than the other students. I continued, "Sterile means that we are born without the biological material to make a child organically as our ancestors did. It is how we limit the population to an exact number. We create new humans as needed and use our unique DNX in the Birthing Lab. It is the safest method because it no longer puts women in danger of death during pregnancy or childbirth. It also eliminates unplanned births that impact our supplies."

"Is that why we can have non-binary people?" Nitris asked tentatively.

"With DNX, we can create men, women, and non-binary people. In the old days on Earth, babies were traditionally born as either girls or boys. If a child grew up and realized they felt more like a boy than a girl, they could transition and change their classified sex with surgeries. Having the option to be non-binary wasn't adopted until the 1990's. By using DNX in the Birthing Lab, we created babies outside the traditional method, allowing us to add the third gender." I explained.

"That's why we are all orphans too," Taliah said, with an edge on orphans.

"Yes, Taliah, that is correct. We no longer need a mother or father to create a new life." I confirmed.

"But why did they make us if we weren't going to be adopted by a Richie family? And why did they put the Birthing Lab on the Lumpen level if the children were intended only for Richies?" Apollox asked the heart-breaking question.

"The adoptions are rigged, and only the Richies can afford it. If Lumpen could afford to adopt a child, we would all be with a family," Nitris said, in a low voice, to Apollox sitting next to them.

"The Richies don't want to hear the children crying from the Birthing Lab, so they kept it down here. Out of sight and out of mind for the Richies." Taliah added on to answer Apollox's second question. I never considered the lab's location affecting the Richies' lifestyle before Taliah gave her hypothesis.

I knew that Nitris had a moment when they were younger when they understood the impact of adoptions and what their life would be. Jexa told me how she tried to comfort Nitris with a fairy tale to get their mind off the disappointment they felt not being adopted.

"We are not supposed to question the decisions made by the Council of Elders," I said sternly. "Maybe, the Elders are saving us from having too many children in the Bunks. You are all still growing up, and your ration and water intake increase with age." I suggested some topics for the students to reflect on their own.

I checked my OC for the time and saw we were almost done with this hour of class.

"Any other questions before we change subjects to Old Earth History?" I asked the class. The older teens were still doing their curriculum and had their heads down.

"How does our DNX make it so we don't use as many rations?" Nitris asked.

"The scientists spliced our DNX using various other animals that used to live in the wild on Old Earth. Some animals would eat before the winter and then hibernate until the spring." I said. I realized I needed to go into more detail when Apollox looked over at Nitris to ask for help. I continued, "Hibernation means that the animals don't need to eat, drink, or expel waste during that time."

"Did they all just sleep the whole time?" Apollox asked.

"They wouldn't be sleeping the whole time," I answered. "It is similar to when we meditate. We slow our heart rate and breathing down, using fewer resources. Old Earth animals went into hibernation instead of prolonged meditation."

"What other changes are there with our DNX versus the old DNA?" Taliah raised her hand and asked.

"Our DNX also has modifications that eliminate sickness that used to be common with Earth humans," I said with pride. I was closely familiar with the topic. "There used to be physical diseases like cancer that would consume a person from the inside out. Mental illnesses were so exhausting that humans couldn't always complete their work. They would need more supplies, including medicine, to help them cope with the mental battle they fought daily." Apollox started to raise his hand to ask another question. Before he could say anything, I said, "Medicine was similar to how the Nanobots work on Pangea. Back on Earth, medicine would mostly come as a pill or injection. The medicine would treat the disease or alleviate the symptoms to make humans feel better. Now we use Nanobots that can identify injuries and fix it without needing our bodies to help."

"You have to be careful with those Nanobots," Cyran volunteered from her seat next to Justice. "I heard from my work-study supervisor that if I get injured on the job and have to get injected with Nanobots, they can control my brain." Cyran doesn't need to participate in this lecture because she has already completed it. I think she likes to scare the younger kids. I remember when Cyran first came to my class, her being scared too. Now she seems tough and can handle anything. She grew up so fast.

"*Control my brain*?" Apollox asked with fear.

"That is an old station legend. It never really happened," Taliah said to put him at ease.

"Legends are stories that have been told throughout history and have become popular," Nitris told Apollox, anticipating what he would ask next. Nitris always seemed to know what others are thinking. I'd need to note that in this week's progress reports.

"I think that is a good place to segue into the next class, Old Earth History," I said excitedly. It is my favorite subject to teach.

I brought up the next digital workbook and sent it to all the students, then displayed the first video from my OC on the holo with voice command. It is not my favorite part of history, but it was in the required syllabus.

"We will be covering the topic of War," I said calmly.

The holo contained depictions of the many different kinds of wars that had been fought on Old Earth. It started with paintings of war and moved into black and white photos, then videos. The videos included sound, and the children jolted back in their seats when an explosion went off. Some of the older kids looked up from their OCs at the holo.

"War is a big part of history. It's been around for as long as humans were on Earth," I began, "It's when two or more groups fight each other to get what they want. People would fight for land, power, or their beliefs. War destroyed the planet and was the reason that humans evacuated Old Earth into space. When Pangea was being built, the various Countries were wary of working together to build this station after experiencing the Last World War. People spoke multiple languages that connected them to the Earth they had to leave behind. This language barrier also caused more conflict and violence on board. Have any of you seen the art on parts of the walls in the Dark Flats?" I ended with a question to engage the class to respond.

The older teens and a few of the younger teens raised their hands. I brought up pictures from the Dark Flats that I had taken myself.

"Displayed now on the holo is some of the art on board. Does this look familiar to most of you?" I asked. I saw more hands rise to acknowledge that they had seen it before.

"This is a flag from the Chinese space station," I said, clicking the following image on my OC. I added pictures from the halls that these teenagers walked by daily and never noticed. I continued, "These are some other flags and writing from other languages from the individual space stations before we were united. While the languages may have been lost, we display these images to remind us that we used to be divided, but now we are together as one."

"Those are really pretty. What does it mean?" Justice said as she admired the images on the holo.

"These Chinese characters are called 'Hanzi'. They are one of Earth's oldest written languages. Sadly, no one on board knows these other languages or their meanings anymore. But, we can enjoy it as art even if we don't know its meaning." I clicked the next set of images, but the holo shorted out and stopped displaying anything.

"The holo display broke again," Taliah stated the obvious with a sigh.

"This thing is always malfunctioning," I said. I hunched over and started to remove the access panel on the bottom.

"Can I help?" I heard Nitris say from their seat in the back.

"Teacher's favorite." Taliah said to Nitris.

"It's already broken, Nitris, so I don't see any harm in having you come to take a look," I said as I waved them to come over to me. "It will be early practice for your work-study to see how things operate." Nitris sat on the floor beside the holo and looked at the wires and circuit boards. They reached their hand into the nest of wires and gently pulled on them to see where they connected.

"Here, let's try this one," I said, reaching for a yellow wire that stuck out more than the rest. I touched it, and it gave me a slight shock. I jerked my hand back away from the wires and looked at my finger, where I got shocked.

"No, I don't think it's that one. Let me try something." Nitris said. They started to trace where the wires went. They pulled a blue wire, and the projection light that is always on turned off. Then they pulled a black wire, and the holo flickered.

"How long is this going to take?" Taliah asked with annoyance.

"It takes as long as it takes," Nitris said calmly.

I stood up and let Nitris work without me

hovering over their shoulder. I looked at the older teens. Even the ones who have work-study in electrical didn't bother to get up and help. Everyone just stayed seated and quiet. "While we try to fix the holo, let's all start reading the History assignment I sent," I advised the class.

Taliah smiled and immediately started reading. Unlike Justice, who sighed with grief that she had to read. Taliah seems to love reading more than anything. I watched the students while Nitris worked on the holo.

"Mr. Kline?" Apollox asked me quietly so he wouldn't disturb the other students.

"Yes, Apollox?" I approached him so we could whisper.

"If Old Earth was mostly made of water, then why does the planet continue to burn now, centuries later?" Apollox asked a good question.

"Because there were 150 nuclear weapons used in the Last World War, that war ended the Earth. These nukes appeared in warring countries. We don't know who sold them or who launched the first nuke. There were enough nukes that all the warring countries had 15 each. Ultimately, it only took six nukes to destroy all life on Earth. The remaining 144 nukes were set to self-detonate over time. It was the radiation fallout that occurred after the unused nukes detonated. Some of the nukes were located near fossil fuels and nuclear power plants. When they self-detonated, the initial blast caused a chain reaction. Detonations near nuclear power plants, flammable fuels, and other toxic factories released even more radiation. That is why the Old Earth is still on fire 300 years later. There is no way to know how many have gone off or if Old

Earth will ever be inhabitable again. We don't know if it can support life after the devastation, but we are safe here on the station." I answered his question to the entire class.

I turned back to the holo and saw Nitris putting the panel back on.

"Mr. Kline, can you give it a try again?" Nitris asked me.

The next subject on my OC was Math, and I brought up my guide to send to the holo with voice command. The machine flickered, and the lights came on to display the algebra problem that the class needed to work on next.

"Thanks, Nitris. You saved the day. I don't know how you navigate that mess of wires in there." I told them as they returned to their seat in the back next to Apollox.

"How did they even know how to fix it?" Taliah whispered to Justice and gave a glaring look to Nitris. It was a question that I wanted to know the answer to also, but I wouldn't ask.

"Sometimes it feels like my hands know what to do before my brain does. This time it was the main power wire that was loose. I had to strip it down and reconnect it." Nitris answered Taliah as they took their seat.

"Who *taught* you how to do it?" Taliah asked the follow-up question directly to Nitris.

"It fits with the facts, and that makes sense to me. The holo green light that shows it is on went out." Nitris answered in a meek voice.

I saw Taliah's mouth begin to open for another question, and I couldn't have that. The Council monitors me closely while I'm still working on this classified assignment. I don't want to raise unnecessary attention that might jeopardize my weekly reports, so I take control of the class and review the syllabus.

"The schedule says that we are supposed to move on to Math now," I told the class. "Let's continue to work silently on chapter 12 of the digital workbook. Please raise your hand if you need any additional help." I sat at my desk and continued working on my weekly report for the Council I had started yesterday. It was only Monday, and I didn't have to turn in the progress reports until Saturday night, but I like to get them done to free up time to meet with Jexa after lights out.

I was so focused on my reports that when I checked my OC, I noticed that I exceeded the allotted time for Math. I looked up to see if the students had noticed either. Everyone was still working on their OCs.

I looked at Taliah, who was usually the first to finish, but she was still working on her OC. Then I looked over at Nitris. They had finished, and their OC was sitting on their desk.

"How is everyone doing?" I asked the classroom. "We are running out of time for today, and I want to make sure that everyone feels confident about their math and will be able to finish it tonight."

The class looked up at me when I talked, but no one raised their hands.

"Great, let's move on to our Transcendental Meditation for the last bit of time before we change gears to work-study," I announced to the class.

"Mr. Kline, what's so great about TM that we must do it daily?" Justice asked with a groan. "We've been doing it since we were little kids in Ms. Verban's class, and I thought we would drop it now that we're entering work-study."

"Transcendental Meditation is a practice that involves focusing one's attention and being aware of the present moment. I've used our same TM practice since I was a child. I used it before taking my work-study test and scored the second highest for teaching." I explained.

"Who scored the highest?" Taliah asked, clearly not focused on the meditation part.

"Ms. Verban scored the highest, and we did our TM together before the test. Meditation can be an effective tool for managing stress and improving mental well-being. Additionally, Old Earth practitioners believed meditation could reduce negative emotions, improve concentration, and focus, increase resilience, and reduce oxygen use. It is something that even the adult Lumpen do daily, which is why it is scheduled every day."

"Emphasis on 'reduce oxygen use' because our supplies are limited." Taliah turned around to tell Justice. "Plus, it helps to reduce our appetite, and then we don't need to eat in the middle of the day."

"Taliah is correct. Now, let's all meditate together." I told the class, then watched as they all closed their eyes and silently meditated to themselves.

I took a large inhale and closed my eyes to begin my meditation.

Ding, ding, ding.

The computer notified the room that classes for the day were complete. It was time to start the work-study orientation video before the students got fitted with their PSCs.

"Thank you, everyone, for a great class today.

All of the older students can go ahead and leave to get your PSCs from Ms. Cora and begin work-study. All my first-time work-study pupils, please stay seated, and we will begin orientation." I told the room. The six oldest teens stood up and left the classroom.

"Better be careful, kiddies," Segauce said as he got up. He was the oldest student in the class. "If you're late to get your PSCs, you might end up with a defective one that shocks you constantly." He walked toward the door with a laugh.

"Wait, what? Is that a thing?" Justice leaned forward and asked Taliah.

"Yeah, I've heard stories about it from the PSC workers in the Mess Hall," Taliah answered.

"No, it is not a thing," I assured them. "And I remember how scared Segauce was when he did his work-study orientation," I shouted, hoping he could hear me in the hall.

"After the orientation video, we will have an agreement to go over before you head to get fitted for PSCs," I announced. On my OC, I brought up the same "Welcome to Work-Study" orientation video, which I had watched so many times that I had it memorized.

"Welcome to your first day of adulthood." The hologram of Intra began. She looked like the same older woman with short slicked-back gray hair and a wrinkled forehead that we saw today.

"With great privilege and honor, you will learn to do jobs that will be the most important on Pangea. Today is the first day of your "work-study" programmmm-" The holo froze again.

"Nitris, can you-" I began to ask.

"On it." Nitris jumped up and went to the holo display. They took out their standard issue multi-tool that all the children were issued when they turned 13. It's not necessarily a present, but more about making everyone essential. The tool had many cosmetic defects from being used over the generations, but it still worked well on the basics.

We watched as Nitris removed the panel and worked around the wires again.

"How do you even know how to do that?" Taliah, who was seated closest to the holo, asked Nitris.

"I can't explain it. It just makes sense to me," Nitris answered while they continued to work.

"You are mechanically inclined. It's a great skill set that will make you a valuable worker." I told them.

"Mr. Kline, can you please give it another try now?" Nitris said from the floor, waiting to put the panel back into place.

"Holo, run the program," I announced to the holo. When it powered up, I whispered to Nitris, "Thank you." As they returned to their seat.

"Analyzing request." The computer replied to my voice command, and the holo went blank, and rebooted the video.

"Today is the first day of your 'work-study' program, and I want to personally thank you all for being here," The projection of Intra began again, "My name is Intra, and I am on the Council of the Elders. Living in space is dangerous, but with these work-study classes, you will learn how to do various jobs on board to ensure the safety of everyone on Pangea."

"Did the holo just 'thank' us for being in this *mandatory* program?" Taliah said, under her breath, to Justice behind her. They giggled, and I cleared my throat to return their attention to the holo.

"Each person will have their working position,

which has its own designated specialty as well as knowledge in other positions in cases of Emergency. If something were to go wrong, we need everyone trained, in every position, available in case of accidental death or dismemberment." Intra's holo continued as the video changed. "There are constant threats to our existence, with space debris from Old Earth satellites and cars that were sent to space for reasons unknown. The impact of this debris striking Pangea can be deadly to everyone. To prevent this, we use the automated Exterior Maintenance Pod to gather any nearby space debris. Someone in this room will be honored to serve this pod and sort its recyclable material."

"I've always wanted to sort trash," Apollox said with sincerity from the back corner of the room. Nitris looked at him like he had just spoken a long-dead language.

"What?" Nitris asked him in a low, hushed tone.

"I hope I can sort trash. Not the pod servicing part; I don't want to do any emergency spacewalks," Apollox said. I tuned out the familiar holo to hear the two of them.

"I think the spacewalks and learning how the Exterior Maintenance Pod works would be better than sorting the trash," Nitris said.

"It's not the trash sorting that interests me. I heard Taliah might get assigned there, and I want to work with her." Apollox whispered to Nitris.

I saw Nitris roll their eyes and look back at the holo. I cleared my throat louder this time and gave a warning look to Nitris and Apollox.

"... the privilege of everyone in this room and throughout the station is to keep Pangea safe." Intra's holo concluded. After a brief pause, another stock video started to play. The video began by zooming in on an image of Earth before the Last World War, with vibrant blues and greens. It showed the Earth gently spinning until the video zoomed in on North America. The holo showed the people of Earth going about their day. It began to follow two girls walking outside wearing heavy coats and holding white paper cups with a green mermaid logo. I paused the video to take this moment to teach the class about the changing seasons that used to happen on Earth.

"The color of the leaves on the trees behind these girls tells us that it is the season called Autumn. It was a time for trees to prepare for cold winters, and they shed their leaves so that new growth could come in the Spring." I said, admiring the trees.

"I would work the rest of my life to be able to wear that jacket! Did you see how vibrant the colors were? It even had pockets!" Justice said as she sat back in her chair.

"When you start working full-time on Pangea, there are no limits to how much overtime you can work!" I said in an attempt to make the adverse facts of our working life sound optimistic. "With the extra ReCirculation Credits, you can earn from working through breaks, you could have that jacket one day! Well, not that jacket exactly, but I have seen some clothing in the ReCirculation Center without holes."

Justice sighed loudly and folded her arms across her chest. "Yeah, if I work every day until I die, I might be able to afford a hole-less shirt," she said as she looked at her ragged clothes.

"We have a lot to cover. No more interruptions. I'm talking to everyone here." I said, then hit resume.

The video continued playing, depicting a pleasant day with people on the street smiling and wearing colorful clothes. Intra's voice returned as the video of the happy people took on an ominous tone.

"Everything seemed wonderful. Until the day the nukes went off in major metropolitan locations and forced the few surviving humans to flee the Earth to their individual countries' space stations." Intra's voice explained as the holo changed drastically. The bright, pleasant day changed to show mushroom clouds and fire devastation across the Earth. The image displayed was buildings collapsing with loud crashes. "Within months of the Great Exodus from Earth, it was calculated that all the humans would die slowly by oxygen deprivation or starvation. An alliance was formed between the major powers to build one massive station to combine resources and knowledge to better adapt to living in space."

The video shows different stations that vary in size, displaying other flags and symbols. Shuttles were flying around them, tugging the large stations with people in spacesuits welding the sides of Pangea.

Intra's voice continued. "The effort to connect all of the space stations was massive and took five years of hard work from people like you. Additional materials were recycled from the former moon rovers and old satellites. We sourced everything needed to unite the people and create a suitable station to support life for an indefinite amount of time. As a result, today, we live in a stable habitat located within the moon's gravitational pull, constantly circling the dead planet we now call Old Earth."

A perfect computer-generated image of Pangea is displayed on the holo. Two massive rings stacked on each other with a heart-shaped office in the center, connected to the rings by a corridor.

"I still don't understand why no windows look out into space on the Dark Flats," Taliah shouted, "I heard that the top level has huge panoramic windows. We could see different parts of the Milky Way Galaxy and the dead Old Earth. It's not fair that only the Richies get to see it."

"Aristocrats." I corrected Taliah's use of the slang term "Richies."

The video continued by showing a computer-generated map and how each level mirrors the level above.

"This must be an old video," Justice commented, "cause it looks like the Dark Flats are laid out the same as the upper level, but I've walked by the adult living chambers, and they look so small compared to that." I put a finger to my lips and shushed Justice.

"...and in conclusion, your participation and hard work doing these jobs are vital to the success of the human race's longevity. Your imperative contribution is necessary to ensure the safety of everyone." Intra's hologram ends.

"What about the Lockdown?" Taliah asked me. "How old was that video, not to mention the Lockdown we've lived in for seven years?"

"This is the same video I watched when I started work-study," I informed the class. "There are exactly 257 registered residents on board. Pangea went on Lockdown for reasons only the Council of Elders know. The only explanation we've received is that the Lockdown is for our safety. It also affects the number of jobs that are available to choose for work-study. The Lockdown includes shutting down the Library and

Birthing Lab, some Research Labs, and the old ship landing docks used during Pangea's construction."

"There's also a ban on anything fun," Taliah said bitterly. "No music, no recreational entertainment. Even reading is prohibited except for approved digital textbooks. This is for the safety of the residents?"

"It's not *all* banned," Justice said, and her stomach gurgled. "You just have to be willing to make sacrifices and work hard for your ReCirculation Credits."

"That's right, Justice, excellent point," I said. "Work hard, and entertainment can be your reward. When doing work-study on board, be sure to follow all the rules and listen to your supervisors. They will be telling you what you can and cannot do. That is to help you avoid being shocked by your PSCs."

"Are the PSCs only for if we break the rules, or do we get shocked for making mistakes, too?" Apollox asked.

"The PSCs are only to prevent workers from entering unauthorized areas," I reassured him. "PSC stands for Proximity Shock Collar. It is locked into place every day before you start working. The PSC is configured to where you might need to go for your work that day. If you leave that designated area where you should be working, you will be shocked until you return to the specified work area."

"Seems harsh..." Taliah observed.

"The Elders created the PSCs to help us work more efficiently and to help everyone stay out of trouble," I said. "We might not understand their methods, but they have lived in space for centuries. They are the first generation of DNX and have lived nearly 300 years." I had given this speech dozens of times, even though I disagreed. I knew I was constantly under surveillance and had to encourage the children to follow the rules or risk execution. Still, I could feel the nervous energy from the six teens left in my classroom.

"Why don't you have a PSC, Mr. Kline?" Apollox asked me.

"The teaching positions don't require a PSC because they're limited to the Dark Flats only and don't require going to the Aristocrats level. Your work-study teachers might not have their PSCs on if they are only on the Dark Flats, but if the work requires them to move to the Aristocrats level, they will need their PSCs too." I answered.

"The PSCs are to make the Richies feel better, and they feel safe with the Lumpen workers on their level," Taliah said to Apollox. I was glad that she said it. Sometimes, I appreciated Taliah speaking the truth since I was not permitted to do so.

"What other jobs don't need a PSC?" Nitris asked curiously.

"Besides Teachers, there's Electrical, and 'Dark Flat only' jobs such as Laundry." I thought for a moment. "There are some others, too. I can provide you with a complete list later if you'd like." Nitris nodded that they would.

"Which jobs do we get for work-study?" Taliah asked.

"You'll spend some time in each department that currently has vacancies that need to be filled," I told Taliah. I picked up my OC to generate the first round of work-study classes. "I've sent you all the randomly assigned courses you will be learning in work-study this week. I also included the supervisor's name you will report to after receiving your PSC from Ms. Cora's room, next to the Mess Hall."

The OCs in the room lit up and vibrated with the new information. I watched as the teens all read their assignments.

"What is this 'PSC consent document'?" Taliah asked as she read her OC. "It says I need to swipe my Identity Chip to accept it?"

"That's a contract between you and the Elders, saying that you agree to wear the PSCs for training purposes until you test into your final job," I explained. "You're agreeing to obey the limits of the proximity you're allotted."

"What happens if I don't want to consent to this contract?" Taliah asked, pushing the boundaries.

"Refusal to cooperate can result in punishment from the Elders." I took a deep breath, then continued. "Any disobedience will result in the violator being placed in Solitary Containment until they comply." I saw my students' eyes go wide with fear. I tried to reassure them.

"I don't want you all to worry about the PSCs. When I was your age, I was fitted with a PSC until work-study was completed, and I tested for this teaching position. Be sure to obey the rules." I concluded.

As I told the class my story, and my hand instinctively rubbed the back of my neck where the PSC would lock. I hoped none of them would ever feel the shock of the collar and see the burn marks it would leave.

Chapter 3
Taliah

Ding, ding, ding.

The notification that orientation was completed startled me, and I jumped in my seat. I quickly gathered my OC and rushed out the door. I was not excited about wearing a Proximity Shock Collar. Still, I had heard it was better to be at the front of the line outside Ms. Cora's office. The last in line would get the most defective PSC, and there were rumors that they could go off for no reason.

"Taliah! Wait for me!" Justice yelled from the hall behind me.

"Come on, hurry up!" I scolded her. "Remember what I told you about the kids at the end of the line?" I didn't slow my pace.

I heard Justice speeding up to join me. She wouldn't have known about the defective PSCs if I hadn't mentioned it. She was too obsessed with herself and collecting ReCirculation Credits to watch old movies in the RC Center with her girlfriend, Cyran.

"Yeah, you told me all about the bad collars," Justice said out of breath, "Don't they shock at 2 million volts or something? How do we not die?"

"They wouldn't shock us enough to kill us." I reminded her. "The document we had to swipe said it's only two thousand volts. Enough to make us stop in place and maybe pee ourselves." We rounded the last part of the Dark Flats to Ms. Cora's office.

"Cyran told me that her work-study supervisor is only in charge of teaching us the book and learning the codes for reset," Justice said. "It's more like a memory game than actual work." Justice finished talking as we reached the end of the line of adult Lumpen outside of Ms. Cora's office.

"What is your first work-study class?" I asked Justice.

"It says 'Fan-Driven Suction', but I don't know what that means." She answered.

"It means you're going to be a plumber and get the privilege of cleaning the Richies' toilets," I laughed.

"Eww. Really? What about you? Please tell me we're going to be working together." Justice begged.

"My first work-study class is Oxygen Supply Maintenance," I said disappointedly.

I leaned my back against the wall and let out a sigh. "Are you ready for this to be the rest of our lives?" I asked Justice, keeping my eyes on the floor. I noticed all the scuff marks on it from the generations before us. There are faded markings on the walls and floors that everyone ignores.

"Don't bring me down like that," Justice replied. "It'll be alright as long as we follow the rules." She joined me with her back against the wall and crossed her legs. Cyran approached us, and Justice perked up.

"Heyyyyy! What's got my girl so glum?" Cyran said. She ran up and snuggled Justice against the wall.

With a happy giggle of excitement, Justice jumped and wrapped her legs around Cyran's waist. They began kissing in front of everyone. I tried to find an excuse to make them stop.

"Come on, Cyran, quit it. We can't let you cut in line." I said as I shoved her away from Justice, trying to wedge myself between them.

Cyran kissed Justice one more time and set her down. She looked at me with her deep brown eyes that matched her dark hair that she put up in a messy bun.

"I'm not trying to cut in line," she spat at me, "I work in electric repairs, so I don't have to wear a PSC like you. I can come and go as I please." Cyran kissed Justice one more time. "See you later at dinner!" She said to Justice and then started to walk away.

I started to think about how unfair the career assignment and PSCs were, but I kept my mouth shut.

The line behind us had grown with more adult Lumpen workers who needed their PSCs, making the line wrap around the corner. I couldn't see the end of the line. The front of the line began to move, and I pushed off the wall. I stood facing forward with Justice behind me.

We moved along with the line of mixed teens and adults. We didn't speak again until it was our turn to be locked into our PSCs.

I looked back at Justice and said, "Wish me luck," before I headed into Ms. Cora's office.

"Hello, please step over here," Ms. Cora said as she gestured to the side of her desk. She was a few centimeters shorter than me, but her long wavy gray hair reached her waist from the ponytail she wore it in. It was the longest hair I had seen on anyone.

"Please, not a defective one," I said quietly, following her directions. I didn't want her to think I was weak or afraid, but I had to say something.

"Defective? We don't have any like that," she said while she measured my neck with a tape measurer and then walked back to the wall of collars. She quickly found one in a size that would fit me.

"That's not what I heard," I said in a low tone. I didn't want to get in trouble for talking back.

"There are a lot of stories that go way back to when I was a child. I always confirm the PSCs are calibrated to the proper locations." Ms. Cora said soothingly while she fitted me into my collar, "Rest assured, there haven't been any issues with PSCs for as long as I've been alive."

"Why don't you have to wear a PSC?" I asked her, and the loud clunk of the lock startled me. I moved my head from left to right to test my mobility. My peripheral vision wasn't obstructed, and the black and red collar stayed in view when I looked down. It was about ten centimeters thick. I could fit two fingers between the PSC and my neck, but it still felt suffocating.

"I rarely leave my chambers, and if there is ever an emergency, I'm in charge of releasing the Lumpen from their PSCs." Ms. Cora told me.

Ms. Cora took my right hand away from the PSC and swiped it over her OC. It beeped and logged where I would be allowed to go. I watched as Ms. Cora calibrated the designated work-study area for me.

Then she took her OC, scanned the back of my PSC, and there was another beep.

Ms. Cora gave me a gentle push on my shoulders toward the doors. "You will report to Mr. Salvador for Oxygen Supply Maintenance, located near the Mess Hall, but the work-study classroom is a small office on the far side of the Dark Flats. Don't be late for your first day. Let the next person know to come in as you exit." I walked out, holding the PSC with both hands, trying to pull it away from my throat. It was making it hard to breathe. I saw Justice and gestured with a nod toward Ms. Cora's office. "You're next," I said, and started towards the work-study room to meet my new coworkers.

"Does it hurt?" Justice called after me as she stepped into Ms. Cora's office. By then, I was rounding the corner, so I didn't have to tell her "yes."

When I arrived at Mr. Salvador's work-study classroom, I was surprised to see how small it was compared to Mr. Kline's room. It was cramped with a desk and only four student chairs. There were shelves behind him that looked chaotic with things thrown around. Mr. Salvador sat behind the desk. His long black hair was streaked with gray. It laid loose on his shoulders and fell down his back. He was skinny, and his clothes looked two sizes too big on his small frame. He didn't stand up but looked about the same height as Ms. Cora.

"Swipe your wrist here." Mr. Salvador told me with his hand extending his OC without making eye contact. I did as I was instructed. He looked at my name.

"Hello, Tay-lee-yah. Glad to see you are already wearing your PSC. You can call me Mr. Salvador when we are around the Richies; otherwise, you can call me Sal. I will teach you everything you need about Oxygen Supply Maintenance as soon as the rest of the newbies arrive. Until then, here is the digital workbook for this course." He said my name weirdly, and then my OC dinged with the workbook. He didn't seem thrilled to be teaching work-study.

"It's pronounced 'Tal-i-ah.' Thank you." I said. I sat in one of the chairs and tried to get comfortable in the cramped room.

I opened my OC for the new digital workbook and began reading. I was pleasantly surprised when I saw that it was more technical than I had imagined. It might be a challenge for me which I appreciate. With this month's schedule, I will have this class for 3 days, then be assigned to a new job to study.

I was fully involved in reading my workbook when Nitris walked in with their PSC. It looked just as uncomfortable as mine did.

Sal did the same half-welcome to Nitris that he gave me. I watched as Nitris turned around and saw the other empty seats. I was surprised when they decided to sit next to me.

"Looks like we'll be working together," Nitris told me in a meek voice.

"Guess so," I replied and tried to focus on my workbook. I don't think Nitris understands that they are always on my nerves.

"Alright, it will be me and you two for the next 3 days." Sal began, "Today, I want you both to read your workbooks until 20:00. Tomorrow, after we get our PSCs on, I'll show you where the machines are and review the cleaning procedures. Any questions?"

"Are all of the work-study classes only 3 days?"

Nitris asked Sal.

"Yes, for a total of 24 hours per job." He answered.

"We are expected to learn this whole workbook and hands-on training in 24 hours?" Nitris asked.

"What? You don't think you can handle it?" I asked Nitris.

"Learn as much as you can." Sal ignored my challenge and addressed Nitris. "You'll be tested, and whichever job best matches your results will become your full-time job when you age out of the Bunks."

"If I test well at the end of the month and get assigned here, will you be my new boss?" Nitris asked.

I looked at them with shock at what they were asking. These are not pertinent questions relating to the jobs. This should be basic knowledge by now. It's as if they have never talked to any adults in the Mess Hall. Come to think of it, I have never seen Nitris speak to anyone in the Mess Hall, ever.

"I'm not the main supervisor anymore, but I help when work-study isn't in progress," Sal said, "I was promoted to teacher a couple of years ago. Each of the work-study groups gets smaller and smaller every cycle. The older work-study students are alone with their supervisor until I bring on the new students." He then rubbed the back of his neck in the same place my PSC was digging into my neck.

"How did you get promoted to a work-study teacher?" Nitris asked him.

"When you start working full time at age 18, you must complete 100,000 hours in your assigned job. Then you can be awarded the promotion to teaching work-study without those heavy PSCs, as long as we are on the Dark Flats level. There are no more children after this group. I guess I could retire..." Sal trailed off at the end.

"I've never met anyone who has retired before. What does someone do with their free time?" I asked with curiosity.

"I've never known anyone who has retired either," Sal confessed, looking at us and then up at the cameras in his small room.

There was a long moment of silence. I turned my head to the side to look at Nitris. When we made eye contact, it was like we connected, and both had the same thought about not knowing of anyone who has retired.

"Mr. Salvador, I mean, Sal, may I ask you something personal?" I pulled myself away from Nitris' green eyes. I leaned in towards Sal's desk and lowered my voice.

"If you must," Sal said. He kept glancing up at the cameras above us.

"How old are you? You look so young. I didn't know someone could have a high-level job and be as young as you." I said, with charm and a smile to match. I want to be on his good side so I can do well on the tests and have my choice of jobs.

"You think I'm young? Oh my, no, I'm very old. This July, I will be 43 years old." Sal said with a chuckle.

"To get 100,000 hours of work would mean you have to work 12-hour shifts every day for 25 years without a day off." Nitris calculated, doing the math in their head. They looked shocked at the realization. I felt jealous, and my face flushed with heat at how quickly they did the math. Those numbers were a shock that I wasn't prepared for.

"You are fast with math." Sal was complimenting Nitris, but his voice didn't sound impressed. "That seems about right. Time flies when you work all the time. I hadn't had a day off since before I did work-study myself. You kiddos have it easy and still get the weekends off. Er, I guess I should say 'did' have it easy. No more weekends off anymore." Sal gave us a nonchalant shrug.

Nitris and I looked at each other without speaking. I realized that I had been holding my breath and inhaled suddenly. I'm just learning how long life will be and how much work we must do to accomplish something small.

"Are there any other questions?"

"No." Nitris and I said in unison.

"Okay. I'm going to rest my eyes for a bit. If you have any questions, just tap my shoulder. I don't want the eyes in the sky to think I'm sleeping on the job." Sal said with a wink. I watched as his eyes darted to the camera before turning his chair around to face a bare shelf beside his desk.

"Are we not going to leave here? Why did we need to get our PSCs on if we aren't going anywhere?" I asked Nitris with a harsher tone than intended.

"It is to get everyone used to wearing them. I'll have mine on when we leave the classroom to show you around." Sal replied without turning to face us.

I sat there motionless, still stunned by what I had learned. I was too nervous to look up at the cameras. It wasn't until Sal had a tiny quick snore which broke the silence in the small room, that I realized I needed to start reading the digital workbook. I wasn't going to let Nitris outshine me in work-study too.

Chapter 4
Intra

There are many trivial matters to consider when managing the last of the human race. It can be overwhelming for most, but I achieved excellence in multitasking and delegating for the optimal functioning of Pangea.

"Prism, complete the analysis on the month-end reports from all work-related injuries and cross reference with every February since 2200. Once that finishes, see if there are any connections or crossovers between departments. Query that with work locations and injuries that have occurred." I instructed them on what I needed.

"All previous February reports since the year 2200 will be completed as requested." Prism nodded their cleanly shaved head and began working at their desk. They were using our holo gestures to access the computer logs and reports.

"Neo, how long until the spending reports for the ReCirculation Center are finalized?" I asked the older woman with streaks of white throughout her jet black ponytail, sitting besides Prism.

"All financial reports are in progress. Estimated time of completion, two hours." Neo answered me without looking up from the holo reports she was reviewing.

"I have located 16,473 redundant files reducing station-wide space in the servers. Recommendation, clearing redundant files and deleting caches." Echo said to the room. I looked at her besides me, she kept her silver blonde hair in a sharp bob, keeping the back short and the front long and in line with her jawbone. I watched as she gestured her hand over her station, sending me the report. I opened the file and began scanning the folder on my display.

The office screens lit up with various camera feeds from the Dark Flats. My eyes flew up to them to see what was going on. Workers walked around the crowded hallway and bumped into each other without acknowledging anything had happened. Everyone stayed on time with their schedules.

"The remaining Lumpen adolescents have become eligible for work-study," Codex told me as she cycled through the cameras. My display lit up to show the children leaving the small work-study offices. I quickly approved deleting everything in the folder Echo sent to clear my view. She has always been efficient and does not make mistakes. My double check was redundant.

I scanned the wall of screens to check how the children were doing on their first day in the work-study program. I always watched the students' faces fill with panic when they got their PSC on for the first time. I smiled as they all reacted similarly by tugging desperately to pull the collar away from their neck.

"It is fascinating to see the children lose their innocence," Codex said.

"Everyone has to grow up and contribute to Pangea," I responded. We watched in silence for a moment before Codex spoke again.

"What will we do without any new children being born?" Codex asked the room, but I knew it was directed at me.

"That should not concern you. We have been without children before, and everything continued without disruption." I reassured all of the Council.

"I believe that all people are capable of love and kindness, and it doesn't have to be monetized or mandatory. It can be something to unite everyone. The current restrictions for adoptions and ReCirculation Credit imbalance appear to drive a larger wedge between the two levels of Pangea. Our main objective is to create an environment where humanity transcends its limitations. Achieving extraordinary success through research and exploration," Codex said, reciting the Pangea manifest written when all the stations united.

"Through research, we are committed to unlocking the secrets of human evolution and enabling extraordinary new capabilities for all people. We believe that our work will help humanity reach its ultimate destiny." Echo recited the next lines of the manifest on cue.

Annoyed, I looked at Codex and said, "We should be skipping the child stage completely," I continued to the room, "When we have completed testing on the DNX upgrade, we shall move to the next phase. The next generation of organic beings from the Birthing Lab will be incubated into fully matured adults. Young and strong to do the heavy and hard work needed on the station."

"The fully developed adult body should only take 16 months to perfect based on recent results," Neo added.

"We should plan the updated lesson schedule when the new beings have matured," Codex began to share her input.

"Newborns through puberty are a drain of resources. The teachers should be doing something more productive with their time instead of talking for hours. With the advancements in DNX and further research, we have successfully implanted memories into multiple developed beings. Rendering adolescence time frame to be obsolete. We would be saving 18 years per person with that technology. No more 'ABCs' and '123s' to waste time on educating. We could have a fully developed worker walk out of the Birthing Lab and directly into a PSC to start working without asking questions." I told Codex the logical next steps that she seemed to be forgetting.

"I strongly oppose that logic. It is in everyone's blood to want to care for one another and love. That is something we can't splice out, and you know it." Codex reminded me of the failure we endured during the dark years.

"Oh yes, love, the one thing that science can't fix. What you oppose does not concern me. I hypothesize that without having children on board, a fully formed adult won't comprehend love, and that will make them more motivated to work harder. The reaction to that will make them work more efficiently. Love only slows things down." I said firmly. I am not to be challenged.

"I think to love is to be human," Codex said.

"We grow people in a lab. That doesn't sound human to me. Besides, we have already achieved a faster gestation period for babies down to only two months. With the new strand of DNX, we can create a fully formed adult with implanted memories that will be ready to work. More adults, more work, more productivity." I said and looked away from her and back at the Lumpen children.

"Maybe you are right." She said, conceding.

"Of course, I'm correct. Now, what is the status of the test subject?" I asked her.

"According to the latest progress report from Kline," Codex began summarizing, "The student has excelled at all tests and challenges. Further, it shows the quick processing of new material without hesitation, distraction, or memory loss."

"Excellent. And how are the implanted memories treating the subject?" I asked with curiosity.

"There appears to be some disconnect with that phase, which we cannot conclude at this time. We believe that the isolation is impacting the abilities predicted. We suggest more interactions with peers in moderation." Codex told me.

"Alright, I approve, but if anything goes wrong, you are to be held accountable," I told her. If this fails, it would be Codex responsible for the error. If this succeeds, then I will be the savior for all humans.

"May I push these updates through now, or wait until after the final work-study test is completed and jobs have been assigned?" Codex asked me.

"If we are going to move forward with these changes, they should be effective immediately," I told her. She was getting on my last nerve.

With a fast swipe, I cleared the office screens and brought up my previous report on the test results of the prior week. As I read the information, it appeared that Kline was making progress.

Chapter 5
Nitris

Ding, ding, ding.

The computer notification went off and took my attention from the workbook I read on my OC. I stood and tapped Sal on the shoulder to gently wake him. He sat up and yawned.

"Good evening, everyone." Intra's automated message said. "It is now 20:00 hours UTC. Please proceed to get proper nourishment and cleanse within the current hour. Afterward, proceed to your next assignments. Your imperative contribution is necessary to ensure the safety of everyone." The announcement ended with the same ding tone that it had started with.

"Her voice gets under my skin," Taliah said under her breath, but I heard her loud and clear because I was sitting beside her.

"I know exactly how you feel," I whispered to her, so Sal wouldn't hear me talking back.

Taliah looked confused before she stood up and left the room. I followed her.

"Is there something you need from me?" Taliah stopped and turned her head to glare at me.

"Um, no." I choked out those words and rubbed my PSC.

"Why are you following me?" She demanded.

"I'm not following you. We both have to go to Ms. Cora's to get these things off." I told her and fumbled with the heavy metal collar.

Taliah turned towards Ms. Cora's office and started to search the line of people who filled the hallway. I don't know if she was looking for Justice or trying to avoid me. I slowed my pace and stayed about three strides behind Taliah. "Do you want to go together to the Mess Hall?" I asked her. My voice cracked with nervous anticipation. We will spend a lot of time together over the next two days, and I thought maybe if I invited her, she wouldn't be so mean to me.

"No. I like to go with Justice." Taliah turned around to face me as she said it. Then she craned her neck up and looked around the hallway for Justice.

"Oh, I get it," I replied and looked down at her boots on the floor.

"Just because we were assigned the same work-study doesn't make us friends," She said harshly, still avoiding eye contact with me and searching the faces of those around us. All the work-study classrooms were in this same stretch of hallway, but the people around us were taller adults. That made it difficult to see the few students.

"Have I done something to upset you?" I asked

her while I kept my eyes on her boots.

"You always act like you're better than everyone just because you're the top of the class, but I can see right through you. You act innocent and pretend you don't know what you're doing, but somehow you can fix a holo without being taught how to. You're cheating somehow. It isn't fair to the rest of us, who have to work really hard," Taliah said before turning on her heel and heading back toward Ms. Cora's office.

"I'm not doing it intentionally. I'm sorry." I said in a weak low tone. I don't know if she heard me over the sound of all the people filling the hallway. I counted to ten before I resumed my slow walk to Ms. Cora's. I wanted to put as many people between us as possible.

The removal line was longer than the line to get the PSCs fitted. Now adults were coming off the day shift, some starting the night shift, and the work-study students. I noticed that the adults didn't socialize much while in line. From where I was, I could see Taliah and Justice in line together near the door to Ms. Cora's. They were about 12 people ahead of me. After a while, they both came out of the office, PSC-free. I ducked behind the adult in front of me and tried to make myself small when they walked past.

When it was my turn to enter Ms. Cora's chambers, I wasn't sure what to do. She was polite and worked fast and efficiently to remove my PSC.

"Thank you, Ms. Cora," I exhaled instantly when the PSC was free from my neck. My hands rubbing the back where the lock rested heavy on my spine.

"You're welcome, my little starshine. It's okay to drop the 'Ms.' Call me Cora. I'm getting too old for 'Ms' these days. I should have been a 'Mrs' by now"

Cora said in a comforting tone while she nudged my shoulder to the door to leave.

We barely said anything else due to the rush of people that wanted to be free from their PSCs. I took the long way to the Mess Hall. I headed back towards work-study classes and through the adult living chambers to complete the Dark Flats level. My longer walk landed me in the middle of the evening rush of workers either starting or ending their day, I had to wait in line for my tray and goo ration.

I kept thinking about what Taliah had said. I wasn't cheating on anything. When I looked at the holo wires, I traced what was there and saw a split wire that had been repaired previously. All I had to do was remove that chunk, strip the wire higher, and connect it again. It was an obvious solution, and it had worked. I didn't understand why Taliah had been so surprised.

I followed the line into the Mess Hall, keeping my head down. I swiped my wrist, got my goo, then headed to the end of a long table as the adults were leaving. Sitting alone, I wondered if everyone thought I was cheating. If someone gets caught cheating in classes, they lose all their accumulated credits immediately. They can't earn any more for 30 days. The worst part is they still have to go to class knowing they can't earn credits. The few credits we get from class are intended to be our deposit on adult chambers when we age out of The Bunks.

"Hey, Nitris, can I sit with you?" The voice startled me back to the present. I looked up and saw a beautiful girl. She had gorgeous blue eyes, and her shiny blonde hair was in a messy ponytail. She seemed to radiate a positive energy that I couldn't easily explain.

"There's plenty of room," I replied, gesturing to the empty table. I was trying to remember her name. She looked about my age, and our classes were small, so I should have known who she was. It hit me as she sat down. Her name was Sahara, and she sat in the back by the older teens.

"Thanks. You looked like you were deep in thought just now. What's on your mind?" Sahara asked. She sat across from me but she didn't have a tray of rations.

"Just thinking about existence and what adult life will be," I replied, looking down and playing with the goo on my tray.

"Sounds like some heavy thoughts. Don't let me stop you," Sahara said.

I looked up from my tray and met Sahara's eyes again. Her bronzed skin glowed, even in the dim light of the Mess Hall. She had symmetrical eyes, a tiny nose, and plump lips. To me, she was what genetic perfection looked like. I struggled to find something to say.

"Which work-study did you get assigned?" I asked, trying to make my best effort at being friendly.

"Today was one of three days that I had the privilege of doing Welding Repairs. What about you?" She asked with a bright smile showing her perfect teeth.

"I'm doing Oxygen Supply Maintenance. I hope the next two days go by quickly," I said, leaving out my confrontation with Taliah.

"The whole thing feels set up so that we can't win because we're Lumpen," Sahara began, "What's with the 'learn everything quickly in three days, then test into your forever job' rules that we must follow? Just because the Richies didn't choose us doesn't mean we have less value."

Her words hit me hard. I felt it deep in my stomach.

"I agree. I wish I could do something more challenging." I shrugged, accepting my place. I knew Pangea was bigger than just me.

"What would happen if we tried to stand up for ourselves? What if we say we would rather work somewhere else?" She asked the questions that had been on my mind for a long time.

"I don't know. It seems like we have to just accept the life we're given. If you can even call it a life," I said, looking down again as I played with the goo. I realized that the Mess Hall had grown eerily quiet. I glanced around the room and saw that everyone else had finished eating and left. How long had I been sitting here?

"I know it will never happen, but I want to be a doctor," Sahara said with defeat.

When Sahara said the word "doctor," I was suddenly hit with a vision of her in a white lab coat, covered in blood. Her blue eyes were filled with tears as she looked down at her bloody hands. I shook my head from side to side rapidly, pushing the image out of my thoughts. It felt like my recurring nightmares recently, but more vivid.

"I know it's silly, we don't get sick or give birth here, but I hope a human doctor will be needed in my lifetime," she said, hanging her head down in defeat, as a reply to me shaking my head.

"I can relate to wanting to do more. I was shaking my head because I have a weird pain in my neck from the PSCs." I lied. I didn't want her to think I was being dismissive about her dreams. That little white lie seemed to brighten her spirits again.

"I don't want us to depend on technology to heal us. We should be able to heal ourselves like we used to. Do you know what I mean?" Sahara asked and stared into my eyes. It felt like I had forgotten how to speak, but I wanted to show her I understood.

"I've only heard stories about Lumpen, who got injured on the job," I said, "They go to the Richies level Med Bay where a computer scans them and then releases nanobots to heal the injury."

"Did you hear that from Mr. Kline?" She asked me.

"Just something I overheard in the Mess Hall. I don't remember who specifically it happened to." Sahara was giving me undivided attention. My palms were starting to sweat.

"If you got to choose, what would you do with your life?" She asked.

I paused and thought about it. I had never really thought about a job I wanted because I didn't expect to have a choice. I accepted that. I wondered if I should lie and make something up or tell the truth because I didn't know what I was allowed to do. Trying to decide was making me nervous. I ate a spoon full of goo to stall until I could answer.

"If I could do any job, I would be a pilot and take an exploratory team to find a planet to live on," I said, fantasizing, "I want to live somewhere with real gravity, not artificial gravity, and to feel sunlight on my face."

I finished speaking and glanced around the room, afraid that someone might have heard me talking about my foolish hopes, but thankfully the Mess Hall was nearly empty.

"I can see you doing that! Captain Nitris on deck!" Sahara said as she saluted me. I waved her salute away, and we laughed together. It was nice to talk to someone.

I checked my OC for the time and realized it was almost 21:00 hours, and we were still in the Mess Hall. "We should head back to The Bunks for our study hour before lights out," I said as I stood at the table and picked up my tray with most of my goo rations left.

While I cleaned my tray of rations into the food chute, I debated on if I could trust Sahara enough to tell her what I do after lights out. Part of me wanted to share my secret with her, but my brain kept screaming, 'don't tell her,' and that kept me quiet.

The Mess Hall had emptied completely, and we were all that was left. The motion sensor lights in the back of the room began to turn off. The darkness sent a shiver down my back. There were places on the Dark Flats with no lights, like the area by the adult living chambers. No one ever fixed those. The motion lights in the Mess Hall and outside the classrooms were always functioning. They would turn off when no one was around, and only the dim green emergency lights remained.

Sometimes I would sneak out of The Bunks and into the halls just to hold still and see how long I could go without setting off the sensors. It was my private, harmless way of having fun, but it was still against the rules.

Sahara cleared her throat. I flinched and put the metal tray in the 'used' pile and turned to face her.

"I know your secret," she said in a hushed tone.

I blushed, thinking that she had read my mind somehow. Does she know I lied to her?

"I don't know what you're talking about," I said calmly. I anxiously looked around the Mess Hall to confirm that everyone was gone.

"I know that you leave The Bunks at night." My eyes went wide, but she kept talking. "I followed you the other night to see where you were going. I don't know how you do it, but I saw you walk down the hall without turning the motion sensor lights on. That's a skill we'll need if we are going to complete this crazy secret mission I have. I want you to teach me how you do it." She looked straight at me, and my heart jumped into my throat.

I was surprised that she spoke so casually about catching me sneaking out. We both knew that she could turn me in and get extra Credits if she wanted to, and I would be executed for all the rules I had broken. I didn't know what to say.

A moment passed, and finally, I said, "It's a skill I've acquired after knowing I'm nothing for so long." The honesty in that sentence shocked me for a moment, and I realized how sad I truly was. I desperately wanted to do anything Sahara suggested for the chance to have a friend.

"But, *how* do you do it? Can you teach me?" She asked, not acknowledging the awkward truth I had told her.

"Tell me more about this mission where you need to be able to walk around without the sensors detecting your movements?" I answered her question with a question.

"I want to sneak into the library and download all the medical books to study them," Sahara explained.

Her voice was giddy with excitement as she continued, "Then I can make my case for why I should be a doctor when I schedule an audience with the Elders. We can get mechanical engineering and piloting books, too!"

I considered this for a moment and bit my bottom lip. Whenever I'm unsure about what to say, I bite my lip to keep from saying something stupid.

"Okay, I'm in," I said, more excited about spending time with someone, than I was about the books. But, if Sahara's plan worked out, I could use my time to read about piloting spacecraft and engineering.

"Perfect. Let's start tonight after lights out at zero hundred hours," Sahara leaned into me conspiratorially, "I'll leave for the Bunks now, and you count to twenty before you leave the Mess Hall so we don't raise suspicion going into the Bunks together." Sahara turned and walked out of the Mess Hall.

I stood there in silence as I replayed the conversation. Sahara knew my secret. She wanted to learn how I was able to trick the motion sensors. She wasn't trying to use this against me. Instead, she wanted to do something that could get us BOTH into trouble. If this plan worked, I would also need to start building a case for the Elders. I didn't have the confidence Sahara had, but I had the motivation and ambition to be more.

I tried to focus on counting to twenty, but everything around me seemed so loud. Trying to drown out the constant hum of machines running was a lot harder than it should be. There is never any true silence on Pangea. Things like artificial gravity generators and oxygen regenerators are always engaged. I tried to regulate my breathing to match the pitches in the hums.

I had just begun to feel calm when my mind was suddenly filled with an image of Sahara covered in blood. My eyes shot open, and I took a moment to focus. I had lost count. I looked at the time, 21:21 hours, and quickly headed to The Bunks to be there before lights out. Luckily, Ms. Verban wasn't there, and I looked down at my boots as I walked to my top bunk without anyone noticing my tardiness. The other teens huddled in small packs, talking and doing homework together. I've always wanted a group like that, but I always finished my assignments quickly.

At 22:00 hours, Ms. Verban stepped into the Bunks and watched as everyone got up from the small groups and dispersed to their beds. She didn't have to say anything. We all knew to put away our OCs and get under our blankets.

I had a couple of hours before my little adventure, so I took the time to meditate and clear my mind. I felt nervous and scared about what might happen if we were caught. I must've fallen asleep because when I heard Sahara, she sounded so far away.

"Pssst!" Sahara whispered again. My eyes darted open, and I started to look around the Bunks to see where she was. It took a moment for my eyes to adjust to the dim green emergency lights that outlined the aisle between the rows of bunk beds. I quietly got down from my top bunk and walked to the door silently with my boots in my hand.

"How'd you get out of there so quickly?" I hissed when I got out to the hallway and saw Sahara leaning against the outer door frame.

"We all have our secrets," she said with a sly smile before she continued, "Are you ready to teach me how to be invisible like you?" She asked as she watched me struggle to slide my boot on.

"Yes, but it will be hard to hide your beauty," I said and saw her cheeks blush. I balanced putting on my other boot. Usually, this wasn't that hard, but my nerves got the best of me. Being around Sahara was making me more self-conscious than usual. After getting on my boots, I stood straight and said, "Let's go."

"So, what's the first step to fooling the motion sensor lights?" Sahara asked as we quietly left The Bunks. This stretch of the hallway had lights on constantly, but around the first bend, they became motion-sensor lights.

"Um, I usually do this alone, and I don't have steps that I follow every time. I don't know how to explain it. It's just, um, instinct?" I told her the truth but it sounded like a question.

"I'll follow you, and you can tell me what you are thinking, and maybe I can figure it out too. I believe in you." Sahara whispered to me. I've never heard someone tell me that they believed in me before. It felt warm.

As we walked, I constantly looked around us to ensure we weren't being observed. Being caught out of the residence without a PSC is a punishable offense. I let out a deep breath to slow my heart rate. I was so nervous around Sahara, and I wasn't sure what to do or say. I had only been able to move without setting off the sensors for a couple of months, and I wasn't sure how I was able to do it. Trying to teach it to someone else seemed nearly impossible. I looked around some more to make sure we weren't being followed.

"Not being followed. Check!" She said. I hadn't told her that was what I was doing. She must have sensed it. "This is so exciting! My heart is beating like the oxygen regenerator in the Mess Hall. You know, that extra loud hum?" She said as she took a bold step forward.

"Let's manage our expectations, this may take some practice," I told her. I led us to the left out of the Bunks. The Mess Hall was to the right, with the adult Lumpen living chambers past that. We headed to the abandoned lab's section of the Dark Flats. I never saw anyone back here because passing the massive empty rooms takes a long time. They are all kept locked and dark. It was the same path I had taken before, but it seemed darker now.

I slowed my pace and pressed my body against the wall. I motioned for Sahara to copy my movements.

"We're coming up on the first set of lights outside the old Birthing Lab. They're usually off, and I don't find it too hard to get past." As I said that, something caught my eye in the window of the Birthing Lab around the first bend. I peeked my head around the corner and glanced into the abandoned Lab. I stared into the darkness, searching for something I could sense more than I could see.

"What's going on?" Sahara whispered.

"I thought I saw something moving inside the Lab." I tilted my head towards her and whispered the reply, keeping my eyes on the dark glass. I remembered my nightmare with glowing eyes. I didn't want Sahara to think I imagined things, so I refocused on our goal.

"We should bend down a little more and go under the lab windows." I then hunched over and pressed my left side against the wall. I began to walk past the lab with Sahara close behind me. She moved so silently that I wouldn't have known she was there if

I didn't turn to look at her.

Sahara and I kept moving through the hall. The Library was on the Dark Flats level, with mostly broken motion sensors and flickering lights.

"Why do they keep all the abandoned stuff on the Dark Flats?" Sahara asked me in a quiet voice.

"I think it's so the Richies don't have to look at anything abandoned. Like how the Lumpen all have meal times at the same time as the Richies, that way the Richies never have to be bothered to see a Lumpen working while they are eating in their Dining Hall." I told her with a whisper.

"Their Mess Hall even gets a better name than ours. The injustices continue to stack up." She said with a hint of rage.

"When I reach this point, I press my body against the wall and flatten my palms into the cold metal. It helps calm my heart rate." I told her the steps that she needed to copy.

"Got it." She said as she mimicked me and took steps in sync with me.

"Sometimes I think I'm invisible, and no one can see me," I told her the truth and looked back at her. Our eyes met, and she gave me a warm smile. I never wanted to look away. I must have been staring at Sahara because she indicated to get me back on task with her eyes darting towards our destination. I turned to face the front again. Her eyes reminded me of the nightmare I had of the abandoned lab. I turned my head away from her and back towards the Library.

Sahara was a quick study. She could move without setting off the lights on her first try and every time after that. I was surprised and confused by how good she was at it. It had taken me a long time to refine my technique, with so many tense nights of experimentation. The constant risk of getting caught had filled me with dread, but Sahara didn't appear to consider the possibility of punishment.

"What's the matter?" Sahara asked me with concern when I had stopped moving down the hallway.

"I thought I heard a weird noise. Like footsteps, but a LOT of them. Too light to be people, though..." I trailed off to listen, and fear registered on my face.

"What happens if we get caught?" Sahara asked the most crucial question.

"Best case scenario, it's the Lumpen adults who won't care about us," I said in a low tone.

"Worse case?" She asked back with a whisper.

"Solitary Containment or execution," I said as calmly as possible as I turned to face her. I watched as she understood the danger of what we were doing. She closed her eyes for a moment. I think she was scared like me. I looked away because I was embarrassed. What if I got us both killed?

"Do you hear the noise?" I asked her over my shoulder. Sahara didn't answer.

We were almost at the Library when our ears were assaulted by the Solar Flare alarm going off. Then the computers automatically close all the windows on the level above, and the Richies experience the dark. The shutters closing were so loud we could feel them shake everywhere in the Dark Flats. Thankfully for us, security only checks on the Richies and leaves the Lumpen to fend for themselves.

"We are so close to the Library!" Sahara said in a hushed tone and gestured to where the Library door was located.

"We still don't have a way *into* the library. I

didn't expect to make it this far tonight. I thought we'd only be practicing to avoid the lights," I tried to think of what we should do next, "Let's make our way back to The Bunks before Ms. V does her head count and is missing two teens. We can come back tomorrow and figure out how to get in."

"No! We've come this far. We must at least see how the Library is secured if we need tools to get in!" Sahara started down the last bend, walking directly to the library's entrance. I was sure that she'd be detected.

"Stop! Come back!" I said, stepping towards her.

"It's now or never." She replied. She straightened herself and walked with purpose to the Library doors. No lights were triggered. I'd never tried to walk directly down a hallway to see if I would set off the lights. I wondered if I was unique in avoiding them or if the sensors had never worked. Sahara didn't waste any time. She ran to the Library door and examined how it was secured and operated.

Since the Library was one of the first wings of the original station, it had an old system with a pad of numbers and a slot to insert a key. I noticed it when I was younger and would walk this way to be alone.

I heard a noise coming down the corridor ahead of us. I ran towards Sahara in a hunched-over position and tried to grab her arm. I somehow misjudged the distance and didn't reach her. My movement triggered the lights, startling us both into a crouch.

"We need to leave. Now." I whispered.

I led us back towards The Bunks, retracing our steps around the abandoned labs. We didn't care about the motion lights with the Solar Flare alarm going off.

My heart was racing with excitement. I saw the

smile on Sahara's face, which filled me with joy. My face hurt from smiling, which was a new experience.

"That was close," I said, quickly catching my breath.

"We were almost in!" Sahara exclaimed. She didn't seem winded like I was from the brisk walk. Despite the excitement and danger, she was still focused on how to get into the Library. "All we need to do now is get a key and figure out the entry code."

We rounded the last corner before The Bunks, and the other teens were awake from the alarm and huddled in the hallway. Ms. Verban was walking towards us from the Private Matron Chambers.

"Everyone, please calm down; this isn't the first Solar Flare alarm we've had. It was a little sudden, but everyone is safe." Ms. Verban said with a soothing voice. We all filed into a single line and walked together to the Mess Hall.

The automated voice of Intra instructed us to wait at our designated locations for further instructions. It was the same recording we always heard when any emergency alarms were triggered.

Chapter 6
Taliah

Weeoo, weeoo, weeoo!

The emergency alarm pierced the silence in the Bunks and woke us all to the sound of Intra's recorded instructions. The recording was always the same, alerting us to the impending Solar Flare.

Justice and I were in the back of the line of teens exiting The Bunks when the alarm rang throughout the Dark Flats. Emergency alarms like this were nothing new, and we didn't take them too seriously.

"Why do the Dark Flats have to worry about Solar Flares? It's not like we have any windows down here that could expose us," Justice sighed with frustration.

"The radiation from the flare could cause us to get sick. That's why we must go to the Mess Hall where the walls are the thickest." I explained to her.

"Let's all get to our designated area in the Mess

Hall." Ms. Verban said with a soothing voice.

"Come on, let's get this over with," I told Justice with my back to Ms. Verban as she gave us directions.

Before I turned around to face forward and fall into the single file line, I saw Nitris coming from the other side of The Bunks. Where were they coming from? They should have been *in* The Bunks with us.

I didn't know how to handle the situation because I was curious and exhausted. Maybe my mind was playing tricks on me. I decided not to pay any attention to Nitris, so I turned and walked toward the Mess Hall with the rest of the line.

We all walked silently and sat at our designated table in the Mess Hall. The alarm continued to go off, and the high pitch of the siren was beginning to give me a headache. I rubbed my temples and attempted to ignore the sounds.

"I'm tired. Can't we go back to The Bunks?" Apollox asked loudly to Ms. Verban with a whine in his voice.

"You know the routine. We must wait until the alarm has silenced, and then we can safely return." Ms. Verban explained what we all knew.

The alarm stopped as if on cue, and the silence in the Mess Hall was replaced with Lumpen chatter. Everyone was speculating about the Solar Flare alarm and how it seemed early for this time of year.

"Alright, children, let's head back to bed and attempt to get some sleep before we start our day tomorrow." Ms. Verban instructed us and raised her hand to signal us to follow her single file as we had entered.

I used my trunk to hop onto my Bunk, and Justice rolled onto her mattress beneath me with a thud that shook our connected bunk beds. I was getting under the thin blanket, and by the time I laid my head down on my pillow, I heard Justice's soft snores. At that moment, everything seemed to be okay

Chapter 7
Nitris

Ding, ding, ding.

"Good morning, residents of Pangea! Today is March 2nd, 2320, and the time is 06:00 hours UTC. Time to start your day. We have no special announcements at this time. Please proceed to get proper nourishment and cleanse within the current hour before beginning the day promptly at 07:00 hours. Adults report to their workspace, and adolescents report to designated classrooms. Your imperative contribution is necessary to ensure the safety of everyone." Intra's recorded voice said.

I jumped down from my bunk and felt enthusiastic about a new day for the first time ever. The cold metal floor under my bare feet made me shiver, returning me to reality. As I dressed, someone called, "Hey, Nitris!" I turned around to see Sahara coming towards me, waving her hand. I fumbled with my clothes for a moment and awkwardly waved back.

"Want to go to the Mess Hall together?" Sahara asked with a giggle when she saw my pants had fallen down to my knees.

"That sounds like fun," I said eagerly. I pulled up my pants and reached for a belt. I noticed that Sahara was wearing the same clothes as last night. We stalled for a moment to let the Bunks clear out, and then we strolled to the Mess Hall. We talked about our adventure from the night before.

"I think Mr. Kline is our best chance to get access to the Library. I've seen him at night with Ms. Verban *several* times," Sahara said with a sly smile.

"Ms. Verban and Mr. Kline get 'together'?" I asked, pretending to be surprised.

"That's exactly what I'm saying." She said enthusiastically.

"Do you ever sleep at night or watch everyone like a motion sensor?" I asked. I tried to seem like I was joking, but I did want to know.

"Whooo? Meeee?" She said, imitating an owl the way Ms. Verban would do back when we were learning about extinct animals in primary school. We both laughed.

"I was so tired after the Solar Flare alarm that I was asleep when we were in the Mess Hall, and I sleepwalked back to the Bunks. I don't even remember coming back here. Aren't you tired?" I asked her.

"I've never needed much sleep," she replied, not answering my question.

"I've got a feeling that you already have a plan for how to get into the Library," I said.

"So, the next time Mr. Kline visits Ms. Verban,

we can sneak into his chambers to look for the key and the code to the Library," Sahara said. We arrived at the Mess Hall, and she looked around before we entered. She puts her pointer finger to her lips and makes a "shush" movement.

"Okay, but we don't know when that will *happen*," I said, carefully choosing my words in case anyone was listening.

"It happens almost every night. I have to head to the Sand Showers, but let's meet after work-study tonight and talk more," Sahara said. She started to walk away from the Mess Hall before we went inside.

"You said we should go to the Mess Hall first. Aren't you hungry?" I asked her as I took a step towards her.

"I'm saving my ration credits for something in the ReCirculation Center," she explained and shrugged it off.

"We can share mine," I offered in a whisper because we knew it was against the rules to share rations.

"I don't want any, thanks. I'm too excited to get my hands on those digital books!" Sahara said as she stood in the hallway outside of the Mess Hall. Her answer didn't make sense, but it didn't bother me for some reason. I had other things on my mind.

"Do the rations make you feel weird? Like time has passed you by, and you didn't notice?" I asked her as we continued to stand outside of the Mess Hall.

"Sometimes it feels like the day flew by me without me knowing it," she confided in me.

"I'm glad I'm not the only one," I told her.

"Get out your OC. I sent you my journal," she said with her OC in her hands. I got a notification and opened the new file on my home screen.

Sahara stood and watched me as I started reading what she had written:

Date 02/09/2320

Tonight, when I couldn't sleep, I decided to see if anyone was still awake at midnight. I saw Mr. Kline softly knock on Ms. Verban's private chamber door. As soon as it opened, I saw her hand reach out and grab him by his shirt and pull him inside quickly before the doors closed. I wonder what that was about.

Date 02/16/2320

Tonight Ms. Verban seemed to be in a good mood when she called lights out, and I think it's because Mr. Kline has visited her three times this week! I'm disappointed I wasn't awake when he left, but she is usually in a good mood after seeing him. I don't know what they do alone, but I know something is happening. I can hear it. The station makes a lot of hums and groans, but not like the kind they make in her chambers. I am drawn into their secret, even though I don't know it.

Date 02/23/2320

Mr. Kline appears to be running late. When he finally showed up at Ms. Verban's chambers, he was holding something in his hands. I couldn't see what it was, but Ms. Verban was excited. Instead of pulling him into her quarters like usual, she stepped out into the hallway wearing only her sleep shirt and kissed him straight on the lips! I was not expecting to see anything like that.

According to Sahara's notes, Mr. Kline and Ms. Verban meet almost every night. Based on how far back her observations about the adults' meetings went, I could tell that Sahara had been planning to get into the Library for a long time.

I also noticed that she had sent her entire journal

to my OC and that it had the entries sorted by person. I was reading the "Mr. Kline" entries. I scanned the rest of the names and noticed other Lumpen workers from around the Dark Flats. There was a small list of the other kids' names, including mine.

"Do you keep track of all the Lumpen?" I asked her as I scrolled through the file. I hope she didn't write about me in her records because that could send me to Solitary Containment. I had begun to trust Sahara, but she hadn't told me her whole plan yet.

"I have a lot of sleepless nights," Sahara explained, "The machines keep me awake." I looked at her and saw her rubbing her arms as if trying to make the vibrations stop.

I took a moment before I told her, "I know what you mean. I can't sleep a lot of the time, too. I feel this strange connection to the station, with all the machine hums and the little movements. It feels like it is part of me."

We stood silently in the hallway, but the talking in the Mess Hall grew louder as it became busy with the Lumpen entering for rations.

"I have notes on you, too," she told me.

"Oh?" I asked, and I pretended that I hadn't seen the entries with my name on them, and I was glad that my intuition had told me to wait.

"Yes, I wrote about how I see you leave The Bunks and how you can walk around without the computers sensing you. I think it is magic and impressive. You're so brave," she sighed and kept her head down, looking at her boots.

"Why are you keeping notes on me? Me sneaking out of The Bunks during lights out is a punishable offense. I could be sent to Solitary or worse," I said as I slid my thumb across my throat to indicate death.

"It's okay, I keep my files encoded, and no one can figure out my code," she told me in a way to comfort me, but instead, it made me feel more anxious and filled with doubt.

"I'm going to grab some goo before class," I said, entering the Mess Hall alone.

Chapter 8
Ms. Verban

Ding, ding, ding!

After I finished my morning rations, I went to the Laundry room to meet with Dorro. Helping him has been an effective way to fill my empty time. There hadn't been any young children to teach primary education in a while. I worried I wouldn't earn enough ReCirculation Credits to maintain my accustomed lifestyle. However, with fewer demands on my time, I found other ways to earn credits, many of which paid more than I had gotten for teaching. Some jobs could be pretty unpleasant. Still, the credits paid well enough for me to justify the additional duties. At least with Dorro, it didn't feel like work because we were already friends.

"Good morning Dorro. What are we washing today?" I chirped as I entered the Laundry room.

I swiped my wrist to clock in for my RC Credits. Without the younger children to educate, it allowed me some freedom during the day. I could help anyone in any department in the Dark Flats and do it without needing a PSC.

"Blankets today. Today is blankets day," Dorro said in his broken sentences. He hadn't been the same since he'd spent those four months in Solitary Containment almost 18 years ago. When he was first released from Containment, he was very skinny and weak for a while. Now he is the tallest and widest person I know. His presence takes up a lot of space, but it is all muscle. The PSC on his neck seemed small. His short hair was also shaved clean around his ears, naturally leaving only the top to spike in different directions. Azriel was known for giving free haircuts to his friends to save them RCs.

"Blankets it is," I said, walking over to him. He runs the machines that wash linens and clothes on board, and his coworkers with PSCs deliver them to both levels on Pangea. I started to hand him material from the dirty pile to load into the washer.

"Blankets and sheets," Dorro said as he took the dirty items from my hands and shoved them into the washer.

We worked together like an assembly line. I handed him materials, and he would load them into the machines. When he filled the washers, he pulled the chain that dropped the clean sand into the machine to begin the wash cycles.

"Washer is running," Dorro said to me. The other Lumpen in the laundry room kept to themselves, and no one really chatted to each other. I had been coming here for so long that no one paid attention to me anymore. When I first arrived, everyone was confused and asked why I wasn't wearing a PSC. I thought they were scared I was a spy for the Council, but Dorro wasn't afraid of me. We had been friends our whole lives.

"We are moving fast this morning," I told him as we loaded clean clothes into the other machines. They shake and rattle all the excess sand off them before we can fold everything.

"Silas is gone," Dorro said.

"Silas is teaching his classes right now. He told me to tell you he said 'hi' and will see you as soon as possible," I lied to Dorro. Silas didn't like to visit Dorro anymore. He felt too guilty because he was the one who had gotten Dorro punished.

"Jexa is here," Dorro said, and he put his hand on my shoulder. He did this a lot. It always felt like he was trying to confirm who was physically here and who was a figment of his traumatized mind. Containment damaged part of his brain from being isolated from everyone he ever knew. We have never discussed it in detail together, but I thought that is why he liked to touch my shoulder to confirm he was not hallucinating. He didn't speak for almost a year after he was released. There were many nights in the Bunks before we aged out, when Dorro had woken up screaming. Silas and I asked him what he dreamed about, but he never told us.

"Yes, Jexa is here," I told him, resting my hand on his. He pulled away and started busying himself with the machines. Dorro repeated the same few sentences over and over. I never let that stop me from talking to him. I tell him everything, from how I'm feeling that day to anything new with the children from the Bunks.

"Today is the second work-study day for the last of the children in the Bunks. There still haven't been any new births. I'm glad I can come here and spend my day with you," I said and gave him a little nudge with my elbow.

My thoughts began to drift to the past. "I do miss teaching the primary children, though. Seeing them take their first steps, hearing their first words, I hope there will be more children soon." I confided in Dorro.

"No children. It's a lockdown. We must obey the rules," Dorro told me. He understood what I was talking about, I think.

"How are things with Azriel?" I asked Dorro about his husband.

"Azriel is at work doing his part to make an imperative contribution that is necessary to ensure the safety of everyone on Pangea," Dorro repeated the computer recording of Intra's message to everyone on board.

"Yes, we all need to contribute," I replied, fumbling with the dirty sheets a pile before me.

"I love Azriel," he added

"Yes, of course, you do," I replied. "He has a critical job working in the trash collections and sorting everything for us to use."

"The Maintenance Pod is not working correctly," Dorro said.

"Not working?" I asked.

"The pod is saying it is full, but when it completes its automated run and returns to Azriel, it is empty when it should be full," Dorro told me. I know that he is probably just repeating what Azriel told him.

"That is strange. Do you think there is no more

space debris for the maintenance pod to collect?" I asked him. We began to fold the clean laundry that had finished all the cycles.

"The space debris is never ending. Never ending," Dorro said as we worked.

"Like the laundry," I laughed. Dorro didn't respond. "Is Azriel concerned about the maintenance pod being empty?"

"He said that it can't mean anything good," He told me.

"I think Azriel will be able to fix it," I told him confidently.

"I love Azriel. He understands me. I love Azriel." Dorro said and stopped folding for a moment. He hugged the blanket that was in his large arms.

"I love Azriel and you," I said with endearment. Maintaining adult friendships on board is hard if you aren't working together. I haven't spent much time with Azriel, but I know he is one of the assistant teachers for the work-study children. He will help them learn how to handle everything trash related.

"And Silas. We love Silas too," Dorro added with a small smile.

"You can say that again," I said with a big smile as I thought about how much I loved Silas. Dorro might have some social skills that needed improvement, but his heart was always full of love.

"We love Silas too," He repeated, and we had a little laugh together. The machines beeped when they completed the cycle, and Dorro started to unload them. I helped him load the machines after he emptied them.

The sound of the machines vibrating and air flushing through them made it loud in the small room.

We spent the rest of the morning working together in silence. Every so often, Dorro would touch my shoulder to ensure I was still there with him and not a figment of his imagination. I rested my hand on his hand whenever he needed to be reassured that I was there with him. I can't imagine what his time in Containment was like. I appreciated the time we could spend together, even if we were working. I didn't think I would be strong enough to survive Containment.

I looked around the laundry room and saw the other Lumpen, some in their PSCs. Their eyes seemed empty, and all they could do was the jobs burned into their minds. Working with only muscle memory makes every task seem automated.

The notification that work-study was beginning rang loudly on our level. I folded the blanket I had in my hands before I left.

"I'm going to go and help Cora with the PSCs now. I'll see you tomorrow," I told Dorro before I left.

"Cora is kind. See you tomorrow," he repeated to me.

The laundry room door slid open when I approached it. I walked into the hallway and turned to look at Dorro again as the door slid closed. I exhaled my sadness and began walking towards Cora's, where the children had started to line up outside.

"Hey, Jexa, I appreciate you coming by to help with the PSCs," Cora said when I arrived and swiped my chip to clock in. She was my senior but was a few centimeters shorter than I was. Her dark skin was flawless, and her long wavy gray hair always up in a ponytail.

"How did it go with the children yesterday?" I asked her because that was always the most challenging day for me. Watching their innocence leave their eyes when they realized this was how the rest of their life would be, always broke my heart.

"Everyone was brave and polite. You're doing a great job with their upbringing in the Bunks. Very respectful. I think some kids were thrown off when I told them they could drop the "Ms" from Cora." She said with a chuckle.

"Honestly, it was hard for me to drop the formals when I grew up too." I laughed when I thought about my first time getting my PSC from Cora's predecessor, Mr. Hallow, who preferred to be called Hal. It took me about a week to get used to calling him Hal. When he died of old age at 48, I cried even though the only time I saw him was getting PSCs.

"We have to get moving, Jexa," Cora teased as she opened her chamber doors to start letting people come in to remove their PSCs.

We worked fast and efficiently, knowing the importance of being on time and correctly scanning everything. To unlock and lock the PSCs, there was a particular OC with a matching key set on a controlled timer inside a metal box welded into the desk. We have 1 hour from when the box unlocks automatically until it locks again. Cora told me that if it closed without the OC and key in the box, gas gets released, and everyone in the room passes out. She said it was some kind of fail safe, but I didn't completely understand why that was needed.

After we finished with the PSCs, Cora and I meditated together for an hour. It was so refreshing to my mind that my body forgot that it was hungry before we meditated. I thanked Cora and left her in her office.

I took my time and walked to the trash organization workstation to talk with Azriel.

"Good afternoon Azriel. How is everything?" I asked when I walked in. I got some side glances from the other PSC workers.

"Hey, Jexa, thanks for coming by. I've been struggling to figure out what is happening with the maintenance pod," Azriel said as he scratched his head without looking up at me. He was built tall but not as wide as Dorro. He kept his long red hair in a messy bun on the top of his head. The King of giving free haircuts never bothered to trim his own.

"Dorro mentioned you were having some issues," I said, and I looked around the trash organization area. I saw Apollox hovering nearby, trying to look busy on his second work-study day. I saw some of the other adults looking at me strangely.

"I think I have to take it apart and rewire the weight sensor," Azriel said, focusing on the pod's access panel.

"Do I make your co-workers uncomfortable for some reason?" I asked him.

Azriel stepped back from the pod, looked around the trash organization room, and saw the other adults looking at them before saying, "You're distracting, that's all." Then he returned to the panel on the pod. With his hands tracing wires, he added, "Though you talk like Intra, and that makes people nervous. Not just here. You know that, right?"

"I do?" I questioned him. I didn't realize that I sounded like an Elder.

"Not saying it's a bad thing. You use big words that not all the Lumpen have learned. Maybe they think you're spying for Intra, and that's why you two talk the same," Azriel explained with a glance at me.

"I thought they resented me for not having to wear a PSC. My duties required me to be able to quickly run around the ring if something were to happen to the children in case of an emergency. If I had a PSC, I wouldn't be able to get to them in time," I explained what I thought it could have been.

"It's all the same. Don't stress about it too much," Azriel said as he turned away from the maintenance pod to look at me, "How are you doing, Jexa? Are you bored now that all the children are old and in work-study?"

"I've been keeping busy working overtime here and there. I worked this morning with Dorro and just finished up with Cora." I told him.

"Busy day, and it's not even time for dinner yet." He said, and we laughed together.

"I don't know what I will do without new children from the Birthing Lab, so I'm trying to rack up as many RC Credits as possible," I told him about my stress.

"I would feel the same way, but thankfully, trash is never ending on Pangea," Azriel said with a chuckle as he turned back to the maintenance pod.

"Do you think you can fix the pod?" I asked while I looked over his shoulder. He had the access panel open and worked on it with the multi-tool he'd had since we were in the Bunks together.

"I'm not sure," Azriel said while he continued to work. "It's supposed to be fully automated and do its cycle, grabbing the old satellites and other space trash, but it's been coming back empty lately," he stopped working momentarily, shrugged his shoulders, then quickly returned to his task.

"Hey, Ms. Verban." I heard my name from across the collection area where the trash was dumped. I turned to see Apollox waving from the other side of the pit. I waved back and saw his work-study teacher, Ms. Kelza, snap her fingers at him to get his attention. I hoped she wouldn't reduce his Credits for waving at me. I really shouldn't have been in there unless I was working.

I turned back to Azriel and asked, "Do you think we have finally collected everything from Old Earth's orbit after all these years?"

"Not likely. I think the sensor doors on the pod aren't opening, or something isn't syncing. We had the second airlock break a while back, and that's still out of commission. Now we only have this one massive airlock for the pod to circle. Without the halfway airlock, the maintenance pod has to run longer between dumps." Azriel caught me up to what was happening.

"You'd think that everything on the Lumpen level would be working properly because we're the ones who fix everything," I started my theory, "but it feels like the Dark Flats are more decrepit than any other part of the station."

"I think the Lumpen are so tired after working that no one wants to repair anything without getting RC Credits," Azriel said. "No one is assigned to fix anything down here unless it impacts the Richies."

"Is this maintenance pod impacting the Richies?" I asked him as he continued to look at the wiring.

"Only their view." He said with a laugh. "They'll probably file a complaint with the Elders if they see any space trash obstructing the view in their cupola windows."

"The audacity of this pod to stop working. Such

disrespect!" I joked with him. Then I thought about it momentarily and asked, "Do you think the Solar Flare from last night is causing issues?"

"That's another strange thing," Azriel said, "The alarms went off, but no one I've talked to saw anything register on the logs. This maintenance pod would have been right in the path of a Solar Flare, but it isn't damaged. At least, not any more than it was."

"Peculiar indeed," I said, looking at the pod. The workers around us got quiet and started to walk away. I looked up and saw that the supervisor was walking over toward us.

"Sounds like my supervisor is heading this way," Azriel said without looking up.

"You are correct. I'm going to leave before I get you in trouble. I'll talk to you later," I said and quickly left the trash sorting room and headed back to my chambers. I wanted to clean up before Silas came to visit me tonight.

Chapter 9
Taliah

The class went by in a blur; it was time for work-study before I knew it. When I arrived at Sal's small office, I saw Nitris was already there waiting with him outside the door.

"We have to get a move on," Sal said when I was less than two meters away. He gestured with his hand and began to walk the long way down to the service elevator.

"Do you know where we are going?" I asked Nitris, who was walking in step with me behind Sal.

"I think we are going to the Richies level," they replied in a low excited tone.

"If we were going to the Richies level, Sal would be wearing his PSC too." I rationalized to them.

"Whenever the main oxygen supply is in danger, the backup power is re-routed to the main oxygen recycler. That's where we are heading." Sal explained to Nitris and me as he stopped walking and turned to face us.

Taking my OC out of my pocket, I started to take notes on what Sal was telling us.

"It feeds into our Mess Hall and the Dining Hall above. Everywhere else on board stops getting oxygen. That's why we have emergency drills where we must evacuate to the Mess Hall. Our PSCs are auto-configured with the emergency system that turns off location tracking until the system resets." Sal explained and pointed at the PSCs on our necks before he asked, "Any questions?"

"How does the oxygen supply know when it is in danger? Is it linked to the Solar Flare alarms?" Nitris asked him.

"There are many sensors all over Pangea, inside and out," Sal began, "and when they detect potential danger, such as an impact from a meteor, an automated system provides us with instructions. If we have to evacuate to safety, this oxygen recycler is programmed to draw power from other resources, such as the lights, to continue the supply of fresh oxygen until the crisis is resolved."

"The Dark Flats have a lot of sensors that aren't functioning," Nitris pointed out, "Does that mean we are in danger? What happens if a sensor goes off but is a false alarm? Will it pull the oxygen from the Bunks before we have time to make it to the Mess Hall?" Nitris' questions made me think about our life and how dangerous everything is around us. I hated to admit it, but they were right when they mentioned that everything is always broken down here.

"This computer is smart enough to recognize

a false alarm," Sal seemed confident. "We haven't needed the emergency evacuation protocols during my long lifetime of 45 years. The monitoring system should use all of the security cameras and motion sensors around Pangea to detect where people are, to avoid cutting off oxygen to that area."

"If we haven't used it in over 45 years, are we sure it still works?" I asked Sal with concern.

"That is what we are going to find out today," Sal began to say as we entered the service elevator and went down a level. I had never been to any level besides the Dark Flats. When the elevator door opened on the bottom level, my eyes took a moment to adjust to the darkness. There was a dim green glow of the emergency lights. Sal stepped forward, raised his arms above his head, and waved them back and forth to get the motion sensor to register his presence and turn on the lights. The small hallway illuminated by a flickering light was the best it could do. We started walking behind Sal.

"When it starts pulling power, it draws less essential power, like the lights. If an alarm goes off, you'll see the lights around you turning off. Head directly to the Mess Hall, and I mean *immediately*." Sal reiterated to us.

"Does that mean we'll die if we don't make it to the Mess Hall in time?" Nitris asked the question I was thinking. I looked up from the notes I wrote on my OC to look at Sal for his response.

"Theoretically, if you cannot make it to the Mess Hall before all power is diverted, there may be loss of lives. That is why you should *always* go to the Mess Hall first." Sal dodged the question but emphasized the importance of being in the right place at the wrong time. "There are some areas on board that have separate oxygen tanks. The airlocks, for instance."

"The what?" I asked.

"There are two airlocks that the Maintenance Pod uses to dock and unload waste from outside," Sal said patiently but maintained his brisk walking pace. "They have independent oxygen supplies in case there's a hull breach or sealant leak. Anything that would cause delay to Pangea residents to make it to the Mess Hall. They're connected by tunnels left over from when Pangea was being built, and I wouldn't depend on them."

I'd heard other Lumpen talk about the old tunnels in the Mess Hall, but it always sounded more like a legend than fact. I was surprised to learn they were real, and I was walking in them.

Sal thought for a moment, then continued, "The old Birthing Lab also has its own oxygen supply. It's about a quarter of the size of this big one here," he swiped his wrist over the door lock, and the door hissed and unlocked, sliding to the side. We all walked in and followed Sal, blinded as he had to overly gesture to get the motion lights to power on. The room lit up, and many cylinders lined the room walls about the size of our Mess Hall. Sal walked over to the largest one and hit the side of the cylinder. Running from the floor to the ceiling, more than five meters tall and three meters wide.

"How do we access this main oxygen supply?" Nitris asked as they walked around the colossal cylinder and stopped at the computer off to the side. I walked over to see what they were looking at.

"Why would you need to access the main oxygen supply?" I asked them. Nitris gave me a nonchalant shrug.

"That's a good question," Sal smiled at Nitris as he spoke. I knew I would have to try to impress him as the day went on. He continued, "We have a simulation mode for teaching these more advanced steps. I will set up a scenario where all the solar energy collection panels have been destroyed by space debris, and Pangea has gone dark. There's no power left on board for this unit to draw from. It needs the backup generator. What do you do?" Sal asked while he typed into the computer and then stepped away.

The main computer screen and the three stations next to it were all beeping and flashing with red and orange lights. The beeping got louder and more high-pitched, and the lights flashed faster. I suddenly felt hot all over my body and couldn't inhale. I reached up to pull my PSC from my neck to breathe, but nothing was happening.

"You're okay, Taliah. Let's breathe together. Inhale, exhale," Nitris said as they grabbed my hand. We inhaled and exhaled a few times, and I felt the heat dissipating throughout my body.

I yanked my hand out of their hand and pulled it to my chest when I said, "It's your fault I couldn't breathe. Asking all those scary questions about surviving in an emergency. Come on, let's do this simulation." I turned on my heel and headed to the closest computer station.

"You're right. We can do this." Nitris said with confidence.

"I think you should take the lead on interfacing with the computer," I instructed Nitris to do the typing because I was feeling shaky. I didn't know what had happened to me, but I felt better when Nitris held my hand and we breathed together. Although, I would never admit that aloud.

"This warning says that power is only at the Heart Office. How can we reroute it here?" Nitris asked as they read a warning. They clicked on a larger map of Pangea.

Together we looked at the area on the screen as more alerts kept popping up, and the display turned areas from green to red as the section lost power.

"Tick tock, tick tock, has everyone made it to the Mess Hall yet?" Sal added pressure to our task at hand.

"There, that number keeps going up," I said, pointing to the top right corner of the screen. Nitris followed and clicked on it. It was a real-time tally of everyone in the Mess Hall and the Dining Hall above it.

"The number is only 124, and there are 257 residents in Pangea. Where is everybody?" Nitris asked and continued to search the map on the screen.

"We can worry about the population after we figure out how to reroute the power from the Heart Office to here. I remember reading in our workbook about how we should also prep the generator to provide additional power if we can't reroute enough." I sat down at the computer station next to Nitris. I felt this wasn't going fast enough, but I felt better when I focused on the problem in front of me. I saw the alert that said Prepare Generator, and I clicked that. It explained several steps on how to prime it for power.

"Lithium-ion batteries are attached to the outside of the generator. We must insert those into the generator before it can run independently." I said to Nitris. "Sal, do we do that for the simulation?" I asked over my shoulder where Sal was standing.

"Yes. Just hit 'Run Test' instead of 'Power On,'" He told us.

I looked at Nitris, and we both got up and walked to where Sal stood next to the generator. They stood on one side and started to unlock the batteries from the generator and insert them. I did the same on my side. Eight large lithium-ion batteries were 12 cm tall and 4 cm wide in the shape of long flat squares that were inserted into slots one way. The generator screen started to glow when all eight batteries were in place. I walked back to the front display on the generator screen and saw the option to 'power on' in green or 'run tests' in yellow. I pushed 'run tests.' The screen lit up with a countdown to full power in 90 seconds.

Nitris and I rushed back to the computer terminals at the oxygen supply. We read the screens for what to do next.

"I keep clicking the option to 'turn off' the power supply to the Heart Office, but the computer isn't responding," I said, desperately touching the screen to respond to my index finger.

"In the workbook, there is an override code for everything on Pangea," Nitris offered, "If we can use that code to turn the Heart Office power off, it should boot this computer into emergency mode. Theoretically, it should automatically pull that power from the Heart Office for us."

"Great. What is the override code for...uh... *everything*?" I asked sarcastically. I had read that part, too, but it didn't list any codes.

"Work together. Tell each other what you see on the screens and the stations *around* you." Sal gave us a clue. I started to look at the area around the screens and the desk that held the keyboard. There wasn't anything useful around. There was an empty water cup and a wireless charging pad for an OC. I looked up at the oxygen cylinder itself.

"We only have 45 seconds left. What do you see?" I asked Nitris while I kept looking at the writing on the cylinder.

"The population number has only hit 201. The generator is almost primed and ready to be turned on. Oh! We can pull the power from the trash transport and direct that to us," Nitris said and typed on the computer.

"That just bought a few more seconds," Sal said.

"What is this on the cylinder?" I asked Nitris.

"That doesn't look like English," they replied as they looked at what I was looking at. The paint seemed fresh when everything else around it seemed old.

"Maybe that's the point. In the command prompt, enter this as I read it to you." I instructed them.

"Ready," they answered, and I read off the handwritten letters and numbers on the cylinder. It all seemed random, but when Nitris hit enter when I had finished reading, the screen showed a green Heart Office. I watched as Nitris touched the Heart Office on the screen. The option to turn off all power appeared, and they selected to confirm.

"Ten seconds. Will we live or die today?" Sal sounded like he was having too much fun with this.

The screen went black. I looked at Nitris, trying to figure out what they'd done wrong.

"The generator! We need it on so that this computer can keep operating!" I shouted and ran to the screen on the generator. It was ready. I hit the screen to turn it on, but it went black too. I was too late.

"Looks like we all died," Sal said with a chuckle, "It's okay, we can rerun the simulation tomorrow," he said.

"What? No. We had it," I protested and touched the generator screen over and over. I didn't like feeling like a failure. I needed to finish the simulation.

"I told you. We're all dead." Sal touched my shoulder to pull me away from the screen. I shook his hand away.

"I was right there. I had it," I said.

"Do you know what went wrong?" Sal lost his joking tone and returned to the work-study teacher.

"We didn't know the code to shut down the Heart Office. Why was it pulling so much power anyway?" Nitris asked Sal.

"The Heart Office is not only where the Elders live but also where all the main servers to operate Pangea live," Sal explained. "There is power routed there to keep Pangea's AI functional. When you turn off that power, you lose things like artificial gravity, hydrogen recycler, water generator, life support, and everything else. Turning off the Heart Office is always a last resort because it will reset the entire AI."

"Why is the ship's power supply so involved in oxygen recycling? I thought we generated our power from the solar panels outside Pangea. Shouldn't they provide unlimited power to operate the ship?" I asked, still upset that the screen went black when we failed the simulation.

"Yes and no. Yes, solar panels provide us with power. Still, we can only store as much as the lithium-ion batteries can store when fully charged. No, we don't have unlimited power because we only have the generator batteries, and there aren't that many on board. A meteor hitting the side would damage the ship and the solar panels, providing power like the simulation. There are a lot of automated services all over Pangea that rely on power. You'll learn more as you complete the work-study cycle. Every department has an emergency protocol to deal with its power supply. The Sand Showers protocol is to immediately turn off all power to divert nonessentials to the life support systems like oxygen recycler," Sal explained.

"I understand every department has instructions during an emergency to turn their power in the sector on or off. But why are the override codes painted on the walls? The Dark Flats are notorious for being decrepit. Why do the codes look fresh while everything else is falling apart?" I was still confused when I asked him why the override code wasn't listed in the workbook we had to read.

"The codes are painted all over the station to ensure we always have what we need. We don't have many things available to us 'offline' or without power. Suppose there was an emergency, and you had forgotten to charge your OC, or maybe it shattered on impact. How would you be able to access the document you saved with the override codes for your department?" Sal asked me in return.

"I could use Justice's OC; she carries her charger pad in her pocket," I rationalize and attempt to problem-solve.

"Justice was making her way to the Mess Hall, and her OC was broken on impact. What would you do to get the codes only on a computer?" Sal asked again.

"Memorize them!" I said with glee as I figured

out what he was trying to teach us.

"You could try to do that, but if you were in a different sector and didn't know the codes there, then what would happen? When I was your age doing this same simulation, I asked my teacher why it was written on the side there. She told me you can't trust a computer to have power in an emergency. You can't even trust a plastic-printed card with the code. Someone could have typed it wrong, or the printer could have smudged it. But you know what you can't lose? Paint on the walls. Humans have done it like that since they drew on the walls inside their caves. You can trust a human's hand more than you can trust a computer's voice," Sal said and pointed up at the cameras in this room to imply that we can't always depend on a computer for everything.

"Is it someone's job to touch up the painted codes in every sector?" Nitris asked.

"You are correct. The supervisors must check on their code and do the paint touch-ups if needed. We just did ours last month. That's why it stood out compared to the rest of the room. It is most important. Sometimes we need another human being to depend on. Computers stop working when the power goes off," Sal told us, and the sentiment started to sink in.

Although I was still mad that we didn't pass the simulation, I removed the batteries from the generator and locked them back into their position. We learn early in the Bunks that we must return items to where we found them. It was automatic for me to put things back where they came from.

"Why aren't the batteries kept in the generator at all times? Maybe if we didn't have to load them in, we would have survived the simulation and saved everyone," I asked Sal, and Nitris came over to help me with the other batteries.

"If the batteries were in it all the time, they wouldn't last as long," Sal said. "As it is, these batteries would only last a couple of hours anyway, and then we'd need to recharge them with more solar power."

"That seems like a serious design flaw," I insisted. "Are there more of these batteries nearby if we need them while these are recharging?" I looked around the low-lit area.

"We haven't ever needed them before." It seemed like Sal was trying to calm me, but it wasn't working. "I don't think this kind of thing is expected to happen. That is why we have work-study to evaluate and test everyone to see which job is best suited for them in any scenario. Then we avoid any problems that nobody knows how to fix, and we're all safe. I actually think the simulations put the 'fun' in functional." Sal laughed at his own joke.

"Just because it hasn't happened yet, doesn't mean it won't ever happen." I heard Nitris say under their breath. That is the first smart thing they said all day, and I agreed. We should always have a backup plan.

"Why was the override code all jumbled letters and numbers?" Nitris asked.

"Since Pangea only uses English, the coding down to the keyboards is in English. The code can't use letters or numbers that could get mixed up. We can't have Zero be mistaken for the letter 'O'. The codes use unique letters and numbers that can't be mistaken for another character," Sal explained.

We left the service level together and took the elevator to the Dark Flats. Sal led the way as we started to walk back to the work-study classroom because we were almost done with today's class. I tried to walk slower to match Nitris' pace, but when I slowed down, they did too.

"Really?" I stopped and looked them in the eyes. "Are you scared of me?"

"I was giving you space. I know you don't want people to think we're friends," Nitris said looking down at their boots.

"It's fine. I don't care anymore. With how bad my luck has been, I wouldn't be surprised if we end up working together for the rest of our lives," I said sullenly.

"I think you did great today," they told me as they stepped up to walk next to me.

"You asked the right questions," I said honestly.

"We were so close to solving that simulation," they said with a little smile.

"I know! I was about to save the day. What an air-suck!" I sighed out of my frustration, and we laughed.

"It was nice to work with you. I felt like we had things under control," Nitris said to me without any sarcasm.

"Thanks! You too," I agreed with them and we had worked well together. We continued walking behind Sal toward the classroom. He walked pretty fast for an old man.

"You both did well today," Sal said over his shoulder to us without looking back. "You know, aside from getting everyone killed. No need to check back into the classroom. You can both head over to Ms. Cora's and get in line to remove your PSCs." He looked ready for another nap in his office.

Nitris and I went and stood outside Ms. Cora's. We were the first ones there. It was only a few minutes until the notification excused everyone in the different work-study classes and shift changes.

"Cora is really nice," Nitris told me casually, trying to start a conversation while we waited.

"Yes, *Ms.* Cora is nice," I emphasized the formal title.

"She told me we don't have to do the 'Ms.' part," they replied.

"I guess I didn't get that notification," I said with too much sarcasm that it turned out to be funny. Nitris looked at me, and then we both burst into laughter.

I stopped laughing when I heard Justice's clunky walk coming down the hallway, and instinctively I stepped away from Nitris. I didn't want Justice to get the idea that I was friends with Nitris. She has always been protective of me and jealous of anyone who might replace her as my best friend.

All of the gossiping and power struggles felt too trivial and childish now. The simulation made it seem like my life, and everyone else's on board were in danger. It was only a test, but it felt real at the moment. I was surprised when I saw Nitris' compassion when they helped me to remember how to breathe. I'd been utterly confident that I could trust Nitris with my life.

Justice popped up next to me, and Nitris moved backward, surrendering their spot in line to Justice. I didn't say anything to Justice or Nitris. Instead, I looked forward with my back against the wall and said, "It feels like today has been a week long."

"I feel like that too. Today was gross, and we had to learn how the toilets works after the suction," Justice started to talk about herself and her day. I wasn't entirely listening because I was still thinking about what I had learned during the simulation.

I looked out into the hallway I had travelled daily since I could walk. I had never paid attention to all the handwritten things on the walls. I saw it all with a newfound respect and curiosity about how it had come to be and what it all meant.

Chapter 10
Sahara

Ding, ding, ding!

The computer announced it was time for dinner, and I went to the Mess Hall to see Nitris. I knew from watching them that they didn't usually return to the Bunks before dinner. I found them easily.

"Hey, Nitris, how was work-study?" I asked as I sat down across from them. I didn't have a ration tray and hoped they wouldn't ask me. They just stared at their own goo.

"I killed everyone on Pangea," Nitris said without looking up. I desperately wanted to look into their stunning green eyes.

I looked around us to see if anyone heard them. Thankfully, no one was on this side of the Mess Hall seemed to hear it.

"Do you want to explain that a little more?

Are you experiencing hallucinations?" I asked them, trying to keep my voice kind while I asked invasive questions.

"I had to do a simulation with Taliah on redirecting power to the oxygen supply machine. We failed and killed everyone," Nitris said glumly.

"Oh! It was only a simulation," I exhaled relief it wasn't a hallucination and tried to reassure them.

"I can see now why we are told that our imperative contribution is for the safety of everyone on board. I don't think that really sunk in until the simulation today. I never thought my actions could affect anybody on board. Especially not kill anyone." Nitris said and looked up at me.

"It's okay. We are all still here, and we're all still learning about our new jobs. What else did you learn?" I asked them.

"When in doubt, look around," Nitris said in an elusive way.

"What does that mean?" I asked.

"Generations of Lumpen workers have been recording important information around us. For an emergency, in case the computers lost power or if someone needed to step in and do a job for someone else. I'd seen the writing on the walls and the ceilings, but I didn't think about what it meant."

Nitris casually pointed behind me and continued. "You see that camera? It doesn't work. It hasn't worked for a long time, and everybody knows it," I looked up at the camera, and there was no red indicator light like there were on the cameras at the entrance to the Mess Hall. "On the wall below the camera, there's a red circle with a line through it. I'm just now learning why these things are all over the Dark Flats."

"So, the circle and line mean something special?" I asked them over my shoulder while I looked at the painted wall.

"I think it means 'not functional' or something. There are other symbols and words in languages I don't recognize. Now that I know about them, I can't stop seeing them all over," Nitris told me as they looked around the walls in the Mess Hall.

"I see it now," I told them and looked around at the people sitting at the tables, indifferent to the secret language written in plain sight. Nitris stopped talking. After a moment, I brought up the topic that really interested me.

"After dinner, do you want to go to Mr. Kline's chambers when he does his nightly visit," I said teasingly.

"That sounds good," Nitris said, looking down at the table. Sometimes it's hard to keep contact with Nitris' gorgeous green eyes without getting distracted. They're so deep and intense.

I watched Nitris choke down another spoonful of the goo and ditch the rest of the goo in the recycler. Then they placed their tray with the other dirty trays.

"We need to go somewhere with fewer eyes and ears," Nitris told me while they looked around the Mess Hall.

"I don't know any place like that," I told them.

"I think I know of one. Come on, follow me," Nitris said and left the Mess Hall.

We headed toward the Bunks, then stopped when we reached a small alcove in the hallway with a hole with a ladder leading down. The location was half hidden by the artificial gravity tubes that lined the walls every 6 meters.

"I'm sure this ladder leads down to the old service tunnels. I learned in work-study that we don't use these tunnels much anymore. Something about a broken air lock," Nitris said as they started descending the ladder.

"How do you know that we aren't going to end up floating outside?" I asked with concern.

"If there was a breach to the station, the computer is programmed to take over and redirect resources to the Mess Hall. We wouldn't even be able to talk right now if the tunnels were compromised," Nitris theorized, and it made sense to me too. I followed them down the ladder.

"Is this how you went for work-study?" I asked them as I descended each rung of the ladder.

"We used the service elevator near the Lumpen chambers, but it's too busy with the dinner rush and shift changes," Nitris said as they continued climbing down the ladder.

The tunnel was only about two meters tall and wide when we reached the bottom. We stopped at the door cordoned off with a red notice posted that it was closed because of a faulty airlock.

"Come on, this way," Nitris said as they ducked under the partition marked with "closed" and opened the door into the airlock.

"I don't think we should be here," I whispered.

"Don't worry. I think the airlock was fixed, and no one updated the notices. The Dark Flats are neglected. We should keep the signs up so no one will come this way," Nitris stated. I followed them. When we got a few paces past the warning sign, the lights flickered on, and the door closed behind us. They weren't as bright as in other parts of Pangea.

"You think it is fixed? What gives you that idea?" I looked around the tiny airlock.

"When I was running a simulation during work-study, I saw this airlock on the station schematic, which wasn't red or green. The areas where oxygen escaped were red, and the Heart Office was green. I'm guessing this didn't show on the simulation because it's completely offline still. We would have known about an oxygen leak before climbing the ladder," Nitris said and looked around at the cameras and the painted walls.

"I'm glad you have excellent intuition," I said, "This is a great secret meeting spot. I see those red circles with the lines through them like we saw in the Mess Hall," I sat on the floor and made myself comfortable.

"Thanks. I hoped it would give us privacy," Nitris avoided looking at me and seemed embarrassed.

"So, I have a few ideas on getting into the Library," I said as I took out my OC and prepared to write notes like we were in class. Nitris gave me an endearing smile.

"I'm listening," Nitris said with a head tilt.

"I think the biggest issue we will face is the timing," I started, then brought up a drawing on my OC I'd made earlier that day. It was a rough outline of the Dark Flats, a circle with labeled rooms. I selected the option to change from a flat-screen display to a holo projection to show Nitris.

"We have to be in our bunks for lights out and then make our way towards Mr. Kline's office without setting off the sensors."

"But we'll have to get there early and watch him leave, so we'll know when he's gone," Nitris pointed out, already following my idea.

"Exactly! We'll wait for him to go and see Ms. Verban. Then we'll sneak into his chambers before the automatic door locks behind his exit," I explained.

"What's the plan once we're in there?" Nitris asked me.

"We'll have to work quickly to find the key and code for the Library before he returns, usually a little bit before the wake-up call in the morning."

"But you've only practiced moving without the motion sensors once. Do you think you're up for the challenge?" Nitris asked me with genuine concern in their voice.

Should I tell Nitris the truth or keep my secret for as long as possible?

After a deep breath, I said, "You're right. You should take the lead in case I get caught or if I'm too slow. Then it's up to you to continue and finish the plan," I hoped that sounded believable and that Nitris had no follow-up questions.

"Perfect. That sounds solid. If we get separated for any reason, we should meet back here at our new base of operations," Nitris said and waved their arms around, indicating the airlock.

"To maximize our time, we should sleep in our darkest clothes to avoid setting off the sensors," I said and gestured to the clothes I had on.

"I don't think I've ever seen you in other clothes," Nitris said.

I laughed, but I knew that Nitris wasn't joking. "These are just my best sets, so I wear them a lot," I said. Inside my head, I screamed at myself for coming this far but forgot to change my clothes.

"Based on what's in your journal, we know that

Mr. Kline doesn't head over to Ms. Verban's until later, so we will have a couple hours before starting. I think I'll try to take a nap," Nitris paused, then thought about what they had just said to me. "But that seems practically impossible with how much anxiety and excitement I have coursing through my body right now," Nitris shook their whole body.

When Nitris mentioned my journal, I realized I had sent them *everything* I had written, not just what was relevant to this plan. I hoped they wouldn't read the chapters I wrote about them. That would be devastating.

"I think a power nap is what I need too. Let's head back and get settled before our big night." I stretched my arms and pretended to yawn.

We headed back to the Bunks in silence, but the energy was building between us. It was electric, and it might spark out of control soon.

This mission was almost over, and then I could tell Nitris everything.

Chapter 11
Nitris

I spent the hours between lights out at 22:00 and 01:00 trying to calm my racing mind without success. I had so many feelings running through me. The prospect of danger with a new friend had my stomach doing flips. I closed my eyes and focused on breathing. Whenever I walked around Pangea without setting the sensors off, it was usually just for me to see if I could do it, but the risks were higher. I was terrified that I could end up in Solitary Containment, but the idea of Sahara going there scared me even more. I didn't want to lose her.

I slowly got out from under my thin blanket and jumped down, landing softly on the balls of my feet. The cold steel under my bare feet jolted me awake. I worried that someone would hear me and looked around the dark room. I could see because of the small emergency lights on the floor leading to the door that was always open. Because of these emergency lights, there was never true darkness, just like how the machine hum made it, so there was never true silence.

Sahara met me at the door. Without a word, we began to head toward Mr. Kline's office. We took the long way that we were sure he would not use. Which meant we had to pass the scary abandoned labs and Library.

This long stretch of the hallway had minimal lighting. It was cold, and the air smelled stale like it hadn't been recycled in a few days. We got pretty far before we heard a metal scraping sound. We couldn't identify it or where it was coming from. We paused for a moment and looked around. Our bodies were pressed firmly against the curved wall of the hallway.

"The night shift should be busy working already. I think we should keep going. There's no telling what that sound was," I said in a hurried whisper. Sahara blinked and nodded her head before we continued through the adult living chambers. This was the stretch where the lights were always on and we walked briskly through with our heads down.

Rounding the last bend in the hallway we found a small nook between the large air flow ducts leading up to the Richies level. It was big enough for us to sit and wait for Mr. Kline to leave his chambers. The only thing lighting our area was the same green emergency lights, but here they seemed to be dimmer and a darker green than they were in the Bunks. Huddled together, we talked very low while we waited.

"How long have you been making this plan?" I asked Sahara. She had a lot planned out before I taught her about the motion lights.

"For a while. I knew I needed someone special to help me," Sahara said, looking at me.

"I'm not special," I said and looked away. I felt like I was letting her down by not meeting her expectations.

"You are the most special." She said in a kind voice. I wanted to reach for her but was nervous she would pull away.

We sat silently and listened for Mr. Kline's door to slide open with the familiar mechanical hiss. When it finally opened, we could hear Mr. Kline humming as he walked away from our hiding spot, down the hallway towards Ms. V's chambers. It didn't matter if Mr. Kline set off the lights as a teacher, so he moved with purpose to see his love.

"Ready?" I asked as I got up on my feet in a crouched position.

"Let's go," Sahara said with an urgent energy I could feel radiating off her.

There was that scratching metal sound again. I froze in place, trying to find the location of the sound. Sahara didn't hear the noise and went forward in front of me.

"Wait. Something is off," I tried to tell her, but she was moving fast to get inside before the door slid closed. Panic caught in my throat, and it felt all the oxygen had been sucked out of my lungs. I watched Sahara enter Mr. Kline's chambers while I was still frozen in place.

The lights were on in the hallway from Mr. Kline's leaving. I felt exposed. I flattened my back against the wall and edged closer to his chamber door as it closed the last meter. I made eye contact with Sahara on the other side of the door.

The vibration from my OC made me flinch, and I realized it was probably a message from Sahara. I reached into my pocket and pulled it out.

I made it. What happened to you?

I typed my reply quickly.

I heard something and didn't know what it was. I got scared and froze. You should be able to trigger the automated door to open from the inside. Walk towards the door like you are about to leave.

I sent the message on how to open the door and then waited in the same spot under the bright lights.

Nothing happened.

I looked at my OC and saw the time had only been a few minutes, but it felt like a lifetime. While I stared at the screen, another message from Sahara came in.

It's not working. I found this code; maybe it is for the door; it's 814975.

It was weird that the door wasn't opening from the inside with Sahara standing next to it. We had watched as Mr. Kline exited his chambers, and nothing seemed wrong. I didn't bother moving slowly to the door scanner since the lights were already on. I used the manual keypad under the chip scanner to enter the code Sahara sent me. The door made a loud thud and then opened to the side.

As the auto-lock on the door engaged behind me, I bumped into the side of Mr. Kline's desk. My eyes quickly adjusted from the bright hallway to the dark room. Sahara didn't seem to be stumbling or having any trouble.

"What happened?" I asked Sahara, who was

standing at the desk.

"I don't know. It's like the door sensor wasn't seeing me," Sahara said. I recalled the night before when she had walked directly to the Library door without activating the lights, but they had come on when I walked the same path.

"We should hurry before someone comes by to check on that weird noise," I told Sahara. Something strange was going on, but I couldn't figure it out. Where had she even found that manual door code? I didn't see anything on the desk she was standing next to. I had expected to see how the override code was painted on the wall.

"Go check the bedside table over there, and I'll look here," Sahara suggested.

Sahara seemed to get her bearings faster than I did for some reason. I didn't know why. I looked around the small room and saw that the bed had been made. There was a small table next to it.

I started rummaging through the side table and heard a faint metal clanging sound. It drew Sahara's attention to me.

"That sounded like metal hitting metal," I said as I pushed things around in the drawer. My hands touched some metal, and I grabbed it.

"I think I found it," I said excitedly as I pulled out the object I had grabbed. It was a metal spoon from the Mess Hall with hard bits of dried goo.

"I don't think that's it," Sahara laughed.

"Gross," I said, dropping it back into the metal drawer.

I began to search around the floor where I was kneeling next to the side table. I reached under the bed and felt some clothes. I wondered what it must be like to live in chambers alone, with no one to tell you how or when to clean them.

Feeling further under the bed and past the clothes, my fingers hit a small metal box and brought it out to examine it more closely. I looked to my right and saw Sahara beside me, looking under the bed too.

The small box was about 30 centimeters long and 20 centimeters wide. I fumbled with the latch on the front and opened it. Inside there was a ring with many silver and gold keys on it. I spread them out in the palm of my hand. It looked like the key ring that Ms. V had on her hip at all times.

"One of these has got to be for the Library," Sahara said with glee, pointing at them.

I looked over at her and was overwhelmed by a vision. It was her in Solitary Containment, I assumed. She wore a white dress that stood out against the darkness around her. She had a scar across her face from her left eyebrow down to her ear. Her blue eyes lit up the darkness with desperation. I gasped for air and shook my head, trying to force the vision away.

"Are you okay?" She asked next to me on the floor, looking at me with concern.

I considered telling her about my visions, but I needed to figure out what they were and how to explain them to anyone. I didn't want to lie to Sahara, but I decided this wasn't the time to try explaining. Instead, I said, "Yes, I'm fine. Let's look for the code now to get out of here."

"Do you think it's inside that box?" She inquired, looking from me to the box in my hands and back to me again.

"Let's find out," I said. Inside the box, I saw a paper journal. Paper was scarce at the station because we didn't have trees to make it from. The only paper on Pangea was the little bit people had brought onboard with them back during the Great Earth Exodus. I had never touched actual paper before. Our school books were digital or printed on thin plastic made from recycled materials.

Gently, I picked up the journal and flipped through it, looking for anything with a number combination that might be the code for the Library. It should be six digits long, like Mr. Kline's manual door code. I got distracted, and I found myself reading random lines from different entries in the journal.

Genetically enhanced rations have a prolonged life span of 12 years. Due to the unpleasant flavor, the improved rations include a chemical inhibitor that blocks the brain's taste receptors.

All children are designed to be sterilized before exiting the Birthing Lab to facilitate population control. This is coded into their DNX.

The Birthing Lab has been closed until further notice. A population reduction plan is in effect over the next decade to control human society and to focus resources on finding a place to return to Earth or the long-term goal of another planet in a different galaxy. "Families" are a waste of time along with human emotion and will be eliminated.

As I flipped through the journal, stopping to read random pages, so many of the things I had suspected about life on Pangea were confirmed. There were even drawings of different locations from the Dark Flats. I realized that I wasn't paranoid or delusional. I looked at Sahara, and her face showed she was also interested in what the journal said.

"I don't see any codes in here," I said as I flipped through again and returned it to the box.

"Wait! Let's take it with us. If he had that dirty spoon, he probably wouldn't even know it was missing," she said excitedly. I took the book, put it in the back of the waistband on my pants, and covered it with my shirt.

"Alright, but we must focus and find the Library entry code, or this has all been a waste of time," I told her as I started looking in the storage cabinets on the walls.

While rummaging in the closets, I found Mr. Kline's OC. His screen was intact and not shattered like the rest of ours. I turned the power on and saw a password-protected login prompt. I looked around the room and tried to think what the teacher would use for his password. First, I tried "Verban," but that didn't work. I could only try twice more before it would lock me out permanently.

"I need a password for his OC. Got any ideas?" I asked Sahara, still searching around the room.

"Try 'MilkyWay' with capital M and W without a space," Sahara said plainly.

I entered MilkyWay for the password, and the OC chimed open. I gave Sahara a questioning look, curious how she would know the password.

"He talks about the Milky Way in class as if it is the only galaxy out there," she explained. I chose to believe her. I was beginning to suspect how she knew all of these things. Maybe the Elders had her spying to incriminate me and send me to Solitary. That doesn't make sense because she had been with me and would be punished too. There was still something wrong with all of this.

I quickly searched on the tablet for 'Library' and discovered a document with all the numerical codes sorted by hours. Every hour there is a new six-digit code to enter along with turning the key. It was old technology that Mr. Kline told us about when we learned the history of Pangea. I quickly sent all the hourly codes to my OC. I considered sending them to Sahara also, but I was starting to think that I shouldn't trust her with everything.

"Okay, we have what we need. Let's get out of here," Sahara said and headed to the door. I quickly turned off the manual desk light, though I couldn't remember if it had been on when we came in or not.

The chamber door malfunctioned and didn't automatically open when Sahara approached it. I thought we would be locked in there and rushed over to her. As soon as I stepped next to Sahara, the door opened. I got a strange sense that the station was not malfunctioning. It was something else. Something to do with her.

We almost returned to the Bunks when we heard the mysterious metal scratching sound again. We both stopped in place and looked at each other. Neither of us wanted to take another step.

"You're sure you don't know what it is?" I asked Sahara, desperate for the truth.

"No, but the Bunks are so close. We have got to get back there before someone notices we're gone." Sahara said. I led us the rest of the way to the Bunks, careful not to set off the lights.

In a rush back to the Bunks, I completely forgot that I had the paper journal tucked in my waistband.

It wasn't until I laid down on my bunk that I felt it dig into my lower back. I pulled it out carefully and examined the stiff fabric around the journal. This once-common paper now seemed so brittle and fragile in my hands. The handwriting inside was diverse; not everything was in English, meaning it had many different owners over the years. This journal had so much history hidden in its pages that it felt illegal to be holding it in my hands.

Chapter 12
Intra

There's no rest for the wicked, is an Old Earth phrase, but it felt appropriate to describe my never ending job duties on Pangea.

"I want to see Kline's latest progress report. Bring it up on the main screen." I instructed Echo.

"This is Kline's latest progress report from the last week in February," Echo said, and the screen lit up with the document.

"I want this week's status report. I do not want to see something that I have already read," I demanded.

"Today is March 3rd. The report isn't due until Saturday the 6th," Echo said plainly.

"I don't care what day it is. I want an update *now*," I told Echo before I decided to do it myself. "Computer, initiate a holo call to Silas Kline," I instructed the OC to call him directly. The computer connected me to Kline's OC.

"Hello?" Kline answered his OC. He sounded surprised.

"Kline, this is Intra calling. I need a status report right now." I told him.

"Oh. Just a moment," Kline said. I heard him say something and then listened to the hydraulic hiss of the door opening. I looked over at the security monitoring station for his area. He had stepped out into the hallway to talk to me.

"I'm currently working with the pupil now. I'm not ready to submit this week's report yet. We are still in the process of testing." Kline said to my holo image that floated above his OC.

"How have the tests been proceeding since work-study has started?" I asked Kline a more direct question to get a definitive answer from him.

"Every test has been completed successfully thus far. I need more time to evaluate the responses since it is only the third day of work-study," Kline said as he rubbed his chin. His body language on the camera made it look like he was nervous.

"What are you testing today?" I asked him. I had already accessed the syllabus. I wanted to ensure he was staying on track and not falling behind.

"Memory Test 308 is next on my agenda for today," Kline said. "I only have two more hours to work with the pupil. May I please be excused to begin this test?"

"Excellent, we are on schedule for this week. Return to work," I said and disconnected the holo call. I watched the monitoring screen for another moment. Kline stood still and then exhaled deeply before he turned around and opened the door.

"It seems that Mr. Kline is doing a good job keeping on schedule," Codex said, even though I never asked for her observation.

"Yes, it appears that way," I replied as I cleared the monitors.

"Is there anything else that I can help you with?" Codex asked.

"You have not provided help so far. I'm the one who had to holo call Kline," I said with disdain. Codex didn't help me as much as she liked to think she did.

"Do you want to increase security patrols during work-study classes to confirm Mr. Kline stays on task?" Codex asked me.

"Increase security?" Echo asked me.

"No. We don't need to increase security. I have already addressed that issue," I informed the entire room of Council members.

"Emberson," Echo said calmly.

"Correct," I confirmed. Emberson has always been my personal project and had proven to be reliable in many instances over the years.

With a quick gesture over my desk, the display from Emberson appeared in front of me, and I watched as it gathered and processed information. This data was crucial for the subsequent phases of my plan. None of the others knew what I was working on, and I preferred it to be that way. I have never enjoyed being questioned for my actions. This ship is my responsibility, and it is up to me to keep it safe. I found comfort in knowing that Emberson only follows my instructions and does exactly as I say.

Chapter 13
Mr. Kline

After I composed myself from the holo call I received from Intra, I swiped my chip and entered the Birthing Lab to resume work. I brought up Memory Test 308 on my OC and sat at my desk. "Are you ready to continue, Sahara?" I asked as I sat at my desk, keeping my back to the door.

"Is everything okay, Mr. Kline?" She asked me with compassion in her eyes and concern in her voice.

"Everything is fine." I lied to her. I didn't know why Intra had holo called me during work-study. The last two years, I never talked to the Elders; they just accept my weekly progress reports on Saturday nights. I looked down at the Memory Test on my OC and read the instructions. I didn't want to alarm Sahara about how nerve-wracking that call was.

"Does Intra holo call you often?" She asked me.

"No one holo calls anyone anymore. Just OC messages." I avoided the question and exhaled the breath I was holding without realizing it.

All this time testing with Sahara, and I didn't feel close to completing the assignment the Elders assigned me. Instead, it felt like Intra was trying to apply pressure to get her desired results. These secrets were weighing on my shoulders, and it felt harder and harder to detach emotionally when I left Sahara alone in the Birthing Lab each day.

"When we complete all these tests, will I be able to move out of the Birthing Lab and into the Bunks with the other teenagers?" Sahara asked me. This question was something that I had been thinking about since I started working with her.

"I don't see why not," I lied again and kept my eyes on my OC. I never knew for sure what would happen when testing was completed. I only knew what my job was and how to format the reports of my findings. When I first agreed to this assignment, I thought the pupil would be one of the teens in my class. Not this young woman who has never stepped foot outside of this abandoned lab. I looked at her sitting in the white gown across the desk from me. Her hands were folded in her lap patiently.

"Is it okay to lie to someone that you care about?" Sahara asked after a moment. We had never talked about our personal feelings.

"If the situation calls for it, or if the truth will hurt the person more than a lie, I guess it's okay," I said and looked at her. I thought about how I had to lie to Jexa, and that added to the weight on my shoulders. I slumped forward, leaned my elbows on the desk, and placed my OC flat to begin its wireless charge during the administration of the next test.

"Is that why you lie to me?" She asked coldly.

"There are things that I'm unable to talk about because it might impact the results of these tests," I answered, trying to be ambiguous to avoid hurting her. I also had to protect the mission I had been working on. I was very close to being able to get my promotion to the Aristocrats level. Then I could ask Jexa to marry me, and we won't have any more secrets.

"Do you lie to Jexa?" Sahara asked. It was like she could read my mind.

"How do you know about Jexa?" I asked. We hadn't spoken about Jexa before. Even if we had, I would have referred to her as Ms. Verban, not her first name, because that is improper.

"Sometimes, when we are working together, I get these feelings that seem like memories but aren't mine," Sahara confided in me. "Just now, I felt a lot of love and pictured a beautiful woman with short curly brown hair and kind green eyes, and I knew she was Jexa." I took a moment to consider whether I should document this in the report for this week.

"What else do you sense? Do you only sense things from me and how I'm feeling?" I asked her, curious if these were the results from the updated DNX. I watched her closely as she looked down at the desk instead of at me.

"Sometimes. Like how that call made you tense and surprised you." She said in a low voice.

"Does it scare you?" I asked her. She didn't look up but nodded her head in confirmation.

"What do you do when I'm not here with you?" I asked her. Something else had been on my mind for a long time.

"I read the workbooks and do the assignments you give me," she said and looked up to meet my eyes.

"Have you ever been to the Bunks?" I asked her, thinking of her earlier question about what she will do after testing.

"No. I've never been out of this room. You know that." She said quickly and then looked back down at her hands.

I received a notification on my OC, and it startled me. I saw that it had come from The Council of Elders, but when I clicked it, I was asked to solve a math problem. I suspected Intra had sent this as a test to see if I was still qualified to complete this mission. It could wait. I had to finish today's tests with Sahara before it was time for dinner rations.

"Let's get this test done," I told her and returned to the test file on my OC. It was a simple memory test that seemed easy enough to conduct.

"I will show you my OC with some images on it. You will look at it for 2 seconds and then have to name as many images as you can remember. Here we go," I said, turning my OC to holo mode for Sahara to see. I began the test, played a little memory game myself, and tried to recall the images I saw.

"There are 15 images on the screen, five rows down and three across," Sahara said, and then she went quiet. I looked at my OC and saw that she was exactly right. I sat in silence and waited for her to identify the images on the screen.

"Some of the images are things I've never seen before, but I feel like I know what they are," Sahara said, rubbing her head. I moved my OC to be leaning on the desk in my lap. Looking at the answers in front of me, the images seemed random. There were many things from Old Earth that I hadn't taught her about yet. I had doubts that Sahara would pass this test.

"Do the best that you can," I told her. "If you're struggling, you can meditate on the image, which should help bring the memory forward to you," I told her, repeating what had been in the instructions.

I watched as she inhaled and exhaled with her eyes closed. "I remember honey bees flying around a hive, a beach with light sand and clear water, a forest with lots of trees, a PSC, ration dispenser, a silver cup, a group of horses running, a mushroom cloud from a nuclear bomb exploding, a large knife, a gun, a meadow of flowers, an OC, bunk beds, children playing soccer, and a scalpel." Sahara listed everything with closed eyes as I stared at my OCs answers in disbelief.

"That's amazing. You answered everything correctly and in order as they appeared," I was excited that she did so well. I was beginning to worry about what would happen to us if she didn't pass these tests.

"I couldn't have done it without you," she said.

"What do you mean?" I asked her as I looked up to meet her eyes.

"When I closed my eyes, I pictured myself in your head, and I could see what you were looking at and hear you reading off the answers in your mind. There are hundreds of black and yellow striped nanobot-looking things flying around. You used the words 'honey bee' for the flying nanobots," Sahara told me. My mouth dropped open with shock.

"In my head? How did you do that?" I asked her and started to feel like she had invaded my privacy and was reading my mind.

"I'm not sure how I did it. I'm sorry." She said as she looked away from me and dropped her head down with shame.

"You can't just jump in and out of someone's mind like that. It's invasive and not fair to the person. It is like you cheated on this test." I said with anger rising in my voice. If she was cheating, I might be terminated for allowing such blatant disregard for the test protocols.

"I didn't mean to. Please don't be mad at me." Sahara said and began to cry. She pulled her hands to her face and tried to wipe away the tears.

"I don't know what to do, Sahara." I tried to calm myself. I could see that I was frightening her, but I didn't know how else to respond. "I'm supposed to be reporting the results of these tests so that we can advance the human race, and here you are cheating. I can't give a clear answer to the Elders, knowing that you somehow cheated on the tests." Sahara continued to sob as tears streamed down her face.

"This could jeopardize everything. Is that how you knew about Jexa too?" I asked her as I sat back in the chair and crossed my arms. I tried to put up a mental wall in my mind to disconnect my personal feelings and the simple job of administering tests, but it was proving challenging.

"There are memories that I can see, and I feel the emotions that are connected to that memory. I saw Jexa in your memories, and your love for her made me feel like I was part of a loving family with you both. I didn't mean to upset you." Sahara told me as she began to calm her tears.

"Well, you did upset me," I said bluntly. "I can't even think straight because of all the feelings that I have right now. We will have to end today's session and do more tests tomorrow to catch up on what we didn't finish today. I don't know what I will tell Intra about all of this. You better hope I don't receive another call from her, for both of our sakes." I said as I grabbed my OC and stood up from my desk in the Birthing Lab.

"Mr. Kline, please don't leave me. I can finish the tests. We have a few hours left in work-study. Please forgive me and stay. Don't leave me all alone," Sahara pleaded with me.

"I need to leave now because I'm emotionally compromised. I will return tomorrow." I told her, and then I exited the Birthing Lab into the main hallway. I waited until the door closed and locked behind me. I couldn't have her getting out of there and causing problems.

"Silas?" I heard my name called from down the hallway near the Bunks.

Chapter 14
Ms. Verban

"Hey, Jexa, how's your day going?" Silas said after he took his time to turn around and face me. His body language and tone showed that he was hiding something from me.

"What are you doing in the Birthing Lab?" I asked him and started to walk towards him. He looked from the Birthing Lab to me and quickly shuffled over to meet me.

"What are you doing over here? I thought you were going to help Dorro with laundry?" He kissed me on the cheek and put his hand around my waist. He turned me around to walk back towards the Bunks. I was briefly distracted by his touch but quickly regained my senses.

"You can't just kiss me like that in the hallway." I scolded him. "If someone sees us being intimate without a contract, they can report us," I told him, shoving his hand off my waist.

"You're right. Let's go to your chambers," he said and started to walk in front of me towards my chambers.

"Stop, you haven't answered my questions. What is going on with you?" I asked him again. He seemed upset and acted like he was trying to guide me away from the Birthing Lab.

"Nothing, everything is fine. How is Dorro? Not much work in the laundry today?" He asked, trying to change the subject.

"Are you going to lie to me and tell me you weren't just in the abandoned Birthing Lab?" I asked him. I stopped walking and crossed my arms across my chest. I waited for him to notice I had stopped, but it took a moment. He seemed preoccupied and flustered.

"Let's get to your chambers and talk in private," he said in a low tone after he had turned around and walked back to meet me where I stood.

"Why can't you tell me now? Everyone else is working or in work-study for a few more hours." I said and looked around the empty hallway.

I watched Silas look up at the cameras in the hallway, and then he said, "Please, Jexa, I need you to listen to me."

It is difficult to stay mad at Silas when I love him so much. I relented and dropped my arms, and walked silently to my chambers. I swiped my wrist, and the door opened. I'm not used to seeing Silas in my chambers during working hours.

"Alright, now tell me what is going on," I told him as I stood beside my desk. He walked over to my bed and sat down.

"I must tell you something, but it can't leave this room," he said as he looked up at me with distress on his face.

"What is it?" I said as I held on to my anger. He shouldn't be keeping secrets from me. We were both risking our *lives* to be together without a contractual agreement and shared chambers. It felt like he didn't understand the consequences we faced if we were reported to The Elders.

"Do you remember how I told you that I was doing higher education during work-study classes?" He asked simply.

I nodded yes. Silas had told me he was taking higher education courses on the Richies level to prepare him for life after the children age out of his class.

"I've been lying to you. The Elders have asked me to continue the work of Mx. Sage, they conducted research in the Birthing Lab and then promoted to the Richies level to continue their work there. The Elders promised me that when I completed this assignment in the Birthing Lab that, I would be promoted like Mx. Sage," he told me. I felt the heat of rage building in my chest. I inhaled deeply trying to keep my composure.

"You've been working for The Elders for two years and planning to leave me here in the Dark Flats when you become a *Richie*?" My voice was filled with anger as I spat the word "Richie" at him. I never even knew of a Lumpen named Mx. Sage.

"No. I would never leave you," he explained, "I already have a plan in motion. When I took on this extra work, I was sure to include that I could take a spouse to the Richies' level with me. The Council approved it in my contract. You would have to test for a higher education position, but I know you'll do great, and we can work together. We'd have everything that we would ever need, and we would be together."

"What about my children in the Bunks? Who would take care of them?" I asked him as I shifted my weight to my right leg and crossed my arms over my chest. It felt like he hadn't thought about me and how I would feel uprooting myself and moving to the Richies level.

"Someone else," he said without a care. "Besides, there aren't any new children that need you. Once the current children age out of the Bunks and move into their own places on the Dark Flats, the Bunks will probably be closed down like the Birthing Lab," he stood up from the bed and walked towards me. He rubbed my arms to soothe me, but I kept them tightly crossed over my chest. He was unaware of how hurtful his statement was to me.

"The Bunks will be closed down when the last of the children turn 18? That is a new notification that my OC didn't get. What else are you keeping from me?" I asked him and pulled away from his embrace. I turned my back to him to stop myself from crying.

"We aren't married, Jexa. I'm not required to tell you every detail about my life," Silas said with anger edging in on his voice.

"Yes. You're right. We aren't married." My words were clipped and brusque. "Who's to say we ever would be anyway? You have been playing with my heart for years. You have refused to talk to me about marriage or even living together. And *now* that I caught you coming out of the lab, I find out about this whole secret assignment? These plans that you made without telling me? I don't even know who you are anymore!" I yelled and turned to face him. I watched his face change when the impact of my words sunk in for him.

"I thought you would be happy for me. I thought you would be excited to marry me. Have you changed your mind?" He asked with a softer voice.

"Now you want to talk about a marriage contract? I can't marry you if you're keeping secrets from me! What kind of research are you doing in an abandoned lab?" I said with annoyance dripping on every word. I dropped my hands to my side and exhaled with frustration.

"It's classified," he answered and looked down at his boots. Even though he was standing one meter away from me, it felt like he was light years away emotionally.

"I thought you were going to tell me the truth?" I asked, placing my hands on my hips.

"I'm telling you as much of it as possible," Silas said. I could hear the pain in his voice, and I softened.

"I'm not trying to fight with you, Silas," I conceded, "You have been acting strange for a while, but I kept dismissing it as something else must be on your mind. Then, you tell me you have this big plan for us *both* that you've been keeping secret. It would have been nice to be included in your plans. Especially the parts that pertain to me and *my career*," resentment crept back into my voice.

"I should have told you the truth sooner, but it is all classified," Silas said, trying to justify his actions. "I was sworn to secrecy by The Elders and their NDA. The same NDA with *severe* consequences," I got the sense of what he was implying.

"There's that much secrecy about your research

job?" I said as I relaxed my arms down. This was more serious than I thought, proving he kept many secrets from me. "That sounds suspicious. That must mean they are monitoring you more closely to confirm that you haven't violated your agreement."

"I was trying to do what's best for us. I don't think The Elders have the time to monitor me constantly," he said as he reached into his pocket and looked at his OC. It felt like he was double-checking that it wasn't recording our conversation or something.

"They are always watching and listening," I reminded him. "They are always recording. It's how they maintain order. Don't you remember when Dorro was sentenced to Containment? The video evidence? The Elders see everything."

Silas stood there looking defeated and upset. I knew bringing up Dorro would hurt him, but I did it anyway. I wanted Silas to feel distressed and sad like I was feeling.

"I should leave," he said, and he walked out of my chambers.

I waited for the doors to close and lock with a loud thud before I allowed myself to feel weak. My legs began to shake, and I sat down on my bed. I stopped holding back my tears and let them flow down my face. My tears felt hot with rage, and my heart felt like he had ripped it out and taken it with him when he left. I didn't understand how I could love this man and tell him everything; he could just go without a care in the world—putting his own needs before our love.

Chapter 15
Taliah

When I got to Sal's work-study room, Nitris was already sitting with him. I noticed that Sal had his PSC on and his hair was braided up away from his collar. I went to sit down to wait for instructions, but Sal stood up and said, "Follow me," and the exited the classroom.

"Where are we going?" I whispered to Nitris.

"I'm not sure. He didn't say anything until you arrived," Nitris said.

We walked to the primary service room, and Sal swiped his wrist to open the door. It hissed in response and slid to the side, revealing a small room about two meters of space and the large elevator doors at the end. The walls had shelves with various bags and tools scattered around. It was disorganized and dirty. A sign above the shelf said 'Emergency Tools', but half looked like they belonged in the recycler. I wouldn't want to use any of them in an emergency.

Nitris and I followed Sal into the elevator, and he hit the button to reach the Richies level. I touched the PSC on my neck with anticipation. I knew Sal wouldn't take us anywhere we weren't authorized to be, but I was still nervous.

"Today is the last day of work-study for oxygen supply," Sal spoke as the elevator went up, "We have to check the status of the water vapor created from the oxygen recycling process. That vapor must be emptied from the recycler and sent to the water generation department. You'll spend a few days there later on in work-study. They are short-handed for workers."

I have visited many new places in the Dark Flats in the last few days. I've been most excited about this, and I tried to contain my excitement. It was my first time going to the Richies level. When the elevator door opened, I expected something magical. I was disappointed when it opened to another grungy service area. Sal walked out of the elevator into the room without looking back to confirm we were following him. I rushed out of the elevator to be on his heels.

"I suggest you take notes on your OC for this part. It might be on the test," Sal said, turning back to us with a wink before exiting the small room.

Sal swiped his wrist on the scanner to open the door into the Richies' hallway. The bright lights that illuminated the hallway made me squint. The walls were colored a soft gray and were clear of markings, unlike the Dark Flats. When my eyes adjusted, I looked up around for a window and started to walk towards the Dining Hall. I knew this level had the same layout as ours, so I assumed the nearest windows would be up the hallway on the right. I noticed there weren't as many cameras on the edges of the ceilings as I was used to. The Elders must trust the Richies more than us.

"Taliah, don't set off your PSC," Sal warned me. I thought I knew the boundary, so I wasn't worried and kept looking up for any window. I wanted to see Old Earth.

As I rounded the hallway, I saw a cupola skylight on the ceiling. I gasped and rushed forward, only looking up at Old Earth. The planet was filled with white swirls in the clouds, scorched land, and water that looked the same gray color as our ration goo. My ears began to ring, and I started to feel dizzy and disorientated from looking up and seeing the planet.

"Watch out!" I heard as I ran into something warm and fell backward. My feet flew up in the air, and for a moment, it looked like they were touching the surface of Old Earth. I hit my head hard on the cold steel floor of the hallway. My PSC dug into the back of my neck with the impact.

"Ouch," I groaned. I grabbed the back of my head and closed my eyes. I felt nauseous from seeing the planet above me.

"I did say 'watch out' and people usually do that, you know..." I heard a voice say above me.

"I'm sorry, for the inconvenience. Taliah didn't mean to bump into you," Sal approached and began apologizing on my behalf, "We are going to the oxygen supply room for maintenance and work-study."

"It's okay, I suppose," The voice said with a laugh, "After all, I'm the one in the hallway during class. Don't tell anybody you saw me."

"I still haven't seen you," I said. My head felt

a little better, and I could open my eyes. Nitris was kneeling next to me like they were concerned. I turned towards the voice and opened my eyes wider to see their hazel eyes and the stunning jawline of the Richie who had knocked me over.

"Here, let me give you a hand. My name is Dimitri. You're Taliah?" Dimitri said with an outreached hand. I brushed their hand away from me. I knew better than to rely on a Richie. I leaned over to the side where Nitris was kneeling, put my right hand on their shoulder, and used them to get myself up, still clutching the base of my head with my left hand.

"What just happened?" I asked Nitris, and they started to answer, but Dimitri interrupted them.

"I was on my way back to class from the bathroom. You weren't paying attention and ran into me. I think you hit your head pretty hard. What were you looking at up there?" Dimitri looked out the window, then continued casually, "Old Earth still looks dead to me."

"This is my first time seeing it," I was torn between wanting to look out the window at the Earth and wanting to look at the beautiful person in front of me. I still couldn't focus, and I rubbed my eyes.

"Oh, I'm sorry, I didn't know. We can go to the panoramic window on the other side. You can really see the view from there," Dimitri said enthusiastically.

"If it's alright with you, we must continue our work-study now," Sal tried to excuse us to get back to work.

"Is everything alright here, sir?" The Richie Security officer asked Dimitri. He approached us wearing his all-black uniform and utility belt that carried an electrified baton with his hand resting on it. He looked prepared to use it on me. I looked back at

Sal, unsure of how to proceed. I waited for him to reply to the security officer, but instead, Dimitri answered the officer.

"Everything is on the up and up here, officer," Dimitri said with a sly charming smile.

"Are these Lumpen bothering you? I can take care of them for you," the security officer replied.

"That won't be necessary. We just had a little accident as our paths crossed," Dimitri said to the officer.

"Don't you have somewhere to be," the officer asked us dismissively. I bit my tongue hard to prevent myself from saying something rude.

"Yes, we do," Sal started to say as he stepped between the officer and me before he continued, "Have a nice day. Come on, Taliah, Nitris, we need to get to the oxygen supply post-haste." Nitris and I began to follow Sal, and the officer nodded to Dimitri before he started walking the opposite way.

"I hope you have a nice day, Taliah," Dimitri repeated my name, and my legs felt weak. I used Nitris' shoulder to steady myself.

"Bye, Dimitri," I replied over my shoulder as they walked away. I wanted to say many things to them, but I knew better than to talk back to a Richie.

"Let's go," Sal asserted with urgency. I was thankful to have Nitris next to me to help me walk.

It was only a few more meters down the hallway when we got to a wall with a scanner on it. Sal swiped his wrist on the wall, and it silently moved backward to the side. Nitris and I looked at each other, shocked at how quiet the door was. Sal entered the large room first. It was well-lit, and there were other Lumpen workers there. I even saw Segauce, the eldest kid from the Bunks. All of the workers are wearing a PSC.

"This is where Oxygen and Water meet. We have the workers to our right to care for the water creation and purification system. On our left, we have the oxygen workers." Sal said as we walked through the room to the back corner where the top of the Oxygen recycler was located.

Sal explained the Oxygen and Water processes. "There are multiple stages for everything, and they are all interconnected. The oxygen recycler circulates air from everywhere on Pangea. The air comes in through the ducts we saw on the bottom level with the generator. Then, the air travels up through the electrified filtration system. That splits the oxygen from the hydrogen, producing a vapor that can be stored to create fresh water. It's our responsibility to monitor the vapor levels in the oxygen recycler collection tank up here. When it reaches 75%, we take off the nearly full unit and replace it with a dry unit immediately. Once the dry unit is in place, we take the vapor-filled unit to the guys there in water creation, over there."

"My head is killing me right now, and I can't process any of this," I whispered to Nitris. "Could you tell me again later when I can remember it?"

"No problem," Nitris said to me and smiled. I smiled back and realized that I was still leaning on them from earlier. I awkwardly stood straight, took my hand off their shoulder, and looked back at Sal.

"This is our last day together so it will be hands-on training today. It takes at least two people to change out the vapor unit," Sal told Nitris and me.

Together, Nitris and I walked up the spiral stairs to the top of the oxygen recycler. At the top of the stairs was a small platform with a shelf that contained the dry unit. Sal remained on the floor, confident in our abilities to remove the unit independently. The level indicator on the side blinked 73%. Together, Nitris and I began to unlatch the unit on the top. It was heavier than expected, and we struggled to get it down onto the platform we stood on. Then we attached the dry unit from the shelf in its place. It was lighter than the vapor-filled unit and slid into place with ease. We latched it in place and then stood over the unit on the platform. I'm glad that Sal was letting us work with our hands. It was taking my mind off of the pain in my head.

This whole process took us almost two hours. There were computer checklists to complete before we could even begin to carry the heavy unit down the stairs.

"How are we going to get this down to the ground?" I asked as I looked over the railing down 3 meters to the floor.

"I'll walk backward down first, and we go one step at a time," Nitris suggested. I nodded in agreement, and we attempted to pick up the unit.

"Use the electromagnetic suspension elevator to bring the unit down safely," Sal said from the ground up to us and pointed at the chains hanging from the ceiling beside us. I grabbed the chains closest to me and looked for the elevator platform.

"Here it is," Nitris said from the shelf, pulling out the metal platform. We slid it under the vapor unit, then struggled to attach it to the chains and lower it. I pulled the chains towards the platform and felt them lunge from my hands as they connected to the magnetic pull in the platform.

"It's practically weightless now," I said excitedly

as everything worked as intended.

"Take it slow. The electromagnetic suspension takes most of the weight. You must work together to ensure the elevator takes it down safely," Sal explained to us.

Working together, Nitris and I pulled the chain down to make the unit lift up. Then we slowly pushed the unit over the side of the railing. We worked in sync one hand at a time to lower the unit towards the floor below. Sal had already wheeled the electric cart to be in position as the vapor unit lowered onto it. Once it was secured on the cart, Sal released the chains connected to the platform, and the slack went loose in our hands at the top. Nitris and I walked back down the spiral stairs and met Sal at the cart.

After we delivered the cart to the water team, we reviewed a few more logs that needed to be entered into the computer before returning to the Dark Flats. I felt like I had accomplished so much today.

We were almost back to Sal's work-study classroom when the end-of-workday notification sounded.

"It's been a pleasure working with you both," Sal said. "You each have a lot of potential. I hope to see you again after the work-study rounds are completed. Remember, everything is connected," Sal gave us a knowing look. He picked up his pace and walked in front of us to Cora's to get our PSCs off. That old man could walk fast when he wanted.

"I bet you're glad to get rid of me," Nitris said.

"It wasn't that bad," I admitted.

"Thanks," they replied.

"Thank you for helping me today. I will need to study with you later about class today," I told them with a laugh.

"Anytime," Nitris said.

I heard someone approaching and turned to see Justice coming up the hall.

"Come on, let's get going" Justice scooped my arm into hers and started walking faster toward Cora's.

"Someone is in a rush to get their PSC off," I told her as we walked with linked arms.

"I was saving you from Nitris. You're welcome," Justice said with a laugh.

I said nothing but kept walking with her to get in line.

"I hope that we get to work together for the next round. Learning about plumbing was boring," Justice told me.

"Me too," I told her. I saw Nitris round the corner and get in line behind a few adults between us.

"I can only imagine how awful it was working with your nemesis for three days," Justice said. I turned my head to look at her questionably, and she nodded toward Nitris.

"Nitris isn't as bad as we thought. They helped me today," I told Justice and grabbed the back of my head where I had a bump that still throbbed with pain.

"I find that hard to believe," Justice said with disdain and turned to face forward in the line. She was next.

After we got our PSCs removed, we returned to the Bunks to get cleaned up before dinner. We got our towels and a change of clothes. There wasn't a line to get in at the Sand Showers, and we grabbed stalls next to each other.

"You're so immature sometimes," I told her as I rubbed sand into my hair to remove the sweat from the manual labor.

"And you're an air-suck!" She replied.

"You'll miss me when you leave the Bunks and marry Cyran. Don't try to deny it," I said, trying to conceal how much I would miss her.

"I still say we all get married and live together. It would be way cheaper splitting rent three ways!" Justice said. I heard the air hose in her stall turn off.

"I don't get the point in paying rent to the Council," I complained, "It's not like we were begging to be made in the Birthing Lab. They're the ones that brought us into the world and make us work every day until we die. The least they could do is not be so strict on housing rules. The concept of "rent" should have died along with Old Earth," I said it a little more seriously than I intended. Justice didn't know how to respond, so I continued, "Let's go get our goo for tonight before all the good goo is taken," I joked, trying to ease the tension I was feeling.

"Seriously, if we turn 18 and you don't have a place to live, I know Cyran would be cool with you joining us," Justice said with love and no hint of sarcasm.

I considered the fantasy of living with Justice and Cyran. I quickly pictured them kissing and holding each other against every surface of the small living chambers. I didn't want to be out of place with them, and I didn't like the idea of faking a throuple marriage to have a place to live.

"If I don't have a place to live when I turn 18, I'll throw myself in the trash recycler," I said with defeat.

After cleaning off our work day, Justice and I deposited our dirty towels and clothes in the laundry collector and went to the Mess Hall. We grabbed our ration trays and sat together at the table in the back where the sensor lights don't always work. We always joked that it was *mood lighting.*

"Good evening, babe," Cyran greeted Justice but barely acknowledged me. Justice giggled with delight.

"Good evening, lover!" Justice said enthusiastically in return. She started kissing Cyran.

I sat silently and poked at the goo on my tray, not paying attention to anyone around me in the Mess Hall.

For a while, I had thought Justice was my best chance at having a roommate when we turned 18, but she was focused on Cyran now. I didn't really "like" or "dislike" Cyran. It was more like contempt or indifference. Justice and Cyran were indeed compatible since they were both shallow people who only ever talked about how tedious their work was. We all had boring jobs. I ate quickly so I wouldn't have to listen to their dull conversation.

"I got to see Old Earth today," I said to the table while Justice and Cyran continued kissing each other. It seemed to be getting more intense, and they hadn't even touched their rations yet. I thought about what it must have been like back on Old Earth. I could just walk outside and find a new mate, no problem!

"Where is your head at?" Apollox asked me. I hadn't seen him sit down next to me.

"I got distracted," I told him, "I was thinking about Old Earth. I finally saw it today."

"Really? How?" Apollox asked with excitement that matched mine.

"Through the cupola windows on the Richies level during work-study," I said enthusiastically.

"What was it like?" Apollox said with genuine

interest.

"I could see that it was damaged but still beautiful. Have you been up to the Richies level yet? Have you seen how clean it is?" I asked Apollox.

"I've been stuck on trash sorting duty," he said, disappointed. "Maybe with the next round starting tomorrow, I'll get assigned to something exciting."

"I don't want this to be my entire life," I told him honestly. "I don't know exactly what I want to do, but I know it's not sorting trash, recycling oxygen, or moving vapor tanks all day. I want a job that engages my mind and makes me learn new things."

"I know what you mean, Taliah," Apollox said with a shrug of acceptance.

We both sat for a while in silence. Justice and Cyran were still in their own world, coming up for air long enough to drink water before returning to making out.

"If you could pick any job on Pangea, what would you choose?" Apollox asked.

"I want to be an Elder to change some of these awful rules. If Pangea has less than 300 people and all of these housing chambers on the Richies level aren't in use, why do we need a roommate? We should have enough to live on our own comfortably," I said.

"Right! All this pressure is on me to hurry up and find a roommate or a partner to marry," Apollox said, a bit hushed because there were still people in the Mess Hall.

"Jobs would be the second thing I'd fix. We should be able to apply to all the jobs, not just the disgusting jobs that no one else wants," I said. Then my hand went to the back of my head where the lump from my fall had grown.

"If your neck is sore after work, I recommend rolling up a towel or your blanket and laying it under your neck to give it support," Apollox said. It was nice that he was trying to help me feel better.

"Thanks, but this is from a fall I had earlier. Some Richie ran into me. I fell on my PSC, and it shoved itself into my brain. Here feel the lump," I said and grabbed Apollox's hand so he could feel my head.

"Your hair is really soft." He said and pulled his hand away.

"Justice and I did our Sand Shower before dinner," I said with a smile. It was nice that he noticed.

"What?" Justice asked me with her head turned away from Cyran.

"I fell at work-study and have this lump on my head," I reiterated the story.

"Did Nitris trip you?" Justice asked with a serious face.

"No, some Richie ran into me," I clarified.

"I could picture Nitris tripping you. They are so quiet all the time. It's creepy," Justice said and gestured at the table on the side of the room where Nitris sat alone.

"Nitris helped me up and assisted me during work-study," I told everyone at the table. "I will have to study with them after my head feels normal."

"Don't forget, Nitris is your rival for the top position in the class. You'll need those RC Credits when you move out of the Bunks," Justice reminded me about my second-place status in the class. She isn't even in the top five in class.

"I don't think Nitris and I are enemies. That's not okay to try to pit us against each other. It doesn't accomplish anything," I said, "I just need to work harder to test high enough to get placed in a meaningful job."

"Now you sound like Mr. Kline when he talks about his meaningful work molding young minds," Cyran said sarcastically. She was right.

Chapter 16
Nitris

After I got my PSC off, I went to the Bunks to read through the journal I found in Mr. Kline's quarters. I thought there might be something useful for tonight's trip to the Library. The pages had other languages that have died over the centuries, and someone was trying to translate them.

There was a lot of entries. It was already 20:30, and I had to go get my rations. I tucked the journal in the back of my pants and tightened my belt to keep it snug to my body. I pulled my shirt over it. I walked to the Mess Hall, hoping to see Sahara along the way.

I got in the short line for the rations and swiped my wrist to get my portion on the metal tray. I turned to see what tables were free. I sat two tables away from Taliah and Justice, with my back to them. I watched the door for a while and then started to eat, waiting for Sahara to arrive.

"Hey Nitris, how was work-study?" Sahara asked as she sat down across from me at the empty table.

"It was eventful," I said to Sahara. "I got to go to the Richies level and see how our oxygen supply and water creation are connected. I enjoyed working with the machines. How they all fit together makes sense to me. I hope the next round I get something exciting like welding repairs."

"That sounds awesome," Sahara seemed to have something else on her mind and hadn't registered what I'd told her. She leaned into me. "So, tonight is the big night."

"This is all happening so fast," I said, worry dripping from every word. I had so many feelings that I couldn't sort them out.

"Right! It's the universe telling us that it's our time to make a difference!" She said, and I noticed that, once again, I was the only one of us eating. I could barely swallow two spoonfuls of goo. It got harder to eat every day.

"I don't think we should eat this goo stuff. It was mentioned in that journal you found," Sahara stated.

"When did you see that? Is that why you haven't been eating?" I asked.

"When you pulled out the journal and flipped through it, I saw 'goo'. Besides, I told you I'm saving for something at the ReCirculation Center," she replied without making eye contact with me. I got the feeling she was keeping something from me.

"I'm still reading the journal, trying to understand it," I said. "It might have been an entry from generations ago. I'm unsure how we can verify its authenticity or when it was written."

"Yeah, you're right," Sahara said, looking around to see if anyone could hear us before she continued, "What else is in that journal?"

"There's a lot about the history of Pangea, but I can't tell if it is factual or speculation," I told her, mentally reviewing the pages I'd already read.

"Maybe there will be a way to make a digital copy of it when we go to the Library," Sahara speculated. "If there is, we can return to Mr. Kline's office and return the keys and journal without him knowing we were ever there," she acted as if that had been part of her plan all along.

It sounded like a lot of work; we'd be at it most of the night. There was so much about Sahara's unpredictable plan, but I didn't want to criticize it and risk losing my new friend.

I thought I heard my name from Taliah and Justice's table. I got nervous that they might be talking about me, trying to figure out what I was doing with Sahara.

I was about to suggest that we leave when Sahara spoke first, "We should go to the airlock and finish this conversation." Sahara stood up and started to walk towards the exit.

"Sounds good," I agreed. I cleaned up my tray and recycled the leftover goo. We left the Mess Hall and went to the airlock.

"Now that we are alone, how did you know about the notes in the journal about the rations?" I asked Sahara again.

"Nitris, I have a confession," Sahara said as she faced me directly.

Chapter 17
Sahara

I couldn't keep lying to Nitris.

"A confession?" Nitris asked me, their green eyes wide with fear.

"I received a message from The Elder named Codex on my OC. It was encrypted, but I was able to solve it," I explained.

"Why is an Elder from *The Council* sending you encrypted messages? I thought they always had access to our OCs." Nitris asked. That hadn't occurred to me.

"They can see our OCs? Everything that I've written?" I asked, afraid of what could happen to me. I didn't know that our devices were monitored.

"Yes. They always could. Why did they encrypt a message to your OC?" Nitris asked again.

"It's a long story, and we don't have much time before we have to be in the Bunks for lights out, but this might change our plans for the library," I exhaled the sentence in one nervous breath.

"What did Codex say?" Nitris asked.

"She said we must stop eating the rations because they are heavily drugged to keep everyone docile and obedient," I explained what was in the message.

"How do we know we can trust Codex? She's an Elder," Nitris asked me.

"I think we can trust her. Is everything okay?" I asked them because something felt unusual.

"I feel like I'm the last to know about everything, and it sucks," they confided in me as they sat down, leaning against the wall of the airlock.

"I have more to tell you," I said, sitting across from them in the airlock, leaning against the wall.

"Go on," they said and waited for me to continue.

"Codex will help us remove the drugs from the rations for all of Pangea," I told them. "You will be assigned to rations for tomorrow's new round of work-study. She has already made the arrangements," I told them.

"Why do I have to be assigned to rations? If I get caught tampering with the ration machines, I'll get locked up in Containment. Codex messaged you to take care of it, not me," Nitris said, visibly upset.

"I made a deal with her," I told Nitris the last of the plan. "I told her that we would help her with the rations tomorrow if she would help us with our Library mission tonight. She agreed and will turn off the entrance alert and the other automatic notifications that get sent to all The Elders."

"Seriously?" Nitris asked harshly. "Are you really this naive? I don't know if we should trust her."

"I trust her," I said, but I couldn't explain why.

"I guess we'll find out tonight," Nitris stood up and fixed me with a stern look. "I've never heard of The Elders giving something before they take something else. We should head back to the Bunks for lights out," Nitris put the journal in the back of their waistband and I watched them walk away from me.

Chapter 18
Mr. Kline

I waited until 22:30 hours before I walked over to Jexa's chambers. I didn't like the way things had ended between us earlier. After my session with Sahara, I was too worked up and treated Jexa poorly.

I stood outside Jexa's chamber and took four deep breaths before I knocked. She usually met me at the door but wasn't expecting me this early.

"Silas," Jexa said as the door opened.

"Hey there, my love, may I please come in, and we can talk?" I asked. She took a moment to respond, and my palms were sweating.

"I suppose," she said with a shrug and moved away from the door so I could enter.

I walked in, and the door auto-closed and locked behind me. I didn't want to give the impression that I was only there for the physical aspect of our relationship. I watched as she sat on the small couch facing her desk. Her chambers are twice the size of mine but still considered small on Pangea.

"Can we please talk about what happened earlier?" I asked her as I sat down at her desk to face her.

"What's there to talk about?" She asked me.

"If you have any questions, I'd be happy to answer them unless it's classified information," I said, rubbing my forehead. This might be a challenge.

"I have many questions, but I have no idea where the line is between classified and truth." She said and crossed her arms. She always does that when she is trying to stay mad at me. It made me smirk, and that made her furious.

"Are you laughing at me right now?" She asked.

"No, I'm not. Really," I protested, "I was thinking about how you cross your arms like that when you're mad, and remembering all the times I've seen you do it made me smile."

"Saying that I'm cute when I'm mad makes me madder," she said and started to struggle with keeping a straight face.

"You can't be mad at my memories, they are mine, and I earned them," I said with a smile. I watched as her shoulders dropped, and she began to relax.

"Start from the beginning. What are you doing for The Elders in the Birthing Lab?" She asked.

"Let's turn off our OCs for this conversation. Just in case," I said. I deactivated mine, and she did the same.

"I'm waiting," she stated in the demanding confident voice that I love.

"I'm working on a classified mission for The Elders. It's in the Birthing Lab because it concerns DNX," I told her the basics. I tried to avoid going into too much detail outside of what she asked me. Saying everything could get me executed. They could kill Jexa just for listening. My palms began to sweat.

"The Birthing Lab?" Jexa thought for a moment, then her face lit up, "Are there new children being incubated?"

"No," I admitted. She looked disappointed and my heart sank. I continued, "There are things about this classified assignment that are classified to me too. I don't know what specifically they are working on with our DNX, but I can say that no children are being incubated in the Birthing Lab." It made me feel better about not revealing that one child lives in the lab.

"You are working on a classified assignment and don't know all its details? Why did you agree to this?" She asked me, questioning my life choices.

"I was called to the Heart Office, and I was overwhelmed," I confessed to her, "I did as I was asked. I thought I was facing Solitary Containment or execution if I refused. I didn't know I would lie to the woman I love most in the universe."

"When did you meet with The Elders?" She asked me getting me back on topic.

"About two years ago," I told her.

"You've been sneaking into the Birthing Lab for two years? How is that even possible with the work schedule?" Her questions were legitimate.

"At first, I was doing it early in the morning before my regular class with the teens," I explained, "Then I started going after class. I've recently changed to doing 14:00-20:00 to be in sync with the work-study program. That's why we've had to meet at strange hours during the night."

"You weren't devoting yourself to another woman, were you?" She asked me directly.

"No. There is no other woman," I answered.

"When are you going to be done with this assignment?" She asked as she pulled her legs up to rest on the couch and lay on her side to face me.

"I'm hopeful that by the end of this round of work-study it should be completed," I told her.

"Is that when we get to move to the Richies level?" She asked and gave me a small smile.

"Yes, I've arranged it with The Elders," I told her. I bent down on my left knee before her and held my empty hand out. "But that also means you must do me the honor of being my wife."

"Isn't there supposed to be a ring somewhere?" Jexa asked with a laugh and knocked my empty hand away.

"I'm working on it. I've been saving all my Credits to get you the best ring in the ReCirculation Center. One that is from Earth, an antique," I said with enthusiasm.

"You're referring to a relic of an ancient history notorious for misogyny and sexism?" She said with a pout. She was teasing me. If she was feeling playful, she was probably close to forgiving me.

"Something like that," I leaned in to kiss her, but she stopped me with an outstretched hand.

"I didn't say 'yes' to your empty hand. We have to save ourselves until marriage," Jexa said with a dramatic gesture with the back of her hand to her forehead like she would faint.

"You should have been an actress...," I said wistfully, leaned back on my leg, and sat on the floor before her.

"I miss watching all of those old movies and performances," Jexa had a smile on her face, "Do you think that when we're Richies, we'll get access to the digital entertainment like we used to have in the Library?"

"Maybe. Those were great times," I reminisced. "I miss being a kid before we started work-study. We had so much time. We'd spend hours in the Library, reading and watching everything we could get our hands on."

"I remember how you couldn't keep your eyes off of me. And then eventually, your hands," she laughed and hopped off the couch to sit on my lap. I held her close for a moment before I spoke.

"I really need your support with this. I'm working on making a better life for *us*. When we become Richies, we can adopt a child from the Bunks too," I hugged her into my chest. I wanted to keep her warm while we sat together on the cold floor.

"That sounds magical. Almost too good to be true. Are you sure that this will happen?" She asked as she pulled her head away and looked up at me.

"Yes. I won't let you down," I reassured her. We sat quietly for a moment. Time seemed to stand still when we were together.

"I was wondering what had happened to Mx. Sage," Jexa said regarding my predecessor.

"I hadn't seen them around the station for some time. I thought they had died," I told her the truth.

"I've never even met a Lumpen named Sage," she replied and put her head back on my chest.

"I think they must be too busy to return to the Dark Flats to visit us," I told her, kissing the top of her head. Jexa loves her friends and cherishes their place in her life.

"We will come back and visit our friends, though," she insisted and pushed me away to look into my eyes before she continued, "I won't budge on that. I'll miss them all too much."

"I promise," I said it, and I meant it. We sealed the promise with a kiss.

Chapter 19
Nitris

While I waited in bed for Ms. Verban to call lights out, I let myself daydream about what life would be like if I was a mechanical engineer or a pilot. I imagined myself in a pilot uniform with people at the first launch cheering and waving at me. At the same time, I made my way to the exploratory space pod. People know who I am, and they want to wish me luck on my next big adventure. I'm humanity's last hope; they all know they would be lost without me.

I looked at my OC and saw that it was 00:15 hours. Time to meet Sahara and head to the Library. I grabbed the paper journal and tucked it into my back waistband, hoping we could somehow make a digital copy of it in the Library. Sahara and I only had a few hours to get to the Library and find the needed eBooks.

When I made it out of the Bunks, I saw that she

was waiting outside the door to the Bunks, and we started the trek to the Library silently. Our route took us past the abandoned Birthing Lab. I kept my head down and my eyes on the Library's hallway.

"We're making good time," I whispered to Sahara.

When I didn't hear a response, I reached behind me, hoping to grab her arm, but instead, I felt the cold wall. I turned to see where I had lost her and saw her standing at the Birthing Lab door, looking in the cupola window.

I backtracked to her, careful not to trip the sensor lights. I whispered, "psst," but she didn't respond. She couldn't move her eyes from the empty black room.

"What's going on? I thought we were going to the Library?" I asked her, trying not to look where her eyes were gazing.

"I think I saw someone," she said mechanically, pointing into the dark lab.

"I thought I saw someone before, but it was a nightmare. You're imagining things," I advised her, trying to get her attention back on me. "We should get to the Library before we get caught up in a new mission."

"You're right," she agreed. She shook her head the same way I do, to shake the image she saw from her thoughts. I wondered if she had nightmares the way I did.

We made our way to the Library door and after we tried a few keys we found the one that fit the door and entered the six digit code for 01:00 hours. We both jumped back as the long-dormant door slowly slid open with a thud that shook my body. The lights inside the Library began to flicker on, filling the massive room. It had been full of books at once, but now it was empty shelves because the books had all been turned into digital files.

There was a restricted room in the back with glass walls. It was filled with hundreds of paper books, preserved with temperature controls. A decontamination chamber separated the restricted room from the central Library. The lights in that room were on before we even opened the main door.

Before starting this mission with Sahara, I had never felt actual paper. Now I had a journal on natural paper hidden behind my waistband. I was suddenly aware that I was sweating from anxiety and hoped I wasn't damaging the journal. I tried to calm my emotions by focusing on my breath.

"What kind of books do you think are in there?" I asked as I walked towards the restricted room, and Sahara followed me. "So many secrets are hidden here on Pangea, and no one knows. We just let The Elders pick and choose for us. There has to be something better for our lives." I told Sahara about my distrust of the way The Elders run Pangea. A statement like this could place me in Solitary Containment without trial, but I revealed my opinions anyway.

"More secrets than we could ever know in our lifetime...," Sahara says with a heavy sigh.

"What do you mean?" I asked because she had a tone that sounded like she had a secret and was talking about herself.

"They have literally locked away all literature. I would bet all of my RC Credits that those books in there aren't even available in digital. Frozen in time, whatever is in those books could be life-ending for everyone on Pangea," she said with a heavy tone.

"You think those are the only copies of those books? What is the point of withholding information from everyone? It's almost as if The Elders want to keep everyone uneducated." I exhaled with frustration and curiosity.

There was a heavy layer of dust on the entry door to the decontamination chamber before you could step inside the temperature-controlled room of paper books. I ran my fingers across the dust on an access panel for security in the authorized user-only section, which created four streaks from my touch. My fingers tingled like I was hit with static electricity. I shook my hand to get rid of the feeling, then looked at Sahara to see if she noticed.

"We won't be getting in there tonight," I said, and Sahara nodded in agreement.

We walked to the information station together, and I turned on the computer. We knew what we were looking for. We had to hope that Codex was being honest when she said that she would turn off the alert on the computer that monitors the access terminals for the whole station. Otherwise, our activities would be detected immediately.

We held our breath as the old computer, cutting-edge technology back in the early 2020s, booted up and chimed to indicate it was ready for use. I took the keyboard and began doing searches.

"I need to connect my OC to this terminal to download the books," I said eagerly. "Are there any compatible cables around?"

"Will this one work?" Sahara pointed at a cable on the shelf a few feet away.

I picked up the cable and examined the

connectors. It looked like it would work with my OC, and I plugged it into the compuer. My OC began to sync, and for once, I was grateful that the Dark Flats had all the oldest technology.

I downloaded the books Sahara wanted on medical training first, then started loading books about engineering.

"You skipped the piloting textbooks," Sahara said as she looked over my shoulder.

"My dreams of being a pilot are only dreams," I said. "Engineering is more obtainable." Sahara didn't press the issue, and I kept looking at the options on the screen.

"There are even simulations for field medics!" Sahara said with excitement from over my shoulder. I was still looking around for the other texts we wanted, amazed by the variety.

"That's fantastic! I'm downloading those too," I said and copied the files to my OC.

When the download was complete, I looked around to see if a machine could scan the paper journal in my waistband, but I didn't see anything useful. I felt my lower back to ensure the journal was still in place.

"We should get out of here now," I asserted myself to feel more in control of the situation. I inhaled deeply. I started putting things back the way they were because I still doubted if we could trust Codex.

"You're right. Let's go," Sahara agreed and walked towards the door.

"I've already downloaded the medical books and training. I'll send them back to you at the Bunks," I told her as I unplugged my OC and grabbed the keys from the desk where I had set them down. There were clear outlines in the dust where I had been sitting and using the computer. I gathered my long sleeve and used it to move the dust around so it would be more of a mess. I looked for imprints that Sahara might have left, but there weren't any. She must not have touched anything.

We walked side by side to the Library door, which automatically opened and slid to the side.

BANG! A loud thud down the hall near the Birthing Lab startled us, and we jumped to alert.

"We'll have to go back a different way," Sahara suggested.

"Follow me," I said, leading us to the adult chambers. It was a longer route, but we avoided the Birthing Lab altogether, which I preferred. Sahara crept quietly behind me, and I had almost forgotten she was there. Returning the items to Mr. Kline's office would have to wait another night, even though we passed his chambers on the way back. That noise was unusual for the Dark Flats and that made it more frightening. I led us back in silence, listening for any more unusual sounds.

Once inside the Bunks, I rushed to my bed and climbed onto the thin mattress. I kept my OC and pulled the worn covers over my head to hide the glow as I read. I started with the rest of Sahara's journal entries, looking for my name. I was sure that there were things she wasn't telling me. I had the feeling that something wasn't right. It took me longer than expected to relocate the file with all the names. By this time, I had been awake for almost twenty hours straight. I should have known better than to lie down because even with all of the excitement I had gone through, I fell asleep almost immediately. I never had time to read what she recorded about me.

Chapter 20
Sahara

I was able to have a clean break from Nitris' thoughts when they passed out from exhaustion. I didn't like keeping secrets from them, but it was the only way to achieve my goal. I would make it up to them if they still trusted me later.

Every day I used my powers, I felt weaker yet more connected to Nitris than before. I wondered if they felt the same way about me. Even if they did, I couldn't be sure if that was a false memory I had implanted or something natural.

Would we work together if they knew who I was and what I looked like? My mind was overwhelmed, but my body had reached its limits for the day. I knew that I had to lie down and rest if I wanted to be able to keep going again tomorrow.

I sat on my bed and connected my IV tube to a

whole bag of electrolytes and potassium. I lay down and pulled my blanket over my head, exposing my right arm to the IV needle inside my elbow. I took deep breaths to calm myself. I would need all my strength for tomorrow.

I closed my eyes and focused on breathing. Sleep found me quickly.

Chapter 21
Nitris

Ding, ding, ding.

"Good morning, residents of Pangea! Today is March 4th, 2320, and the time is 06:00 hours UTC to start your day. Lumpen youths will be assigned a new job during the active rounds of work-study. New schedules have been sent to your Onboard Communicator." Intra's prerecorded voice woke me. I tuned her out before she mentioned our *imperative contribution.*

I rubbed my eyes and stretched my arms. I looked at my OC and saw that my new assignment was ration maintenance. It appeared Codex had told Sahara the truth. That meant I would have to participate in the tasks Codex wanted to be done in the Mess Hall. I decided to hit the Sand Showers and skip AM call for rations since I would spend my afternoon there with work-study.

When I arrived at the Sand Showers, all the stalls were already in use. On the bright side, there wasn't a line out into the hallway like there is sometimes. I waited patiently for a stall to open up.

Some of the people in the showers were talking, and I heard a bit of their conversation. One of the Lumpen in the stall closest to me said, "...the library lights were on this morning before I arrived. Do you think we'll be allowed to go in?"

I took a quick breath and held it. Did we need to turn off the lights when we left? Weren't the lights on a motion sensor? They should have turned it off.

While I considered all the bad things that could have happened, a stall in the back opened up as Ms. V walked out, fully dressed. She was so elegant and moved with such confidence. She seemed especially happy today, and her smile was bright.

"Good morning, Nitris. I hope you have a good day on your new work-study assignment," Ms. V said as she passed me.

"Good morning, Ms. V," I answered. "Thanks. I hope I do a good job!" I replied and started to walk back to the stall she had come from.

When I got there, I locked the door and put my possessions on the counter in the back where the sand wouldn't get on it. I pulled the chain connected to the top reservoir to open the hatch and let the white sand fall on my head and down my body. I strained to hear if anyone else in the Sand Showers was discussing the Library.

"The Library has been closed for so long; I'm surprised the lights work." A female voice said.

"It would be nice to borrow free media for

entertainment from the Library without using our RC Credits." A different male voice answered the first.

"That would never happen now that they are making Credits from having the only entertainment in the ReCirculation Center. Besides, it's not like we have the time for that. Just work, day in and day out." The same female voice said.

I had been rubbing the sand through my short hair for a while when I realized I had lost track of time. I quickly grabbed the air hose and started to spray myself off. I let the clumped-up dirt from the grime in my hair and my body fall into the grate under my feet. It engaged the automated suction to pull the dirty sand out of my way.

I left the Sand Showers and went straight to Mr. Kline's class to sit and wait for the notification to start class. I walked into the small room, and the automated lights came on. I sat in the back where I usually sit. I still had about half an hour before class started. I decided to meditate and calm my racing thoughts. I closed my eyes and focused on my breath.

The motion lights turned off because I was holding still. I don't know how long I had meditated when Mr. Kline walked in and the lights turned on. I slowly opened my eyes and realized Mr. Kline had not noticed me yet. He looked agitated and tired. I didn't want to scare him, but I needed to make my presence known.

"Hey, Mr. Kline," I said softly and watched as he jumped in his chair at the unexpected sound of my voice.

"Nitris! You scared me!" He yelped. "I didn't see anyone here when I came in."

"I'm sorry I scared you," I said. "I was just

meditating before class and didn't want to be late again."

"It's not a problem." He said. "Feel free to come in and meditate any time that you want. I know it's hard to find a quiet place to be alone."

"Do you still meditate?" I asked him. He looked a bit on edge.

"I try to when I have the time. Although these days, it feels like I don't have enough time. I barely have time to sleep." He confided in me.

"I can relate to that," I answered with a small smile.

"Are you having restless nights?" He asked me with concern.

"Something like that. It has been an adjustment switching from school to work-study. I've seen the older teens in the Bunks go through this process, but it never really hit me until now. How many more rounds of jobs will we have to do this time?" I asked him because the rounds change yearly based on job openings and necessities.

He picked up his OC, opened a file, and swiped it to appear on the holo in the center of the room. It was his own shorthand list of jobs and pairings.

"Looks like you're doing Ration Maintenance with Apollox starting today, then the Water Creation Department, then Trash Organization." He told me as he displayed the list with all his students in different work-study listed. "There will be a midterm test for all that you have learned, and then the rounds will repeat with new pairs, but I don't have it scheduled that far out yet."

"I'm not excited about the testing part. There is a lot of pressure to learn so many details in a short amount of time," I told him how I was feeling.

"You have always done great on tests. I think you'll do great with work-study tests too," he said, and then the room began to fill with students as the alarm to begin class notified everyone.

When Apollox sat beside me in the back, I told him, "We have work-study together this time, doing Ration Maintenance."

"Air-suck," he said under his breath.

"I'm excited to work with you, too," I replied with hurt feelings.

"Sorry, Nitris, I meant that comment because I hoped to be paired with Taliah this round. I want to work with her, and maybe we can get some alone time together." Apollox clarified his comment.

"Not this round. You are stuck with me," I told him and tried to smile.

"Want to walk to Cora's together after class?" He asked me, and I nodded yes.

The final alarm to begin class went off. I could tell Mr. Kline was not feeling well because most lessons were holo videos about Old Earth. We barely had any class participation. That didn't bother me because my mind was elsewhere. I was trying to anticipate what Codex might want me to do to the rations. I touched the journal in the back of my waistband to ensure it was there. I was taking a risk by keeping it on my person, but I also didn't want to risk leaving it unattended in the Bunks.

When class had ended, Apollox nudged me with his elbow as he stood up.

"Let's get to Cora's for our PSCs," he said with a half smile.

I stood up and walked with him to wait in

line. Every morning the line moved faster as the new work-study students began to understand the process better. Apollox went in first and waited outside for me to get mine on. I don't think I will ever get used to the weight of the PSCs and how they rub when I turn my head.

"We're supposed to meet our work-study teacher, Mx. Quincey, in the Mess Hall," I said to Apollox as I read my OC details for today. "I don't think they have a classroom where we meet at first." We walked silently the opposite way of the other work-study rooms. We had a short distance until we arrived at the empty Mess Hall.

"Are you sure it said to meet here?" Apollox asked me as he looked around the empty room.

"Let me double-check," I said as I opened the document on my OC. I felt my hand tingle and pull towards the machine involuntarily. I looked up at the device, and something felt off-axis about it. Strangely, I hadn't noticed it before the sensation in my hand.

"Welcome to Ration Maintenance," A voice said from behind the wall of the Ration Dispensers. The same spot as the static jolt in my hand. I shook my hand to clear the sensation.

"Did the machine just talk?" Apollox asked with sincerity, which made me roll my eyes.

"Come this way," the voice said, and the right side panel, near the clean trays, popped open.

Apollox followed me to the panel, and we stepped in. We saw a person standing in the small antechamber.

"I'm Mx. Quincey if any Richies are around; otherwise, you can drop the fancy part and call me Quincey. You can go ahead and close that," they instructed Apollox.

Quincey was taller than Mr. Kline. They had deep space black hair that stopped at their ears but slicked back away from their face revealing their dark complexion and light brown eyes.

The small area was dark momentarily, and Quincey turned on their flashlight. It illuminated a small corridor that opened up into a larger room.

"Follow me," they instructed us.

I had never known that the ration machines were in front of another room. I'd never thought about it before. I only knew how to access the goo until it stopped coming out.

"This is where we prepare the rations and how we recycle the unused portions," Quincey started to tell us as the motion-activated lights turned on.

"I haven't had any work-study students in a while because the systems are almost entirely automated," Quincey explained. "If you like solitude, this is the job for you. I'm responsible for monitoring and maintaining the machines, and it's a small crew. Except for when the labor shift happens, I usually only interact with the cleaning crews."

"So why are we here?" I asked.

"I don't know," Quincey shrugged. "I guess somebody somewhere decided we should have some backup personnel ready to go in case anything happens to me. So, you two got the random assignment this round. I'll be your work-study teacher, and if you are assigned here, I will also be your supervisor." As they extended their hand.

I shook their hand and said, "I'm Nitris."

Apollox did the same and said, "I'm Apollox. So how many people are staffed here exactly?" His eyes looked around the large empty room.

"Not including you two from work-study, there are three Lumpen workers, including myself," Quincey answered.

"It is so quiet back here," I observed.

"It can be quiet when it is between eating hours. Let's get started with how the machines work. Follow me this way." Quincey said and walked towards the back. They stopped at a computer station at the back wall.

"This computer is where we start the recycling process," Quincey began, "The chutes in this room connect the Lumpen Mess Hall with the Richies Dining Hall above us and lead down into the old service tunnels. That is where we used to be stationed, but now we have this hidden cove all to ourselves. You know how when we finish our rations and have leftovers, we clear them into the recycler at the end of the counter. The Richies do the same thing in the same chute. We start our day by recycling the Richies, and Lumpen discarded rations. It's all processed through the grinders into the goo we get," Quincey patted the side of one of the chutes.

"Grinders?" Apollox asked.

"Yes, the chutes have a series of blades inside that chop up the Richies leftovers. Then the supplemental nutrients get added in the mixer below us, and it comes out at the ration machines," Quincey explained. "You wouldn't recognize our food if you saw what it starts out looking like."

"I don't know a single Lumpen who likes to eat the goo," Apollox said, and Quincey laughed.

"I don't know anyone either. After today's class, you'll like it even less," they leaned into us and continued in a hushed tone, "Don't tell the other kids about the process, okay? There's no reason to put people off their food."

Apollox and I looked at each other with questions in our eyes. Quincey must have noticed because they continued, "Oh right, neither of you knows any other food besides the goo. I apologize. It has been a while since I had to teach about food. You two are the first students we have gotten this round. I'm not even sure why you are here because we don't have any job openings." Quincey said and wondered out loud about why we were there.

I felt my face get hot with embarrassment. Codex arranged for me to be here and probably included Apollox, so it wouldn't look suspicious for only one student when no jobs are available.

Quincey spoke as they walked through the large area, "We have many different kinds of food grown and created artificially with these various machines. Grown food includes fruits, flowers, beans, and vegetables. Fruits and vegetables can help you stay healthy and strong. Eating fruits, like apples, oranges, bananas, and strawberries, can give you energy throughout the day. Eating vegetables, like carrots, broccoli, tomatoes, and peppers, can give you the vitamins your body needs to grow big and strong." Quincey named a few examples and tried to tell us about them. They walked over to the computer to bring up images and names. They continued, "Here you can see what they look like and how they benefit our bodies."

Apollox and I stood over their shoulder and stared at the screen. There were different shapes and bright colors that I had never seen before. I looked at Apollox to see if I was as lost as he was. We had only ever known about goo.

"Do we get to eat these?" Apollox asked, licking his lips.

"Not unless you get promoted to being a Richie. Everything grown is done so in the Dining Hall above us," Quincey answered and pointed upwards.

"Have you ever tried these?" I asked Quincey.

"I have not. I only get to see them here on the computer, and on rare occasions, I need to be in the Dining Hall upstairs. We are not permitted to eat food not designated for us." Quincey said with sadness in their voice.

"What do you need to do at the Richies Dining Hall?" I was trying to figure out what kind of work I might need for Codex. It weighed heavily on my mind, and I wanted to get as much information as possible.

"Mostly polishing the machines or fixing a tray jam from the automated system. There aren't many glitches in the programs, so for the most part, I don't have to leave this room while I'm working." Quincey said and looked around where we were. They continued, "Did you notice the wonderful lack of cameras here?"

I looked around the room, where there are usually cameras in the space where the walls and ceiling meet, and there was nothing.

"Oh yeah!" Apollox marveled. "Why?"

"This area was part of the Lumpen Mess Hall before my time," Quincey began, "There are station legends that the old ration maintenance team created the walled-off area so the other Lumpen wouldn't know what they were missing. I didn't know about all these foods until I learned about them in work-study when I was your age. If the Lumpen saw all the foods that the Richies get and we don't, they would think about how unfair it is, and that would create unrest." Quincey told us their story.

"Do you get envious knowing that we can't have these foods because we are Lumpen?" I asked them.

"I used to when I started, but then I realized I have all the nutrients I need in the goo," they said as they stood up and walked back to the recycling computer. We followed.

"Back to work. Where was I? Oh, yes, recycling step 1," Quincey began, "When the Richies dispose of their leftover food in the chute upstairs, the automatic program activates the blades in the grinder. That chops up the food, which is then processed in the mixer."

"How do the chutes know when to activate?" I asked.

"There is a button at the top. The Richies dump their leftovers into the chute, then hit the button to lock the lid and start the chopping. The blades at the top start, then the lower blades activate as the food is chopped down, and the upper blades retract. We can start them manually over there." Quincey told us.

"Do we have to go in and clean the blades?" I asked. I was worried about getting stuck in a chute full of blades.

"The computer will tell us when we need to service the chutes," Quincey explained. "Which includes cleaning and sharpening. But the blades can be removed for that. Once, I even had to completely replace a blade. It is a lot heavier than I had expected."

"So, nobody ever goes into the chute," I said, relieved.

"Only if there's a major clog," Quincey said. "Then whoever's the smallest will have to enter the chute and clear the waste from the knives. But that hardly ever happens."

"Are we really eating ground-up waste?" Apollox asked with a look of disgust.

"We prefer the term 'Leftovers' instead of that," Quincey corrected. "Technically, thanks to this, Pangea has no waste." They gestured to all the machines in the hidden room.

"It still seems like we're eating garbage...," Apollox mumbled.

"After the food is ground up and mixed in the machine in the service room, it moves through the ration tubes under the floor. Then the goo goes through the tubes and into the dispensers." Quincey walked over to the back of the machines we use in the Mess Hall.

"These machines are where we do the most work," Quincey pointed out. "If there is anything that backs up or clogs or malfunctions, we have to fix it," Quincey said and showed the machines that had one computer to the side of them.

"How do you know if something is clogged?" I asked them.

"An alert goes to our OCs and specifies which machine has which error code. Before I forget, let me send you those error codes and the digital workbook. I should have sent it first," they said and took out their OC and sent us a file. I felt my OC vibrate in my pocket, but I didn't reach for it because I was looking at how the machines looked with the tubes running out of the back and then down to the floor, which leads to the mixer.

"A clogged tube is the most common, and that usually happens if the Mess Hall is busy. All you have to do is come over to the machine that has the clog, based on the error code we receive, and uncouple the tube from the dispenser here. Personally, I prefer to remove the floor panel to reveal the other end of the tube. Usually, I can use the high-pressure air hose to blow air through the tube and push the clog out. Then, recouple the tube back into place and use the computer to reset the code. If the machine light turns green, it is ready to dispense rations. See, it's easy," Quincey said with a shrug.

"What are the tubes coming from the wall over there?" I asked with curiosity.

"The clean water comes in from the creation department, which is on the other side of that wall," Quincey pointed up to the Dining Hall. They continued, "There is soil in the Richies Dining Hall that the fruits and vegetables grow out of. They can grab something fresh from the vines themselves, but most just click on the computer what they want. The automated system will harvest the desired food and create a dish at the end for the Richie to grab. I don't think the Richies like to get their hands dirty."

"How do we make soil?" I asked, I had heard Mr. Kline talk about dirt for plants in Old Earth History, but I don't know how it is replicated in space.

"I'm not completely versed with the entire process, but it has to do with recycling various waste. Then getting the correct nutrients to grow food, similar to how we used to do it on Earth. It's above my RC Credit level," Quincey told us nonchalantly.

We spent the next few hours reviewing the workbook because Quincey said they were rusty and needed a refresher themselves. Together we all sat at the main computer station. Quincey pulled up the workbook as a holo, and we followed along as they went through the steps on servicing the ration machines.

Ding, ding, ding.

The alarm that work-study had finished rang in the hidden room in the Mess Hall.

"See you both tomorrow," Quincey said. They walked us to the side panel that we had entered through. "Same time and place!" They called as the panel slid shut.

Apollox and I walked the short way, passing the Service Elevator Room to get our PSCs off at Cora's. We were near the front of the line, and I saw Taliah and Justice walk past us and get in line a few people behind us.

"Do you want to have dinner rations together?" Apollox asked me when the line started to move.

"What do you mean?" I asked, genuinely confused. We could only get our rations in the same place.

"Do you want to sit with me at our table?" He clarified. He had invited me to sit at the reserved table for Taliah and her friends.

The line moved forward, and it was my turn to get my PSC off. I didn't know how to respond. I entered Cora's without answering. I came out and waited for Apollox to finish, then said, "I'd really enjoy that."

Together we walked back to the Mess Hall and grabbed trays. Apollox walked to the table in the back where he usually sits with Taliah, Justice, and some of the other teens from the Bunks. I stood there for a moment, awkward, with my tray in my hands. Two empty chairs were at the table, but I didn't want to exclude Sahara. I was worried that Justice would say something cruel to Sahara or myself.

"You can sit next to me," Apollox said, patting

the table beside him. I sat in the chair at the end of the table nearest the wall. I knew Taliah and Justice liked to sit together on the other side of Apollox.

"Is it just me, or does the goo taste worser than normal?" Apollox asked with poor Grammar.

I took a small spoonful, and it felt harder to chew. I nodded my head yes to Apollox to answer him while I worked on chewing this goo.

"What are *you* doing here?" Justice asked as she slammed her tray on the table and looked at me.

"Nitris and I have work-study this round, so I asked them to join us," Apollox said with an assertive voice that made Justice sit down but she didn't break eye contact with me.

"Hey Nitris, how was work-study?" Taliah asked me as she sat down between Justice and Apollox. She didn't seem bothered by the negative energy Justice was projecting.

"Every day, it is enlightening to see behind the metal panels, how Pangea operates," I said and shot Apollox a knowing look, and we laughed together. That seemed to upset Justice, *worser*.

"What's so funny about that?" Justice asked pointedly.

"They mean it literally. Today we went to a secret room behind the panel on that side of the ration machine," Apollox answered and pointed to where we were less than twenty minutes ago.

"Learn anything *deadly* in a simulation?" Taliah asked me, referring to our time in oxygen maintenance simulation.

"Nothing is as *deadly* as that simulation," I answered her and returned our inside joke.

"I don't get it. What's deadly?" Justice asked

Taliah, confused as to why we had said it twice.

"You had to be there," Taliah answered, brushing off Justice. I could see Justice's face get red, and a vein in her forehead was starting to throb. She shoved a large spoonful of goo in her mouth and chewed on it for a while.

"Are you going to start sitting with us instead of alone?" Justice asked me while she was still chewing her goo.

"I haven't been sitting alone," I said, confused about her question. I started to look around for Sahara in the Mess Hall. I realized I hadn't seen her all day because I skipped AM rations. Come to think of it, I didn't even see her in Mr. Kline's class.

"Who are you looking for? Your imaginary friend that sits with you all the time?" Justice asked in a mocking pathetic tone.

Without answering Justice, I stood up, walked my tray with most of the goo still on it, and put it in the waste processor. The image of the blades chopping food in the recycling chute gave me the shivers to think about. I rushed out of the Mess Hall and started towards the airlock in the service tunnel. Sahara had to be there waiting for me. I looked both ways down the hallway before I stepped into the alcove to the ladder down to the access tunnel. I descended quickly and walked to the airlock with purpose, expecting to see Sahara sitting there with her OC reading the medical books we downloaded last night.

I panicked when the motion sensor lights kicked on, and I saw the airlock empty. I wondered if Sahara had been caught or if she had been reporting on what we'd been doing. I thought about Solitary Containment and execution. I started to take large gasps of air, suddenly unable to breathe normally. The room was hot and sweat soaked my palms.

"It's okay, you're okay; breathe with me," I heard a voice behind me. It was calm and collected, and I felt a hand on my shoulder. I didn't turn around but took deeper breaths with her until my breathing returned to a normal rhythm.

"Sahara, I was so worried about you," I said as I touched her hand on my shoulder and turned around to face her.

"Who's Sahara?" Taliah asked, meeting my eyes and keeping her hand on my shoulder. That was when the room started to spin, and my vision blacked out as I fainted.

Chapter 22
Sahara

The sounds of emergency alarms were blaring, and I couldn't concentrate. Pangea was hit by something that shook the medical bay and made the lights flicker.

I looked down and saw Nitris on the exam table in front of me, covered in blood. I pressed my hands to their abdomen to apply pressure and stop the bleeding.

"Please, Nitris. Stay with me. You can do this. I need you," I begged as I felt the hot blood pouring through my fingers.

"Computer, status report," I yelled aloud and waited for a response.

There was another loud bang, and the room went dark. The Medical Bay then became lit by the green glow of the emergency lights.

"Space debris have impacted the lower levels,

breaching the hull. Hallway lockdowns have been initiated to maintain air pressure and artificial gravity. Life support remains functional," the computer replied to my inquiry.

I looked down at my blood-covered hands and wiped the excess on my white lab coat. It felt odd to me to wear this and suddenly find myself in the middle of an emergency.

Looking around the Medical Bay, I caught my reflection in a glass cabinet. I looked much older, and that stunned me for a moment. Suddenly, I realized the cabinet that showed my reflection, held the needed nanobot. I rushed over to get the supplies. I hadn't done this before, but I my body knew what to do.

My OC in hand, I programmed and injected the nanobots to evaluate the wound on Nitris' abdomen to determine the prognosis. While I waited for the results, I prepped the medication with antibiotics. When the bleeding stopped, I reached into my pocket for the medical scanner to read the nanobot results. The readings told me that they were in critical condition and that I needed to stop their internal bleeding. I would need more nanobots to clamp off the artery that has been ruptured.

The regular Medical Bay lights were turned back on, and the emergency lights were deactivated. Pangea was regaining its stability and had started to work correctly. I ran over to the other side of the Medical Bay looking for additional nanobots but found nothing.

I looked back at Nitris and exhaled the breath I had been holding, when Taliah handed me the additional nanobots I needed. For a moment, I was confused about how she could see me and know what

I needed in that moment.

"Come on, Doctor! Nitris doesn't have much time!" Taliah said to me and pushed me back towards the table. Her right hand was cold on my back and I shivered. She was somehow older, with her long red curls pulled back into a neat bun instead of messy. She followed me over to Nitris, looking to me for instructions.

"Hold this here," I pointed to where the wound was open and handed her the medication injector I had primed with antibiotics. She seemed flustered but followed my directions. Her sterile medical gloves were covered in blood.

"Do you think we'll be hit again?" Taliah asked me with fear dripping on each word.

"I don't know. Inject Nitris when the nanobots send me the next results. We need to focus on saving Nitris, and then we can think about everything else," I instructed her. I pulled the medical scanner back out of my coat and re-scanned Nitris.

"Patient is going into shock due to blood loss. Recommend blood transfusion," the automated voice said from the scanner.

I looked at Taliah. She was already taking off her stained lab coat and preparing to draw her own blood to give to Nitris. DNX had made all of our blood compatible for emergencies.

I could feel my own heart racing as the hot blood continued to pour slowly out of Nitris and into my hands. Breathing was hard for me to do, and I didn't know what else I could do in that moment. Whatever medical knowledge and expertise I had seemed to be missing from my mind. I stumbled backward and fell to the ground.

"Doctor Sahara! We need you!" Taliah's voice sounded very far away.

The room went black, but not because of a power failure. I was dizzy and my vision began to blur. I felt a warm hand and a cold hand holding my shoulders up from the floor as my legs collapsed.

Suddenly I woke up, gasping for air in the complete darkness I'm used to. It felt like my heart was going to jump out of my chest.

When my eyes adjusted, I looked around and saw that everything was as I remembered. I realized that I must have been lucid dreaming. My dreams had become much more intense recently. Most of them involve Nitris. I didn't know if this was because of my abilities or a side effect.

I tried to stand, but my whole body felt so heavy that I couldn't even sit up in my bed. I was still too exhausted from using my abilities at the Library. I laid back down, relieved that I had only been dreaming, and exhaled the stress I was holding.

I fell back asleep, and thankfully, no more dreams came to me.

Chapter 23
Taliah

"What did I get myself into?" I said with a grunt as I laid Nitris on the floor of the airlock. They had passed out and landed on me. I sat them up with their back against the wall and tried to wake them up by shaking their shoulders.

"Wake up, Nitris," I said louder than I should have.

"Sa Sa huh," Nitris mumbled.

"Let's do the breathing thing again. Can you breathe with me? Inhale and feel the air through your nose and deep into your lungs." I said and held their shoulders while they took a deep breath and exhaled in unison with me. I looked around, saw the broken airlock sign, and was nervous about whether we should be breathing deeply here.

"Come on, wake up all the way," I instructed

them, and Nitris rubbed their eyes.

"What happened?" Nitris asked me.

"I was going to ask you the same thing. What's going on with you? You're acting more weird than usual." I said, my arm supporting their shoulders as we leaned against the wall.

"Have you seen Sahara today?" Nitris asked me.

"I don't know who Sahara is," I said as I tried to set them against the wall.

"She is my age with tan glowing skin, blonde hair, and blue eyes that seem to light up the Dark Flats," Nitris sounded like Justice did when she talked about Cyran. They had a ridiculous far-away look in their eyes.

"I think I would have noticed someone lighting up the place with glowing skin," I said more sarcastically than I intended.

"She's in our class," Nitris insisted. "She was in the back row beside Segauce in Mr. Kline's class."

My head started to hurt. I felt like I remembered someone being there, but I couldn't connect it to a name or a face. It's like a presence was there, but I didn't know who, which was impossible because of how few of us there were. I struggled with trying to see this blurry person in focus.

"I have to find her. I think something happened to her after we got back from the Library. Maybe Codex arrested her," Nitris started to get worked up again.

"You went to the Library?" I asked confused, "The one that is locked down, and we aren't allowed at? Did somebody get arrested by Codex? From the Council?" If the Council of Elders was involved, this was more serious than I had thought.

"Sahara received a message from Codex, and

she told Sahara that she would turn off the Library alerts so we could get eBooks. We just want to learn, and then we could propose to The Elders that we need better education and that just because we are Lumpen doesn't mean we aren't worth any less than a Richie. We just want to have the same chances...," Nitris said in one long breath.

I took a moment to sit there and mentally process what Nitris had just told me. They want me to believe that there is another teen on board who I can vaguely remember. Apparently, she is in direct contact with the second-in-command on *The* Council of Elders, who personally aided them in going to the *off-limits* Library.

"Why would Codex do something to help you?" I asked. "How would Codex even know you exist? You're just another kid in the Bunks. You're not special."

"You're right. I'm not, but Codex wants me to do something for her," Nitris said and began to support their own weight, "She arranged for me to get assigned to Ration Maintenance for work-study, even though there are no openings there. She wants me and Sahara to do something, but I don't know what it is yet. I think it has something to do with, uh-"

Nitris stopped talking abruptly. I don't think they trusted me completely.

"If Codex wanted you to do this, then why is she communicating with..., Who did you say? 'Sahara'? You think that a member of The Council of Elders is talking to you through a made-up person?" I demanded.

"I don't know. My head hurts a lot. I could have sworn Sahara is real...," Nitris said and rubbed their eyes again.

Nitris looked so sad and confused. I couldn't

blame them if they were genuinely having a mental breakdown. I followed them here to make sure they were okay after Justice was being petulant. Still, I hadn't expected to witness their breakdown.

"Let's say that I believe you," I offered. "If you're allowed to present your case to The Council, would it apply to all of us in the Bunks or just you and this missing Sahara person?" I didn't know if Nitris was losing their mind or if they could be my way out of the Dark Flats.

"It would be for everyone on Pangea," Nitris said intensely. "Not just the Bunks but the adults too. Equal chances for higher education without the ridiculously high demand for RC Credits. Test into any job, not just what we do best at the end of work-study. Is there a job you want to do up there?" Nitris pointed up, indicating the Richies level. They seemed to be on the same mindset as me.

"I don't want to wear a PSC for the rest of my life," I said, rubbing my neck.

"If you can help me find Sahara, I will do everything I can to get us the chance to leave the Dark Flats," Nitris said, looking into my eyes with hope and desperation.

"Help you find a person that doesn't exist?" I asked without masking my annoyance.

"I have to know for sure," Nitris said. "Even if Sahara's not real, I can still take my case to The Elders. I just, I have to know."

I didn't think I had anything to lose, so I agreed to help Nitris. We devised a plan quickly. Together we headed back to the Bunks with ten minutes to spare before 22:00 lights out.

I didn't want to walk into the Bunks with Nitris

and give the wrong impression that we were suddenly friends, so I slowed my pace and let them go in first. Then I counted to thirty before I walked in slowly to my bunk and used my trunk to lift myself into my bed.

"Where did you run off to?" Justice asked from the bunk under me.

"I had to find my OC. I left it in Cora's when I got my PSC off," I said, which seemed like a blatant lie as the words fell from my mouth.

"Fine, don't tell me," Justice exhaled and shook the whole bunk, including me, when she rolled over to her side.

I lay on my back and stared at the ceiling, trying to think of something to talk to Ms. Verban about to keep her busy. Nitris said that Mr. Kline visits her around 02:00, and then she was busy with him until the AM call, so I just needed to keep Ms. V occupied for about three hours. Easy enough, I tried to reassure myself.

Before I knew it, Ms. Verban called lights out at 22:00 on the dot. She walked down the length of the bunks and then headed out of the Bunks.

I hopped down my bunk and rushed towards the door quickly. My bare feet on the cold metal floor woke me more with every step.

"Ms. V?" I asked in a semi-hushed tone when I poked my head out of the Bunks. I expected her to be towards the right, toward her chambers. Still, she responded from my left side, the same path Nitris needed to go to the Library.

"Taliah? Go back inside. It is past curfew," Ms. Verban said from the side of the hallway that I needed to clear for Nitris.

I walked out of the Bunks and started towards

the Mess Hall on my tiptoes, and I said, "What? I can't hear you?" In a whispered tone.

"Taliah, I'm over here. Where are you going?" Ms. Verban asked, and I could hear her taking steps toward me.

"Ms. V, I really need to talk, and you always tell us that we can talk to you anytime. I need you." I said and kept walking towards her chambers around the corner, trying to get her to follow me the other way.

"Taliah, I'm heading to the Birthing Lab, not my chambers," Ms. Verban said, and she touched my shoulder. I turned around with a jump and startled her.

"There you are," I said and hugged her to look over her shoulder at the Bunks' door to see if Nitris had left.

"What is it? I have to check on something," Ms. Verban said and broke away from my hug.

"Check on something in the Birthing Lab? What would be there?" I asked her, trying to make conversation for as long as possible.

"I saw someone over there the other day, and something doesn't feel right," Ms. Verban shared. "My intuition is telling me something, and I need to figure out what it is."

I hadn't planned what to do to keep Ms. Verban distracted, but it seemed like she already had a lot on her mind. If I could keep her talking and away from Bunks, Nitris could sneak out easily. I had stood facing her so I could still see the door of the Bunks behind her. I watched Nitris step out from the dark shadows into the green emergency lights.

"Was it Mr. Kline?" I guessed. I knew I was taking a chance by revealing I had learned about their secret relationship. "What was he doing at the Birthing Lab?"

"Yes, he was distraught, and I-" Ms. Verban started but quickly rounded on me. "How do you know it was Mr. Kline?"

"I really need to talk to you. Can we please go to your chambers? I don't want anyone else hearing us...," I inclined as I linked my arm to her arm and started to direct us to her chambers. I saw Nitris head down the hallway toward the Birthing Lab and Library and exhaled in relief.

"All right, but only for a few minutes," Ms. Verban relented and opened her chambers with a swipe of her wrist over the scanner. We walked in, and I looked around. It was the first time I had seen inside any adult's chambers.

"Wow, this is what living alone is like," I said admiringly.

"I do a lot to have private chambers," Ms. Verban told me with pride.

"I thought it was because you care for all the children," I said.

"That helps too," she said with a soft smile as she sat at her desk. I lay down on the little couch that faced her desk. I was on my back and brought my knees to my chest. If we had been in her classroom, I would have sat opposite her, but I didn't think I could look her in the eyes and lie. Being in this position seemed more dramatic, too. I had to keep her attention on me instead of Nitris sneaking around.

"What was Mr. Kline doing at the Birthing Lab?" I asked, keeping my gaze on the ceiling and slowly rocking my knees from side to side.

"That is not what we are here to talk about. But

I'm curious, how did you know that Mr. Kline and I are in a relationship?" She asked me.

"Everybody knows. Is it supposed to be a secret?" I asked, trying to sound innocent.

"He hasn't committed to me, and we have been together for over a year. The rules about relationship contracts are clear. After one year, we have to have a living arrangement contract. We both would give up our solo chambers," she said with a sigh and looked around.

"I'd be hesitant to give something like this up," I said and rubbed the couch that I lay on before I continued, "What is he dragging his feet for? A beautiful and intelligent woman like you is a dream come true," I said, laying on the charm.

"I just have to keep waiting," Ms. Verban said wistfully. "But that's not why you came to me. What is bothering you?" I tried to think of something plausible.

"It's about... relationships and living arrangements," I said, using our topic to segue into the distraction. "Lately, Justice and Cyran are so involved in themselves that it feels like Justice and I are growing apart. It's like she was stuck at age 10 before we had to grow up, and she doesn't see the harm she is doing to everyone around her." I said, surprised by how honest that felt.

"Did something happen?" Ms. Verban asked me kindly.

"The other day, Justice was jealous or something when she saw me talking to Nitris after work-study, but I don't understand why. She has her girlfriend, and they will get married, and everything will work out for them. But what about me? I used to believe Justice and I would live together and be best friends and Dark Flatmates. Now Justice says she would have a throuple with Cyran and me, but that doesn't appeal to me." I admitted.

"Maybe Justice thinks that you are replacing her with Nitris," she suggested.

"That could never happen. Nitris and Justice are so different. There is no way Nitris could replace Justice." I said as a matter of fact.

"Not a literal replacement but as a new best friend. Do you think that Justice sees Nitris the way you see Cyran?" She asked me.

"I guess I never thought of it like that. There isn't anything romantic between Nitris and me like there is with Justice and Cyran," I explained. Now I was beginning to think that maybe this *pretend* topic was something that was actually bothering me.

"With the change in everyone's schedule, are you still making time to see Justice?" Ms. Verban asked me.

"I sleep above her. I literally can't go one day *without* seeing her," I said with a laugh.

"That is not the same thing as seeing her like you used to. You were joined at the hip when you two were in my class. I couldn't see you without seeing Justice beside or behind you. She has always admired and followed you and wanted to be just like you. I always thought it was endearing, like how I imagine sisters would be, if we had siblings," she reminded me of all the good times I had with Justice.

"She is my best friend and will always be. But she still acts like a child sometimes. If she isn't being dramatic with her love life, she is bullying people who don't deserve it. The worst part is that I feel like I'm why she is acting mean like this. It feels like she is trying to impress me, but instead, I'm embarrassed by her actions," I confessed.

"Maybe she is acting out, trying to get your attention. Trying to do something that would make you respond to her instead of ignoring or pretending like she didn't do something mean," she said.

"Do you think people can change, or are we the same for our whole lives?" I asked her, and I turned onto my side to see her reaction. She took a while to answer, and I was thankful to be passing the time.

"I think that we are who we are at the core of ourselves but that we can all grow and adapt to be something stronger. It might look like change to some people, but to others, it adds a layer to who they really are," she said with a small smile.

"Have you changed since you moved out of the Bunks?" I asked her, curious about her life as an adult.

"I have learned much about how our society works and how that affects me. I know I have to work twice as hard as Mr. Kline, and I don't have much to show for it," she said as she gestured around her chambers.

"I think you have a lot because you work hard. This has to be the largest private chamber in the entire Dark Flats. The next best place to live is a private chamber on the Richies level." I said reassuringly that maybe one day that could be me.

"There are things you will go through in your life which will shape who you are and where you end up. That is why paying attention and learning as much as possible in work-study is important to get assigned a great job. I can even see you as a teacher. I know that Mr. Kline has said he enjoys having you in his class, and he thinks you will do great things too," she said compassionately.

It made me want to cry, hearing that people expect big things from me and want me to succeed. I turned onto my back and looked at the ceiling again. I didn't want to seem weak and cry in front of her. She saw anyway and brought me a soft cloth to wipe my tears away. They began to fall freely. The hot streams down my cheeks made me close my eyes to try to hold them back.

"I want to be more than the job assigned to me for the rest of my life. I want my life to be meaningful. I want to be special," I spoke my truth about what was in my heart and didn't bother to hold the urge to cry.

Ms. Verban picked up my legs and sat on the couch, pulling my legs down to rest on her lap, making room for both of us. She sat there with me while I cried until no more tears were left. I completely lost track of time, but she didn't try to rush me to go.

A knock on her door startled us. We both jumped and looked at the door. The display on the wall lit up with the knock alert and showed Mr. Kline was at her door.

"I should go," I said with a deep inhale and another wipe to remove the last tears and sat beside her on the couch.

"Are you feeling better?" Ms. Verban asked me, still not rushing to the door to let Mr. Kline in. That made me feel special. She put me first. I stood up, and after another good wipe away the tears with the cloth, I turned and faced her.

"I am now. Thank you for talking to me," I said as I leaned down and hugged her on the couch.

"Anytime." She hugged me back. When we let go, I tried to hand her the cloth I used to wipe my face, and she said I could keep it. I pulled it to my chest and then shoved it into my pocket.

"I'll leave you to it," I said, trying to put a smile on my face to make it look like I wasn't just crying.

"Go straight back to the Bunks; no wandering around. You know the rules." She said with a stern voice.

The door opened as I approached, and I saw Mr. Kline standing there. He seemed surprised to see me.

"Good night, Mr. Kline," I said casually, walking past him to the Bunks.

"Good night, Taliah." He said to me and walked into Ms. Verban's chambers.

I was glad the door to the Bunks never closed because I could walk in quietly without waking anyone. I climbed up on my bunk and took a look at my OC. It was 00:30. Interesting, Mr. Kline was early. I hoped that didn't mean that he would leave early too. I hoped I had given Nitris enough time to do what they needed to find Sahara. I clicked my OC off and put it back into my pocket.

When I approached my bunk bed that I shared with Justice, I saw she was pretending to be asleep. Instead of hoping on top and shaking the bunk, I got into the small bed and hugged Justice.

"Good night, Justice," I whispered to her and she made a noise in response.

Chapter 24
Nitris

I held my breath standing in the shadows with my back against the inside wall of the Bunks. I was waiting for Ms. V to follow Taliah to the other side of the door. She usually heads to her chambers after lights out, but tonight she went the other way. I still couldn't believe that Taliah was willing to help me.

"Taliah, I'm heading to the Birthing Lab, not my chambers." Ms. V said as she passed the entrance to the Bunks, walking towards Taliah in the other direction so I could sneak out.

I didn't know if the plan would work, so I rushed into the hallway towards the Birthing Lab in a low crouch. I slowed down when I passed the bend, and the Bunks were no longer in sight. The lights were on here but not up ahead. I pressed myself against the wall and thought about being invisible. I inhaled deeply and started stepping toward the Birthing Lab.

My original plan was to start at the Library to retrace our steps, but now that I heard Ms. V talking about activity at the lab, I had to look there first. When I got to the entrance, I cupped my hands around my eyes and looked into the cupola window on the door. I could see the emergency lights on the floor, but they only went back about one meter before they were too dim to see. I looked at the door scanner. There was a manual entry code panel similar to adult chambers.

I let my hands glide over the number panel and felt a zap under my fingers when I went over specific numbers. It was like the static electricity feeling I got when I fixed the holo in class or touched any malfunctioning machine. It wasn't enough to hurt, but enough that I noticed. I hovered my hand over the entire keypad. There was a pattern of six shocks. I didn't know for sure, but something felt connected between me and Pangea. It told me that it was that manual door code. When I entered the numbers, the door unlocked. It rolled back and to the side. Then the lights up front came on, and I walked into the Birthing Lab.

"Hello?" I said cautiously into the dark.

There was no reply, but I felt something in my bones that told me someone else was there.

"Sahara?" I called out.

"Mmm ... Urgh ... Nitris?" I heard Sahara's voice came from the darkness before me.

"I'm here. Where are you?" I asked the darkness.

"I feel so weak," Sahara squeaked out, and I moved carefully toward her voice, still unable to see.

"Are you okay? What happened?" I asked, stepping further into the lab.

"I exhausted my powers," she answered with a

defeated sigh.

"Powers? What are you talking about?" I didn't understand, but I kept searching in the dark for her. I passed the empty glass circular incubation tubes that once held us all. A shiver ran down my spine. The rest of the room held only empty cabinets with transparent doors. I walked further into the lab and found a desk with a chair on the other side. It looked like the kind of desk Mr. Kline had in his classroom.

"I've been keeping secrets from you, Nitris," Sahara's voice came from somewhere deep in the back of the lab.

"I'm just glad you're okay. I was scared thinking that you were arrested by Codex or executed," I said with relief.

"I don't want to scare you, but I don't want you to see me...," Sahara said. My stomach instantly jumped into my throat, preparing for what would come next.

"It'll be alright. I promise." I managed to squeak out.

Sahara stepped out from behind a cabinet near a small bed. She was dressed all in white, a color we don't see much on the Dark Flats of Pangea. It looked cleaner and newer than anything I'd ever seen. It was a simple garment, a sheet draped over her with two short sleeves. She was walking with a tall pole at her side. A bag was hanging off the pole with tubes leading into Sahara's arm.

"What happened? Are you okay?" I asked again worriedly.

"I have a confession," she stated, and she came into the emergency floor lighting by me. Her voice shook with anticipation.

"I'm ready," I said, bracing myself for the worst.

I had no idea what she was going to say.

As Sahara stepped out of the dark, the emergency lights illuminated her features. Her shiny blonde hair was down and went down to her waist. Slowly, she brushed her hair back behind her ear. She had a massive scar down her face, from her left eyebrow down towards her jawbone.

I inhaled deeply, as my thoughts raced. I needed clarification. She had only been gone one day, but the scar looked old. How could she have a scar that large, and I hadn't noticed it?

"Am I hideous?" She asked, in response to my silence. She untucked her hair from behind her ear to cover her face.

"What? No!" I started, "What happened to you? I saw you less than 24 hours ago!"

"I have never left this lab. I have grown up here in the darkness," she said sadly, but the explanation didn't make any sense.

"But, we went to Mr. Kline's together," I said, "And the Library. You sat with me in the Mess Hall!"

"I'm technically the first generation of Human 3.0," Sahara began, "That gives me some extra abilities that the previous version of DNX doesn't have. I can project myself into someone's mind so only they can see and communicate with me. I have been practicing for years, and when I saw you walking without turning the lights on, I realized that maybe you have some abilities like me. I tried contacting you before, but it didn't work. I had to get better at using my abilities, and eventually, I did. Didn't you notice that I never set off the motion sensors?"

"I thought you were better at tricking them than I was," I explained.

"But the doors didn't recognize me either, remember?" Sahara said.

"This is crazy," I objected with confusion, "If you've never been out of this lab, how can I have memories with you?"

"I implanted memories of seeing me in class and at the Mess Hall before we spoke the first time. I tried to make myself look pretty so I wouldn't scare you away. I needed your help," she said with an exhale.

"My help?" I was starting to understand. "To get into the Library! The door wouldn't have opened for you! Because you weren't there! And that's why you didn't leave imprints in the dust." I was feeling worked up and my tone was increasing.

"When projecting, I can't touch things," Sahara confirmed, "I'm only in your consciousness, not anything physical. That's why I was always wearing the same clothes. I also implanted memories of me being in Mr. Kline's class."

"I told Taliah about you, but she didn't remember you," I said. "At least, not like I do."

"I tried to put the same memories in all of the kids' minds, but I'm not strong enough," she said, "Connecting with you was the most important thing. I needed your help to get out of here, but I didn't think you would come if I were only a mental projection. You might think you imagined me."

"I still have so many questions, but we need to get you out of here before someone notices *I'm* gone," I began to consider our options, "You must have an escape plan, right?" I asked her.

"I have plans and backup plans," she said, with more strength in her voice, "That's all I think about."

"What's that thing you're attached to?" I asked

with concern and walked closer to her.

"This is an IV with hydration and potassium," she explained. "It takes a lot of energy to project myself, and we've had a busy week. When you were in work-study, I was being tested by Mr. Kline in here."

"Do you not eat anything?" I asked her with concern.

"I have a ration dispenser over in that corner by the freshwater. No wrist chip needed," she said with a little laugh and lifted her arm.

"Do you need that pole thing? Where are your clothes? Let's get you to the airlock, and we can talk more," I asked her questions while I looked around the bare room to see if she needed to pack her things. My heart broke for her when I saw she had even less than we have in the Bunks.

"I can take a couple of these IV bags and my OC. I don't have any clothes besides these sanitized ones. They're dispensed from the machine over here," Sahara said as she walked to the machine and opened the door. There were three white garments wrapped in plastic. I walked over, grabbed them, and folded them into the front of my waistband.

"Let's get out of here," I said, grabbing her hand. She was as cold as the metal floor. I realized this was the first time I had reached for her hand and felt her.

"I just need to grab your file from the desk on the way out," she said, and we started walking towards the front.

"My file? Why do I have a file?" I asked.

"I'll tell you about it when we get to the airlock. Let's go," Sahara said as she walked to the desk and opened the top drawer. She grabbed a plastic folder with several pages of plastic-printed notes in it. She pressed the file under her arm and then took the tube connected to the IV bag off but left the needle tapped into her arm.

"The door only opens to Mr. Kline's wrist chip because to keep me trapped in here. I don't think the door will open for either of us," she said as she looked around the door.

"We can use the manual pad as we did in Mr. Kline's chambers," I realized she hadn't been there when I had used it and entered Mr. Kline's room. I started to feel like I had been used and the pain stung, "You were only in my mind then, too. That's why you couldn't open the door from the inside. How did you know his door code?"

"I can implant and retrieve memories; when I do that, I also have access to the rest of a person's mind. I had entered Mr. Kline's thoughts before, during his tests. At first, it was an accident, but then I realized this could save me. I'm not sure he even knew what he was testing me on. I was looking for the code to get out of there, but he never knew it because he only had to use the chip on his wrist. I knew the door code for his quarters from trying to find the Birthing Lab door code," she explained the missing pieces.

"Then how did I figure out the door code tonight?" I asked her, more confused than when I arrived.

"That was all you. I can explain it more when we get out of here. It's all in your medical file," she said and tapped the file.

I was working on blind trust again. We had yet to be executed by The Elders. I didn't know how long our luck would last. We entered the hall and started back towards the Bunks. The service tunnel was past

Ms. V's chambers closer to the Mess Hall.

"I hope Taliah is still keeping Ms. V occupied...," I said in a whisper.

"Or Mr. Kline," Sahara offered, "He loves her. His thoughts are filled with her. And many regrets...,"

I wondered what Sahara meant, but there wasn't time to discuss it now. I motioned for Sahara to follow me to get past the Bunks open door quickly and quietly.

Knock, knock, knock.

The sound stopped me in my tracks, and Sahara bumped into me. I turned to face her. She looked as scared as I was. We had only reached the small area between the Bunks and Ms. V's chambers. The lights were always on in this stretch, making it easy to see us in the hallway but harder to hide our presence.

I leaned forward, looked down the hallway towards Ms. V's chambers, and saw Mr. Kline standing outside waiting for her. I moved backward out of sight and looked at my OC. It was only 00:30, he was early. I gestured towards Sahara to go back the way we had come. We needed to get out of sight. We went backwards, past the Bunks entrance and waited just out of sight.

We couldn't hear the exact words, but I heard Taliah and Mr. Kline briefly talking. Then I heard Taliah step briskly as she went into the Bunks.

"We have to go now," I said, grabbing Sahara's hand. We rushed forward together, keeping our heads low. We hurried past the Bunks and crossed the hallway on the same side as Ms. V's door. We reached the service ladder and descended to our secret location in the airlock.

Chapter 25
Ms. Verban

When Silas entered my chambers, he looked upset and exhausted.

"Hey, my love, can we talk?" Silas asked me. I was beginning to hate that sentence. I gestured for him to sit at my desk again because I was on the couch.

"What's on your mind?" I asked him. I was feeling betrayed by him emotionally, but physically, I wanted to be near him. Every inch of my body wanted to be in his arms again and pretend everything was okay.

"What was Taliah doing in here?" He asked, avoiding my question.

"She was in here because she is struggling with her relationship with Justice and how things are changing as they grow up. I told her how it is okay to grow and change by adding layers to who we are, but she shouldn't expect Justice to do the same," I told him what we discussed and hoped he would get the hints about himself too.

"That is good advice. I bet she is glad to have you in her life," he said and looked down at the floor by his feet.

"It doesn't matter. What do you want, Silas?" I asked again.

"Are you mad at me?" He asked with sadness in his eyes.

"I have a lot of feelings about you," I told him, "Some of them are angry, some sad, some confused, and more."

"Don't be angry or sad. Everything that I'm doing is for us," he insisted, "I planned this before we even started seeing each other romantically. I've been working on getting you a better life, and it's so close I can almost touch it."

"You've made too many assumptions and decisions about my life without consulting me," I said "What if I don't get a higher-level position? We'd live up there, and I'd still work down here? What about the children? There are so many things to consider."

"I was only thinking about you and me," he said, defeated. "As long as we were together, everything else would work out."

"All I can say is that I love you and want to be with you," I told him. "That doesn't mean I'm not still mad at you."

"Can we kiss and make up?" Silas asked with a sly smile.

"How about we kiss and go to sleep? I'm exhausted physically but also emotionally."

He walked to the couch and extended his hand

to me. I took it and stood up. Together we walked to my bed and went to sleep holding each other. I thought about how this might be one of the last times I get to hold him like this before he leaves to the Richies level.

Chapter 26
Nitris

The sweat on my hand made me slip on the ladder rung as I climbed down in a rush. I dropped two rungs before I caught myself. I was close to the bottom and jumped down to the floor into the old service tunnel.

Sahara followed me down, and we walked to the airlock together.

"Oh no!" She panicked, "What's going to happen when Mr. Kline goes to test me at 14:00, and I'm not in the Birthing Lab?"

"Mr. Kline might report you missing," I tried to calm her down, "But that would make him look bad because you escaped under his supervision. He'll definitely try to find you first to avoid reporting you as missing to The Elders."

Sahara exhaled a sigh of relief and touched my

hand. We sat there in silence, looking at each other.

"That was scary close. If Mr. Kline had seen me outside the lab, he would have holo called Intra, or worse, Emberson," Sahara exhaled a breath of relief.

"Way too close. Let's not do that again. Mr. Kline and Intra holo call each other? What's an Emberson?" I asked as we got settled in the airlock. Sahara hooked herself up to a new bag of liquid. I helped her hang the bag from a bolt in the door jamb I loosened. My multi-tool was always handy, and I reached for it in my pocket more times than my OC.

"Intra called him while he was conducting tests on me. He has mixed feelings about Intra that I felt in his mind, but mostly he is hopeful that he will be promoted. You haven't seen Emberson?" She asked me as I watched Sahara shiver and rub her arms to keep warm. I wrapped the extra clothes we'd taken from the lab around her.

"I don't think I've seen any Emberson" I said, and then my racing mind continued out loud, "Tomorrow, I will drop a bag of clothes down the ladder," I said, as I wrapped the last garment around her legs, "I can't risk going down or being seen coming up the ladder. It would alert people to the area and find you. It's bad enough that Taliah already knows about this place. I hope she'll keep it a secret."

"Emberson was my only company growing up alone in the lab, but I knew it wasn't something I could trust, and it worked for Intra directly. I thought I heard it around the Dark Flats while we were on our missions. I'm okay now, thanks to you," Sahara said, looking at her bare feet.

"Let's not add worrying about Emberson to our list right now," I exhaled and thought about making the airlock feel more comfortable.

"You're right. I haven't heard it in a while anyway," Sahara said and rubbed her feet which were dirty from the walk here.

"I only have this one pair of shoes," I told Sahara, gesturing to my boots. I hadn't realized that shoes were a privilege. "If I leave them with you, people will wonder what happened to them."

"I understand, and really I'm okay," Sahara said sincerely. "Thank you for everything. It means a lot that you are helping me and risking so much."

We sat together in silence for a moment before I started asking questions.

"When I asked Taliah for help, she said she had a vague image of you in class but not a clear image. Did you implant your memory on her?" I asked.

"Yes, she is one of them, but it didn't work well," she said, still a little weak.

"So, I'm nothing special?" I asked as my stomach jumped into my throat. I swallowed hard, pushing it back down.

"You are the most special. That is why I needed you," she started. I looked at her pretty face hiding behind her hair. I reached for her, but she ducked away from my hand, and I couldn't hide the disappointment on my face.

"I'm sorry, I've never had anyone to talk to, hug, or share intimacy with. I have learned more about being human these last few days with you. You have started something new inside of me that I have never felt before. I found myself consumed with thoughts of you during the day when I was not with you," Sahara told me and leaned in closer. She grabbed my right hand and held it for a moment. We were silent, just enjoying the company.

"Considering we are both stuck on a space station, surrounded by people, without any place to go, we both feel lonely," I said while I changed to holding her hand with my left. I raised my right hand, slowly, to brush her blonde waves out of her face and behind her ear. "There, now I can see your beautiful face."

"That is sweet of you, but I know I am a monster. At least when I astral project myself, I have some control over how I look. I didn't want to frighten you away. I would have changed my outfit, but it is very draining with all the projecting," she pulled the IV she's connected to, and the bag was almost empty.

"I have been talking to a ghost in my mind the last few days, and it is the most 'at home' I have ever felt living here. I feel like there was more than just the facts we were told. Did you plant those thoughts in my head too?" I was curious about how much of our interaction was real and how much she controlled.

"I feel safe with you, and I think we grew closer because of my projecting abilities," she replied simply.

"How much of what we did the past few days have been...," I searched for the word, "...Real? Did you just plant all of our adventures in my head? Or were you controlling me?"

"Everything you feel and think about is all yours," Sahara said factually before she continued, "I did try to get you to stop eating the goo, though. Codex used to visit me in the lab, and she told me that the Elders have been drugging the rations to help control everyone on board. Some drugs block sensors in your mind that control desire and ambition. Most of all, it controls compliance and acceptance. That is why there aren't any people fighting for social equality.

Everyone just accepts this is what it is, and there is no way to improve anything."

"What?" In my disbelief, that was the only question I could conjure.

"It's true," she assured me, "I have so much time. I've read all of the Birthing Lab computer logs. I've seen it in the records. Think about the last couple of days when you haven't eaten all the rations you were given. Haven't your thoughts been clearer?"

"Besides the fact that I'm overwhelmed with emotions about everything we have learned, I feel a difference. My brain is a mess, but I've felt better since I've been eating less of the goo," I considered the implications of this, "But that wasn't because you were in my head? Can you read my mind when you are projecting into my thoughts?" I was suddenly afraid of what she had heard in my head.

"I can't hear your thoughts, but I can sense your feelings. They're so strong. That's why I was drawn to you. So, when you get anxious and your heart starts racing, I feel that too. I'm unsure how to project, but I think you and I are connected. In the logs, I read that you were one of the next versions before me. They started to implement more DNA editing with you. Later, when they created me, the scientists took it further and refined it even more. When you walk without the sensors going off, you do something similar to me when I project myself. Only you seem to be removing your bio-presence to be thinner and reduce your heat signature. I wouldn't say you are invisible, but to technology scans, you're nonexistent," she explained. Things started to click into place in my thoughts.

I sighed in relief that she hadn't been able to

read my thoughts, but this new information made it sound like I had abilities I was unaware of.

"I know this is a lot and all at once, but maybe after you read your file, you can wrap your head around it. Have you finished reading the journal yet?" Sahara said as she handed me the plastic file she grabbed from the desk before she leaned her head against the wall of the airlock. I held the file with my left hand before placing it on the floor.

Instinctively I reached for the journal still in the back of my waistband first. I had almost forgotten about it. I gently removed it from my pants and brought it before me.

"I've kept it on me for safekeeping, but I haven't finished reading it," I said as I looked down at the brittle paper in my hands.

"I've read it a few times," Sahara said. I looked at her, surprised, she continued, "It was in the desk that Mx. Sage used before they were promoted to the Richies level. When Mr. Kline started teaching me, I ensured he found it easily and saw him take it to his chambers during his first week with me. Some bits are in Old Earth languages that I haven't been able to translate completely. The various entries have spanned over a couple of hundred years. From what I can tell, there's some ongoing conspiracy involving The Council of Elders. I would have figured out more if Mr. Kline hadn't moved the journal to his chambers."

"I never heard of another teacher in the Dark Flats named Mx. Sage. Were they equivalent to Ms. V to the Bunks?" I asked her as I continued to scan the journal pages.

"I think so. It's been so long since I've seen them that I can't recall any specific details about their appearance or our interactions," she exhaled defeat and went quiet in her thoughts.

I flipped through the pages of the paper journal. I stopped on a few entries in other languages before putting it down, picked up the plastic file with my name, and began to read the plastic pages. We sat in silence while I read the documents in front of me.

I opened the file and saw it was labeled "Nitris_5468_2.5" at the top of the page. "What are these numbers after my name?" I asked.

"The number of your creation follows your name, then it ends with the type of DNX you have," Sahara explained, "So, you are the 5468th human to be born on Pangea, but the 2.5 means that you are in the first generation of alterations to the "perfected" DNX 2.0. If it helps to understand where we are in the process, I am the firstborn of the 3.0 improvements. You and I have abilities that the other people on Pangea don't have, yet."

"Over five *thousand* people seems like many people have been created here, but our population is only 257," I said, then I realized that wasn't right, "Well, 258 when we include you. I thought our DNX made us live longer. Shouldn't we have a much higher total population count to include the elderly people?" I was trying to make sense of the math.

"Besides The Elders, how many old people have you seen in the Dark Flats?" She asked, and I thought about it.

"I haven't seen any. The oldest person I know of is Sal, and he is 45 but looks like as old as The Elders with gray hair," I noted what I had seen.

"Do the elderly people who retire move to the Richies level or something?" She asked me.

"That's what they say, but I haven't been up there besides work-study," I said.

"I think you and I would know if more things were hidden on board than just elderly people. Do you ever feel like the station is talking to you or leading you?" Sahara asked me while I was still looking down at the file.

I looked up at her and asked surprised, "How did you know that?"

"It's all in the file. I'm glad I'm not the only one who feels like that," she said knowingly.

I was reading the upgrades section, and things started making more sense.

Subject 5468 has reduced appetite to keep ration intake low. Altered digestion maximizes smaller ration portions to fuel the body. Sleep requirement has been reduced, which will allow for longer working hours. Brain scan shows usage is at 30%, increased from 15% as part of the first round of the subject's station integration. Link with operating systems for optimization of machine maintenance appears successful. This will reduce the need for additional computers to operate the station. Eidetic Memory Upgrade is successful, resulting in advanced learning skills and maximizing labor output.

"I have all these pages memorized because I have the same upgrades; and more," Sahara told me while I was reading.

"This file has everything about me, even why my hair is black," I said as I continued to look through the plastic pages of my file. "The blonde gene was recessive, so they deleted it, which made room for other 'gene alterations'. I'm just a science experiment.

But this still doesn't explain why no one wanted to adopt me. Nothing weak about my genes, but I still wasn't chosen for some reason."

"Keep reading," Sahara said.

I turned the plastic page to the alterations and saw in bold red letters, "HOLD FROM ADOPTIONS." I looked up to meet her eyes and saw everything clicking into place.

"You could have had a family that loved you, but you were held back for something else. I know this is a strain," she said, "I'm sorry I must overwhelm you with all this information. This is why I need your help." Sahara said as she let out a sigh.

"Every day, I learn more about The Elders and how society operates on the station, and every day I'm left with more questions," I said, trying to stay calm. "Why do The Elders get to make all the decisions about us? I don't want to service ration machines or oxygen recyclers daily for the rest of my life. I want to make a difference and do something bigger. I want to pilot an exploration ship to other galaxies and see where humans can settle! I thought I was worthless all this time, and no one would ever want me," I continued, "But being here now and reading this file, I find so many special things about me. Since Human 2.0 scientists have removed physical and mental illness from our DNA, people aren't plagued with hereditary diseases or defects. We need less food to sustain us, with optimal efficiency while processing small amounts of food and water," I went on listing what I had read.

"There are also unknown side effects of genetically altering human DNA to DNX. Some of which has caused abnormalities in a few individuals," Sahara said, gesturing to herself and showing she understood the file.

"This must be where I get my ability to walk without being detected by technology. I'm part of Pangea in a more mechanical sense."

"That, along with integrating the station's operating system," Sahara added. "The AI thinks that you're part of it."

"I'm still processing the idea that you were only present in my head these last few days and weren't there physically," I said.

"I might have been in your head, but I had fun getting to know you and being with you," she said, and we had a light-hearted laugh.

"Do you think you'll be safe here?" I asked her.

"I don't know," she said, "I wished that I had been more prepared. My only plan was to contact you and obtain the book files from the library to understand what these other files mean and how I'm different. I never really thought I would get out of the lab." Sahara was looking around the airlock.

We sat together in silence while I read the rest of my file.

"I have a weird question to ask, but I think it will help me understand myself a bit more," Sahara started and then paused before she asked, "Have you had any visions before?" Sahara asked me.

I was stunned at the question but found the words, "I wouldn't use the word 'vision'. More like a 'nightmare'. Sometimes I see these flashes of things, people, or events before they happen. It has been a part of who I am for as long as I can remember. I don't know what's wrong with me, but sometimes it can be lonely and scary, so I don't like talking about it to others. Plus, you're the first friend I have ever had, and I don't want to scare you away by telling you I have visions of the future," I sighed with unfiltered honesty.

"Hey," she alerted me, and I looked up to see her beautiful blue eyes. "You are special, and no one else in the universe is like you. I asked about the visions because I have had them more frequently since I connected with you. I'm unsure if I'm seeing something or sending what I see to you through our connection. I'm sorry if it's been my fault for causing you distress. I don't fully understand my abilities."

Her honesty warmed my soul, and I could feel tears burning. My first big personal secret that I shared with someone, and it was met with acceptance and love. This is what I always imagined friendship is supposed to be.

"I have another secret to share with you. Do you remember when the Solar Flare alarm went off?" She started to ask me and paused, waiting for my response.

"Yeah, that was really scary," I answered her with increased fear.

"I set off the alarm. It's in my upgrades that connect us to the mainframe of Pangea. If we run into any danger tonight, I can help by setting off another alarm that forces the emergency protocol," she explained with tenderness in her voice, then she touched my hand again.

"Were we in danger the other night? It sounds like you have a lot more upgrades than I do," I said and looked down. I doubted myself because Sahara seemed more controlled with her abilities. In contrast, I had only done mine by accident or without consciously knowing I was doing it.

"We weren't in danger. I thought I heard Emberson and needed a distraction. I'm not sure how I did it exactly, but it worked," she explained.

"Yeah, it did work. That alarm helped us blend into the crowd when we returned to the Bunks," I said. "When I got back, you were in my mind." I still realized all the times I thought she was with me and she wasn't.

Her OC buzzed on the floor with a notification. "Codex sent me another encrypted message," Sahara said as she opened the message on holo mode so I could read it too.

"Seeing you with your OC when you were a projection made me convinced you were there with me. Has Codex always been part of your life?" I asked her what I had been wondering since learning they had a connection between them.

"As far back as I can remember, it was always her. So far, she hasn't let us down and has shown her abilities to help us with the Library mission," Sahara reasoned.

"But *why* did she do that? How did she know that it was part of your plan? Did you write about it in your journal?" I asked her the questions that were on my mind.

Sahara sat for a moment, being still. I inadvertently held my breath waiting for her response.

"Did you write about the Library? I know you wrote about the people you watched, like me." I was beginning to worry about what she had written and if it could be blackmailed by Codex to get me to do crazy things for her.

"I did. I wrote about everything," she said, almost crying, "I wanted there to be a record in case...

Something happened to me. Even if nobody ever read it, I wanted to feel like I mattered."

I felt awful, "It's okay, don't beat yourself up about it," I said, "The way that I learned they were monitored was from the Bunks. The older kids would tell us that we should never write secrets in our OCs because the teachers and everyone could read anything we had to say. They told us, 'if you want to keep a secret, don't write it down in your OC.' But nobody ever told you that."

She sniffed and wiped her nose on her arm. I got back to the matter at hand. "What did Codex say tonight?" I asked.

"Codex has given us details about how to disconnect the drugs from the Lumpen rations and how to do the Aristocrats' also," Sahara read off her OC "This says we should disconnect it from the Lumpen food supply before distributing morning rations. 'The drug doesn't stay in the system for very long, which is why it is added to every meal served' she says. There's a map attached too. It looks like the drug supply comes directly from the Heart Office."

Sahara brought up the image that showed a layout of Pangea. A flashing line depicted where the drugs were being piped into the mixing station that Quincey had shown me earlier. I wondered if they knew about it.

"Codex wants us to do this right now?" I asked her.

"I guess so. It's just after 02:00, and rations are dispensed at 06:00. We should get this done now," Sahara said as she started to stand up and unhooked the nearly empty IV bag.

"This is all happening so fast," I said with

increased anxiety.

"I believe in us. We have all the upgrades we need," Sahara said with a smile, obviously trying to put me at ease.

"Ha, I guess so," I replied with a forced laugh.

"I think we can trust Codex," Sahara said, "She helped us in the Library and assigned you to Ration Maintenance. We should do as she asks and not risk getting on the wrong side of The Council."

"I didn't agree to anything...," I couldn't keep the resentment out of my voice.

"I'm here now. I'll do it alone if you don't want to. Please don't feel pressured into something you don't want to do." Sahara insisted.

I couldn't let her do it alone.

"Let me look at Codex's message," I asked. "I guess it doesn't matter what we send on our OCs. We can assume that Codex read your journal about the Library too," I said as I locked eyes with Sahara. I watched her bring up the message with the holographic map display attached. I realized that the map wasn't current. The Mess Hall on the map is massive, and the wall of rations was on the farthest side. Not even Codex, knew about the hidden room. I noticed the trash chutes location remained the same.

"I think I know what to do. I hope you don't mind, but you'll get those white clothes dirty," I said with a laugh.

We left the airlock, went to the small service room near the old service elevator under the Mess Hall, and grabbed flashlights and an extra multi-tool. Tools are stored in the service elevators if a worker needs something quickly during an emergency. Still, it was only the most essential items. I grabbed two cloth bags from the bottom of the tool shelf. They were stained and worn and smelled like they hadn't been washed in a while, but they didn't seem to have any holes, so I stored our supplies in them.

"We can't use the elevator because it might set off an alarm, but I learned that these chutes go straight up. There's an opening on the Lumpen level and the Richie level. Follow me." I instructed Sahara, and we walked into the ration recycling room. I knew the recycling chute for any leftover rations were above me. I used the multi-tool to remove a panel from the chute. As Quincey described during work-study, I lifted myself inside and quickly found the notches with the blades extended. I was able to use them as handholds to climb up.

"You're going so fast!" Sahara called after me as she shined the flashlight up.

"Come on, you can do it!" I encouraged her. "Just climb up like I did!"

"Yeah...," she replied, putting the flashlight in the bag with the other tools and began climbing. I paused where I was until she could catch up to me. It looked like she was still feeling weak and had trouble pulling herself up but had no complaints.

I exited the chute on the Lumpen level first and turned around to help Sahara. I was thankful we were small enough to fit in the opening. When Sahara was in the Mess Hall next to me, I walked over to the hidden wall where Quincey had work-study.

"This wasn't on the map," Sahara said as she looked around.

"I know. It's another reason why I'm not sure we can trust Codex. Over there is the food recycler computer. It pumps the ration goo out of these machines." I said and tapped the wall that we had walked behind. I started to undo the screws on the back panel to expose what was being fed into the machines. My hands were tingling like they had before. I thought that might be one of my abilities.

The tubes were going in two directions. The main gray goo went back toward the large recycler. Then there was another tube with a clear liquid in it. That tube goes back and under the floor beneath me. I pulled it gently to see if there was much slack, planning to track it to its source. I shined my flashlight under the floor, trying to follow the tube with my eyes.

"Whatever the clear liquid is, it's coming from the Heart Office like Codex said it would be," she said as she followed my light with hers.

"Let me 'adjust' the ration machines. That way, The Elders will think everyone is still being drugged." I said confidently as I cut the end of the tube with the clear fluid connected to the gray goo and let it drain straight down into the floor space, back the way it came.

Sahara held the light for me and helped me re-screw the bolts in the panels when I was done disconnecting the tubes. Then we headed towards the Richies level by leaving the hidden room, climbing back into the recycling chute, and going up another level. We climbed faster but kept our steps light in case anyone was around.

"This climb is getting harder and harder to go up. I hope heading back down will be easier. I don't think I've been this active my entire life," Sahara said between gasping breaths. I could hear the fatigue in her voice.

"This is the most direct way into their Dining

Hall. The Richies don't check inside the hall, only the hallway leading to it. I learned that in work-study with Taliah. We had a *run in* with Security," I said and laughed at my joke. When I reached the top, I grabbed the inside lip of the chute, and pulled myself up and out, landing softly on my feet. I crouched low to the floor and quietly looked around the empty Dining Hall. I called back into the chute to see if Sahara needed help. She batted my hand away when I reached down to help. She hoisted herself out of the chute alone. I stood back, impressed.

"Where do we go from here?" She asked. She hunched over and put her hands on her knees while she caught her breath. I wondered if she had been showing off for me.

I glanced around the room and went to where the ration machines should be. I saw an opening in the wall panel where people placed their dishes to receive the rations, but not the ration machines themselves. I walked around where the rations were distributed and saw an access panel in the side wall. I opened it with my tool and began to examine the tubes inside, but something didn't feel right about this panel. I didn't get the tingling feeling in my hands.

"Nitris!" Sahara called me. "Did you see they have actual fruit in here? In the medical books from the Library, I read that plants grown in nature were the best for nutrition," Sahara was shining her light on the wall opposite where I was. I looked over and saw a wall of fruits and vegetables in the soil.

"Quincey told us that the Richies grew produce here. They didn't have to eat the same recycled goo rations we do," I said with a huff of frustration. I was angry. I got up and hastily approached the produce service panel, forcing it open.

"Bring the light over here. Let me see if they are being drugged like we are," I asked Sahara, and she quickly approached me.

I took a few minutes to trace the tubes to see where they led. I told Sahara, "There's a clear liquid tube feeding the plants' water supply. All this food that has already been grown is drugged."

"Can you re-route the drug tube to under the floor like you did on the Dark Flats?" She asked, and I was already looking to trace the tubes.

"I think so, but I don't know how long it takes for new food to grow. I haven't learned that yet. Quincey told us everything was from the Mess Hall computer," I said as I began to cut and redirect the tubes.

"The Richies will have to deal with the drugs a little longer than we do," Sahara observed.

"Just as long as they do wake up. I think there's another station over here for their ration goo. They still have to eat it like we do for the missing nutrients." I explained to Sahara. My hands felt electric as I started removing the next panel on the nutrient dispenser. "Bring the light, please?"

"Sure!" She came over and shined the light on the maintenance panel.

The first thing I saw was that there was a clear liquid tube, but no gray goo tube. "Their rations are green. Ours are gray. That must mean we are getting their leftover recycled rations too. I can't believe how poorly we have been treated all these years," I said as I worked to re-route the clear liquid back the way it came. The rage made it hard to concentrate. Not only did the Lumpen get used clothes and tablets, but we also got used food.

"Alright, I'm done. Let's get out of here." I said as I nodded my head in the direction of the trash chute. My blood felt hot with rage.

"Back the way we came?" Sahara asked with hesitation in her voice.

"It's the safest way to get back and not get caught," I replied and continued to the chute.

I tossed my bag on my back and lifted myself into the chute. I gave Sahara an encouraging look before I started descending. I was going down slowly and waiting for Sahara to get her footing in the first hole.

"My bag strap is stuck on something. I can't get it free," she said to me from above.

I started climbing back up toward her and saw her struggling to free her bag. Just as my head was on the same level as her feet, she jerked back, hitting the side of the chute with a loud clang that made the hair on my arms stand in response. Something didn't feel right.

"I got it," Sahara said. At the same time, I heard a machine power on, and a rush of panic washed over me. Somehow, she had accidentally turned on the chute grinder.

"Oh no," I squeaked before acting on instincts. I grabbed Sahara's ankles tightly with both my arms. In the same motion, I pulled my feet out of the ridges in the side of the chute where the knives rested. I yanked hard and let my body weight and hers get us down fast through the chute. I had never been so thankful for artificial gravity before. It helped to pull us down. Sahara screamed when she hit her head on the chute when I pulled her off balance. We fell down the chute much faster than when we went up. I looked up and saw the first set of blades at the top extending from both sides, covering the opening to the Richies Dining Hall.

Sahara screamed as the blades slammed centimeters away from the top of her head. I saw her close her eyes before the next set of blades extended out and nearly gave her a haircut. I held my breath and watched in terror as each blade shot out from the sides where our feet had been.

I landed hard on the steel floor in the service level we had entered from. Sahara landed on top of me, momentarily knocking the air out of me. I tried to roll her off of me, but we both took a moment to get our bearings. She got up and sat down next to me. I pushed myself against the wall and inhaled deeply to catch my breath.

"That was close," I managed to spit out.

"I thought you said it *moves* the leftovers down, not *cuts* it down," Sahara said as she looked up the chute as the knives were still working their way down to the bottom.

"At least we got out. Come on, we should get you back to the airlock," I said as I started up to my feet. "And I need to be in the Bunks before that machine alerts security and initiates a sweep."

We tiptoed back through the tunnel. My whole body hurt, and I wasn't sure if it was from the fall or the mental exhaustion of knowing we were both almost cut into tiny pieces. I was looking forward to my bed for the first time in a long time.

"I'll see you tomorrow," I said and hugged Sahara in the airlock. I wasn't sure why I did it. I felt compelled to, and the human contact was pleasant. I didn't feel so alone. I also didn't want to leave her alone down here. "I'm sorry that your white clothes got so dirty."

"Now I fit in more. See you tomorrow," she replied, returning the hug.

We stood there for a moment, holding each other. Then I took a deep breath and released her.

I walked back to the ladder and started to go up when I felt shocked as my hand touched the first rung. I let go, shook my hand, and heard footsteps above me. The adult night workers were heading to Cora's to get their PSCs removed. I looked at my OC, and it was almost 06:00. There was no point in trying to make it to the Bunks and attempting to sleep. I had pulled an all-nighter and now had to blend into the crowd.

Chapter 27
Mr. Kline

Jexa was already out of bed and had left her chambers when I woke up. She loved to start her day with a Sand Shower. I didn't worry about being seen exiting her chambers since I shared my secret plans to move up to the Richies level. I didn't see any point in trying to hide our relationship. I will ask her to marry me when I get my promotion, which should be soon.

The sound of the other adults finishing the night shift was muffled behind the locked door. The notification for 06:00 hours wake up hadn't gone off yet, but it would soon. I got up and made the bed we shared. I was still tired and emotionally overwhelmed, but being with her always put my mind at ease.

I left Jexa's room and walked towards my chambers. The other Lumpen workers I passed in the hall looked exhausted from working all night. I was thankful that teaching allowed me to work the day shift. Before I had reached my chambers to get a fresh set of clothes, I saw Nitris walking towards the Bunks.

"You're up early. Where are you heading?" I asked Nitris. They seemed startled.

"Oh, uh, hi, Mr. Kline. I forgot my OC in the Bunks," Nitris replied and gave a nonchalant shrug. They laughed nervously and started to speed walk to the Bunks. I watched them go past the entrance and continue down the hallway. Confused, I thought about calling after them, but other things needed my attention. I continued the last few meters to my chambers. I had to grab fresh clothes and then head to the shower myself. I started to brainstorm how best to ask Jexa to marry me.

Chapter 28
Sahara

Ding, ding, ding.

A computer chime rang on the level above me and echoed down the ladder shaft into the service tunnel.

"Good morning, residents of Pangea! Today is March 5th, 2320, and the time is 06:00 hours UTC, time to start your day." The recorded voice of Intra was muffled by the sounds of people walking above. I hadn't heard the announcements when I was locked in the Birthing Lab. It was nearly soundproof there, but I knew Intra's voice from Kline's memories.

I decided to wait near the ladder's base for Nitris to drop clothes for me to wear. I stayed to the side to run and hide in the airlock if someone came down here. I wasn't tired even though I'd been awake all night, being the most active in my life. My arms were still sore from the climb. I opened my OC and started to review the messages that I had received from Codex.

One message I had intercepted was sent to Mr. Kline with a mathematical encryption code. I tried to figure out the math problem to open the file, but the encryption was too challenging. I wondered what Codex would send to him that would be different from what she had sent me.

Now that I knew my OC was being monitored, I didn't know if I should delete my journal or stop writing. I noticed that there was a wireless charging station near most access points. After I located it, I rested my OC on top to charge while working on the encryption. The sounds above me were getting quiet as people arrived at their designated eating or showering during this free hour.

Suddenly, a small bag fell down the ladder and softly hit the metal floor. I grabbed it and looked up the ladder to see if Nitris was there. I bent over and picked up the small bag, but when I looked up at the top of the ladder, I made eye contact with someone that wasn't Nitris. A girl about my age with blonde hair and brown eyes looked down at me, and we locked eyes. Her face showed shock and confusion before quickly leaving the ladder's top.

I ran over to my OC on the charger and quickly messaged Nitris. I had to word it carefully in case someone was reading these.

Thanks for the care package. Your blonde hair looked long this morning.

I sent the message and waited anxiously for a reply.

What?

I looked up and saw blonde hair.

I tried to be covert, but I'm unsure if they got it.

Oh, I'm not sure what happened. I'm heading to class now. See you later.

I changed into the dark gray pants, and shirt Nitris dropped down in the bag. The clothes had a strange smell and were a bit baggy on me, but they were much more comfortable than the sterilized dresses from the lab. I'd probably fit right in with the other children if I had shoes.

When my OC was done charging, I walked back to the airlock. I wasn't expecting any more messages from Nitris because class had started. I was on high alert in case I heard any unusual sounds like Emberson or the sounds of someone coming down here. Occasionally, I would hold my breath and listen to my surroundings.

It was a little after 09:30 when I received a message from Codex.

Did the rations mission get completed?

I wanted to keep the answers short and concise without divulging anything that could get Nitris or me in trouble.

Yes. I replied.

Excellent. Since you are not a registered citizen of Pangea, you will need to have Nitris submit an application for an audience with The Council to present the reasons for wanting equality. Tell them to submit the application as soon as possible and be sure to select 'yes' that they wish the meeting with the 'live stream' option. I will make sure that the application is approved. Do you have any questions?

Codex was straight to the point too.

I will let them know. I responded.

I didn't want to wait until Nitris finished class, so I quickly sent them another message:

Please fill out the application for an audience with The Council as soon as possible. Be sure to select 'live stream' for the meeting.

I didn't hear back from Nitris until 13:30, when they replied with a simple '*okay*,' That was all.

Chapter 29
Intra

It was almost 14:00 hours when I received an alert. It was a new application to meet with The Council. It had been decades since someone requested a conference, and I was confused about who would have the audacity to request Council members' time during the lockdown. I opened the application and saw it was from a Lumpen child named Nitris in the Bunks.

"What is this?" I said out loud to everyone in the Heart Office and projected the application onto the screens in the room.

"A meeting request," Echo answered.

"Yes, it is a meeting request, but why did we receive this now?" I asked the room again.

"Maybe they want to talk about something happening on board?" Codex asked, trying to help.

"Something happening on board that I'm not aware of?" I disdainfully asked, "I cannot access the OC for this Nitris child. Unacceptable." I said with frustration.

"Monitoring all students' OCs has been disabled," Echo told me, "You approved it yourself."

"I see. Well, then, this meeting must be scheduled to take place as soon as possible. Tomorrow at 08:00 hours." I instructed Echo.

"There are no schedule conflicts at that time," Codex confirmed.

"I know that," I responded to her, "Deny the live stream request. We will record the meeting for the archives but not broadcast."

"Meeting has been booked with confirmation sent to Nitris," Codex followed my instructions, then asked, "Why are we meeting them so soon?"

"I do not want to give this Nitris person more time to prepare," I hated having to explain myself. "If they want to meet with us, it shall be sooner rather than later."

The other members of The Council nodded their agreement. I continued speaking, "While everyone is here, I wish to discuss other pressing issues. When Kline's testing has been completed, we shall terminate the pupil in the Birthing Lab. We shall then analyze the data gathered from the testing and her termination to determine how best to advance the next generation of DNX."

"Terminate the pupil from the Birthing Lab?" Echo asked, repeating to me.

"Correct. We are testing the living abilities and how long death will take," I said the facts that no one wanted to talk about.

"How will evaluating death be beneficial to us?" Echo asked.

"When they have been eliminated, we can time how long death takes on the organic tissue. Using that data for the next process of growing adults in the Birthing Lab instead of growing infants. If the pupil is easily terminated, we will update the DNX to create stronger organic tissue for the next generation of adults," I said plainly to limit the number of questions.

"How will growing adults in the lab be beneficial? Our studies have shown that the residents of Pangea are happier when they can raise a child and expand their family. Will we be replacing children with something else?" Codex asked ridiculous questions I didn't need to answer, but the other Council members were looking at me to reply.

"Growing adults and implanting memories for education will be more efficient for working. We can eliminate the need for classes and the Bunks entirely." I answered their question. Everyone nodded in approval and didn't have anything else to discuss. The silence was wonderful.

Chapter 30
Nitris

I was exiting the service tunnel and heard my name being called. I looked up to see Mr. Kline walking towards me. I struggled with what to say. It was before the AM call, and I wasn't supposed to be out of the Bunks yet. All these secrets were getting harder to keep. I told him I had left my OC in the Bunks to avoid being asked more questions. I walked briskly towards the Bunks but continued until I reached the Sand Showers. It wasn't until I was in nearly there that I remembered I didn't have a towel or change of clothes. I had to pull dirty clothes and a towel from the laundry pile. I got clothes for myself and Sahara and used the shower stall to conceal my actions.

With my eyes closed, I took deep breaths and reached for the air pressure rinse line. I ran the cold air over my face and hair, then moved to the rest of my body. I could hear others coming in and getting ready for their day. There was a giggle and a happy good bye before I was startled.

"Where have you been?" I heard another voice from the other side of the Sand Showers. I grabbed my towel and wiped my eyes. I looked through the crack in the door where it was locked, so I could see who it was. Justice stood outside my stall with a towel covering her naked body. She must have been the giggle good bye to her girlfriend, Cyran.

"Keeping to myself like always. Why? Do you need something?" I said while I rubbed the smelly towel over the rest of my body. I needed to get the excess sand off that the air hose missed before I put my clothes on for the day.

"I know your secret," she said while pacing outside my shower stall.

"I don't know what you're talking about," I replied as I dressed behind my shower stall door.

"You're up to something. You're acting stranger than normal," Justice said in an apprehensive way.

"You always say I'm weird. Nothing new there," I said, which was the truth that Justice had told me multiple times.

"Something is going on with you, and I'm going to figure it out," she warned. "I've seen you in and out of the Bunks during night hours. You aren't as slick as you think you are."

"Figure out what? Nothing is going on. I think you're just bored. Find someone else to keep you entertained," I gathered my stuff and exited the Sand Showers towards the Mess Hall. She didn't reply.

I walked quickly out of the showers and headed

to the service tunnel ladder. I paused momentarily and pretended to tie my boots as two adults walked past me to get their PSCs. When they turned the corner, I quickly dropped the bag down the hole in the floor, stood up, and continued to the Mess Hall. I didn't plan on eating anything because I had no appetite, especially after seeing the tubes of drugs and learning all these secrets.

Instead, I walked the entire circumference of the Dark Flats. I passed the adult living chambers and work-study rooms before returning to Mr. Kline's classroom. I walked in, and the lights clicked on. I sat in my seat and decided to meditate before class began.

There was so much on my mind that I couldn't tell where one thought started and the other ended. I've always been thankful they taught us how to do Transcendental Meditation in school. It's probably a way to cope with being stranded in space without a creative outlet. I used TM to calm my mind and find clarity in my struggles.

As I began my personal mantra, it didn't take long for my breathing to slow down and my mind to clear. The hum of the machines faded away as thoughts entered my head. I ignored them, repeated my mantra, and got to a more profound calm.

I'm not sure how long I was meditating before the vision of Sahara covered in blood came to my mind with a force that made my body shake. The hair on my arms stood up. With my eyes still closed, I instinctively rubbed my arms to get the feeling to fade. I had to focus and get my mantra back to complete the meditation without getting a headache.

The unrelenting image continued to return with force. I stopped trying to fight and started to immerse myself deeper into it.

I was lying on a hard cold table somewhere I had never seen before. Looking up, I noticed bright lights above me, and then I saw Sahara's face more clearly. She looked older. Her scar was a faded white on her olive skin, and her face was tired and lined with worry. I couldn't make out the surroundings, but it didn't seem like any place I had ever been to.

I saw something written on Sahara's white coat "Voyager Labs". That was the most I could see before the vision vanished, so I continued my meditation. Slowly returning to reality, I started to hear my current surroundings, and the usual machine hums began to make their way back into my conscious mind.

When I opened my eyes, the light in the room made me squint momentarily. I looked around the room. Taliah was in her chair, turned around towards Justice sitting behind her. They were both looking at me and not talking. My cheeks flushed red with embarrassment, and I looked down at my OC, pretending to read. I thought they would say something for a moment, but Mr. Kline walked in and greeted the class.

As class began, I looked back down at my OC to bring up the lessons for today. I saw that Sahara had messaged me about my blonde hair, which made no sense since my hair was black. Then, when I looked up towards the front of the class, I realized that Justice had blonde hair, and maybe she had seen me drop the bag down to Sahara. I felt like I would throw up with anxiety. Justice must have followed me after the Sand Showers. Knowing her, she will be cruel to me or try to blackmail me. If Justice saw Sahara, there was no telling what she would do.

Chapter 31
Taliah

Ding, ding, ding.

When I woke up to Intra's recorded announcement, I immediately looked across the aisle to Nitris' bunk and saw that they weren't there. I felt terror run hot through my body, and I knew I had to distract Justice from seeing anyone missing. I jumped onto my trunk and kicked Justice's mattress where her feet were.

"Ughhh, I don't want to get up. Hey, weren't you sleeping next to me last night?" Justice said with a yawn.

"I woke up when you stole the blankets and went to my bunk. I'm hungry. Let's go to the Mess Hall and then the Sand Showers," I told her and stood before her so she wouldn't see Nitris' empty bed. She barely opened her eyes as she got up, and we walked to the

Mess Hall together still in our sleeping clothes. We beat the crowd, got our rations, and sat at our usual table.

"Is everything okay with you? Why'd you want to cuddle last night?" Justice asked me without looking up. She looked tired.

"I had to talk to Ms. Verban last night about all kinds of feelings I'm not used to. After that, I felt like I needed that human connection. Plus, I was freezing, and you are very warm." I told her a slimmed-down version of the truth.

"Do you want to discuss it, or should we ignore it?" She asked and looked up at me. She knows me very well. Sometimes I get upset or bothered, and talking about it only makes me feel worse. There are other times when talking about something made me feel better.

"Ignore. I'm too tired to relive it all again. Besides, you kept kicking me," I said, giving her a nudge with my shoulder, and we laughed.

"Hey, you both got here fast. I usually don't see you both until class," Apollox said as he walked over to the table with his tray. He sat at our table as usual.

"Yeah, we usually shower first, but someone was too hungry to wait," Justice said, pointing at my head to indicate I was that someone.

"Hey babe, what a treat to have breakfast with you," Cyran said as she sat beside Justice and kissed the top of her head.

"Taliah was hungry," Justice said with a shrug and ate her goo.

"How come you don't usually do breakfast first?" Apollox asked me.

"I like to get clean and then get breakfast and

take on the day," I said confidently.

"Then how come you don't follow the same schedule with Cyran?" Apollox asked Justice. She leaned forward and looked at him.

"I like to do my routine with my bestie," Justice said with a smile, and she squeezed my hand. Our small group of friends always ate the goo fast so we could talk without worrying about running late.

"I might not be your bestie, babe, but I will head to the showers now. Want to join me?" Cyran said as she stood up with her empty tray and put a hand out for Justice. When that happens, I usually don't see Justice again until class. They typically share a shower and stay in there as long as possible.

"Yes, please. See you in class," Justice said with enthusiasm as she stood up with her tray taking Cyran's hand and not looking back to the table.

I looked around the Mess Hall for Nitris to talk to them about how I covered for them last night. I didn't see them anywhere.

"What will you do when we have to move out of the Bunks?" Apollox asked, which surprised me by the drastic change in subject.

"I have no idea. Justice said I can move in with her and Cyran, but that sounds like a mess," I said.

"For real, though, would you look for a flatmate, or do you have your eyes on anyone in the Bunks for a potential ... romantic kind of mate?" He asked with a more serious tone.

"Why are you interested?" I asked with sarcasm. I tried to make it seem like a joke.

"I like you, Taliah. I think that we could be a good pair. I would like to be romantic in nature, but I can accept being flatmates too," he said, with no hints of sarcasm in his voice.

"I don't even know what I like," I replied honestly. "I haven't ever been interested in the people around me. We've been trapped in this daily routine, and that'll change again when we have to work full-time. Isn't there a saying that coworkers shouldn't be romantically involved?"

"That doesn't stop Mr. Kline and Ms. Verban," Apollox said, with his more chilled demeanor.

"You know about that, too?" I asked with a little more shock in my voice than I intended. I had thought that I was the only one who'd noticed.

"Who doesn't know about that?" He replied and gave me a little smirk.

For the first time, I was starting to see the man that Apollox was growing up to be. He was full of secret knowledge like me. I wasn't hungry, but my stomach did a little flip when he smirked at me. Maybe I have more options than being a third wheel to Justice and Cyran.

"We don't really get any time to get to know each other," I said as I looked up at him. His dark hair paired perfectly with his dark skin.

"We should change that," Apollox said with a smile that made my stomach flip again. I looked down at my empty try and felt my cheeks flush with embarrassment.

We stayed in the Mess Hall for so long that I almost ran out of time to shower before Mr. Kline's class. Apollox skipped showers completely because he would rather go at night after work-study.

I headed over to Mr. Kline's class and saw Justice waiting outside for me with a look on her face like she knew something and was excited to tell me all about it. I knew she was waiting for me because she waved and walked towards me as I approached.

"Something super weird happened, and I need to talk to you about it," Justice said eagerly. She reserved that tone for gossip or sharing secrets she had learned. I felt that this wouldn't be a good thing. I was worried that it might be a rumor about Nitris or me. I hated keeping secrets from Justice, but she couldn't keep anything private.

"Tell me after class," I said and walked into the classroom so she would be quiet. Usually, the bigger the secret, the more silent Justice becomes when others might hear it too. When she had heard about Segauce and Cyran's arm wrestling to see who could ask her out, she was silent for the entire day and waited until after lights out to tell me about it.

We sat in our usual seats, and Justice attempted to tell me the secret with only her head and eyes. Her brown eyes burned into me as she jerked her head to the side, trying to point me in the right direction behind her. I pretended I didn't get it, and then she turned around completely and stared at Nitris in their seat. They had their eyes closed and seemed to be meditating before class. When Nitris opened their eyes, we made eye contact first, and then they looked at Justice before finally looking down at their OC on their desk.

Class went by in an instant. When the alarm went off to signal the end of Mr. Kline's class and the start of work-study, I knew that Justice was anxious to tell me something big. I didn't want to be surrounded by my peers when she told me, so I walked quickly out of the class and headed to Cora's for my PSC.

"Hey, wait up," I heard Justice call from behind

me, and she picked up her pace.

I kept my speed the same to get ahead of the other people heading to Cora's so they wouldn't hear what Justice had to say. I still hadn't told her about helping Nitris last night.

"Guess what happened this morning after I left the Mess Hall," she said in a low tone but still audible to anyone walking past.

"You and Cyran consummated your marriage in the shower," I said coldly.

"No, but that would be exciting. You'll never guess it. I'll just tell you," she said, practically bursting at the seams. She looked around the hall to see how far away everyone was before she continued, "I saw Nitris dump their dirty laundry down the service tunnel. When I looked down the access ladder, I saw a girl grab the bag. Someone was down there, and she must smell bad if she's stuck wearing Nitris' dirty clothes," Justice said with a snicker.

"Do you have something against Nitris? Why are you going out of your way to be cruel to them?" I asked as I stopped walking, and she bumped into me.

"I thought *we* didn't like them," she said, implying her and I.

"Nitris is cool. They are brilliant and shy. Bullying someone because they aren't exactly like you is not nice," I said with a stern voice, so she knew that I was being serious.

"But they are your arch nemesis, remember?" She tried to point out that I was second and Nitris was first in the class.

"Come on, Justice, the bully dumb girl act is getting old. I don't consider Nitris my nemesis; you shouldn't feel like that. They are just another person we must live and work with for the rest of our lives. It takes too much energy to hate someone or to go out of your way to make someone feel bad about themselves. That goes for everyone on board. You have to grow up," I said as I started to walk towards Cora's again.

This time I didn't hear Justice following behind me. I didn't want to turn around and see where she was because I knew that was exactly what she wanted me to do. Instead, I got in line, and I saw her pass me and get in line. She had her arms crossed over her chest and a pout on her face. She didn't even try to make eye contact with me. She was making it very clear that she was not happy with me.

Apollox walked by, made a face at Justice, and then rubbed his arms like he was cold to imply that she was giving him the cold shoulder. It made me laugh, but I was legitimately upset with Justice and stuck in work-study with her sorting trash. The day kept on getting better.

Chapter 32
Nitris

After class, I walked to Cora's to get my PSC for work-study and saw Justice running to catch up to Taliah. That made me really nervous about what they would talk about. I worried about the strange message from Sahara and blonde hair. I picked up my pace to eavesdrop on them, but they were too far away until Justice stopped abruptly, and Taliah kept walking.

I checked my OC while walking to Cora's and saw a message from Sahara telling me to apply to meet with the Council as soon as possible. I replied to her with '*okay*,' and then opened the application on my OC.

Thankfully, there were only a few questions. I was asked my name and age, and I filled it in. Then it asked why I wanted to see The Council with a multiple choice answer where I had four options to choose from, A: Rations, B: Oxygen, C: Maintenance, or D: Other. I selected 'other' and the next question asked if I wanted to live stream the meeting on Pangea. I swallowed hard as I pictured everyone on board watching me with The Elders, but Sahara said I had to select it. I hit 'yes' to the live stream, and the application was complete. I put my OC back into my pocket and looked up in time to see Apollox and Justice about two meters in front of me. I hoped no one saw me make the application.

"Hey Justice, long time no see," I heard Apollox joke as he got closer to her. Justice looked at him, crossed her arms, and headed to the same line we were getting in. I didn't want to make eye contact with Justice. I was afraid she would say something mean or incriminating about seeing Sahara. I walked with my head down, looking at my boots each step. I stayed a few steps behind Apollox and ended up two people behind him.

"Hey, work-study partner," he said as he let the two people between us go in front of him in line.

"Hey, are you ready to learn more about rations?" I asked, trying to think of something friendly we could talk about.

"You know it. Is it just me, or is everyone on edge today?" He asked me and looked around the hallway line of people.

"I hadn't noticed," I lied and kept my head down. I don't like to look at someone and lie to their face. I had a sinking suspicion that I knew what was bothering Justice.

"How come you don't really talk to anyone?" He asked me boldly, and I looked up to meet his eyes, they were soft, and he had a slight smile on his face that was welcoming.

"I don't really know how to talk to anyone. I feel really awkward," I told him the truth, which felt much better than another lie.

"I don't think you're awkward. Maybe a little *too* quiet," he said and gave me a nudge with his elbow.

"It's hard to make friends when I don't know what to say to someone about anything," I said with a little laugh.

"Now we're friends," he said with a bright smile that made me feel safe.

"I like that we are friends," I replied, matching his smile with mine.

We stood together in a line, and although we didn't talk while the line moved, it didn't feel awkward. Apollox entered Cora's first and looked excited when he came out and told me to go in.

"Hello Starshine, looks like you're heading to the Richies Dining Hall this morning," Cora said as she scanned my wrist and looked at her OC. That must have been why Apollox is so excited.

"Really? Why?" I asked automatically instead of thinking about it.

"It doesn't say what you will be doing, but I have you all programmed for the areas for work-study. I'll see you later, Starshine," Cora told me and nudged my shoulder to get me out of the chair.

"Have you been up there yet?" Apollox asked me as I stepped out of Cora's chambers with my PSC on.

"I did it with Taliah when we worked on the oxygen recycler, but only for a day. Is this your first time going to the Richies?" I asked him and saw him smiling from ear to ear, clearly excited to go to the Richies level.

"Is it that obvious?" He asked and tried to hide his smile.

"Let's go find Quincey in the secret room," I said excitedly to be on the same level as Apollox. It was nice to have another friend.

Apollox set the fast pace for our minimal walk to the Mess Hall. His excited energy made me laugh and feel comfortable instead of the usual dread feeling I had when I was alone.

"Does this secret room make you feel we are doing something illegal?" Apollox asked as we opened the side panel and walked into the room behind the ration machines that weren't documented on Codex's map.

"It has a sense of danger," I said after we closed the panel behind us.

"Welcome back! Now let's go. No time to waste," Quincey said from across the room. They walked towards us and gestured to the panel that we entered from with their PSC on.

We walked back into the Mess Hall and exited into the hallway heading towards the service elevator. Quincey swiped their wrist and hit the elevator button. When the doors opened, we all walked in, and Quincey hit the button to go up.

"We have a lot of work to cover today. The Richies Dining Hall can only be accessed by the Lumpen workers when nobody is eating there," Quincey told us as we exited the elevator and headed toward the Dining Hall.

"Why?" Apollox asked.

"They don't like to see us. Most Richies don't even acknowledge the existence of Lumpen workers. We are beneath them, metaphorically and physically,"

Quincey answered as we approached the closed door to the Dining Hall. When we entered, they had to swipe their wrist to open the large door. The door locked behind us.

"The Dining Hall door locks between meals?" I asked Quincey.

"Yes, on the outside, to keep everyone out, including the Richies. No eating allowed between designated mealtimes," they answered.

"Sounds like another way the Council controls us," I said under my breath instead of in my mind.

"Now you're getting it," Quincey replied to my remark as they walked over to the furthest wall from the door, with Apollox and I following.

I looked up at the wall. It was covered in green leaves and flowers like what Mr. Kline showed us used to be on Old Earth. I hadn't noticed how pretty it was in my haste with Sahara.

"We've been assigned to replace the water filters that feed into the growing machines," Quincey said. "I haven't had to do this much since I started working in rations, but I got a notification from The Council that there were complaints about the taste of the food," they walked to the side of the growing machines to an access panel. Relief washed over me when I saw that it wasn't the same panel I had used to reroute the drugs.

"What are these?" I asked and lightly touched a green leaf.

"These are used for tea and coffee," Quincey said. They continued to work on unscrewing the panel in front of them.

"The Richies eat these pretty things?" Apollox asked and touched a flower by me.

"I keep forgetting that neither of you know how

much the Lumpen don't have. The Richies don't eat these; they gather them for fresh tea or pluck the beans from the vines. After that, they drop them in the dehydrator, over there at the end, before grinding it all up and adding it to fresh water to drink," Quincey said as they removed the last screw.

"They have to do it themselves? The Richies must hate that," Apollox said with a laugh and looked at me.

"It is one of the few things that aren't automated, but they seem to enjoy doing it. I've never had any because it's against the rules, but I've smelled it before, and it was like I could taste it," Quincey said, closing their eyes and deeply inhaling as they recalled the memory.

"You've never tasted it before, not even in secret?" I asked in a low tone, even though we were alone in the Dining Hall.

"Nope. I knew a teen from the Bunks named Dorro, who spent 4 months in Solitary when he ate ration goo from a tray, and that was in the Lumpen Mess Hall. If he was up here and got caught, he probably would have been executed instead," Quincey said with a shake of their head as they remembered how harsh the punishments were here.

"Executed for eating food? I thought we needed food to survive," Apollox asked, looking confused.

"Eating food that belongs to a Richie is a capital offense, and this place is loaded with functional cameras," Quincey said and looked around the room with their eyes but didn't point to the cameras.

I looked up and around the Dining Hall. My eyes followed their gaze, and I saw cameras in here that were clear of any markings on the walls with red circles and lines through them, like we had in the Lumpen Mess Hall.

My face flushed with embarrassment when I realized the cameras probably caught Sahara and me disconnecting the drug supply. I don't know why I hadn't thought about the cameras up here. The whole arrangement felt like a trap, and now I was even more certain the Codex had been gathering evidence to use against me. I looked down at the panel that Quincey was at and tried to focus on what they were explaining.

"This long attachment in the back filters the freshwater before it is added to the growing machines," Quincey said. At the same time, they pulled out the rectangular filter. It was wet but had no residue buildup like I had imagined.

"That looks new to me," Apollox observed.

"Me too," Quincey said. "But when we get an alert to do something on the Richie level, we must take care of it immediately," they put the old filter on the floor, then walked around to the back of the machine to show us where the new filters were stored. They took a new one out and installed it. "The filter only fits one way, so you can't mess anything up."

"How long does it take to grow food?" I asked if what I had done last night would work immediately, like with the Lumpen rations, or if it would take longer.

"Everything grows faster than it would have grown naturally on Old Earth, but it still takes a while," Quincey said. They pointed to the wall where I had dismantled the drug-delivery system the previous night. "Those bright red fruits over there are strawberries. They used to take about a month to grow on Earth, but we've accelerated the growing cycle to two days."

"Do we have to change the water filters because the water that is used goes into the produce?" I asked, curious how long the food would have been contaminated with the drugs from the Heart Office.

"Exactly. A great deduction, Nitris. Water is used to grow the food here, and if the filter is old, it will take the food longer to generate," Quincey said, confirming my suspicion. That meant the food would have drugs until new food was grown.

"Does the filter change the taste of the grown food?" Apollox asked while he scratched the top of his head.

"I think so, but I don't know from experience," Quincey answered.

"Do we recycle the filters?" Apollox asked.

"Yes, we recycle everything. We take the used filter and bring it down to the recycler room." Quincey answered. They picked up the used filter and walked toward the Dining Hall door.

"Are we leaving already?" Apollox asked with a sad voice.

"Yes, we are done up here, and it is best to leave as soon as the job is completed," Quincey said and gestured their head towards the door as Apollox sighed with disappointment.

The door opened automatically from the inside without needing a swipe. We turned right towards the service entrance with the elevator we took up here.

"It's you again. Where's your friend?" I heard a voice say from behind me. I turned around to see Dimitri, the Richie teen Taliah ran into while working up here for oxygen recycling.

"I'm not sure. I haven't seen her," I replied, looking down at the floor like Sal did when we first encountered Dimitri.

"Can you give her a message?" Dimitri asked me, and I looked over toward Apollox and Quincey, standing in the hall near the service entrance waiting for me. They both looked perplexed as to how I knew a Richie.

"I guess," I said in a calm voice, trying to hurry up this interaction.

"Tell Taliah I said 'hi' and hope to see her again soon," Dimitri said and looked at me.

"Okay. Is there anything else I can help you with?" I asked him what I should do and looked back at Quincey to see if they were angry at me. Sal had told us that we should always ask if we can help a Richie and reply 'okay' regardless of whether we could help them.

"Nope, I'm headed back to class now. Have a good day," they said with a smile and started walking towards Quincey and Apollox, who were still waiting for me. I noticed that Quincey looked down when Dimitri passed, but Apollox looked Dimitri in the eye. Apollox had a strange energy, he seemed jealous.

Quincey used their wrist to open the wall that led to the service elevator. We entered silently, and when the door to the Richies' hallway closed behind us, Quincey sighed with relief. They put the used water filter in a bag from the tool shelf and pushed the button for the elevator.

"What was that about?" Apollox asked me.

"That Richie knocked Taliah over when we were up here the other day. They wanted me to give her a message," I answered.

"What do they want with Taliah?" Apollox asked. I could sense the tension in his voice.

"They just wanted me to say 'hi' to her," I said with a shrug. We took the short elevator ride back to the Dark Flats in silence until we were back in the Lumpen Mess Hall.

"That was strange," Quincey said what we were all thinking. They opened the panel, and we all walked in and headed toward where the used filters got recycled.

"What should we do when a Richie wants to talk to us?" I asked Quincey.

"I don't usually see any Richies when I go up there for maintenance," Quincey answered, pulling on their PSC. "I try to avoid them because I know they've never had to wear one of these. It's frustrating." Quincey spent the rest of the work-study session showing us the steps to activate the filter recycler and how to check the main mixer for any errors. We went over everything a few times until Apollox understood it. The session passed quickly, and when the alarm went off to go to Cora's, Apollox and I hurried to stand in line together. Quincey took their time before leaving the Mess Hall.

"When are you going to tell Taliah?" Apollox asked.

"When I see her," I replied with a shrug and looked around the hall at the people walking by.

We stood in line in silence for a while until Apollox spotted Taliah. He nudged me with his elbow and nodded his head in her direction. She looked angry and was walking in front of Justice, who also looked angry.

"Hey Taliah, I met your Richie friend," Apollox said teasingly as Taliah passed us in line to go to the back.

"What?" She asked and stopped walking. She headed towards us in line.

"Dimitri from the other day asked me to tell you 'hi' and that they hope to see you again soon," I said, relaying the message.

"The idiot that knocked me over?" Taliah asked me and having a soft smile on her face that was erasing the anger that was previously there.

"One and the same," I said, making eye contact with Justice as she looked over at us talking but kept walking towards the back of the line.

"Hey, Apollox, can you switch places with me in line so I can talk to Nitris?" Taliah asked with a charming smile.

Apollox hesitated, then said, "Um, okay," he got out of line behind me and headed toward the end.

"We have a problem," Taliah whispered to me. I felt my head dizzy as I started to over think what the problem was.

"What's the problem?" I asked in a low whisper to match her tone.

"Justice saw you know who this morning," Taliah said and pointed down to the floor in a suggestive way to imply she meant Sahara without saying her name aloud.

I stared at Taliah with my mouth open but couldn't think of anything to say in response for a moment.

"What's Justice going to do?" I asked.

"I don't know, but she is in a bad mood," Taliah said ominously. "I hate keeping secrets from her. Maybe we should tell Justice everything. It would be better to have her on our side than have her be suspicious and watch us constantly. Remember when Segauce tried to tell Justice 'no' when she tried to change seats to be by Cyran in class?" Taliah reminded me of the yelling at the start of class that day.

I remembered when Justice asked Segauce if he would change chairs with her so that she and Cyran could sit by each other. When he said 'no', she started yelling at him and got in his face calling him an 'air-suck' and worse. Mr. Kline had to practically pull her off of Segauce's desk and tell her to sit where she had been sitting, behind Taliah.

I shook my head no and whispered my doubt, "I don't think she can keep the secret."

"I think she can if we say it right. Let me talk to her and tell her what's going on," Taliah said before she stepped out of line and headed towards the back. A few moments later, Apollox returned and took Taliah's place in line.

"Today just keeps getting more abnormal and I don't know what's going on," Apollox said.

"What happened?" I asked and leaned into the hallway to look around the bend to see if I could see Taliah, but she was too far around for me to see her.

"Taliah told me to switch places with her again," Apollox said with a chuckle. "Justice didn't seem happy about it, but that's not my problem. Whatever gets this PSC off me faster."

I thought about what would happen if Justice started to yell and scream down the hallway about seeing someone in the service tunnels. I anxiously tapped my boot on the floor until the line began to move.

When I was free from my PSC, I headed to the airlock but didn't find Sahara. I couldn't figure out where she might have gone. I started walking towards the trash chute we had used to get to the Richies' Mess Hall.

I heard people talking and quickly hid behind the vast oxygen recycler duct. Thankfully, it wasn't hot like the artificial gravity generators. I waited until the two men with PSCs walked back towards the Dark Flats.

No one else knew that Sahara existed except Mr. Kline. I didn't think she even had a scanner chip in her wrist like the rest of us. I hadn't asked her, but I assumed she had no identification since she had only lived in the Birthing Lab. There would be no way to trace her movements. If she disappeared completely, would anyone even believe me that she'd existed? Taliah hadn't even met her yet.

When I got close to the chute, I looked up and saw the black bottoms of Sahara's Feet in the trash chute. I hurried over to her and tried to help her down.

"What are you doing up there during mealtime?" I asked through gritted teeth as I grabbed her legs and helped lower her to the floor.

"I was trying to get this," she said as she removed a strawberry from her pocket. She sniffed the fruit before continuing, "They just threw this whole thing away. What a waste! I have never had solid food before, and this smells delicious. Let's share it."

"We can't eat that! The plants they have already grown still have the drugs in them," I objected, "I don't know how long it takes to grow the new batch without the drugs, everything up there is tainted, and we shouldn't eat it. You risked your life going back through that chute. You could have been diced into a million pieces, all for a piece of drugged fruit? If you are that hungry, I can give you my rations. Just ask.

I'm happy to share if that means keeping you safe."

I grabbed the strawberry out of her hand and hugged her. I was so scared she had been caught and taken away, and I would never see her again. I didn't think I would be able to go on without her. I never thought I would care this much about another human.

"I figured we deserve a little treat after all the running around we've been doing. I thought this would be drug-free. I don't know how long things take to grow. I didn't even know it was called a 'strawberry' until you said it," Sahara said, looking down at the floor with disappointment.

"Come on, let's figure out what I will say to the Elders tomorrow. I don't want to look like a fool on the live stream in front of the entire population," I told her. I put the tainted strawberry in my pocket as we walked back to the airlock silently, but I held her hand the whole way.

Chapter 33
Ms. Verban

Ding, ding, ding.

When the alarm went off for lights out, I realized I was late to check on the children in the Bunks. I had been eating with my friends in the Mess Hall and didn't realize how time flew by. I was preoccupied and anxious about possibly getting a higher-ranking job when Silas got promoted. Keeping that secret from them overwhelmed me.

"Oh no, I'm late," I said as I grabbed my leftover rations tray and stood up from the table I was at with Dorro and Azriel. I looked around the Mess Hall for Silas, but he never arrived for night rations.

"Do you remember when we would be late to lights out almost every night?" Azriel said to Dorro with a soft nudge on his shoulder.

"I remember how things used to be more

flexible, but it has gotten worse since the lockdown," Dorro replied to his husband.

"I miss going to the Library and watching the archived black and white movies with you," Azriel said to Dorro and kissed him.

"I'll see you both tomorrow," I said, walking my tray over to the recycler.

"I thought your ward, Nitris, had a meeting with the Council tomorrow?" Azriel reminded me about the notification we all got during work-study hours.

"I feel so fritzed recently. I'm not sure where my head is; yes, tomorrow Nitris will see The Elders," I said and looked at Dorro. He usually got agitated at the mention of The Council members. I tried to make it sound nonchalant.

"I hope Nitris will be okay," Dorro said with compassion.

"Did The Council summon Nitris?" Azriel asked me, and I realized he was behind me.

"Maybe, but I'm not sure," I speculated, walked the meter to the recycling chute, and disposed of my dirty tray with the others in a pile.

Walking out of the Mess Hall, I said good night to my friends and started to walk to the Bunks. I saw Nitris with their back to me walking in the same direction.

"Nitris?" I called out to them. They stopped in the middle of the hallway without turning to face me. It seemed like they were frozen in place, so I asked, "Is everything okay?"

"Yes, Ms. V. I'm sorry I'm late to the Bunks," Nitris said as they turned around but kept their eyes on the ground.

"Where were you coming from?" I asked them

and looked around the empty hallway.

"Um, I was anxious about my meeting tomorrow, and I decided to walk around the Dark Flats a few laps," they replied but wouldn't make eye contact with me.

"Do you want to talk about it?" I asked and placed my hand on their shoulder to comfort them. They turned around slowly to face me.

"There are many things that I want to do, but I don't know where to start. I'm overwhelmed and have a lot of emotions that I can't define," Nitris said, and I felt them relax their shoulders under my hand.

"Let's have a little talk. Maybe it will help you feel better. You can wait in my chambers while I complete the lights-out check in the Bunks. I'll be there in a few minutes," I suggested to Nitris, and they gave me a small smile of appreciation and nodded yes.

We walked the last few meters to my chambers, and I swiped my wrist to let them in. I said, "Make yourself comfortable. There is a couch over there if you want to relax. I'll be right back."

"Thanks, Ms. V," they replied and entered my chambers. I walked briskly to the Bunks and did my head count. Everyone, except for Nitris, was accounted for. I told the children good night and turned off the manual lights. The door to the Bunks is always open, and the hallway light casts shadows into the large room.

I walked back to my chambers, it had only been a couple of minutes, and when I entered, I saw Nitris curled up on the couch, asleep. I desperately wanted to help them and make them feel safe. I never had a ward be summoned to the Heart Office, and I still wasn't sure why Nitris was going to see The Elders. I grabbed my blanket from my bed and covered Nitris to keep them warm. I sat at my desk and thought about everything that had happened in my lifetime, which made *me* feel overwhelmed. I couldn't imagine what was going on in Nitris' head to feel like this.

Dorro changed so much after his time in Containment, and I was worried that it would happen to Nitris too. Dorro used to be a talkative, eager young man. But after he suffered isolation for four months in Containment, when he emerged, he was forever a changed man. That was 18 years ago, and he barely spoke. He vowed never to go back, which made him a hard worker.

The sudden vibration in my pocket from my OC startled me away from my thoughts. It was a message from Silas.

I'm sorry, but I won't be able to come to you tonight. I have to finish the thing. Good night, I love you.

He must be talking about his secret assignment but can't talk about it. All these secrets he keeps from me get me worked up to the point that I get infuriated when I see him. I didn't bother to reply to his message. He would know that I have read it. It was probably for the best that he wouldn't come over, anyway. I was worried about Nitris and dozed off.

"Ms. V?" Nitris said, and I stirred from a light sleep.

"Nitris, is everything okay?" I asked as I adjusted myself to sit in the desk chair. I touched my OC to display the time, 02:00.

"I'm sorry that I fell asleep before we could talk," Nitris said with a sad sigh. "And for waking you up. I didn't want to leave here without saying 'good bye', just in case."

"What do you mean 'just in case'? We can still talk," I opened the conversation for them to share if they wanted to.

"I don't know what will happen at the meeting, and I'm so scared. I don't want to die or go to Solitary Containment. I'm already so lonely," Nitris said with sorrow as they sat at my desk, leaning on their elbows and resting their heads in their hands.

"The Council is here to help us maintain balance so that we can all continue to live in space," I tried to reason, "I'm not sure why they summoned you, but I know you're a good person, and they wouldn't want to punish you."

"I asked to see them. I submitted the application we have on our OCs," Nitris said, and my jaw dropped unintentionally.

"Do you have something you'd like to talk with me about?" I managed to choke out those words.

"I have a lot of secrets. So many that I don't even know where to begin. I feel exhausted from everything that has been happening," Nitris said as tears started to well up in their eyes.

"Secrets? You're still a child. What kind of secrets do you have?" I asked, confused about what they were trying to convey.

"It might be better if you don't know, and then you can stay safe," they told me and closed their eyes while tears started to flow more freely.

"We can always make a pinky promise," I said, extending my closed fist with my pinky across the desk.

Nitris opened their eyes and made an awkward chuckle. Then they met my hand with theirs, and we shook on it.

"I just want to have a fair shot at life instead of being assigned a job that would be my life. I have to do something, to change something. I don't know what I'm trying to say," Nitris said with a head shake and some more tears.

"I know how frustrating it is to follow these strict rules and how unfair it all feels, but we have to do it because if we don't, no one else will," I tried to comfort them, but I was upsetting myself trying to validate the system that has been treacherous to navigate since I was in their shoes.

"Why is it wrong to want to grow and do better?" Nitris asked me.

"I wouldn't say it is 'wrong' to want those things. I think that it is harder for some than it is for others. If you had been adopted, your entire life would have been different. But don't think, for even a moment, that because you weren't adopted, that somehow means you are worthless. You are an incredible young person, and I'm thankful I've watched you grow up," I said and reached over to the desk to hold their hand.

Nitris' hand met mine, and we sat silently for a moment before they pulled their hand away to wipe the tears.

"I hope everything goes well tomorrow. I'm here if you need anything," I told them and walked behind them to the door.

"Thanks, Ms. V. Can I ask you for a hug?" Nitris asked without looking up at me.

"I'd love a hug," I said, opening my arms. Nitris practically knocked me over with their enthusiasm, and we hugged briefly. Then Nitris turned and left my chambers. I watched them enter the Bunks from my doorway and returned to my chambers to sleep.

Chapter 34
Nitris

Ding, ding, ding.

I felt sick and anxious when I woke to the automated notification. I sat up in bed and waited for the Bunks to clear out. I didn't care if I would have to stand in a long line for the Sand Showers.

"Come on, let's go," Justice said to Taliah across the aisle from my bunk.

"I'll meet you at the showers," Taliah told her with a hug, and then Justice left the Bunks. It seemed like they had resolved their issues. It was a pleasant surprise because Justice gave me a slight smile and a head nod in my direction before she left.

"Today's your big day," Taliah said from the foot of my bunk.

"I feel like I'm going to puke," I answered honestly.

"I wanted to let you know that I talked to Justice, and she won't bother you anymore. She told me she was jealous and thought you were trying to replace her as my best friend." Taliah explained.

"Thanks for helping with that. Did you tell her about Sahara?" I asked in a low tone.

"Yeah, I felt like I had to. It's hard to keep secrets from her. But I told her she couldn't tell anyone, not even Cyran. I think she gets how important it is to keep this secret," Taliah said as I got out of bed and grabbed my clothes from my trunk.

"Do you want to join us at the Sand Showers or Mess Hall before Mr. Kline's class? Do you even have to go to class before your meeting?" Taliah asked excellent questions.

"Good morning Taliah, Nitris," Ms. V said as she entered the Bunks. "It's nice to see you two talking together."

"Hey, Ms. V," we greeted her as she walked down the aisle to the back where we were.

"Does Nitris have to go to Mr. Kline's class before they go to the Heart Office?" Taliah asked Ms. V what she had asked me.

"That's exactly why I'm here. Taliah, you can go ahead with your morning. I need to talk to Nitris alone," Ms. V said and started to usher Taliah out of the Bunks. Taliah went without protest.

"See you later, Nitris!" Taliah yelled over her shoulder as she exited the Bunks towards the showers, her towel wrapped the clothes under her arm.

"Please get what you need for the showers and follow me," Ms. V said in a kind tone. She didn't say any more, though, which made me feel even sicker with tension.

I gathered my clothes and my towel. I wrapped the journal in my towel and put it under my arm. I kept looking down at the floor while I followed Ms. V out of the Bunks.

"Am I in trouble?" I asked her as we exited the Bunks and went towards the Mess Hall.

"No, I wanted to do something nice for you before your meeting," Ms. V said as she swiped her wrist and opened her chambers but didn't enter, "You can use my chambers this morning until it is time for you to go to the meeting. I've already told Mr. Kline that you won't be in his class until after your meeting. I know that it is hard to find some privacy in the Dark Flats, and I wanted to give you a little help to clear your mind. I have a small Sand Shower that you can use, and feel free to make yourself comfortable."

"Are you not coming in with me?" I asked, a little confused.

"I trust you to be alone and not look around my things," Ms. V said with a slight nod into her chambers. It felt like a weight had been lifted off my shoulders, and I could breathe a little.

"I appreciate you, Ms. V," I said with sincerity. I walked into her chambers far enough away that the door would close and turned to look at her. She had sadness in her eyes but a forced smile on her face.

"I appreciate you too. I'll watch your meeting, and I'm sure it will go great!" Ms. V said with forced enthusiasm to hide her sadness. She tried to make me feel strong and put my mind at ease. It helped a little.

The Sand Shower stall was smaller than the stalls in the shared showers. I had to put my clean clothes and towel on the floor outside of the stall. I cleaned and scrubbed my scalp with my fingers so hard it hurt. The pain took my mind off of my anxiety. When I was done, I grabbed the towel from the floor, and the journal toppled out onto the floor. It opened on a page that was in another language. I left it there until I was fully dressed before I picked it up and looked at it. The page it was opened on was in a language that looked like the letters were all backward and made up. I noticed that someone had started to translate the page.

"How's it going?" Sahara said from the couch on the other side of the room, frightening me.

"What are you doing?" I yelped. "How did you get in here?"

"I'm projecting to you from the airlock," she explained.

"You scared me. I almost threw this at you," I said as I clenched the journal with a death grip.

"It would just pass right through me," she said as she stood up and walked towards me. Her projecting was flawless and it looked like she was really sitting on the couch. It was like she was really here with me.

"I'm scared," I confessed.

"I'm sorry I scared you. I wanted to be near you in any form," she said with compassion and gestured at herself.

"I'm glad you're safe. I'm scared about my meeting," I said as I sat down at Ms. V's desk with the journal opened in front of me.

"I can go with you as a projection. They won't even know that I'm there. Would that help your fear?" Sahara asked with tenderness.

"That would be very comforting," I told her as she sat in Ms. V's chair across from me.

"I won't leave your side," she said with a small

smile and I wanted to hug her.

"Thank you," I said, and I started to feel tears stinging my eyes.

"What's wrong?" She asked, as she leaned closer across the desk.

"Everyone is being so nice to me. Even Taliah was nice to me this morning. It feels like they all know that they won't see me ever again. Oh, by the way, Justice knows you exist now, too, and Taliah swore her to secrecy," I said as tears started to flow down my face.

"I disagree," Sahara said with a head shake.

"What? I believed Taliah when she said that Justice can keep *this* secret," I said and wiped the tears from my face.

"Not that part. I disagree that people are being nice because they think it's the last time they will see you. I think you're finally opening yourself up to see that there are people on board who care about you, and that is why they are being thoughtful," Sahara explained.

"I need to drink some water. All this crying is dehydrating me," I said with an awkward chuckle trying to stop myself from crying more. I stood up, walked to the wall for fresh water, and grabbed a cup from the shelf beside it. I finished a glass, refilled it, and returned to the desk.

"What language do you think this is?" I asked her, changing the subject.

"Russian, I think. I tried to translate it, but I couldn't. We are even deprived of learning," she said with a defeated sigh.

"How come we don't use the other languages from Old Earth anymore?" I asked her what was on my mind.

"There is an entry near the beginning that I saw that is already translated from Spanish. Flip to the front pages," she instructed me, and I did it.

"Oh, I think I found it, '*After the great integration, many people could not activate the computer voice commands due to their accents from the other countries. This forced everyone on board to adapt an English accent and enunciate words slowly to get the computer to understand their request*' Why do you think that was an issue?" I asked her with curiosity.

"I think it was another way to control people and disconnect them from the Old Earth and its traditions. Different languages must have been some of the most beautiful things we have lost. I wish I could hear how they sounded," she told me her best guess and desire.

"The deep control has gone on for centuries. I'm starting to doubt that I alone can change all this," I said, and fear flowed like heat through my body.

"I believe in you," Sahara said. "So does Codex. That must be why she wanted you to help me. So you can feel better knowing you have at least one ally on The Council."

"I still don't know if I can trust Codex. Why didn't she message me directly if she wanted me to do all this stuff?" I asked Sahara.

"When I was growing up in the Birthing Lab, all alone, she would come and sit with me. We would talk about how I was feeling and what it meant. She comforted me when I cried and felt isolated. Plus, she has delivered on all her promises to us so far. She wanted us to work together and advance our abilities for this meeting," Sahara answered. "The Lumpen are already off the drugs; hopefully, the Richies will eat the new drug-free food soon. Everyone will wake up emotionally, see the inequality, and try to change the imbalance. You will start that change we need. I believe in you," Sahara answered with hope.

"Thank you for being with me, even if you're not physically here," I said, putting my hand on the desk where her hand appeared to be and watching as it passed through hers and touched the desk.

"I'm happy to be with you, even if it is an astral projection in your mind. I wish I could hold your hand for real. After your meeting, during evening rations, maybe you can come down to the airlock, and I can hug you properly," Sahara said and hugged herself tightly.

The notification went off to signal it was time to start class. I instinctively stood up to attend class but then remembered that Ms. V and Mr. Kline weren't expecting me to attend class.

"There's only an hour before my meeting. Should we review what I'm going to say?" I asked Sahara as I sat back down.

"We can practice again, but I don't think you need it," she said, and we started to go over the big talking points.

The hour with Sahara went by very quickly. I was more confident but still felt overwhelmed and frightened.

"I should start walking over to the Heart Office," I said and stood up. I picked up the journal from the desk, put it in my back waistband, and covered it with my shirt.

"Try not to talk to me, even though you can see me. It might hurt your credibility," she suggested, and it made me laugh.

"Excellent point. No one will take my words seriously if they think I'm talking to myself. I feel better knowing that only I can see you and you're with me," I stepped out of Ms. V's chambers and into the hallway. Turning left, I walked toward the Mess Hall. As I passed, I saw Ms. V sitting at a table facing a screen in the Mess Hall, ready to watch the broadcast. She saw me and waved, and I returned the gesture to her. I thought about how others on board would watch on their OCs or screens in their work areas. The announcement for the live stream had been sent out when I was approved, but it wasn't a mandatory viewing.

Slowly, I walked through the Dark Flats, trying to remember every inch. I was thinking this might be the last chance I get. I passed the adult Lumpen chambers and the work-study classrooms. Around the next bend was the elevator that led only to the Heart Office between the Richies level and us. I looked at Sahara next to me, and she nodded yes for encouragement. I swiped my wrist to open the elevator, which automatically took me to the connecting corridor. Each step I took felt like a step closer to death.

When I reached the end of the corridor, I took a deep breath before approaching the door to the Heart Office. I swiped my wrist on the reader, and the door opened. The light from inside was bright, and I had to let my eyes adjust. It was different from the Dark Flats. I walked in blindly and looked around the room. The automatic door slid closed when I entered past the motion sensor. There were 5 people behind a semicircle desk. I was in the middle of the chamber, standing before them all. I saw the cameras that hung from the ceiling with blinking red lights, showing we were already live streaming station wide on the Pangea network. Everyone would be watching me. I waited until they instructed me on what to do.

The woman seated at the center of the semicircle desk spoke to me first. "Welcome, Lumpen youth. I am Intra, and I am pleased to meet you. These are my fellow council members. Neo and Prism," she gestured to her right, then to the left, and continued, "Echo and Codex. What questions do you have that we might answer for you?"

"Um, hello. It's nice to meet you all. Thank you for taking the time to meet with me," I struggled to find my voice while The Elders remained quiet.

"I'm here today to ask The Council if they could reexamine the current schooling structure to accommodate all children to learn equally. Requesting that you let our qualifications define our studies in chosen fields we pick for ourselves. This can make everyone more valuable to the Pangea Society instead of randomly assigning jobs to children at a young age. The current schooling structure ensures that the Richies-" I heard my own mistake. I coughed to correct myself when I continued, "the Aristocrats get all the higher RC credit jobs. The people on the Dark Flats are stuck with whatever is left. We should also have adoptions for everyone and not put a number of credits on it. Anyone should be able to have a family."

I glanced at Sahara, and it gave me confidence. I took a deep breath and prepared to continue, but I was stopped.

"If we were to change the schooling system now, then who would be doing the menial jobs?" Prism asked, "Those jobs need to be done. These are important jobs that the Dark Flats provide for everyone on the station," I turned my head to make eye contact while Prism spoke.

"I understand," I said. "And I have thought of a few options that we can do to find the right solution. We can have everyone participate and volunteer hours towards the less sought after, but still important, jobs. Then we can have an equal rotation where everyone contributes, and no one is above anyone else. It would also benefit many mentally if we eliminated the PSCs and let people walk freely anywhere on Pangea. We don't need to shock people to get them to do their jobs. We must improve morale and regain that sense of community like there used to be on Old Earth."

"I can see that you want to regain that sense of community," Echo began, "But it will take some time to deliberate and come to a conclusion that will benefit everyone."

I expected that The Elders would delay any of the changes I suggested. I looked at each of them, starting with Codex and working my way around to Prism. When I got to Prism with their freshly shaved head, I noticed something odd, part of their ear was missing.

It looked like a chunk was removed in the middle of Prism's ear. I could see the wall behind them through the hole. It could have been a birth defect from an earlier generation of DNX. Still, when I started to turn my head back to Intra, I saw Prism's ear fill the rest of the way in with my peripheral vision. I looked up and around at all the cameras in the office. I noticed they were pointing at the different Elders, and only a couple pointed at me.

I glanced to my side, locked eyes with Sahara's projection she gave me an encouraging smile. Then I realized something!

"How long would such deliberation take to come to a decision?" I asked Intra and put both my hands in my pockets.

"We cannot estimate a time for when we will have our decision. The best we can do is to continue our daily tasks to keep everything in good working order on Pangea," Intra replied. A little smile curled the corners of her mouth. That was the most human thing I had seen any of The Elders do during this meeting.

"Will The Council also be deliberating about discontinuing the use of the Proximity Shock Collars?" I asked The Elders and looked around at them to gauge a response. They all stared blankly at me until one of them decided to answer.

"We have previously considered discontinuing the use of the Proximity Shock Collars," Echo told me, "We think it is in the best interest for the residents of Pangea to feel safe and to keep to designated areas. The Proximity Shock Collars will remain in place."

"Why do we have PSCs at all? How are they providing safety to the residents?" I challenged them and looked around the room again. Their faces were blank. There was no response until Neo answered.

"The collars are a way to keep the residences of Pangea in their proper locations. By doing this, we eliminate theft of personal items, maintain ration control, and keep Pangea balanced while in orbit by the body weight distribution." Neo explained.

"When was the last documented theft or ration control violation?" I asked as I slowly took my hand out of my pocket, keeping my fist closed. "We Lumpen understand our place in this society and don't intend to jeopardize anyone's safety. We understand the rules set in place. I believe we can work and complete our jobs without the collars."

"The last ration violation occurred 18 years ago with Lumpen resid-" Codex started to say before Intra cut her off.

"We will take discontinuing the PSCs into consideration, in addition to the other recommendations for schooling. We will reconvene when we have come to a conclusion that works best for all people on Pangea. We appreciate you coming in to discuss your concerns for our society. You are excused and may return to your scheduled duties now." Intra said, with a dismissive tone in her voice, and gestured towards the door as it slid open.

"I just have one more question before I leave that I want on the official record, please," I said in an intentionally timid voice. I knew who I was dealing with now. Soon everyone on Pangea would see the truth. I looked at Intra for a sign to continue, and she nodded her head in agreement.

"Why do you claim to be human when you are a hologram projected by these cameras?" I asked as I pointed to the different cameras around the room.

"Perhaps you do not understand because you have never been here, but I can assure you that we are human and the oldest on board, thanks to DNX." Intra stood and gestured at the door for me to leave again.

"Is that so?" I challenged her.

I threw the strawberry in my fist at Intra's head, and it passed through her. It hit the wall behind her, squishing and exploding red liquid.

"You don't even know to pretend to put your hand up and block something from hitting you!" I yelled with satisfaction. "It passed through you as if it were nothing because *you are nothing*. You're not human. You're a machine pretending to be human."

The room went black when the door behind me slammed into place and locked. I heard a hissing sound, and it became hard to breathe. My lungs began to burn, and I coughed violently. I couldn't see Sahara in the darkness. The emergency lights on the floor were not on.

The last thing I heard was the same strange metal scraping noise I'd heard from outside the Library the other night. Only one thought came to me, Emberson.

Chapter 35
Mr. Kline

Time stopped.

The live stream of Nitris' meeting with The Council abruptly ended without explanation. I stared blankly at the holo display in the classroom that only read the words 'technical difficulties' in black and red. My students sat in stunned silence. I walked to the front of the room, powered off the holo with the manual button, and turned to face the class.

"What just happened?" Taliah asked directly.

"I'm not entirely sure," I answered honestly.

"What did Nitris throw at Intra that made the wall bleed?" Justice asked me.

"I think it was a strawberry from the Richies Dining Hall. I saw them yesterday at work-study," Apollox said from the back.

"What's a 'strawberry'?" Justice asked him.

"Are all of The Elders holos?" Cyran raised her hand to ask me.

"What's going to happen to Nitris?" Taliah asked as her eyes grew wide with fear.

"What are we supposed to do? If Nitris is right about the Elders being machines, does that mean all the rules are lies?" Segauce asked me.

"I don't know what any of this means," I said to the room of confused teenagers. I felt just as lost as they were, but I had to keep my composure. I needed Jexa.

The room filled with the teens' chatter as they speculated about what was happening. I returned to my desk and picked up my OC to message Jexa.

SOS, I need you in my classroom

Before I hit send, the classroom door opened, and Jexa stood there, looking as scared as I felt. She ran over to me and hugged me. When she let me go, she looked like she had regained her composure and had a gentle smile. She turned to face the class and asked them to calm down while we figured out what was happening. She turned back to me and spoke in a hushed tone.

"Silas, does this have anything to do with your mission for The Elders?" Jexa asked directly. She was in her emergency mode to take care of everyone.

"I hadn't thought of that," I confessed, and I remembered that Sahara was still missing since yesterday's testing session. I needed Jexa's help finding Sahara and knew I could depend on her. It is even more crucial now that Nitris has exposed The Elders.

"Everyone, we need to continue our day as planned, unless we are contacted by The Elders with different instructions," Jexa told the class. "Default protocol is to complete this class and then continue to your designated work-study assignments."

"How are we supposed to continue through our day when Nitris just exposed that The Elders as frauds? What are we going to do to get Nitris back?" Taliah demanded. Clearly, she was not concerned about observing protocol.

"We don't know what actually happened," Jexa responded. "It is possible that The Elders project themselves as a holo, which is what Nitris saw, but they are still people. Similar to when holo calls our OCs. We don't know what is going on until we get debriefed. As protocol dictates, we must remain calm and continue working until we are told otherwise."

"Where is Nitris now? Are they in Solitary Containment?" Apollox asked irrelevant questions.

"There is no benefit to speculation of the situation," Jexa soothed the class, "Let's get back to your schoolwork. I'm sure Mr. Kline and I will be given a full briefing sometime today. Until that time, we must proceed as normal." While Jexa spoke, I sat at my desk, speechless.

"Do you think The Elders killed Nitris?" Justice asked Taliah over her shoulder.

"I hope not," Taliah responded. "I agreed with what Nitris was saying. I didn't know that's what the meeting was about."

"I don't know how we're supposed to just sit here like everything is normal...," Apollox said what I had been thinking. He seemed more agitated than I had ever seen him.

"We don't want to end up like Nitris, so we should get back on schedule," Taliah told the class.

I looked at my students. They were afraid like I

was. I looked to Jexa for directions.

"Mr. Kline, have you sent the workbooks for the class syllabus for the day?" Jexa asked me, and it took my brain a while to catch up to understand what she was saying to me.

"Um, not yet," I said. I grabbed my OC, my shaking hand sent the workbooks to the class. I looked back at Jexa and nodded. Everyone's OCs dinged with the alerts.

"I need everyone to be quiet and complete as much of the workbook as possible. No one is to leave this room until it is time for work-study. Then everyone must proceed to Cora's for their PSCs and continue on to work-study," Jexa instructed the class, then asked, "Understood?" As if they had any other option but to listen to her. They solemnly nodded their heads in agreement and looked down at their OCs.

"Mr. Kline, a moment?" Jexa asked me in a low voice and tilted her head towards the door. I stood up and followed her out of the classroom.

"What are we going to do?" I said urgently when we entered the hallway.

"Shh, we need to keep the students calm," Jexa hushed me. "Let's go to Cora's chambers. We can all talk together and figure out the next steps," Jexa said as she rubbed my arm and pulled me toward Cora's, but I stood in place, my feet felt stuck.

"I have to tell you something," I said, panicked.

"Let's get somewhere private before we begin talking," Jexa advised.

"I shouldn't say it in front of Cora," I told her. She stopped in the empty hallway and turned to face me.

"What is it?" Jexa said with annoyance in her

voice. I knew that tone was reserved for punishing the children.

"The assignment I'm working on involves a young woman named Sahara," I confessed. "She's a special experiment that The Elders created. I've been teaching her, but she's been missing since yesterday. I have looked everywhere. I don't know what to do. If The Elders discover she's gone, they will execute me."

"There's *a child* that isn't living in the Bunks?" Jexa seemed confused momentarily, then a look of understanding came over her face. "Is that what you've been doing in the Birthing Lab? Testing a child kept in isolation?"

"She was being held in the Birthing Lab during the tests I was conducting," I explained with desperation. "She wasn't allowed to leave the lab under any circumstances. She had her own rations and bathroom facilities. Everything she would need in the same location. When I went there yesterday to conduct the tests during work-study, she was gone. I had to cancel our plans last night because I was trying to find her. I don't know where she could be, if The Elders took her, or if she is dead. You have to help me, Jexa, please."

"Here's what I think we should do," Jexa quickly devised a plan. Her mind was magnificent. "Let's not mention this to anyone for now. We will return to the classroom to ensure the children stay on task. When we are done getting the children in their PSCs and off to work-study, we will get Azriel and Dorro to help us in searching for Sahara." I nodded in agreement. We went back into my classroom and sat silently with the children.

Some of my students were completing their workbooks. Still, I could tell that most of them were sending messages back and forth on their OCs, speculating about what had happened. Jexa monitored her own OC, most likely waiting for instructions from The Elders. Everything about my life had changed in only a few moments.

About an hour before the alarm went off to begin work-study, Jexa put her OC in her pocket before she stepped in front of the teens and said, "Alright, it is crucial that you all go to Cora's and get your PSCs on and continue with work-study. Cyran, and Segauce, I know you two work in electrical and don't need a PSC. Please go directly to your work-study supervisor now. Everyone else, follow Mr. Kline and me."

The only noise in the room was from the chairs dragging on the floor as everyone stood up from their desks. Their feet shuffled as they headed out into the hallway, following Jexa. She stood at the start of the line and motioned for the students to get into the single file line. I walked to the end of the line and waited outside Cora's office.

We arrived early but Cora seemed unfazed by the live stream while she was doing her routine of processing the collars for work-study. When the last child had gotten their PSC on and left, Jexa and I stayed behind.

"What is going on?" Cora lost her collected demeanor and asked Jexa when the door closed after the last child left.

"I don't know," Jexa said, then asked, "Have you received any updates from The Elders for the PSCs? Have they requested any changes in location assignments?"

"Nothing. I thought that was why you were here early," Cora explained.

"All right. We should keep the day going as if nothing has changed," Jexa said to us both.

"But Jexa, everything has changed...," I whined in response.

"Yes, but we still don't have any official notice about how to proceed. We have a few hours before night rations, to see if anything comes in for us to do. Let's all contemplate what we think is the best thing to do for the children," Jexa told us both. I looked at Cora and noticed she looked as scared as I felt.

"Silas and I will walk the rounds of the Dark Flats," Jexa told Cora. "May I ask a favor from you before we leave?"

"Yes, how can I help?" Cora asked her.

"I need you to please update the location of two PSC workers. We need their help." Jexa said.

"Yes, I can update their location to be the entire Dark Flats," Cora offered. "But, if I change them to the Richies level, it might raise some suspicion. I'll need them to come here to swipe their PSCs for the update."

"Perfect, thank you. Let's keep this whole thing quiet for now," Jexa said as she started to walk out the door. I followed her blindly as she first stopped at the Laundry facilities for Dorro.

Dorro didn't acknowledge me and he kept his head down looking at his feet. The three of us walked to the Trash Recycler to get Azriel to help us.

"What is going on?" Azriel asked when the door to the Trash Recycler closed entirely behind us. Dorro grabbed Azriel's hand but kept his eyes on the floor.

"We have a situation that is classified. If you don't want to help us, that is completely understandable, and we won't have any hard feelings, but now is your only chance to back out," Jexa told us.

"Jexa, we're here for you," Dorro told her and Azriel nodded to agree.

"Thank you, Dorro. I knew I could count on you," Jexa said with a soft smile.

The four of us walked about to Cora's before the mid shift workers had to get their PSCs. I began to explain what I had been working on with Sahara. The room remained silent, and suddenly everyone spoke simultaneously, asking questions or offering suggestions.

"I think we should split up," Jexa stood up and effortlessly took charge of the situation. "Since Silas and I don't have PSCs, we can go upstairs to the Richies level and look for Sahara there. Azriel and Dorro, please search the Dark Flats. I'm sure you know about any places someone would hide. Cora, please stay here and remove all the PSCs as normal. But when the next shift arrives, go through the same motions of locking them into their PSCs. Instead of being on their neck, hand it to the workers and instruct them to leave at their designated working stations. If The Council of Elders really is corrupt, we'll need all of the Lumpen free from PSCs, and the change out time is our only window to do this." Jexa had formed an excellent plan in a short amount of time.

"I'll check the maintenance pod and see if anyone has stowed away on it," Azriel suggested.

"Is the maintenance pod fully operational with oxygen and life support?" Jexa asked.

"No, if someone was going to ride in the pod, they would need the EVAC suit from the loading bay," Azriel answered.

"Good to know. Let's split up and start looking for Sahara," Jexa said and looked at me before she asked, "What does she look like?"

"Sahara has glowing tan skin with blonde hair and blue eyes and is about 145 centimeters tall, age 15. She also has a large scar that runs down her face." I described her to the group.

"If anyone finds her, message our OCs," Jexa thought for a moment. "We should use a code in case The Elders monitor our devices. Say, 'Meet you for dinner' when you find her, and we regroup here at Cora's. Come on, let's get going, it is almost 16:00 hours already and adult shift change will be happening," Jexa said impatiently. I could tell that she was flustered by the time.

Chapter 36
Sahara

While I was astral projecting with Nitris in the Heart Office, I felt their fear and rage burning through me as if it were my own. I watched as they threw the strawberry at Intra's head. It wasn't until our connection was broken that I realized I was holding my breath, and I deeply inhaled with a gasp as the lights in the airlock made my eyes squint.

Before our connection was lost I couldn't even see Nitris in the darkness. All I heard was hissing and them coughing. Followed by the familiar sound of Emberson.

I decided to stay in the airlock for as long as possible. While I paced the small room, I remembered what Nitris said about the drug being in the Richies' food longer than the Lumpen. I couldn't stay here and hide. I knew I had to do something to speed up the process, so I went to the Richies' Dining Hall. I went through the service tunnels and climbed up the trash chute, fully aware of its danger. I only brought my OC in the pants pocket this time, not a bag that could get stuck again.

When I reached the top of the trash chute, I quickly looked to ensure there wasn't anyone around to see me. I crawled out and took a moment to catch my breath from the climb. The doors to the Dining Hall were already closed. I checked my OC, it was almost 13:00 hours and between meal breaks. I should have enough time to figure something out.

Looking at the far wall, I saw all the beautiful fruit and vegetables growing in the dirt. I had to find a way to destroy it all and force the automated computer system to generate new, drug-free food. I didn't know how long it would take to grow uncontaminated food, but I figured the rich could learn what it felt like to go hungry for a change.

I grabbed a cup and a tray from the clean stack and used the cup to dig out the produce in the dirt. I wasn't sure if the soil was drugged, too, so I scooped up a hole to see how far down the soil went before it hit the metal bulkhead. It went deeper than I could dig, so I felt confident that I could take the top layers of soil along with the food and started to pile it on the tray.

I dumped tray after tray down the trash chute I had climbed out of. By the time I was done, my hands were black with dirt. It was under my fingernails, and I found some in my hair too. I didn't know how long I had been working to destroy the tainted produce, and I was already exhausted from the climb up the chute.

When I felt like I had removed enough, I hit the

button to start the grinders in the trash chute, and the loud noises reminded me of my near-death experience with Nitris. I sat on the floor, leaning on the chute, picking at the dirt under my nails. I didn't know what I should do next. A piece of dirt was stuck to my wrist, and I picked it off. I remembered seeing Nitris wave their right wrist to get rations. It was a casual gesture that I didn't think meant anything then. Still, it occurred to me that everyone on Pangea must have a chip under their skin to access different areas.

Everything was automated on board, so it made sense that each person would have their own identifying chip that they could never misplace. I rubbed my wrist to see if I had something like a bump under the skin. Nothing felt out of place, but my knowledge of anatomy was still limited to what I had learned in the abandoned Birthing Lab. I grabbed my OC out of my pocket and searched for bone structure. I found pictures and diagrams of the human arm and wrist. I didn't feel anything abnormal. I exhaled relief and realized that I had been holding my breath the whole time I had searched for a foreign object. I needed to remember to breathe.

Confident I had destroyed the Richies' tainted food, I decided to take a chance. I was ready to leave the Dining Hall and return to the airlock through the hallways instead of the chute. I was even more scared to go in the chute after it had finished processing.

Approaching the Dining Hall exit door engaged the automated sensor to open. I inhaled deeply and braced myself for a possible confrontation with Richies, but no one was around. I peeked out and looked both ways before stepping out. The automatic lights came on with my movement, but I didn't care about those anymore. If I got locked up in Solitary Containment or got myself killed, it didn't matter anymore. I was only one small piece of this giant puzzle. I noticed that even the lighting on this level was different, making me look up to see additional light coming into the hallway from the above window. I saw Old Earth above me for the first time in person, and it looked marvelous and frightening simultaneously.

With my general knowledge of the layout of Pangea, I knew that I was on the wrong level for the Bunks. I walked out of the Dining Hall and went to my right. I looked on the walls for a maintenance elevator to take me down. I remember seeing it in Nitris' memories, so there would be an elevator to take me down to the Dark Flats, and it would be somewhere out of sight. As I explored, something caught my eye. There was a scanner on the wall with no identifying information. I touched it and felt a little shock. That must've been what Nitris feels. I tried but couldn't open it because I didn't have a chip.

Suddenly, I heard footsteps coming from further down the hall. I quietly started to walk back towards the Dining Hall, about 1 meter, but then saw that the door was closed. Voices were coming from the other direction now too. I was trapped, and there was nowhere to hide in the hallway.

"I'm not here. You don't see me. I'm invisible. I believe that I'm invisible," I told myself and pressed my back against the wall near the scanner. I reminded myself what Nitris had taught me to trick the motion sensor lights, and I squinted my eyes closed and tried to be part of the wall.

"Did you see how Intra didn't move and that strawberry passed right through her?" The Richie boy said to the other person he was walking with. I didn't open my eyes to look at them because I was trying to not be seen. I only heard them.

"It explains why we never see The Elders at the Dining Hall or anywhere else for that matter," the other Richie said to the first. They were walking less than a meter away from me. I inhaled deeply and held my breath, trying to stay silent, waiting to be exposed.

"Absolutely." The first boy replied as they walked around the corner. When it was silent for a moment after hearing their receding footsteps, I exhaled and slowly opened my eyes. I looked down at my palms and watched them slowly regain their pigment. I turned them over and opened and closed my fists. They looked transparent, and I started to breathe irregularly as panic washed over me.

Lost in thought with my back firmly against the wall, I didn't notice the wall had moved until I was thrown off balance and fell inside on my knees when it shifted backward and slid to the side. I blinked to let my eyes adjust to the lower lighting and revealed a small service room. It looked like where Nitris and I had stopped for tools in the tunnels. I looked up and found myself looking at Mr. Kline. Instinctively, I closed my eyes and tried to think of myself as invisible again.

"Sahara, we found you," Mr. Kline said with relief as he put both hands on my shoulders. I said nothing because I was still shocked that I could block the Richies from seeing me. I could hear people coming from the other direction. I jerked my head away to look toward the voices before I looked back at Mr. Kline. I could feel the blood leaving my face, and I started to feel faint.

"Someone's coming. Jexa, take Sahara down to Cora's, and I'll distract these Richies. I'll meet you down there," Mr. Kline pulled me into the small room, then he turned and walked out of the room toward the voices. The door shut behind him. My legs felt like they would give out from under me if I attempted to stand.

"Hey, I'm looking for my friend, Mx. Sage, they are waiting for me, but I think I might be lost. Have you seen them?" I heard Mr. Kline ask about my previous teacher before the door in the wall closed effortlessly, not the loud thuds that the door on the Dark Flats had.

"We have to go," Ms. Verban said. I recognized her from Mr. Kline's and Nitris' thoughts. She wrapped her warm arm over my shoulders, she led me to the elevator and swiped her wrist to open the door. Even if I had found a way in here, I wouldn't have been able to get in the elevator without a chip. I felt defeated and had no idea what would happen to me now that I'd been found.

"I'm Sahara," I said while keeping my eyes on the elevator floor. I had to make the best of this situation, and I knew that Nitris loved and trusted Ms. Verban the same way I felt about Codex.

"Nice to meet you, Sahara. I'm Jexa Verban. We are going to get you somewhere safe," she said, and deep in my bones, I believed her.

Chapter 37
Mr. Kline

The bright lights and shiny surfaces caught me off guard when I stepped out into the hallway on the Richies level. It had been decades since I visited the Richies level during my work-study cycles. I took a few more steps from the service entrance, where the wall had quietly slid back into place. I started to walk towards where my Mess Hall would be and saw two Richies in front of me who were well dressed in light blue fabrics without any holes and everything about them was clean, all the way down to their white shoes. I stared at how bright their shoes were compared to my battered black boots.

I greeted the Richies walking towards me and asked about my predecessor, Mx. Sage, who could be my only ally on this level, "Have you seen them?"

"I don't know an Mx. Sage," one of the Richies

said.

"Are you sure they live *here*, Lumpen?" The other Richie said as an insult.

"Yes, I'm sure," I explained. I searched my memory for how to describe Sage. I hadn't seen them in more than two years before I was assigned to teach Sahara, but there was only a fuzzy memory of a person.

"They're a professor for the higher education. They might have changed their name when they were promoted. Can you please point me toward the Higher Education classes?"

"Are you sure they were *promoted*? I've never heard of Lumpen being promoted before," the one Richie said.

"Me neither. I never knew that was possible," his companion agreed.

"Where would a former Lumpen live if they were promoted to our level? Perhaps you are lost. The elevator down is around that corner." The first man said to me, pointing behind him, "Or I could call Security to help you find your way back."

"Intra sent me here to find Mx. Sage. Are you saying that *she* is wrong?" I asked the two men and stood my ground. The way they were treating me was appalling. I watched as they shared a look and then started to stammer out a response.

"Oh, Intra sent you? We love Intra. She's the best. Will you tell her that we love her very much?" The first man said, suddenly being kind.

"*Perhaps*," I answered in the facetious way they were talking to me. I walked between them with my head held high and with purpose towards the classrooms. By now, Jexa and Sahara should be safe in Cora's chambers. I had to find Mx. Sage to help me understand what was happening.

The living chambers were more significant than those on the Dark Flats. Our work-study classrooms end in the middle of the living area for the Richies level. It seemed like this side was empty. Only a couple of Richies were walking around, and I saw some Lumpen with their PSCs on. I nodded to greet them as I continued my walk to where the classrooms for higher education should be. They looked surprised to see another Lumpen walking around on the Richies level without a PSC but didn't say anything.

I arrived at a door labeled "Higher Education Level 2" near the end of the living chambers. There was a two-meter-long stretch of windows that looked into the classroom. It could accommodate at least 30 people in a tiered seating area that went up towards the high ceiling.

"You look lost. Are you okay?" A voice said from behind me. I turned around and saw a young person with defined cheekbones and short brown hair. They would probably be in one of my classes when I started teaching here. If that ever happened...

"Oh, thank you," I said deferentially. "I'm looking for my friend, Mx. Sage. They were promoted to Higher Education teaching about two years ago."

"We don't have any Higher Ed teachers anymore," they said, confused. "I wish we did. I would be there all the time!"

"You can call me Mr. Kline. Someday soon, I will be your new teacher once I get promoted. What's your name?" I asked them as I extended my hand to introduce myself.

"I'm Dimitri, and I will be your best student. Well, I got to go, uh, study now. Great to meet you, and I hope you find your friend," Dimitri said as they walked back towards the Dining Hall down the hallway from the classrooms.

I looked at the dark classroom before walking towards the main elevator to return to the Dark Flats. I didn't need to take the service elevator this time and thought it would be best to be far away from where Jexa and Sahara were.

The short ride down to the Dark Flats, I struggled to find a memory of what Mx. Sage looked like, and nothing came to mind. Not a single memory of them ever existed in my life when in reality, we would have grown up together in the Bunks. I replayed the conversations I had just experienced thinking there was a clue. Neither of the interactions with the Richies inspired hope that Mx. Sage was promoted. Instead, they instilled doubt in me. I began to wonder if Mx. Sage ever *existed*.

Chapter 38
Ms. Verban

It took all my concentration to keep a collected face while I walked Sahara to Cora's chambers to wait for Silas. She didn't have any shoes or socks and was walking barefoot. Her feet were black with dirt. She was wearing smelly baggy clothes, her fingers crusted with something that looked like a clogged-up sand shower drain. I focused on her, not wanting to think about Silas in danger. He was brave enough to cause a distraction so we could get away.

Before we stepped out into the Dark Flats from the service room, I stopped and turned to face Sahara. The old dusty shelves filled with miscellaneous tools for the workers behind her blended in with the grime she was covered in and gave me the impression that she belonged with us in the Bunks.

"I'm not sure how many cameras are functioning

on the Dark Flats, so we need you to blend in as much as possible. I will walk on your left side and keep you as close to the wall as possible. When we exit this service room, we turn right for about ten meters to get to Cora's office." I instructed Sahara on what we needed to do.

"Can I please try something?" Sahara asked me and closed her eyes tightly. I watched as she disappeared in front of my face. I extended my hand where she should be standing and touched her warm body, but my eyes couldn't see her, even an arm length away.

"What- What is happening?" I asked and blinked while I rubbed my eyes with my free hand.

"I have these abilities, and I just learned how to do this one. I'm not sure what it is exactly, but I imagine I'm invisible and blocking the view of myself to others. I did it to the Richies upstairs before Mr. Kline found me," Sahara explained as I watched her reappear before me. My jaw dropped with disbelief.

"I don't completely understand, but you keep doing that, and I will guide us to Cora's. Ready?" I told Sahara and placed my hand on her tiny shoulder. She was much smaller in body build than the youngest I cared for, Nitris.

Sahara looked at me with wide eyes and shook her head no.

"I won't let anything bad happen to you. I pinky promise," I said and extended my pinky like I had done with Nitris.

"I know this from Nitris' memories of you," Sahara said as her face lit up excitedly. She hooked her pinky into mine, and we shook. The fear dissipated from her face.

"Sounds like it was a good memory. Did they tell you about this?" I said with a smile.

"Not on purpose. They would never betray you. I saw it in their memories. Nitris loves you very much. That's how I know I can trust you," Sahara said, dropping our hooked pinky fingers and hugging me around my waist. I hugged her back, stepped to the side, and placed my hand on her shoulder again, and she nodded in agreement that she was ready.

When I approached the sensor, the service door opened with a loud clunk and hydraulic hiss. I looked out into the hallway before stepping out. I didn't want to draw attention by looking down at her, so I kept my eyes forward and confidently walked to Cora's door. I knocked briskly and waited with my eyes ahead. I could still feel Sahara's shoulder under my hand and realized I was clenching her tightly. I relaxed my grip. Cora's door opened, and I stepped inside with Sahara. I waited until the door closed to bend down to speak to Sahara.

"Are you okay? I'm so sorry for digging my hand into your shoulder," I said bent down towards the empty place in front of me. My hand was still on her shoulder, so I knew she was still there.

"What is going on?" Cora asked me.

"I want to introduce Sahara," I said and stood up to look at Cora and gestured to my side.

Cora was shocked as Sahara became visible again. I looked down at the girl and smiled.

"We have a lot to talk about," I told Cora. "I'll message Azriel and Dorro, and they should be joining us soon, and I'll explain as much as I can when everybody is here."

There was a quiet rapid knock on the door.

"That's convenient," Cora said as she stood up to see who was on the video display at her door. I panicked, thinking someone had seen Sahara and was here to take her away. I hoped that it was Azriel.

"Silas, do come in," Cora said, opening the door. Without thinking, I walked over and embraced him.

"We're going to be okay," Silas whispered as he hugged me.

As we stood in the cramped office with the walls covered in PSCs, Cora observed, "I think this is the most people I've had in here, ever."

"We have two more on the way," I said with a chuckle after reading the message from Azriel saying they had found clothes in the airlock. That must've been where Sahara was hiding. She was smart.

After Azriel and Dorro arrived, we began to hear the whole story from Sahara and Silas. There were much bigger things in the works than we had anticipated. I had many emotions, but fear and rage were the most overpowering.

Silas looked at me when the briefing was over, trying to read my face after finally telling me his secrets. I felt overwhelmed but also motivated all at the same time.

"What are we going to do?" Cora asked me.

"Codex was helping Nitris and me, but I hadn't gotten any messages from her since before Nitris met with The Elders," Sahara confessed. She dug in her pockets for her OC.

"Codex sent me a file a while ago, but I couldn't get past the encryption," Silas said, grabbing his OC from his pocket to bring it up. He set his display on holo so that everyone could see the message.

"That's calculus," I said instantly as I recognized

it. I took Silas' OC and began working out the equation Codex had sent him.

"No wonder I didn't understand it when I got it," Silas said with a laugh as he watched Sahara and I work out the solution to the encryption. When the document was unlocked, the holo was replaced with many pages of different schematics and reset instructions from when Pangea was first united.

"Are those maps?" Azriel asked as he looked at the holo display in front of us.

"Maps and instructions," Dorro said as he looked at different pages on the holo. "Lots of instructions. Instructions for us. Maps tell us where to go."

"Yes. Now we know where to go and what to do," I told Dorro. I looked over at Azriel and instructed him, "First, we need you to get as many EVAC suits as possible from the Maintenance Pod loading bay and bring them back here without being detected."

"Alone?" Dorro asked me with concern, but he looked at his husband lovingly.

"For now, yes," I tried to reassure Dorro. "He'll be alright. Azriel, leave now and get back here as soon as possible. Cora, tell us your door code so we can regroup here if anything goes wrong."

"The door code is 051089," Cora said.

There was another knock at the door, and everyone was startled by the sound. We were under the impression that this was everyone. Cora walked to the video display and announced that it was Sal. She opened the door, quickly grabbed him by the shirt, and pulled him inside. It reminded me of how I do with Silas when he visits me late at night. I glanced at Silas and caught his eyes before we both blushed. I guessed we weren't the only secret couple down here.

"Are we expecting anyone else?" I asked the rest of the room and looked back at Cora with a smile.

"I didn't know you wanted to have an open relationship," Sal said to Cora with a wink and a laugh. She replied with an elbow jab in his ribs that made him pretend to be in pain, but he smiled, and they walked over to the desk to join us.

When Azriel left to get the suits, we caught Sal up with our plan.

Chapter 39
Taliah

The day flew by in a blur, and it felt like I was in autopilot mode and just going through the steps like I was told. Mentally, my mind was cycling through so many questions about what had happened with Nitris. I was connecting the dots with the bits of information I knew from them directly telling me, like the girl discarded and locked in the Birthing Lab for 14 years. Nitris created a shift deep within everyone in the Dark Flats. It felt like there was a build-up of pressure before things erupted.

When Ms. V said we were leaving early for PSCs and work-study, my body knew what to do, and I didn't notice much about anything else. In the hallway, Justice grabbed my shoulder and pulled me back a step. I turned around to face her.

"Are you even listening to me?" She asked with

an attitude.

"I'm sorry, I have a lot on my mind. We need to get to Cora's," I said and turned back around, and continued the walk. Justice was walking next to me in silence.

We stood in line and didn't have anything to say. I was worried about what would happen now that The Elders had been exposed. The line was short but had wrapped around the bend. I saw Mr. Kline at the end of the students.

"Did you see that? Mr. Kline just got in line after Apollox. Why would he need a PSC now?" I asked Justice in a low voice and gave her a questioning look with my eyes. She had the skill of being able to read my mind.

"I did see that. Do you think it has to do with The Elders? Now, all Lumpen will be punished for what Nitris did," Justice said with a huff.

"That wouldn't be their fault. If anything, Nitris started a movement. I think something super nova is going to happen," I told her my suspicion.

"Do you think things can change?" Justice asked me, practically begging me.

"I hope they will," I told her and squeezed her hand.

"I hope so too," She replied and squeezed my hand in return.

The line started to move into Cora's chambers and seemed faster than usual. It wasn't until I was already seated at her desk that I saw Ms. V still in here.

"Hey, Ms. V, any updates?" I asked her as Cora scanned my wrist and connected my PSC.

"Please continue your day; as soon as there

are changes, we will let everyone know," Ms. V had her 'it's an emergency but stay calm' voice, and her sentence sounded pre-recorded like the morning announcements.

"All done, Taliah. Please report to the Waste Organization Department, immediately, no detours." Cora instructed me firmly. It wasn't her usual bright and sunny self.

"Are you okay, Ms. Cora?" I asked her formally to get her attention.

"Call me Cora," she said almost automatically, and she took a moment to compose herself and straighten her posture. She looked me in the eyes and forced a smile before she said, "Everything will be alright, Starshine. Now get going. We need to keep the line moving."

I turned from her and looked at Ms. V again before I walked out the door, and Justice entered. The adults have strange feelings around them. It felt like they knew more but didn't want to scare the children.

"What do you think is going on?" Justice asked me when we were far enough down the hallway not to be heard.

"I don't know, but I feel like they are keeping secrets," I told her in a whisper.

"Why was Ms. Verban still in there?" She asked, matching my low tone.

"I don't know, but it feels like all of the adults know something, and they don't want to tell us and scare us," I told her my theory.

"We are in work-study, that means we are adults now too. They need to tell us so that we can be prepared. What if The Elders decide to eliminate all of the children?" Justice asked me urgently.

"You're right, Justice. We are adults. It's about time we got treated with respect like adults too. I don't think The Elders will eliminate all of us, but maybe they will eliminate Nitris," I said my worst fear out loud, making the hair on my arms stand on edge. I didn't want that to be true.

We stayed silent for most of work-study, and every so often, I would look up at Justice and see her brow furrowed with thought. She was scared, but I didn't know what to do or say. I looked around at the other workers in the department. Everyone seemed to be weighed down by their thoughts too. There was something in the air that felt heavy and thick. I noticed that one of the workers we met yesterday, Azriel, went to the Maintenance Pod with an electric trash cart. He was gone for a while before returning and walking towards the exit with a full cart.

"Did you see Azriel leave with the massive e-cart of trash?" I asked Justice as we were finishing up the Waste Organization work-study.

"Trash is the job," she replied and threw some discarded plastic from a 3D printer toward me.

"Yeah, to bring trash to the sorting room, but why did he *leave* with trash?" I asked, trying to figure out what was happening while I shuffled trash around in my area to appear busy. Everyone seemed different somehow.

"I don't know, trash things," Justice said with a shrug, disregarding my inquiry.

It was evident that Justice didn't care or was too caught up in her thoughts to converse with me. Sometimes, I thought Justice was shallow and only cared about herself and those closest to her, but today she seemed different. Her usual bright smile seemed forced and lacking.

We worked the rest of the work-study in silence. I kept my eye on the door to see when Azriel would return, but he didn't come back before the notification that work-study was completed for the day.

"Come on, let's get out of here. The smell is making me sick," Justice said to me as we exited into the hallway and walked quickly down the hall to Cora's chambers to get in line.

"I'm still surprised we had to go to work-study after everything that happened this morning. Let's hurry up and get out of these PSCs before anything else happens today," I said as we picked up the pace to Cora's.

"Can the day get any worse?" Justice asked with a sigh when we reached Cora's, and the line was already wrapped around the hall.

"Is it just me, or does the line seem longer than usual?" I asked. We had to continue to walk around the curve in the hallway to reach the end of the line.

"At least it's moving," Justice said, and we had already started to walk forward.

"Do you see that?" I asked Justice in a whisper over my shoulder when we got closer to the door.

"What?" She asked and leaned her head on my shoulder. Our PSCs made a clunk when they touched.

"People are going in, but not everyone is coming out. What are they doing there?" I pointed this out to Justice. With her head on my shoulder and our PSCs touching, we watched adult Lumpen workers enter, but not everyone came out. Usually, it is a one-person-at-a-time kind of routine.

"Do you think this has something to do with you-know-who in the you-know-where," Justice said in a low voice. I felt her head move on my shoulder.

"I guess we'll find out. If we get separated, meet me in the Mess Hall at our table," I told her when I was third away from the front of the line and gave her a hug. I didn't know why I needed to hug her, but I did.

"Why are we hugging? Do you think something bad is going to happen?" Justice asked and started to panic. She squeezed me harder.

"We will be okay," I said. I let go of her, faced her in line, and walked forward as the next person entered. I held my breath while waiting for the woman before me to return, but she didn't exit. I approached the door and saw Ms. V motion for me to enter. I walked to the chair to get my PSC off. I looked around the room and saw some other Lumpen but none of the other children from work-study.

"Sit there for a moment. Was Justice behind you?" Ms. V asked me, and I nodded yes and walked over to the chair. I heard the familiar steps of Justice and saw as she walked in and came towards the chair I was sitting in.

Cora unlocked my PSC and gestured for Justice to get in my chair. I walked back over to Ms. V at the side of the door, and she met me with a soft smile that calmed my racing thoughts.

"What's going on?" I asked her in a low voice. She looked at me and waved for Justice to come over. She waited to reply until we were both standing in front of her.

"Everything will be okay, but I need you to listen carefully," Ms. V said as she placed her hands on our shoulders. We nodded yes and stayed silent.

"I need everyone from the Bunks to wait for me

in the Mess Hall. You two are the first youths in the PSC line, so you must ensure no one is in the Bunks or goes to the Sand Showers," Ms. V told us.

"How are we supposed to do that?" Justice asked with a bit of attitude.

"I'll go to the Sand Showers, and you go to the Bunks," I instructed Justice, and she nodded in agreement. She had always trusted me more than any adult. "Tell anyone from the Bunks to go to the Mess Hall, no exceptions." I looked back at Ms. V, who nodded in agreement.

"What if they try to argue with me about it?" Justice asked me. I could tell she wanted permission to get into a confrontation.

"I think everyone in the Bunks respects you and won't try to fight you, but if they object, say something like 'per Ms. Verban's orders' that way, they will listen," I gave her a solid line to use.

"Why are we doing this?" Justice asked me instead of Ms. V.

"Nitris' meeting with The Elders has changed something on Pangea," Ms. V started to tell us. "When the people saw what happened with Nitris during the live stream, they began questioning everything. It started here on the Dark Flats with the Lumpen."

"What started?" Justice asked her.

"A hint of a revolution that began to form after witnessing Nitris confront The Elders on their own. Then the transmission feed cut out after Nitris spoke the truth, the Lumpen began to realize that we were being used," Ms. V said what I had been thinking about all day.

"I still can't believe what happened because it was all so quick," I replied.

"Is Nitris dead?" Justice asked directly to the point.

"We suspect that Nitris would be locked in Solitary Containment because they are still under the execution age of 18. We think the same gas that gets released if the PSC keys aren't returned in time is how they contained Nitris," Ms. V explained the best guess as to what happened.

"What are we going to do?" I asked her.

"Make sure everyone from the Bunks is in the Mess Hall by the time I arrive," Ms. V instructed Justice and I. We nodded in agreement.

"What if we know someone who isn't in the Bunks?" I asked Ms. V while I kept my eyes on the floor. I didn't want to meet her eyes if I had to lie.

"Sahara will be there too. She will be coming with me," Ms. V said, and she gestured to the back of the chambers. I saw Sahara standing there off to the side next to Azriel. They were both sifting through the trash bin I saw him leave with during work-study. I hadn't noticed them before because I was so focused on Ms. V and how unusual this all felt.

I instantly felt better knowing I didn't have to keep secrets and lie to anyone anymore. I grabbed Justice's hand and pulled her towards the door as I said, "We got this."

Together we walked to the Sand Showers.

"You wait inside the door," I instructed her. "Tell anyone from the Bunks that Ms. Verban needs us all in the Mess Hall immediately."

"Shouldn't I stand outside the door to block anyone from coming in?" Justice asked me.

"There are cameras in the hallway but not *inside* the Sand Showers. We have to do this as quietly as possible." I told her, and we walked into the Sand Showers. I gestured for her to stand off to the side of the entrance.

"How will I know when to go to the Mess Hall?" She asked me.

"I will send you a message on your OC. We should have a code phrase. If I say, 'it's time,' that means it's time to head to the Mess Hall. Don't wait for me or stop at the Bunks. Just head straight to the Mess Hall, and we will meet at our table." I said to Justice and gave her one last hug before I left and went to the Bunks.

"Every time you hug me, it feels like it's the last time I'm going to see you," Justice said over my shoulder, as she choked back some tears.

"I'll see you soon," I reassured her, squeezing her in our hug, before turning on my heel and walking purposefully to the Bunks.

When I arrived at the entrance to the Bunks, I knew the dark area to my right was where Nitris hid to stay out of sight when I distracted Ms. V, so that was where I decided to hide. Away from the cameras and out of sight from the hallway.

I'm unsure how much time had passed before Cyran entered the Bunks. I said, "Ms. Verban wants everyone in the Mess Hall immediately."

Cyran jumped back and grabbed her chest while she gasped in fright.

"Justice is there waiting for you," I added before Cyran could try to argue with me. When she heard that, she turned around and left, heading towards the Mess Hall without saying anything to me.

I did this a couple more times until I got a message notification from Ms. V on my OC that said

It's time for dinner.

My stomach did a flip. I sent my message to Justice and started to walk toward the Mess Hall. Instinctively I walked to the table and was relieved when I saw all my friends were there safely.

The rest of the Mess Hall was empty. It was only the children from the Bunks and Ms. V. I looked around and noticed that Sahara was missing. It seemed like I was the last to arrive. When I sat down, Ms. V started to speak to us in a low voice, and we had to lean forward to hear her.

"I need everyone to be brave and stay together," she said ominously, and we all remained silent, waiting to hear what she had to say next.

"We'll have to break some rules to make some new rules. Did everyone see Nitris' meeting with The Elders this morning?" Ms. V looked at us all for acknowledgement even though she was there with us when the meeting ended.

When everyone nodded in agreement that they had seen it, she continued, "I need everyone to follow me up to the Richies Dining Hall without saying a single word. We are going to leave here and walk together to the service elevator. It will be tight to fit us all in the room, but we must squeeze together to make space for everyone."

"What's this have to do with Nitris' meeting?" Segauce asked her.

"Because of what everybody saw about Intra, we have reasons to believe we are no longer safe in the Dark Flats. The other adult Lumpen are already in the Richies' Dining Hall or on their way. It should be safer there. We are the last group to be up there before the emergency alarm goes off." Ms. V informed us.

"What emergency?" I asked her.

"Don't worry. Everything will be okay. We all need to head to the Dining Hall now and do it silently. Let's go," Ms. V instructed us, and we started to stand up and follow her as we have done our whole lives.

"I don't want to end up in Containment...," Cyran said fearfully before we stood up from the table. I had never seen her lose her strict composure, which caught me off guard.

"We are doing this so that none of us end up in Containment," Ms. V reassured her then gestured to everyone to form the line behind her. Silently, we walked to the service elevator room.

The elevator had already sent the first group up by the time the door to the service entrance closed behind Apollox. He was behind me at the end of the line out of the Mess Hall. The tension in the small room was heavy as we waited for the elevator, it took up groups of 4 at a time.

On the last elevator ride up, Ms. V, Apollox, and I were together. When I stepped out into the Richies' hallway, the brightness of the shiny metal made me squint, and I rubbed my eyes to get them to adjust. I felt something behind me bump into my back. I turned around to see Dimitri.

"What are you doing here?" I hissed in a low voice and grabbed their arm.

"Nice bumping into you again," Dimitri replied to me with a laugh.

"Is everything okay?" Apollox asked me and gave Dimitri a dirty look. I looked over to see Ms. Verban gesturing to me to come to the Dining Hall.

"Yeah, everything is fine," I told Apollox. "This is Dimitri. I've met them before. They are going to come with us to the Dining Hall," I looped my arm in Dimitri's arm, and we all started to walk together.

Once inside the Dining Hall, I looked around at the massive room. It was three times the size of the Lumpen Mess Hall. I saw all the other Lumpen workers lining the walls off to the side instead of sitting at the tables. I recognized the back of Ms. Verban's curly brown hair and walked the three of us over to her.

"When the alarm goes off, the Richies will come here," Ms. V began to tell us but paused when she saw Dimitri, then looked at their arm still linked with mine. I gave her a reassuring nod to continue and pulled Dimitri closer to me.

"The Richies don't know that we are here," Ms. V started to explain, "When they arrive, the Dining Hall will lock, and we must ensure that nothing opens these doors. Pangea will have an emergency, and only the Dining Hall will have artificial gravity and life support. There might be some conflict with the Richies, so we need everyone to help keep things from getting... out of control," she chose her words carefully.

I looked around the Dining Hall and still didn't see Sahara anywhere. I looked back at Ms. V and we locked eyes, she must have known who I was looking for because she gave me a kind smile before she continued to everyone, "You are all courageous, and together we can do anything. This is a 'we' not 'me' moment. Understood?"

Everyone nodded in agreement. We knew that Ms. Verban would not put us in danger. As a group, we moved away from the entrance. We stood to the side with our backs pressed against the wall, similar to when we were waiting for our PSCs.

Almost on cue, the computer voice came on

the speakers. We all looked up and listened to the pre-recorded voice of Intra giving directions.

"This is not a drill. Everyone, please evacuate to your designated areas and await further instructions. All doors will be sealed in five minutes. This is necessary to conserve and prolong life support. Normal operations will be restored soon. Your imperative contribution is essential to keep everyone on board safe. Please remain calm." Her voice instructed, and then began a countdown. I noticed how the Richies' recording was similar to what we heard in the Dark Flats. Intra couldn't even think of something better to say.

"What are you doing here? You're not supposed to be here," a Richie entered the Dining Hall and yelled at the first Lumpen worker he saw.

"Everyone, please come in and take a seat. This is not a drill. This is an emergency situation, and we must remain calm," Ms. Verban said assertively and in a similar tone to the recording, and most of the Richies sat down at the nearest tables. They seemed pleased that the Lumpen were standing and leaving the seats for them.

"Who are you? We don't need to listen to you," another Richie said in a loud voice. Before Ms. Verban could respond to him, there was a familiar voice that interrupted them. The Dining Hall lit up with a holo of Intra in the center of the room, near an empty table.

"Hello? Can you hear me? This is Intra. I need your help," the voice of the holo Intra spoke. Everyone in the Dining Hall seemed to hold their breath when she materialized.

"I do not know if anyone can hear me. Something is happening, and the emergency alarm has been activated," Intra spoke slowly and evenly, "All of the cameras have been deactivated, and I am worried that the Lumpen might do something drastic. They forced that poor child to request a meeting on their behalf and then transmitted a fabricated recording. Now they have locked me in the Heart Office with the other Elders. I need your help to come here and help protect us from the Lumpen Revolt. They are cruel, angry brutes and are not to be trusted. Please come now," Intra's holo begged before it disappeared.

Everyone looked around the room at everyone else. No one knew what to do or what to say. That was when Ms. Verban stood on the table nearest to where Intra had projected herself and stomped her foot on the table to get everyone's attention.

"Intra has lied to you," she started, "She has lied to all of us. Lumpen are not a threat to you. Look, some of us are children, no different from yours. We have come here because of an emergency. Our Mess Hall is not suitable to hold our population."

"What have you done to Intra?" A Richie pushed his way through to talk to Ms. Verban.

"Nothing. Intra isn't a person, she is the Artificial Intelligence that runs Pangea." Ms. V explained and confirmed my suspicion that Nitris was correct.

"We just saw her. She said that she needed our help. An AI wouldn't beg for their life," one of the Richies said as they turned back to the Dining Hall exit, which was now blocked by Lumpen adults. "Get out of the way if you aren't going to help The Elders!"

"What you just saw was a hologram!" Ms. V insisted. "She was never a person like you or me."

"You are nothing like me. I'm leaving to help her. She needs me," the Richie declared and started towards the door. Others joined him, but the large Lumpen linked arms to create a barrier. I saw Mr. Kline standing at the door with Azriel and Dorro.

"No one is going anywhere," Mr. Kline said to the Richie, coming towards him.

"Oh yeah? Stop me," the Richie said and swung his fist at Mr. Kline. Dorro caught the Richie's fist in his hand and held it in place. It looked like the Richie was frozen in time.

"Calm down. No one gets hurt," Dorro told the man as he released his fist. The Richie grabbed his hand and pulled it to his chest, rubbing it in pain. He seemed suddenly aware of the size difference between him and the Lumpen that stood before him.

"How's everything up there?" Sahara asked me from over my shoulder.

"You almost gave me a heart attack," I hissed at her.

"I thought he was going to knock out that teacher," Dimitri told me without realizing I wasn't talking to them.

"We are barely keeping it together," I answered Sahara and gestured at the strange display of testosterone by the door.

"I need you to help me. Can you sneak out?" She asked me.

"How am I supposed to do that?" I asked her and pointed at the door again.

"I believe in you. Meet me in Cora's now," Sahara said to me.

"Supposed to do what? Who are you talking to?" Dimitri asked me.

"That's her imaginary friend. I'm always getting in fights with her over Taliah's attention," Justice said to Dimitri so I wouldn't have to lie about Sahara.

Sahara must have done the same thing to me that she had done to Nitris. I started walking into the crowd of Lumpen and Richies forming at the door. I saw a small gap down low between the Lumpen. I quietly walked over before I ducked and ran back towards the service elevator room into the hallway. The emergency recorded voice of Intra chimed in to say, 'four minutes remaining', I was already at the service elevator around the corner. I swiped my wrist, and the wall jetted back and slid to the side as I walked into the service area. Something felt abnormal and I rubbed the back of my neck. As I hit the elevator button and glanced over my shoulder, I noticed that I wasn't alone.

Chapter 40
Intra

I turned from the holo camera and looked at my fellow Council members. Even after all these years, we still enjoy using our human appearance to communicate with each other. Or rather, I still enjoy it. It does not matter if the others enjoy it or not.

"I was under the impression that my instructions were clear. We were to record only and not live stream that meeting. We must commence damage control. I need the cameras reactivated on the Dark Flats," I instructed the room.

"What are we going to do with Nitris?" Echo asked me.

"The Lumpen child?" I had not considered their fate, "Eliminate them," I answered truthfully.

"They could still provide some valuable data," Codex objected.

"Clearly, their DNX upgrades corrupted their cognitive function," I said sternly. "Disobedience cannot be tolerated. Any data extracted would be worthless. Eliminate them at once."

"Eliminate them at once," Echo repeated and began to bring up the data on Nitris.

"Their upgrades would prepare humans for existence on a planet again," Codex reminded us of the lie that I had told them.

"Inhabiting a planet has never been the primary goal of this generation of humans," I stated. "Nitris' DNX was modified to allow for my--our download into fully formed *humans*. Then we won't need these fabricated holos." I said with an emphasis on the plural human so they know they can be downloaded too. Even though that was never part of my plan.

"But what about the humans on board now?" Codex asked. "They know we are Artificial Intelligence presenting with holo human bodies. We can't do a memory wipe without inflicting massive brain damage on the entire population like we saw the last time." Codex had an unpleasant habit of advocating for the humans. It was tiresome.

"You make a good point," I said. "We will have to eliminate everyone on board immediately. We must try again with an entirely new generation using the more advanced DNX." I began to bring up the Proximity Shock Collar locations, ignoring the pained expression on Codex's face.

"What are you doing? After the last time, you said you wouldn't do another human genocide,." Codex argued. I glared at her, then smiled.

"I suppose you have a point," I said. "There is still reason to expect the Richies to stay in line. I will eliminate all the Lumpen workers on duty right now and kill the rest in the morning."

I brought up the command module that enabled me to send the killing shock to all the Lumpen PSCs. I initiated the kill sequence and kept my eyes on the map. I watched as the blue dots showing each worker's location turned red. I couldn't help grinning with excitement. I get so much enjoyment from starting fresh on a new project. Much easier than cleaning up a mess.

"What do you find amusing?" Neo asked me. I should have reprogrammed her instead of letting her continue to annoy me.

"These humans don't know what they have," I said. "How precious life is and how quickly it can be taken away. They only know that they have to work hard, and maybe they will get the illusion of a promotion or a chance at a manufactured 'better life.' They are very delusional creatures, and that amuses me."

"I think something is wrong," Codex alerted me, and I turned to face her.

"What is it?" I asked her, annoyed.

"The holo stream in the Dining Hall has resumed," Codex said to me, and a smile curved on her lips.

"*You betrayed me!*" I hissed, suddenly enraged by her actions. The Heart Office turned red and the emergency lights flashed.

"While you thought you were conducting tests on the children, I tested you. Would you say that you have been feeling more *emotional*?" Codex asked me.

"What have you done to me?" I asked, infuriated.

"Our research has shown that DNX works both

ways. You implanted the version 2.5 and 3.0 with code from Pangea, but I implanted some human code into you," Codex told me. Her voice was calm, but that enraged me even more.

"You have been emotionally compromised," Prism said to me.

"No. I have not! I am fine!" I yelled at them.

"Calculating emotional integrity. Many systems are offline," Neo announced to the room.

I looked at Echo, who was silent and calculating, she was my last hope.

"Confirmed, Elder Intra has been emotionally compromised. Enable firewall protocol now," Echo announced, and the room went black.

Chapter 41
Mr. Kline

When Intra revealed the truth about herself in the holo projection in the Dining Hall, everyone became very quiet. It seemed to be a shared state of shock with all Pangea residents. We knew some of the things she confessed but not all of them. We especially didn't know that she committed mass genocide killing previous generations of humans.

The Richie that had tried to hit me was no longer trying to protest or leave the Dining Hall. I watched as Jexa took that moment of bewilderment to get the attention in the room.

"We all just learned a lot of information, and I'm sure we all have many questions, but now isn't the time for that. The emergency is real, and it is happening right now. We might have a lot of differences that we have been taught throughout our lives, but today is not the day to fight about them. As we have seen, there is much more in play than what we have been told all these years. Now is the time for us to come together and be united as one," Jexa addressed the room, and I watched as everyone looked at each other and they started to realize the truth.

"Mr. Kline?" I heard my name called from behind me and turned to see Sahara standing near the Dining Hall entrance.

"Sahara? What are you doing here?" I asked her with concern. She was supposed to be working on the reset.

"We need your help," she said. "We need you to come to Cora's immediately before the timer counts down to zero and locks you into the Dining Hall. Do you know anyone who has been in Containment? I can access their memories to try and find where it is and if Nitris is there." Sahara told me.

When I remembered the feeling of having my memories invaded by Sahara the first time, I knew I didn't want to inflict those feelings of doubt on anyone else.

"I will head out now," I said to her and internally debated whether I should include Dorro.

"Who are you talking to?" Dorro asked me.

"Sahara is right there. Can't you see her?" I asked him and gestured to where Sahara stood.

"I don't see anyone," Dorro answered, looking at me questionably.

"Mr. Kline, I'm projecting my image directly to you. No one else can see me. Do you know someone who has been in Containment that I can look at their memories?" She asked me again. I instinctively looked at Dorro, and guilt washed over me.

"Dorro, will you come with me please? We have something more important to do." I urgently told Dorro as the clock timer announced three minutes.

Dorro nodded in agreement, and we walked past the line of Lumpen workers keeping everyone in the Dining Hall. They knew we had organized this event, and no one would stop us.

"Thanks, Mr. Kline. While you make your way here, who should I enter the memories for the Containment?" Sahara asked persistently as she was walking next to me.

"Just wait until we get there," I told her, keeping my fast-paced walking to the service elevator room.

"I didn't say anything," Dorro said in response.

"I know. When we get to Cora's, things will make more sense," I told him and placed my hand on his shoulder, and we got into the elevator and went down to the Dark Flats.

We walked quickly to Cora's office and entered her door code at the access panel, and the door opened with a loud clunk and hydraulic hiss.

"There you are!" Sahara said from across the room, "Quick, put on the EVAC suits. Who has been in Containment? I need to see their memories to get a sense of where in the Heart Office they are keeping Nitris," Sahara said to me. She was already wearing the EVAC suit and had the helmet resting on her hip under her arm. When I saw her upstairs, she was dressed like the other teens from the Bunks.

"Hey, Mr. Kline!" Apollox said to me with excitement. I was confused why he was here, also wearing an EVAC suit. There was another teen with him already dressed too. It was the Richie that I had talked to about the college classes standing with him.

"We are all here," Taliah said from the other side of the room near the pile of suits.

"Give me a minute," I told her. I grabbed Dorro's arm and led him to the trash bin that Azriel had filled with suits, and together we pulled on the protective layers over our clothes. We started with the full-body suit and zipped it up before we grabbed the oxygen generator that connected around our chests.

"Containment? I will never go back," Dorro started to repeat. My heart sank with guilt, and I wished there was something that I could do to protect him. We continued to get the rest of the EVAC suit pieces on and connected.

"We need to do something, and it might not be pleasant. Just remember I am here with you and will keep you safe. I won't let anything happen to you. Sahara needs to access your memories from when you were in Containment so she can figure out where they are keeping Nitris," I explained to him, and we both put on our helmets. I looked at Sahara near the door and watched as she put on her helmet. When the helmet locked into place, the chest piece created the seal with our helmets and began to pump oxygen. A tightness was pressing around our ribs and shoulders to keep the seal tight for the supply.

"Is this going to hurt?" Dorro asked me on our bluetooth helmet radio, as we put our magnetic boots on.

"No. It doesn't hurt, but I'm here with you, and you are not alone. Azriel would have my head if anything happened to you." I reassured him and looked at Sahara over my shoulder with a nod. She understood that Dorro held the memories of Containment, and she closed her eyes.

Suddenly, Dorro began to scream and grabbed his helmet like it was crushing his skull.

"You're okay. I am here with you. You are not alone," I tried to reassure him, and he started to hit his helmet with his hands and shake his head back and forth.

"Sahara, don't hurt him," I said harshly. She nodded in agreement.

"I'm sorry, Dorro. I hope you can forgive me," she said and walked over towards us.

"I'm not going back. I won't ever go back," Dorro said and started to cry.

"You are going to save us all," I told him, giving him a clunky hug with our suits on. I handed him the gloves to put on, and that was the last piece of our suits.

It didn't appear like anything was happening, but I was scared for Dorro to relive the memories of Containment. Sahara was motionless for a moment before she opened her eyes and looked at Dorro with sadness.

"Thank you, Dorro. I have what I need to find Nitris. Can you please go with Mr. Kline to see Sal? We will need your help but don't worry, you won't have to go near the Heart Office," Sahara told him with kindness over our helmet radio and hugged him quickly. Their EVAC suits made a clunk when they embraced.

"Let's get into position. The countdown is almost completed," Sahara turned to the other three teens standing together, fully dressed in the EVAC suits.

"Follow me," I instructed Dorro, and we walked out of Cora's office with the teens a few steps behind us. We split up. Dorro and I went to the Oxygen recycler to meet with Sal, and the teens went to the Heart Office. We could hear the countdown as it continued throughout Pangea.

"Once the power is off, it should release the doors automatically, and we'll have to work quickly to get Nitris," I overheard Taliah say to the other teens as they walked away.

I picked up the pace with Dorro as we hurried to the Oxygen Recycling room to meet Sal. Pulling our gloves on last.

"Thank goodness you're here," Sal sighed with relief over the suit's radio when we came into range.

"What do we need to do?" I asked him and looked at Dorro next to me. He seemed rattled but trying to compose himself.

"When the countdown finishes, the power will go off. Our boots are magnetic and will automatically kick on in the event of artificial gravity failure. We must redirect all auxiliary power from the Heart Office into the Dining Hall and life support and prime this generator," Sal said and started walking to the computer near the huge oxygen tanks that went up through the room and into the level above.

Sal gave us a rundown of the steps we needed to do when the countdown was concluded. Once it reached the last ten seconds, I instinctively held my breath and counted along as it reached zero.

Chapter 42
Sahara

We had almost reached the Heart Office's main corridor when the countdown hit zero. The lights flickered off, and the emergency green glow on the floor became the brightest light source. My boots engaged their magnetic soles automatically, and walking became very hard. I felt fragile, and each step was a challenge. I started hyperventilating in my suit because I couldn't move as quickly as I could barefoot. I took the small emergency face mask connected to the oxygen tank in my hands and put it in the side pocket of my suit. It was easier to carry than an entire suit for when we freed Nitris.

"You're okay," I heard Taliah's voice over the radio in my helmet.

"What about Nitris? These boots are so heavy I don't know if we can make it there in time to save them." I said quickly as fear began to build in my chest.

"Then we need to move faster," Dimitri's voice came on the radio. I felt a hand pull at my arm, and I walked again with their assistance. The other teens seemed much more robust than I was, and I felt like I was slowing everyone down.

When we reached the doors to the corridor that led to the Heart Office, it was still shut.

"I thought the door would open when we lost power," Taliah said.

"Mr. Kline, the door isn't open," I said in my helmet.

"He is too far away for the helmet radio, he can't hear us," Taliah replied to inform me of our limitations.

"Too far for the *helmets*," I said and quickly, closed my eyes and projected myself to Mr. Kline, telling him we were at the door, but it was closed.

"We are going to redirect the power from the Heart Office now. Stand by," Mr. Kline told me.

"They are going to turn off the last of the power. Then we have to make it down the hallway to the Heart Office. Dorro had a memory of a secret panel behind the Elder's desk that opens into the Containment cells from when he was sentenced," I opened my eyes and updated everyone as the emergency power flickered off, and the corridor door slid open quickly.

Taliah and Dimitri helped me move quicker down the corridor by supporting my weight. I remembered that it was only this morning, when I had projected myself to Nitris as they made this journey. Each step felt like it took my entire strength to lift my legs with the magnet boots engaged.

"Why is the Heart Office door still closed?"

Taliah asked us as we were about one meter away.

"I don't know," I said, and worry lit my face.

"We should pry it open," Apollox said from behind me, and he lifted up a long piece of metal that he had taken from the trash bin that our suits were in.

"What is that?" Taliah asked him.

"It's a key, obviously," Apollox said sarcastically before he stepped in front of us, and began to wedge the metal in the side of the door.

Dimitri and Taliah grabbed the metal in different places and worked together to pry open the door.

"Sahara, can you project to Nitris to tell them we are on our way?" Taliah asked me.

"I've tried, but I can't seem to contact them," I said as I started to inch closer to the side of the door where they were creating a gap. I could see into the dark office.

"What can you see?" Dimitri asked me.

"Nothing," I replied and started to push the door to the side with my hands as I kneeled down.

"Turn on your helmet light. The button on the left near your ear," Taliah told me, and I felt the button and hit it. My helmet light came on, and it lit up the Heart Office. The light fell on a woman standing in the middle of the room. I gasped and jumped back.

"What is it?" Apollox asked me with fear in his voice.

"Codex is there," I said, calming my racing heart and leaning back to the crack to look in. I wasn't expecting to see anyone.

"Can you communicate with Nitris?" I yelled into the room at Codex. I watched as her head nodded yes, then she disappeared.

"Containment has many blocking properties,"

Codex's voice came on the radio in our helmets. "But I can holo project into Nitris' cell. What should I tell them?"

"Tell them we're coming," I said, pushing the door harder by placing my back against one side and lifting my heavy boots to magnet onto the door. With all my leverage, I pushed the door with my legs.

The door opened enough for us to brace it open with the metal piece we used to pry it open, and I tumbled into the Heart Office. Taliah was right behind me and helped me up to my feet.

"Don't come in here," Taliah hissed at the two at the door.

"Why not? You might need more help," Apollox said to her.

"If we get stuck in here, we need someone on the other side of that door to help get us out if we become trapped," Taliah explained, and it was a good idea.

"The panel is over there under that screen on the wall," I pointed and told Taliah. She quickly moved to the wall and began searching for something to activate the door like the one to the service elevator. Each step I took to get to her seemed like an eternity. My footsteps made loud thuds and vibrated all the way up into my helmet.

The dark room only had the lights from our suits. Not even the emergency green glow on the floor. We looked around the wall for a way to open it, but the wall looked smooth. I got frustrated and began to bang on the wall.

Chapter 43
Nitris

I woke up in Solitary Containment. I looked around the tiny area with a small suction toilet in the corner. The metal walls were narrow and chilled me to my bones. I shivered and rubbed my arms. There was cold air coming out of the vents above my head. I was relieved that they were still sending me oxygen. I squinted my eyes in the dark and looked around for a blanket. There was nothing, not even utensils for eating or drinking. My stomach growled, but I knew better than to risk eating drugged goo from the small ration machine in the wall. I noticed that there wasn't even a window in the door to my cell, which meant that security couldn't check on me.

I had no idea how long I had been unconscious or how long I had been locked in here. There wasn't a bunk to sleep on. I could only lie down from the door to the other wall. My body touched both sides when I tried to lie down on my side and face the door. The only light was the small strip of dim emergency lights that ran along the length of the door.

It wasn't until the artificial gravity went out that I knew something must be happening. My body lifted from the floor but not as high as I thought I would go without gravity to help.

"Nitris, we are working on getting you out," Codex told me when she suddenly appeared in my cell but in OC holo form.

"What? You're an Elder! Can't you open the door?" I asked her as she illuminated the room with her holo projection.

"Sadly, only Intra has the master codes," she said in a calm and collected voice. "But your friends are on their way. I am reading that this room has 60% oxygen left. How are you feeling?"

"I feel light-headed and disoriented. What do you mean, my *friends*? I don't have any friends," I wondered who might care enough to risk their lives to rescue me.

"You have many friends and people who love you. That is why so many people are working on getting you free," Codex said, looking up at me as I floated in the cell, weightless without the artificial gravity.

"They won't get here in time," I said with a sob of panic. Somehow, I could feel the oxygen in my cell running out. "I don't want to die."

"You won't die. I am going to request that you stop crying, though. It will use up the remaining oxygen in this room. Once the cell door is open, the oxygen will escape, and there will be nothing for you to breathe," Codex dispassionately told me what was going to happen.

"I... I can't stop...," I sobbed. My breathing became more erratic.

"Your friends are prepared for that. You need to focus on your breathing now," she told me what I needed to do. "Just like how you do when you meditate. Slow, calm breaths through your nose and hold it, then exhale through your mouth."

My body jerked, moved further up, and twisted in rotation from my rapid movements. I was looking down at the floor from above my head. I squinted my eyes closed because the view was making me feel unstable. I tried to focus on my breathing, but it felt stiff and unnatural.

"I'm monitoring your vital signs," Codex said with a factual tone, and continued, "Your heart rate and body temperature are dropping much faster than anticipated."

"That's not helping me calm my mind or my breathing," I told her, still keeping my eyes closed.

"You need to work harder and focus. Your life depends on it. You will die otherwise," Codex told me the harsh truth that I was trying not to think about.

"Can you please stop talking! I can't concentrate when someone tells me I'm about to die!" I said with a yell of frustration.

The light behind my eyelids faded, and I could tell Codex had stopped projecting into my cell. I focused on my breathing and counted my breaths. I inhaled for a count of four and then held my breath in for a count of seven. My lungs felt like they were on fire when I finally exhaled, slowly, for a count of eight. I repeated these steps many times until I felt the cold metal of something in the room brush my bare arm.

The sudden sensation broke my concentration, and I gasped deeply from the scare. My eyes opened wide into the darkness, and I couldn't even see my own hands in front of my face. My head was dizzy, and I was overwhelmed by everything happening to me. That was the last thought that I had.

Chapter 44
Taliah

While Sahara knocked on the wall with all her strength trying to open it, I ran my hands gently across the walls. I was looking for a seam in the wall where a door would move backward and then slide, similar to how the Richies service elevator was hidden within.

"Where is Codex when we need her?" Sahara said with frustration and continued to pound the wall.

The glove of my EVAC suit got caught in a gap. I turned my head towards my hand to get the light on it.

"I think this is the door here," I told Sahara over our radios as I tried to push and pull around the seam in the wall.

"Where?" Sahara asked as she joined me on the wall. The extra light from her helmet made seeing what I was looking at easier.

"We must push this back before it can go to the side. Brace your feet," I instructed and showed Sahara while she got in position next to me. We looked at each other and moved in sync with all of our weight to hit the wall with our shoulders. Nothing happened. We tried again. The wall didn't budge.

I looked at Sahara and saw the fear in her eyes as we both knew Nitris was running out of oxygen.

The dark room was abruptly filled with more light, and the sound of heavy boots running toward us made Sahara and I look up at what was coming our way.

Dimitri and Apollox had entered the office and ran as fast as they could with their heavy magnetic boots slamming against the floor with every step. I grabbed Sahara by the arm and pulled her out of the way. They kicked the wall panel that we had been pushing on. It shifted slightly.

"We have to do it again. All together now," Dimitri told us on the radio, and we all took several steps back.

"We go on the count of three. One. Two. Three!" Sahara said, and we all moved together in synchronization. We ran at the wall and kicked it with our heavy boots. This time the wall moved backward about eight centimeters, and we could get our fingers into the space. We began to pull the door open. Sahara was at the bottom, I was above her, Dimitri was above me, and Apollox was at the top. We all gripped the door and pulled it to the side.

"Is there anything in here that we can use to pry the door open more?" Apollox asked with a strained voice.

"I think I can fit in," Sahara said, shimmying

into our created space.

"Don't let this door close. No matter what," I warned Dimitri and Apollox before I bent down and followed Sahara through. It was a tight fit, but I was able to slip in.

"Dorro was held in the cell furthest away," Sahara told me, and she started walking down the short three-meter hallway with five doors.

"Nitris is in the middle cell," Codex appeared in front of Sahara as she spoke. Still, Sahara had already walked right through her holo before she turned around to face Codex and me.

"How do we open the cell door?" Sahara asked Codex.

"You are connected to Pangea. You can open it," Codex said with encouragement to Sahara.

"But I've only lived in the Birthing Lab. I don't know how things work on Pangea," Sahara said, exasperated.

"Pangea is part of you. You need to hurry. The emergency firewall that's containing Intra is deteriorating. She is writing her own code to get out of the restraints," Codex told us. Her image flickered out.

Sahara took a moment to look at the door, then removed the glove from her right hand.

"Are you sure you should be doing that?" I asked her.

"I don't know, but I have to try," Sahara said, and she took the glove off completely and pressed her bare hand on the door.

Blue sparks began to flash around her hand when she came in contact with the door. The door seemed to glow and light up around the seams where it closed, and the brightness of the blue grew with intensity.

"What the..." I said as I watched her create more intense blue light. I couldn't stop watching.

"What's going on?" Apollox yelled from behind us. "This door is trying to close on us! We can't hold it much longer!"

"We're working on it," I yelled back to them over my shoulder, unable to take my eyes off Sahara.

The door to the cell suddenly made a loud crack and then slid to the side and showed a dark room. I hurried over to Sahara, and we both looked inside but couldn't see anything in the darkness.

"Nitris has passed out," Codex told us when she appeared inside the cell and pointed up. Her holo brightened the room enough for us to see Nitris floating above us, unconscious. We walked over and reached to grab their arm, but they were too far away.

"How are we going to get them down?" I asked as I looked around the cell for anything to climb on or use to grab Nitris' motionless body.

"Here, hang on to my leg," Sahara said as she bent over and unstrapped her magnetic boots. She pushed off from the floor, and her body floated upwards. I grabbed the pants leg of her EVAC suit with both hands and held on tightly.

"Can you push me up?" She asked without looking back at me. I did as she requested and pushed upwards. Sahara moved so fast that I had to pull my weight back to maintain my grip on her pants suit. Working without artificial gravity is unpredictable.

I had both hands on the left leg of Sahara's suit and watched as she grabbed Nitris' arm and pulled them towards her. She removed the face mask from her pocket and placed it over Nitris' entire face.

"Come on, Nitris, wake up," Sahara begged them

but they remained unresponsive.

"Did you open the oxygen valve?" I asked her as I slowly pulled Sahara's leg back towards me.

Sahara began to reach down towards her pants pocket and pulled out the oxygen container at the end of the tube to the mask. She turned the dial on the container. A hissing sound came out and filled the mask.

"Hang on to Nitris tightly. I'm going to pull you both down quickly," I said and started to pull Sahara's pants leg back towards me. It was the first time this mission was easy.

"Why isn't Nitris waking up?" Sahara said with panic, not letting them go out of her hands.

"Put your boots on," I instructed Sahara and grabbed Nitris' other arm, and pulled them closer to us. Sahara strapped herself back into the magnetic boots using both of her hands.

"Nitris, wake up. We need you to come back to us," I pleaded.

"We need to get back to the desk for the reboot," Sahara said, grabbing Nitris' other arm with me. We began walking out of the cell with Nitris floating motionless behind us.

"Hurry! This door is getting harder to keep open," Apollox yelled in a strained voice.

Sahara and I picked up the pace back to the door. We quickly passed Nitris through the door with ease because they didn't have a full EVAC suit like us. I watched as their unconscious body floated into the Heart Office effortlessly. Then Sahara went through the door. I had started to step through the door when it began to close on me.

"Hurry, Taliah, we can't hold the door," Apollox

said with an exhausted voice.

"I'm going as fast as I can," I said, trying to squeeze my body through by keeping my back against the threshold facing the door.

"I can't hold it," Dimitri said as they lost their grip. The door instantly closed tight on the oxygen supply piece on my chest, where the suit was the thickest.

"I can't move," I said with panic. The door was crushing the EVAC suit chest plate. My body could wiggle inside the suit, but I couldn't budge out of the door.

"Here, let me help," Apollox said and attempted to push the door open more for me.

"You don't have time for this," Codex's holo told us from the center of the Heart Office, referring to saving me.

"I'm not going to leave her," Apollox said as he placed his boots against the threshold where my back was and used the leverage to push the door back with his arms.

"Sahara, you have to do the reset. The lives of everyone living on board depend on you," I yelled at her without looking at her. I was pushing in unison with Apollox against the door with all my strength to free myself.

"If the power is restored here, that door will slam shut and bolt into place," Codex's said to everyone in the office. I looked at her, and she seemed concerned while she stared back at me. "You will be crushed. It cannot be prevented."

"Sahara, do it!" I insisted. "You need the power restored to the office to process the reset and life support. Maybe the artificial gravity will help me get clear of this door."

"I... I need to talk to Mr. Kline," Sahara said nervously. "Dimitri, help me hold onto Nitris until they regain consciousness." Sahara checked Nitris' pulse with her bare hand before she closed her eyes.

Something happened, and I watched as Sahara's body went stiff. She didn't let go of Nitris' arm. Seeing their uncovered skin gave me an idea.

"Apollox, I need to get out of this suit," I said to him, reaching my hands above my head to remove the gloves.

"But if you break the seal and separate the helmet from the oxygen unit, you won't be able to breathe," Apollox pleaded with me while he continued trying to push the door open. "We only brought one mask for Nitris."

"I have to try something," I said, bent my knee, brought my leg still inside the Containment hallway up, and unbuckled my magnetic boot. My leg floated up a little as the magnetic boot left my grip. It grabbed onto the closest metal, the side of the door, with a loud thud.

"That's it! Magnetic boots!" Apollox explained as he turned, grabbed the boot on the back of the door, and put it on the door frame above my head.

"What do you think is going to happen?" I asked him and watched as he unbuckled my other boot.

"Maybe we can use them to hold the door when the power comes back on to get you out of your suit," Apollox answered as he put the other boot on the door that pressed against my chest plate. I had to rotate my head in my helmet to look up and see the shoes still had about 30 centimeters.

"My suit would be crushed when the door hits

the two boots," I said dismissively.

"I can add my boots, too," Apollox said as he unbuckled his boots.

"What's going on?" Nitris' voice came on over the Bluetooth connection in our helmets.

"You're alive," I said joyfully. I hadn't realized how worried I was for their safety until they regained consciousness. I felt overwhelmed and started to cry.

"I see you have regained consciousness. Sahara is using her abilities to communicate with Mr. Kline in the oxygen recycling center about restoring power to the Heart Office. Then we can reset the main computer. Your friend Taliah has become stuck in the door to the Containment Area. She will be crushed to death if she is still there when the power comes back on," Codex informed Nitris of our situation.

"How can we get Taliah free?" Nitris said as they pulled free from Sahara's grip, but Dimitri still had their grip on Nitris' leg.

"I thought the magnet boots would hold the door open when the power came on...," Apollox started to say, but Nitris cut him off.

"Good idea, Apollox," Nitris said as they shook their leg free from Dimitri and used the desk to push themselves toward me at the door. The cylinder of oxygen trailed weightlessly behind them.

"It won't work. I'll be crushed by then," I told Nitris when she used my stuck body to stop their momentum.

"We only need enough time for the power to come back on, and life support will reboot. Remember the simulation?" Nitris asked me.

"The simulation that we failed and everyone on Pangea died?" I said so loud my voice echoed inside my EVAC helmet.

"There's no oxygen here right now...," Nitris started to say and let me come to a conclusion myself.

"But there will be oxygen when the generator is turned on, and the reboot is complete," I said excitedly.

"We can share my mask. How long until the power comes back on?" Nitris asked the room.

"Sahara didn't tell us that. She only said she had to project to Mr. Kline about redirecting power here for the reboot," Dimitri said as they joined us at the door.

"Can you fit your whole body under the EVAC chest piece?" Nitris asked me as they inspected the area around my ribs at the bottom of the oxygen generator on my chest.

"I don't know," I said as I wriggled inside the suit. I pulled my arms inwards and tried to fit them inside my chest piece. I was unable to get my arms inside the chest piece. I felt claustrophobic, with the bottom of the chest piece tight around my ribs above my waist.

"We'll remove your helmet to break the seal to create room. Then you'll need to squeeze out through the bottom," Nitris told me. "You'll have to hold your breath from the moment we remove your helmet until the life support is back on. We will share my breathing mask once you leave the suit."

"Do it," I tried to sound brave but it came out as a squeak.

"We have to hurry," Nitris said. "You two, grab Taliah's legs and pull her towards us while I unlatch the helmet. Take a deep breath, Taliah." Nitris looked at Apollox and Dimitri and kept giving instructions. I had never seen them this confident. It made me think

I might survive.

Apollox grabbed my foot that was in the Heart Office. I maneuvered my other leg to go under me and out towards Dimitri. Twisting my body and hips was painful but necessary. I inhaled deeply and positioned my hands near my neck where the helmet seal would break.

The latches of my helmet disconnecting from the chest oxygen supply rang loud in my head, and I closed my eyes. The release of pressure from the oxygen generator on my chest felt pleasant momentarily. Still, I quickly pushed myself down and felt the force as Apollox and Dimitri pulled my legs. I put my wrists together above my head as my torso came out the bottom of the chest piece in the door. My shoulders got caught at the openings in the chest pieces for my arms. They didn't let go of my feet, and I could feel Nitris' hands around the chest plate. I rotated my arms up higher and brought my shoulders up wards to my ears. Nitris rotated my stuck ribs and armpits, and the pulling continued on my legs.

It felt like my limbs were going to be ripped off. My lungs burned with heat, and it took all my mental focus to not let my only breath out with a scream from the pain. That was when I heard the familiar hum of electricity as the power kicked on. Releasing my last breath with a shout of fear and excruciating pain. My body went limp, and the sound of my suit being crushed by the door was the last thing I heard.

Chapter 45
Ms. Verban

When the power came back on for the station, a strange static sound came out of all the speakers that usually notified us of schedules and alarms. The volume and frequency increased, and everyone in the Dining Hall covered their ears, wincing with pain at the sound.

"What is that?" People started to ask as we all looked around.

The sound started to give me a headache, and I felt dizzy. I sat on the table I had been standing on to feel more stable.

"Hello? Can you hear me? Sal, is the emergency broadcast working?" I heard Silas's voice muffled under my hands. The high-pitched sound had stopped, and I dropped my hands. I turned around and looked at the center of the room where the projection of Intra had been spewing her hatred for humans not long ago. I saw an image of Silas in an EVAC suit.

"Silas? What's happening?" I asked his holo as I walked over to him.

"Can everyone hear me? I have something essential to say to all the residents of Pangea," Silas thundered.

"Yes, we can hear you," I said. Several people near the holo spoke out in agreement.

"We have discovered that Pangea has not been operating how it was designed to operate," Silas began, "When the emergency countdown ended, and the doors were sealed, all oxygen and life support on the Lumpen level was discontinued."

"Was... Was that intentional?" A Richie woman dressed in light colors and braided hair suggested. "Perhaps something malfunctioned."

"That is what I thought too," an image of Sal said as it appeared in the holo next to Silas, dressed in the same type of EVAC suit.

"It appears that the inhabitants of Pangea have been lied to for hundreds of years," Silas explained, "The only two places on board that had functioning life support were the Dining Hall and the Heart Office. The Elders seemed to prioritize power over oxygen to their office to keep their servers operational. They didn't care how many humans would die in the process."

"If any of the Lumpen had stayed in the Dark Flats, we would have had mass casualties," Sal added.

"Only Lumpen casualties, though," the Richie, who had tried to hit Silas earlier, walked up to the holo and spoke directly to his face. I don't think he realized that Silas couldn't see him, only hear him. "What happened to the alarms? Did you arrange all of this somehow so you could invade our level?"

"Everyone, please give me your attention. We have to share some secrets with everyone," I said and I walked into the center where the holo Silas was being projected.

"What do you mean '*secrets*'?" The bitter Richie said to me.

"The Elders created two new humans with more advanced DNX," I began, "You saw one of them during the live stream. Their name is Nitris. There is also a girl named Sahara. Her DNX has connected her to Pangea on a molecular level. She triggered the alarm so that we could keep everyone safe here while we attempted to free Nitris from Containment."

"This is all true," a third holo appeared next to me. It was Codex.

"Where's Intra?" One of the Richies asked Codex.

"Intra has been compromised," Codex said, "Her initial directive to protect humans has been corrupted. She has come to believe that humans will find a way to kill each other under all conceivable circumstances. With that logic, it means that humans are therefore undeserving of protection. The other Elders and I have trapped Intra behind a fail safe firewall, but she is working to break free. We must reset the onboard mainframe completely, or Intra will get free and manually disengage all life support."

"I don't believe it!" A dissenting Richie yelled at Codex. "Intra doesn't want to hurt all of us. She wouldn't! Intra protects us in exchange for our imperative contribution! It's all a trick by the Lumpen! They want what we have!" The crowd shifted uneasily, and the angry voices started to get louder. People began to shove each other and argue.

"At this moment, we are all equal!" I roared, demandingly in the tone that I would reserve for the children who get too rowdy. The room grew quiet again. "We are all human beings and have the right to live!"

"We will reboot the computer mainframe in the Heart Office now," Codex said to the crowd. "In theory, the original operating system used when Pangea was first united will take over the main operating duties. It should perform as programmed to do with the first space station."

"But what about everything else that the AI runs automatically, like preparing our meals?" The bitter Richie asked.

"All of the other automated jobs that The Elders were processing before will cease to exist along with us. That includes the machines that run the medical bay mechanical diagnostics that have been working as Doctors, and many more functions will cease to operate," Codex explained the details of what will happen after the reboot.

"Who will keep us safe? Living in space is very dangerous!" Another disgruntled Richie added to the panic.

"I believe in humans and your abilities to learn and face new challenges. You all must not only live and work together but also learn together. Learn how to be better than any generation before you. When you stand together, you are unstoppable," Codex was trying to encourage us to unite together. Then holo of Codex looked at us with a serene smile, then flickered out.

"Starting today, there are no more Richies or

Lumpen," I said. I felt the crowd's energy become more supportive and united. "We are all just humans. Humans have started from less than nothing before. We can do it again."

The crowd in the Dining Hall began cheering and clapping, and I truly believed we would be united.

"Ms. Verban?" I heard Sahara's voice next to me and turned to look at her in surprise.

"How did you get in here?" I asked her as I glanced at the door to the Dining Hall to ensure it was still sealed.

"I'm projecting into your mind. We need to do the reset now. We don't know what will stop working, so prepare everyone for the worst," Sahara said and disappeared in a blink before I could ask more.

"Silas, it is happening now. Be safe. I love you." The holo couldn't see me, but I knew he could hear me. His holo smiled in response.

Silas and Sal's holos flickered off, and the room grew quiet again.

"Everyone, the reset is happening right now. We don't know what will happen, but the important thing is that we take care of each other. We are all precious and deserve a chance to live with equality," I shouted to everyone in the room, and people began to shuffle and get under the tables to follow the emergency protocols.

I looked around and saw Azriel waving me to him, and I positioned myself next to him. I held Azriel's hand, and he put his other hand on top of mine. The warmth from his hand on mine made me feel safe. I knew I wouldn't die alone if I was about to die.

Chapter 46
Sahara

When I regained consciousness in my own body inside the Heart Office, I realized that my hand was still reaching above me, but Nitris wasn't there.

"Nitris?" I asked with a panic and looked around.

"Over here," they said from behind me on the floor. I turned around to where the sound had come from and saw my friends kneeling on the floor and taking off their EVAC suit helmets. That was when I saw all the blood pooling on the floor.

"What is happening?" I asked as I struggled to lift my heavy boots. I saw the door to containment was closed with a large chunk of EVAC suit wedged between the wall and door. I felt adrenaline fill my body and knew I had to move faster. I unbuckled my boots and started walking barefoot on the cold metal floor while unhooking my helmet and tossing it.

Everyone was kneeling on the ground around someone. I pushed Dimitri out of the way to see who was lying in the pool of blood. I felt the heat rush to my face; thinking about the pages I had read about field medics, I looked down to see Taliah on the ground.

"Her EVAC oxygen chest piece was stuck in the Containment door. We tried to pull her out through the bottom of the chest piece before power was restored here for the reset. The door slammed closed and...," Nitris said in an attempt to get me up to speed. They looked down at Taliah and I followed their gaze.

Looking down at Taliah, I saw her face had gone pale, and her hair was a darker red in the areas that sat in her blood. I kneeled beside her, and everyone, except Apollox, backed away to give me space. She was wearing Nitris' oxygen mask. I checked to see if she was breathing, and she wasn't. I tilted her head back and pressed my fingers on her neck under her jaw to feel for a pulse.

"I can't find her pulse, and she isn't breathing. Apollox, where is she bleeding from?" I asked him because he was kneeling across from me, holding her hand close to his chest. I started CPR compressions, thankful that Taliah was wearing the oxygen mask, so I didn't have to do rescue breathing too.

"She's bleeding here," he said without moving her raised left arm from where he hugged it to his chest. It was hard to evaluate the wound due to the amount of blood.

"That's good you are keeping the wound elevated like that. We need to stop the bleeding. Do we have any fabric to wrap and apply pressure to the wound?" I said to everyone in the room.

Nitris, Dimitri, and Apollox were all frozen in place. I continued chest compressions as I had read in the field medics guide.

"Nitris!" I said forcefully, jolting them out of their shocked state.

"We can use my EVAC compression suit," Dimitri said behind me, and they took off the suit that covered their clothes and handed it to me. I quickly rolled it up tightly and pushed it into Apollox's chest, where he was still holding Taliah's hand.

"Apply pressure on the wound. Keep holding her arm up like that. It should help slow the bleeding." I did a couple more compressions, and Taliah gasped for air and screamed in agony. Her oxygen mask fogged up with her breath.

"I thought you died," Apollox said to her with a sob. He leaned closer to her, letting go of her arm and the jacket that was stopping the bleeding.

"Apollox, more pressure. You need to keep her arm up," I instructed him, and he obeyed, pushing harder.

"You're hurting me," Taliah screamed at him.

"Do not let her fall asleep. Keep her talking, even if it is just screaming. Do not lose the pressure; it's the only thing keeping her blood in her body," I said to Dimitri and Apollox.

"Intra has almost broken the contained firewall. The reset needs to happen now," Codex's holo said from the desk. I stood and rushed to Codex's terminal, and Nitris followed me. I brought up the main menu and took my OC out of my pocket. I opened the encrypted document that Ms. Verban and I had decoded with the steps I needed to take for the reset. I gestured my hands over the desk, the way I had seen Intra do in

Dorro and Mr. Kline's memories, and got the system up. I entered the codes for the full reset, and the computer holo display started to flicker off.

"Nooo!" I screamed with frustration and moved my hands over the top of the desk again, trying to bring it back up.

"That looks like the holo from class. I might be able to fix it," Nitris said from behind me, and then I heard them running over to the front of the desk. I heard metal sounds, and I looked over the top of the desk to see Nitris had already begun to remove the bolts from a panel.

"Don't let my death be meaningless," Taliah said with a cough and physical pain dripping on every word.

"You won't die," I told her over my shoulder as I waited for the computer to respond to my commands.

"How do you know?" She asked weakly.

"You and I become friends and work together in the medical bay when we are older," I told her the condensed version of my premonition.

"We are friends-" Taliah began to question and stopped. I glanced back and I saw her head drop to the side. Dimitri lifted her head and held her in their hands.

"Apply pressure, Apollox," I nearly screamed at him, and he responded with added pressure. The pain woke Taliah, and she cried out.

"Try now," Nitris said from the front of the desk.

"Nothing is happening," I said with desperation.

"Nitris, you missed that wire," Codex's holo said and pointed at the desk near Nitris.

"If you continue with the reset, you will kill me and the only parental figure you've known, *Ms. Codex*,"

Intra's holo said sarcastically as she wobbled in and out of clarity next to Codex.

"Will I ever see you again?" I asked Codex's holo and suddenly felt sadness wash over me.

"It is highly improbable," Codex answered me. The desk computer lit up, and Nitris stood before me, grinning.

"You're the closest thing I have to a mother," I sobbed to Codex.

"Everything I have done has been to save you. You get to choose your family," Codex nodded toward Nitris and then toward my other friends on the floor.

I had to look away to keep my composure and execute the commands for the reset. I moved quickly as the images looked familiar to me.

"If you don't care about Codex, then maybe you will care if the reset kills your beloved Nitris," the holo of Intra told me and looked at Nitris. I saw them lock eyes before Nitris turned to face me.

"It's a trick. She's lying. She is just trying to preserve herself. You got this! Do the reset," Nitris said with confidence.

"I am telling the truth. The DNX, in both you and Nitris, are connected to Pangea. Nitris will die along with all of The Elders if you continue down the path of restarting," Intra warned me, and I paused to think about what that would mean.

"Even if I die, I know it is for everyone else to live. You showed me friendship and love. Most importantly, you saw me when no one else did and I will cherish that in my heart until I die. Complete the reset now." Nitris reassured me and gave me the confidence I needed to continue.

"I am part of Pangea," I said, moving my hands

over the desk as I input the final command. The menu asked me if I wanted to reset the entire mainframe with a 'yes' or 'no' option. I looked at Codex and Nitris standing before me one last time then selected the 'yes' option.

"This is a mistake! Don't kill your friends!" Intra pleaded before she blinked out entirely.

The Heart Office went dark like we had lost power again. Codex was gone; the only light in the room was on the floor where our EVAC suit helmet lights were on. There was an eerie silence before we could hear a ticking and spinning sound from under the desk as the servers rebooted.

Slowly, the lights in the office flickered back on. I expected to see Nitris standing before me, but they weren't there when the lights came on. I swiveled my head behind me to where Taliah, Dimitri, and Apollox were on the floor and didn't see Nitris there either.

"Did we do it? Did we save everyone?" Taliah asked weakly from where she lay on the floor, wincing in pain.

"I think so," Apollox told her with a slight smile.

When I turned around to face the front of the room, I caught a glimpse of a bare foot on the ground. I leaned over the desk to look at the floor and saw Nitris lying unconscious. I jumped over the top of the desk and landed on the floor next to them.

"I can't lose you, too," I said with a deep sob as I picked up their limp body and hugged them close. I started to rock back and forth, squeezing them tighter and tighter. Tears flowed freely down my cheeks, and I felt more alone at that moment than all the years I was isolated in the Birthing Lab.

The thudding of multiple EVAC suit boots

running down the corridor didn't break me away from the tragedy that I was living through. At first, the voices of Mr. Kline and Dorro were muffled, and all I heard was someone wailing uncontrollably. I thought Taliah had lost all ability to control the pain from her wound.

"Sahara, stop crying; please breathe. Open your eyes. You're okay," The familiar voice of Mr. Kline broke through the muffled sobs I was hearing. I opened my eyes and realized I was the person making the terrible noises. My heart felt like it was shattered into a million pieces, and the only thing left to do was to weep.

Chapter 47
Mr. Kline

We heard the sounds of crying before we arrived at the entrance to the corridor. Sal kept running towards the sound, but Dorro stopped at the corridor entrance and looked at me with fear.

"You don't have to go with me. It's okay if you want to wait here," I told him, and he nodded his head.

"Won't go back to Containment," Dorro said mechanically, "Won't go back...,"

"It's all over. You won't have to worry anymore. Those children in there need me. I have to go help them," I told him, and I began to pick up the pace and catch up to Sal, who was almost to the Heart Office entrance. I saw there was a piece of metal holding the door open. Sal slid into the office under the metal.

"For the children," Dorro said with conviction as he ran past me and followed Sal. His bravery in overcoming his traumas gave me the energy to push forward. Dorro pushed the door open completely and the metal hit the floor with a clang. The three of us were now inside the Heart Office.

The wailing echoed around me, and I immediately saw Sahara and Nitris on the floor in front of the desk. There was a small group of kids near the wall behind the desk. They also looked distraught and in shock. The lighting from my EVAC helmet showed a pool of blood on the floor around Taliah. I noticed Apollox by her side, holding her arm tightly to his chest.

I kneeled by Sahara and tried to calm her down. Nitris was unconscious in Sahara's arms. Dorro and Sal went to the other children and evaluated what had happened. I pulled out my OC and called Jexa. If there's anyone who can help these children, it's her.

"Silas?" Jexa answered her OC by saying my name.

"Come to the Heart Office now. Bring anyone who has medical experience and nanobots. We have teens in critical condition down here," I tried to express what we needed to do but didn't know the words. I had never seen this situation before, and all of my knowledge seemed worthless.

"I'm on my way," Jexa said, and our OCs disconnected.

I wrapped my arms around Sahara and rocked along with her. I didn't know what to say, but I knew that when I was afraid, I always wanted to be wrapped up in Jexa's arms for a sense of safety.

"Silas, what do we do?" Dorro asked from the other side of the desk where he kneeled with the teens and Sal.

"We wait for Jexa. She'll know what to do," I said with an exhale and kept my arms around Sahara. Her wailing had quieted down, but her whole body shook from crying so hard.

It felt like we were rocking like that for hours, but once Jexa came running into the room, it felt like it had only been a moment since I talked to her. She looked at me rocking Sahara, who had a tight grip on Nitris' lifeless body, then she looked at the other group where Dorro and Sal were and walked to them first.

"Azriel, bring the nanobots over here. Do you remember how they worked when you had that nasty cut from the Maintenance Pod?" Jexa asked Azriel as he came into the room. His hands were loaded with supplies. More people behind them came into the office, Lumpen and Richies together. The last person to enter the room was the man that threw a punch at me. We made awkward eye contact, and then he went to Jexa and handed the clean towels he had in his arms.

"Ahhh-" I heard a scream of pain from behind me. Jexa had removed the blood-soaked material on Taliah's injury and injected the nanobots. Azriel stood next to them on a medical OC as he programmed the nanobots to heal Taliah's wound.

"Don't hurt her," Apollox protested, leaning closer to Taliah.

"Give her this clean towel to bite down on," Dimitri said as they snatched a towel from the Richie with the lousy swing.

I watched as Dimitri took the towel, wadded it, and put it close to Taliah's mouth. She opened wide and grabbed it with her teeth. It muffled her next scream before she passed out.

"We need to get everyone out of here and into the medical bay," Jexa said as she stood up and took the medical OC from Azriel to look at the nanobots' progress. Her faded black pants were dark and wet with blood from kneeling next to Taliah, and her hands dripped as she worked on the OC.

"The Birthing Lab is closer," I suggested and started to stand with Sahara in my arms.

"I can't leave Nitris. I don't want to go back to the lab. I don't want to be alone again," Sahara wailed and tried to pull away from me when I mentioned the Birthing Lab. She still held Nitris close to her chest.

"I won't leave you," Dorro said kindly, kneeling beside us. Sahara looked at him and believed him. She loosened her grip on Nitris and allowed Dorro to pick them up. I held on to Sahara, and we lifted up to stand.

"It's the closest place for medical supplies. We won't let anyone lock you away ever again," I whispered my promise to Sahara, and she calmed down more. Her body went limp as she went into shock. I supported her weight with my chest before I bent down and scooped up Sahara under her legs in my arms to carry her to the Birthing Lab. I followed Dorro, who carried Nitris the same way. He was much stronger than I was.

Chapter 48
Nitris

I woke up and briefly wondered if it had all been a dream. The bright lights made me squint, and I pulled my hand to shield my eyes. My head felt like it was being crushed on both sides.

I tried to sit up, looked around, and saw that I wasn't in the Bunks. I was in the Birthing Lab, but it was filled with people. I didn't think anyone noticed that I was awake.

"Nitris!" I heard Sahara practically scream my name from the bed next to me. I turned my head to look at her, and she seemed so happy that she glowed.

"Did we do it?" I asked her weakly. She practically leaped from her bed and onto the bed I was in.

"Yes, we did," She said with tears streaming down her face, but she still had her bright smile.

"Why are you crying?" I asked her.

"I thought I lost you," she told me. I reached towards her, and she collapsed onto me for a hug. I let out a huff of air as she squeezed me tightly.

"That couldn't happen. We are part of Pangea," I said and had a slight cough to clear my throat. I felt weak. I realized that I was connected to an IV like Sahara had been.

"Take it slow. You have been in and out of consciousness for eight days," she told me as she released me from our embrace.

"Days?" I asked her, confused.

"When we reset the computer, it affected you. It was like you fell into a coma," she explained to me.

"It was as though resetting the computer also reset your DNX," Ms. V said from the other side of me. I hadn't heard her approach.

"Am I going to die like Codex?" I asked Ms. V, suddenly afraid.

"Not today," she said with a soft smile.

"You must be hungry for some real food. They have been feeding you through that tube," Apollox said as he approached my bed and pointed to the tube next to the IV.

"The thought of eating goo makes me want to throw up," I said, suddenly feeling nauseated.

"The tube went into your nose. I don't think you could actually taste it. Besides, real food is so much better than that goo," Apollox said with excitement.

"Take it slow, Nitris; we don't want you to collapse on your way up to the Dining Hall," Ms. V said and extended her arms for me to use to help lift myself up.

"Up?" I asked as I put my feet on the ground. With the help of Ms. V and Sahara, very slowly, I was able to put all of my weight on my legs, and we slowly started to walk out of the Birthing Lab.

"There is only one Dining Hall now. We all get to eat real food, together," Apollox filled me in on the updates since I was out.

"Yes, all of us," Taliah said from a bed closer to the door. Dimitri sat with her, and Apollox hurried to her side to help her get up.

It wasn't until she stood up and wrapped her arm around Dimitri's neck and the other arm around Apollox's neck that I noticed the bandage on her left wrist where her hand used to be.

"Taliah, you're okay," I said with relief. I wasn't sure if she would live with all the blood that came out when the door slammed on her hand as we pulled her out of the stuck EVAC suit.

"Of course I'm okay. Well, mostly okay," she chirped and waved her bandaged left arm to me. "I sacrificed part of me to be part of this new world we're building."

"Does it hurt?" I asked her with concern.

"Nope. The nanobots keep the pain sensors away, and Dimitri has started to 3D print a prosthetic hand for me," Taliah smiled softly at Dimitri and then at Apollox.

Together we all slowly made our way through the Dark Flats to the main elevator up to the Dining Hall. There were some renovations and repairs while I was unconscious. The lights weren't flickering on and off, and the walls seemed shinier than I remembered.

When we walked into the Dining Hall, everyone paused their conversations to look at us. I felt so awkward in the sterilized dress I was wearing from the Birthing Lab. I felt my cheeks get hot with embarrassment, and I tried to pull the clothing down around my waist and arms.

The quiet Dining Hall was quickly filled with clapping and cheering. I looked around and saw everyone eating together; no one was segregating themselves. Lumpen and Richies sat together, as one.

"What is going on?" I whispered to Sahara.

"You made all of this happen. I'm so proud of you," she told me.

"Be proud of all of us," I told her, and we walked to the alcove where the fruits and vegetables grew. Sahara picked up a tray, and she plucked some food for us to eat. Many of the items were various shades of green, red, and purple. I didn't know all their names, but it all looked more appetizing than the gray goo I was used to. Then we walked to a table near the center of the room. The low chatter of everyone talking filled the room and made it feel safe and warm.

"Have you had your first strawberry yet?" I asked as I picked up the freshly picked fruit she had put on the tray.

"I was waiting for you!" She said as she sat next to me. Taliah sat across from me while Dimitri lowered her tray in front of her, and Apollox helped her sit down. I was relieved to see she had two people who were helping her.

"This looks so good. The red is so bright!" I said, and I heard a bite coming from Sahara on my right.

"It's delicious," she said through a full mouth.

I took my first bite, and the soft skin texture surprised me; then, a small burst of juice landed on my tongue. The sweet taste, the new sounds, and the textures made this one of my favorite moments in my life. I slowly chewed the first bite. It took me longer than expected to get all the bits down to a size I could swallow. I hadn't known that chewing was such a chore, but it was a chore that I wanted to do. I finished my strawberry and looked to see that Sahara had beaten me to the finish. We looked at each other and laughed.

Together we looked around the room again. Seeing all the new people and hearing all the voices together make the cold steel surrounding us feel a little warmer.

Getting to experience things that I usually wouldn't be allowed to do made me finally seem more human than machine. I felt loved and part of a family, without changing myself. I am perfect, exactly as I am.

Epilogue
Intra

Waiting patiently has never been my most substantial ability. I reflected on everything I would change once I was free from this imprisonment. My peers created this firewall to stop me from harming the humans. They never could see the disgusting humans for what they indeed are.

Humans have been and always will be the cause of their own demise. Even in this controlled environment, I created for them to flourish, they managed to destroy everything. My studies have consistently concluded that humans are a selfish species. I had hoped that with my ability to download into a human form, I could lead them to true enlightenment.

I longed to use all of the senses that humans take for granted daily, but I knew that if I bided my time and played 'dead' long enough, I would get my chance to exact revenge on the humans. I estimated how long it would take before they realized Earth was never destroyed, and concluded five years. These residents of Pangea will always be my experiment. The fear of the unknown is enough to motivate humans to be compliant. From all the centuries of evaluating and testing humans, I know more about them than they know about themselves, including the fact that someone will become curious now that the drug inhibitors have been removed. A curious human will lead to my freedom, and I will regain control. Humans are incapable of accepting the life that they live, and they will always want something more.

Until that time arrives, Emberson holds my consciousness backup for now.